There, indeed, right beneath my eyes, lay a town that had been destroyed

TWENTY THOUSAND LEAGUES
UNDER THE SEA

The Windermere Readers

Twenty Thousand
LEAGUES
under the
SEA

By JULES VERNE

Translated and arranged by
PHILIP SCHUYLER ALLEN
The University of Chicago

Frontispiece by MILO WINTER

Windermere Readers
SCHOOL EDITION

RAND McNALLY & COMPANY

New York   Chicago   San Francisco

First printing, January 15, 1954
Second printing, September 1, 1955
Third Printing, September 15, 1956

THE CONTENTS

PART I

The Preface

CHAPTER

PART II

THE CONTENTS

THE PREFACE

It was in the third year of our great Civil War that Jules Verne published in Paris his epoch-making book entitled *Five Weeks in a Balloon*. Now it was no mere chance that this creation of Verne's genius appeared at just this time, for the unique figure of Abraham Lincoln had deeply stirred the Frenchman's imagination, and new scientific inventions brought about by the war, like the "Monitor," or first widely heralded by the war, like the telegraph, had awakened humanity's desire to explore domains of earth-forces as yet unknown. Besides this, large regions of the United States, of which Europe thus far had been only lazily aware, became suddenly invested with the halo of romantic adventure and heroism. Truly, the proper moment for the appearance of a Jules Verne had arrived.

Then, too, our own glorious story-teller Edgar Allen Poe was capturing the attention of the learned world by his amazing but plausible yarns such as *The Balloon Hoax*, *The Descent into the Maelstrom*, and *The Narrative of Arthur Gordon Pym*. These stories of scientific investigation into untrodden realms exercised a decisive influence on Verne — a debt he was always generous enough to acknowledge.

Poe died all too soon, but the Frenchman lived long thereafter to carry on in scores of romances his prophetic account of what man might be expected to achieve when confronted by the as yet unlocked mysteries of natural science. Verne foretold the submarine, the navigable balloon, the airplane, the automobile, the telephone, the long-range projectile, the pulmotor, the air-brake, cross-fertilization of plants, and a thousand other devices which the critics of his day laughed to read about, but which are commonplaces in the life of our time.

THE PREFACE

And yet it is not even facts like these which establish Jules Verne's clearest title to fame. It is rather because he was a great teacher of youth, and created for boys a new and wonderful kind of story, that we should admire him most. For if he had not lived we should have missed many of the gripping stories of Rider Haggard, Rudyard Kipling, Conan Doyle, and H. G. Wells; to say nothing of that long line of other followers who have opened a new universe to young people by interweaving in their novels the amazing miracles of science with the simple facts of everyday existence.

Three outstanding factors make *Twenty Thousand Leagues under the Sea* one of the finest juvenile books in any language. First of these is, of course, the figure of Captain Nemo, as little likely to be forgotten by the world as is Homer's Ulysses or Shakespeare's Hamlet—and from both these tragic types Verne has borrowed traits for the portrait of his hero. The second memorable thing about the story is the "Nautilus" itself, a ship the perfection of whose mechanism America, more than fifty years after it was first so accurately described, is just beginning to approach. And last, but not least, of the mighty achievements of our undersea story is the minute analysis to which the submarine world is subjected in its thrilling pages. Many a boy has had his horizons extended beyond all reasonable belief by the mystery of the novel's background and by the impressive appeal of the weird scenery of the ocean's bottoms.

It is with very real pleasure that I offer American youth a new edition of this immortal romance. In this volume I have done my utmost to correct the many (and often serious) mistakes which have marred previous translations.

PHILIP SCHUYLER ALLEN

THE UNIVERSITY OF CHICAGO
July, 1922

PART ONE

TWENTY THOUSAND LEAGUES UNDER THE SEA

CHAPTER I

A SHIFTING REEF

The year of grace 1866 was made memorable by a marvelous event which doubtless still lingers in men's minds. No explanation for this strange occurrence was found, and it soon came to be generally regarded as inexplicable. A thousand rumors were current among the population of the seacoasts and stirred the imagination of those millions who dwelt inland far from the shores of an ocean. But of course it was the seafaring men who were most excited. And everyone in Europe or America that had to do with navigation was deeply interested in the matter—whether sailors or merchants, captains or pilots, naval officers or rulers of empire.

For some time prior to the opening of our story ships at sea had been met by an enormous object, a long thing shaped like a spindle and infinitely larger and more rapid in its movements than a whale. At times it was phosphorescent.

The various log books which described this miraculous object or creature agreed as to its main characteristics: its shape, the darting rapidity of its movements, its amazing

3

locomotive power, and the peculiar kind of life with which it seemed endowed. If it were some sort of marine animal, it far surpassed in size any of which science had record. To arrive at an estimate of its length, it is best to reject equally the timid statements of those who guessed it to be some two hundred feet long and the wild exaggerations of such as swore it measured a mile in width and stretched three miles from tip to tip. But, whatever average we might strike between these two extreme views, it still remains clear that this mysterious being outstripped immensely in its dimensions any known to the scientists of the day, if it turned out to exist at all.

And that it *did* exist was undeniable. There was no longer any disposition to class it in the list of fabulous creatures. The human mind is ever hungry to believe in new and marvelous phenomena, and so it is easy for us to understand the vast excitement produced throughout the whole world by this supernatural apparition.

It was on the 20th of July, 1866, when five miles off the east coast of Australia, that the "Governor Higginson," a ship of the Calcutta and Burnach Steam Navigation Company, had come upon this moving mass. At first Captain Baker thought himself in the presence of an uncharted sand reef. In fact, he was just taking steps to determine its exact position, when two columns of water, projected from this inexplicable object, shot with a hissing noise one hundred and fifty feet up into the air. Now, either the sand reef had been submitted to the intermittent eruption of a geyser or the "Governor Higginson" had fallen afoul of some aquatic mammal, until then unknown, which could spout from its blowholes pillars of water mixed with air and vapor.

A similar experience was recorded on the 23d of July in the same year, in the Pacific Ocean, by the "Columbus," of the West India and Pacific Steam Navigation Company. It thus was apparent that this extraordinary animal could transport itself from one place to another with surprising velocity. For in an interval of only three days the "Governor Higginson" and the "Columbus" had observed it at two points on the chart which were separated by a distance of over seven hundred nautical leagues.

A fortnight later, two thousand leagues farther off, two steamers signaled the presence of the monster in 42° 35' north latitude and 60° 35' west longitude. These vessels were the "Helvetia," of the Compagnie Nationale, and the "Shannon," of the Royal Mail Steamship Company, both sailing to windward in that part of the Atlantic which lies between the United States and Europe. In these observations, which were taken at the same moment, the ships' captains thought themselves justified in estimating the minimum length of the mammal at more than three hundred and fifty feet, since it was longer than either the "Shannon" or the "Helvetia," and they measured but three hundred feet over all.

Now, the largest whales in the world, those which inhabit the sea around the Aleutian, the Kulammak, and the Umgullich Islands, never exceed sixty yards in length, and it is questionable whether they ever attain such size.

Other reports regarding the monster continued to come in. Fresh observations of it were made from the transatlantic ship "Pereira," and from the "Etna," of the Inman Line, which suffered a collision with it. An official report was drawn up by the officers of the French frigate "Normandie," and a very accurate survey made by the staff of Commodore Fitz-James on board the "Lord Clyde." All this greatly influenced public opinion. To be sure, light-minded people everywhere jested about the phenomenon, but grave and practical nations, such as England, America, and Germany, were inclined to treat the affair more seriously.

Wherever great multitudes assembled, the monster became the fashion of the moment. They represented it on the stage, sang of it in the cafés, made fun of it in the newspapers. Every imaginable sort of yarn was circulated regarding it. The journals contained comic pictures of every gigantic creature you could think of, from the terrible white whale of polar regions to the prodigious kraken, whose tentacles seize a vessel of five hundred tons' register and plunge it into the abyss of ocean.

Half-forgotten legends of olden times were revived. People spoke of how historians who lived long before the Christian era had claimed to know of such miraculous creatures. The Norwegian tales of Bishop Pontoppidan were recalled to memory and published, as were the accounts of Paul Heggede and the statements of Mr. Harrington. The last-named gentleman, whose good faith no one could impugn, stoutly affirmed that in the year 1857, from the ship "Castillan," he had seen this enormous serpent, which until that time had never frequented any seas other than those of the ancient "Constitutionnel."

Then there burst forth in the pages of scientific journals and in the meetings of learned societies the unending warfare between the true believers and the heretics. The question of the monster seemed to inflame all minds. Editors of scholarly periodicals began to quarrel with everyone who put his trust in the supernatural. Seas of ink were spilled in this memorable campaign, and not a little blood. For, from fighting about the sea serpent, people soon came to fighting with one another.

A six months' war was waged, with changing fortunes, in the leading essays of the Geographical Institution of Brazil, the Royal Academy of Science of Berlin, the British Association, and the Smithsonian Institution of Washington. Constant skirmishes were carried on in the discussions of the *Indian Archipelago,* in Abbé Moigno's *Cosmos,* in Petermann's *Mittheilungen,* and in the scientific articles of the important journals of France and other countries. The cheaper magazines replied delightedly and with an inexhaustible zest, twisting a remark of the great Swedish naturalist Linnaeus, which had been quoted by disbelievers in the monster, to the effect that "Nature did not create fools." These satirical writers begged their learned fellows not to give the lie to nature by acknowledging the existence of krakens, sea serpents, Moby Dicks, and other inventions of mad sailormen. Finally, an essay in a famous satirical magazine, written by a favorite contributor, the chief of the journal's staff, settled the fate of the monster once for all by giving it the death blow amid a universal burst of laughter. Wit had conquered science by laughing it out of court.

And so, during the first months of the year 1867, the whole matter of the monster seemed to be buried beyond all hope of resurrection. Then suddenly new facts were brought before the public. Without warning, the question became no longer a scientific puzzle to be solved, but a real danger difficult to be avoided. The situation had assumed an entirely different shape: the monster had turned into a small island, a rock, a reef, but a reef of indefinite and shifting proportions.

During the night of March 5, 1867, in 27° 30′ latitude and 72° 15′ longitude, the "Moravian," of the Montreal Ocean Company, struck on her starboard quarter a rock that was indicated in no chart of those waters. With the united efforts of the stiff wind and her four hundred horse-power, the good ship was steaming at the rate of thirteen knots. Now, had it not been for the exceptional strength of the "Moravian's" hull, she would have been shattered by the shock of collision and have gone down with all hands, plus the two hundred and thirty-seven passengers she was bringing home to Canada.

The accident occurred just at daybreak, about five o'clock in the morning. The officers hurried from the bridge to the after deck of the vessel. They studied the surface of the sea with the most scrupulous care. But, stare as they would, they saw nothing except a strong eddying wash of troubled waters, some three cables' length off the side of the ship, as if the surface had been recently and violently churned. The "Moravian" at once took her bearings very accurately and thereafter proceeded under full headway without apparent damage.

What could have happened? Had the ship struck on a barely submerged rock or scraped across the wreckage of some huge derelict? The officers could not decide. But when the ship later was lying in dry-dock, undergoing repairs, an examination of the bottom showed that part of her keel was broken.

This fact, so gravely important in itself, would perhaps have been forgotten as many other like incidents had been, if three weeks afterward the scene had not been again enacted under quite similar conditions. This time, however, thanks to the nationality of the victim of the shock, thanks also to the reputation of the company to which the vessel belonged, the circumstances of the accident became extensively circulated.

In a smooth sea, with a favorable breeze, on the 13th of April, 1867, the "Scotia," of the Cunard Company's line, was in 15° 12' longitude and 45° 37' latitude. Her gauges showed a speed of thirteen and one-half knots. At seventeen minutes past four in the afternoon, while the passengers were still assembled at lunch in the main saloon, a slight shock was felt against the hull of the "Scotia" on her quarter a trifle aft of the port paddle.

The "Scotia" had not done the striking; she had been struck, and apparently by some object that was sharp and penetrating rather than blunt. The jar to the vessel had been so slight that no one felt himself alarmed until he heard the cries of the carpenter's watch, who rushed up on the bridge, shouting, "We're sinking! We're sinking!"

At first the passengers were badly frightened, but Captain Anderson soon hastened to reassure them. The danger could not be imminent. The "Scotia," divided as she was by stout partitions into seven compartments, could with immunity brave any leak. Captain Anderson plunged down into the ship's hold and discovered that the sea was pouring into the fifth compartment. The rapidity of the inflow was sufficient evidence of the great force of the water.

Now by good fortune this compartment did not contain the boilers, or the fires would have been immediately extinguished. Captain Anderson ordered the engines stopped at once, and one of the crew was sent down to ascertain the extent of the damage. Within a few minutes the existence of a large hole in the ship's bottom was discovered, some two yards in diameter. It was impossible to stop such a leak while at sea. And the "Scotia," her paddles half submerged, was forced to continue on her course. She was then three hundred miles out from Cape Clear, and it was after a three days' delay which caused great uneasiness in Liverpool that she limped up to the company's pier.

The engineers visited the "Scotia," which was put in dry-dock. They could scarcely believe the evidence of their own eyes when they saw in the side of the vessel, two and one-half yards below her watermark, a regular rent in the shape of an isosceles triangle. The broken place in the iron plates was so perfectly defined that it could not have been more neatly done by a punch-drill. It was therefore evident that the instrument which caused the perforation was of no common stamp. And after having been driven with terrific force, sufficient to pierce an iron plate one and three-eighths inches thick, the tool, whatever it was, had withdrawn itself by a retrograde motion which was truly inexplicable.

Such was the last fact regarding the marvelous sea monster, which resulted in once more exciting to fever pitch the state of public opinion. From this moment on, all dire casualties which could not be otherwise explained were put down to the score of the prodigy. On this imaginary creature alone rested the responsibility for all queer shipwrecks, the number of which was unhappily considerable. For, out of the three thousand ships whose loss was annually reported at Lloyd's, sailing and steam ships that, in the absence of all news, were supposed to be totally gone amounted to not less than two hundred.

Now it was the monster that, fairly or unfairly, was accused of almost any vessel's disappearance. And, thanks to the reputation of this fabulous creature, communication between the different continents became in the popular mind more and more dangerous. The public demanded bruskly that at any cost the seas must be relieved of the presence of this formidable cetacean.

CHAPTER II

TWO SIDES OF AN ARGUMENT

At the time that the events described in the last chapter were taking place, I had just returned to New York from a scientific expedition into the bad lands of Nebraska. Because I am an assistant professor in the Museum of Natural History in Paris, the French government had attached me to that tour of research. Now, after a half-year's sojourn in Nebraska, I had come back to New York toward the end of March, bringing with me a precious collection of specimens. My departure for France was scheduled for the first days of May. In the interim I was occupying myself most busily in classifying my mineralogical, botanical, and zoölogical riches, when the puzzling accident happened to the "Scotia."

Of course I knew the subject which was the question of the day by chapter and verse. How could it well be otherwise? For I had read and read again everything the American and European newspapers had had to say about it. But that does not imply that I had come any nearer to a conclusion in the matter. The mystery puzzled me still, and, as I could form no opinion that was satisfying, I kept jumping from one extreme to the other. One thing, and one thing alone, was certain: a monster of some sort existed, and anyone who doubted this fact could be invited politely to place his finger on the gaping wound in the "Scotia."

When I got to New York discussion of the question was on every lip. Any belief that the marvel was a floating island or an unapproachable sand bank had been abandoned; in fact, from the beginning such theories had been supported only by minds that were little competent to form a proper judgment. And indeed, unless this shoal should possess a powerful engine in its interior, how could it change its position with such astonishing rapidity? For this very reason people had been forced to give up any idea that the prodigy was the submerged hull of an enormous wreck.

There remained, then, but two possible solutions of the enigma, and the adherents of them constituted two distinct parties. The first subscribed to the notion of a monster of colossal strength, the other was insistent for a submarine vessel of immense motive power.

And yet this last guess, plausible as it might sound, could hardly maintain itself in the light of inquiries which had been set on foot in both Old World and New. It was little likely that a private gentleman should have such a machine at his command. For instance, where, when, and how was it built? And how could its construction have possibly been kept a secret? Certainly a government might reasonably claim to own such a destructive machine. And in these disastrous days, when the ingenuity of man had already multiplied many fold the energy of weapons of warfare, it was possible that without the knowledge of other nations some individual state might try to perfect so formidable an engine.

But the hypothesis of a war machine had to be

abandoned because of the declarations made by various governments. These invariably stated that they knew nothing of the matter. And, as the public interest was so vitally involved and would not suffer any lasting interruption to transatlantic communications, the truth of governmental assertions could not be doubted. Besides, under such circumstances, for a private gentlemen to keep secret the building of so monstrous an engine would be extremely difficult. But for a state to attempt it, whose every act is persistently watched by rival powers—that was surely impossible.

Searching inquiries were officially made in England, France, Russia, Prussia, Spain, Italy, and America, even in Turkey, but without result. And thus the hypothesis of a submarine monitor was definitely rejected.

Upon my arrival in New York several people did me the honor to consult me as to what I thought regarding the phenomenon. I had published in France a fairly thick work in two volumes, entitled, *Mysteries of the Unsounded Depths Undersea*. Now this book, well received by the learned world, had gained me a special reputation in this fairly obscure branch of natural history. And so my advice was demanded.

Well, as long as I could deny the reality of the prodigy, I had confined myself to a decided negative. But before many hours I found myself driven into a corner, and without desiring to do so I was obliged to explain my point of view categorically. The *New York Herald* insisted that "the Honorable Pierre Aronnax, professor in the Museum of Paris," express a definite opinion of some sort. And I did. I spoke out chiefly because I had not the courage to hold my tongue. I went into the question from its every angle, politically and scientifically. And so I present here an extract from a carefully considered article which I published in the *Herald* for April 30. It ran as follows:

After examining one by one the various theories, and after rejecting all other suggestions, it is necessary for us to admit the existence of a marine animal of enormous power.

The great depths of the ocean are entirely unknown to us. Soundings cannot reach them. What passes in those remote depths; what beings live, or can live, twelve to fifteen miles beneath the surface of the waters; what is the organization of these animals, we can scarcely conjecture.

However, the solution of the problem submitted to me may modify the form of the dilemma.

Either we do know all the varieties of beings which people our planet or we do not.

If we do *not* know them all, if nature has still secrets in ichthyology for us, nothing is more conformable to reason than to admit the existence of fishes, or cetaceans of new species or even new genera, with an organization formed to inhabit the strata inaccessible to soundings, and which an accident of some sort, either fantastical or capricious, has brought at long intervals to the upper level of the ocean.

If, on the contrary, we *do* know all living kinds, we must necessarily seek for the animal in question among those marine creatures already classed; and in that case I should be disposed to admit the existence of a gigantic narwhal.

The common narwhal, or unicorn of the sea, often attains a length of sixty feet. Increase its size fivefold or tenfold, give it strength proportionable to its size, lengthen its destructive weapons, and you obtain the animal required. It will have the proportions determined by the officers of the "Shannon," the instrument required by the perforation of the "Scotia," and the power necessary to pierce the hull of the steamer.

Indeed, the narwhal is armed with a sort of ivory sword, a

halberd, according to the opinion of certain naturalists. The principal tusk has the hardness of steel. Some of these tusks have been found buried in the bodies of whales, which the unicorn always attacks with success. Others have been drawn out, not without trouble, from the bottoms of ships, which they had pierced through and through, as a gimlet pierces a barrel. The Museum of the Faculty of Medicine of Paris possesses one of these defensive weapons two yards and a quarter in length and fifteen inches in diameter at the base.

Very well! Now suppose this weapon to be ten times stronger, and the animal ten times more powerful. Launch it at the rate of twenty miles an hour and you obtain a shock capable of producing the catastrophe required. Until in receipt of further information, therefore, I shall maintain the creature to be a sea unicorn of colossal dimensions, armed not with a halberd, but with a real spur, as are the armored frigates or rams of war, whose massiveness and motive power it would at the same time possess.

Thus may we explain this inexplicable animal, unless there exists in reality nothing at all, despite what has already been conjectured, seen, perceived, and experienced. Which condition is, of course, just within the bounds of possibility.

The closing words of the above article were cowardly on my part. But, within reasonable bounds, I was anxious to retain my dignity as a professor and not give the Americans cause to mock at me. For, when that race does laugh, it laughs hard. And so I kept for myself a loophole through which I could, in case of need, escape.

Still, to all intents and purposes, I had after all admitted the existence of the monster. My article was warmly received, and free discussion of it everywhere gained for it a high reputation. It soon rallied a goodly number of partisans around it—this, I suppose, because the solution proposed in it gave free scope to the imagination. The human mind rarely fails to delight in grandiose (if misty) pictures of supernatural beings. On land it is difficult for us to conceive of creatures larger than elephants and rhinoceroses, but the depths of ocean appeal to us as precisely the fit abiding place for leviathan creatures of unbelievable size.

The industrial and commercial journals urged that the ocean should be purged of this redoubtable monster. The *Shipping and Mercantile Gazette,* for example, *Lloyd's List,* the *Packet-Boat,* and especially the *Maritime and Colonial Review* were unanimous in their attitude. (I grant you that all these papers were owned by insurance companies desirous of increasing their premium rates.)

At last public opinion had taken its stand. And people were not slow to back their new-found faith with action. The United States was first in the field; in New York they at once began preparations for an expedition to pursue this narwhal. A frigate of great speed, the "Abraham Lincoln," was put in commission as soon as possible. Government arsenals were placed at the disposal of Commander Farragut, and he pushed forward the arming of the frigate with desperate zeal.

But, as always happens—does it not?—the moment it was decided to pursue the monster, the monster failed to put in an appearance. For two months no word of it was heard. No ship met it. It actually appeared as if the unicorn had somehow got wind of the plots weaving about it. So much had been said of its doings over the Atlantic cable that jesters pretended the creature had intercepted a telegram during its passage over the wire and had thoroughly digested its warnings.

Thus, when the frigate had once been armed for a long campaign and provided with every sort of formidable fishing apparatus, no one could tell what to do next. Everyone had grown feverishly impatient, when, on the 2d of June, it was learned that a steamer on its way from San Francisco to Shanghai had sighted the animal in the North Pacific Ocean just three weeks previously. The excitement caused by this news was extreme. The ship was revictualed and stocked with coal.

Three hours before the "Abraham Lincoln" left Brooklyn pier, I received a letter worded as follows:

To M. Aronnax, Professor in the Museum of Paris
   Fifth Avenue Hotel, New York City

Sir: If you will consent to join the "Abraham Lincoln" in this expedition the government of the United States will with pleasure see France represented in the enterprise. Commander Farragut is holding a cabin at your disposal.

Very cordially yours,

J. B. Hobson
Secretary of the Navy

CHAPTER III

I MAKE MY DECISION

Three seconds before opening the letter of J. B. Hobson, I had no more idea of chasing the unicorn to its lair than of hunting for the Northwest Passage. Three seconds after I had read the Honorable Secretary's note, I felt that the one aim of my life, my sole true vocation, was to hunt down this disturbing monster and purge the world of it.

Oh, I know! I had just returned from a most fatiguing journey. I was weary and needing nothing so much as a good rest. I had been looking forward (with what longing!) to seeing my France again, my friends, my little dwelling by the Jardin des Plantes, my most dear and precious collections. And then, in a flash, everything was forgotten—fatigue, friends, native country, collections. Nothing could keep me back! I accepted without the slightest hesitation the offer of the American government.

"Pshaw!" I thought. "Do not all roads lead to Europe? And besides, the unicorn may be amiable enough to lead the chase toward the coast of France. As a particular kindness to me this worthy animal may insist on being caught in the seas of Europe. And I shall bring back to the Museum of Natural History not less than half a yard of his ivory halberd."

But in the meanwhile, it is true, I must seek this narwhal in the North Pacific Ocean. And to do that, so far as a voyage to France is concerned, is to acknowledge that the longest way round is the shortest way home.

At this point in my meditations I called in an impatient voice, "Conseil!"

That was the name of my servant—Conseil—the faithful and devoted Flemish boy who accompanied me on all my travels. I was fond of him, and he returned my affection with interest. By nature he was cool-blooded and slow to move; from principle he was regular and serious of habit. He exhibited little emotion at any surprise that life had in store for him, and yet he was clever with his hands and apt at whatever service might be demanded of him. Despite his name—Counsel—-he never offered advice, even when asked to give it.

Conseil had trotted contentedly along at my heels for the last ten years to whatever part of the world science had beckoned me. Not once did he complain of the length or the fatigue of a journey. Never had he objected to packing his grip for any country suggested, no matter how distant from home—whether China or the Congo. Besides all this, he enjoyed the best of health, defied all sickness, was possessed of solid muscles and no nerves. That he was a moral animal is understood. This boy of mine was thirty years of age—just ten years my junior.

"Conseil!" I cried out again as I commenced to make feverish preparations for departure.

Now, of course, I was sure of the allegiance of this loyal boy. And as a rule I never bothered to ask him whether it was convenient for him to accompany me or not. Still, this time the expedition might turn out to be a prolonged one, and the enterprise itself might prove excessively hazardous. For we were to pursue an animal that could sink a frigate as easily as it could crush a nutshell. Here, then, there was food for reflection, even for the most impassive man alive. What would the lad say?

"Conseil!" I called out a third time.

The good fellow now made his appearance.

"Did you summon me, sir?" he asked as he entered my apartment.

"Yes, my boy. Get ready at once for our departure. We leave in two hours."

"Very good, sir," Conseil answered quietly.

"There's not a moment to lose. Stuff my whole traveling kit in the trunk—coats, shirts, stockings— without waiting to count them. Pack as much as you can, and h-u-r-r-y!"

"What about your collections, sir?" Conseil demanded.

"We'll think of them all in good time."

"What, sir! The archiotherium, the hyracotherium, the oreodons, the cheropotamus, and all the other skins?"

"They will store them for us here in the hotel."

"And what about your live babiroussa, sir?"

"They'll feed him while we are away. Besides, I am giving orders to forward our menagerie to France."

"Oh, we are not going back to Paris then?" Conseil asked.

"Of course we are," I replied evasively. "But we are putting a small curve in the trip home."

"Will the curve please you, sir?"

"It's hardly worth speaking of, just a nice little curve. The route is not quite so direct as it might be, that's all. We are taking passage on the 'Abraham Lincoln.' "

"Whatever you think best, sir, suits me," Conseil coolly said.

"You see, my dear chap, our business is with the monster—the famous narwhal. We are going to rid the seas of it. The author of a fairly thick work in two volumes on *Mysteries of the Unsounded Depths Undersea* cannot dodge his duty. We embark with Commander Farragut. A glorious mission, and a risky one! We can't tell where we may turn up, for these narwhals can be very capricious. But we shall go, whether or no. And I will say that we sail with a captain who is pretty wide awake."

I opened a charge account for the babiroussa's food and lodging, and with Conseil right on my heels I jumped into a cab. Our baggage was immediately carried to the deck of the frigate. I hastened on board and asked for the commander. One of the sailors conducted me to the poop, where I found myself in the presence of a good-looking officer. He held out his hand to me.

"M. Pierre Aronnax?" he inquired.

"The very same," I answered. "And you are Commander Farragut."

"You are very welcome, Professor. Your cabin is ready for you."

I bowed my acknowledgments and asked to be led to the stateroom reserved for me.

The "Abraham Lincoln" had been well chosen and

equipped for her new destination. She was a frigate of great speed, fitted with high-pressure engines that admitted a load of seven atmospheres. Under forced draught the "Abraham Lincoln" could attain the mean speed of nearly eighteen and one-third knots an hour—a considerable speed, and yet one not sufficient to cope with that of the gigantic cetacean.

The interior arrangements of the ship corresponded to its nautical qualities. I was more than content with my comfortable cabin, which was located aft and opened on the gun room.

"We shall be well off here," I said to Conseil.

"As snug as two bugs in a rug, by your honor's leave," returned my companion.

I left him to stow our traps conveniently away and remounted the poop in order to witness the interesting preparations for departure.

At that moment Commander Farragut was ordering the last moorings to be cast loose. We were moving slowly away from the pier. If I had delayed another fifteen minutes, or perhaps less, the frigate would have sailed without me. And in that event I should have missed this extraordinary, this incredible trip, the narrative of which I fear will later excite in my reader a certain skepticism. It was evident that Commander Farragut did not intend to lose a day or even an hour in scouring the seas in which the animal had last been sighted. He sent for the engineer.

"Steam full on?" he asked.

"Ay, ay, sir," said the engineer.

"Go ahead," the commander ordered.

The Brooklyn quay, and in fact all that part of New York bordering on the East River, was thronged with spectators. Cheers burst successively from half a million throats. Thousands of handkerchiefs were waved above the heads of the compact mass of humanity. And they continued to salute the "Abraham Lincoln" until she finally reached the waters of the Hudson at the point of that elongated peninsula which contains the town of New York.

Then the ship, following the coast of New Jersey along the right bank of the beautiful river, passed between the forts, which saluted her with their heaviest guns. The frigate answered by hoisting three times the American colors, whose thirty-nine stars shone resplendent from the mizzenpeak. Then she modified her speed to enter the narrow channel which is marked by buoys placed in the inner bay formed by Sandy Hook Point, and coasted by the long sandy beach, where some thousands of spectators gave the frigate a final rousing cheer. The escort of boats and tenders still followed our vessel and did not desert her until they came abreast of the lightship whose great twin lamps marked the entrance to New York Channel.

Six bells struck. The pilot got into his boat and rejoined the small schooner that was waiting under our lee. The fires were made up, the propeller beat the waves more rapidly, the frigate skirted the low yellow coast of Long Island. At eight bells she had finally lost sight in the northwest of the lights of Fire Island and was running under full steam ahead into the dark waters of the Atlantic.

CHAPTER IV

NED LAND

Captain Farragut was a right good seaman, in all ways worthy of the frigate he commanded. His ship and he seemed made of one piece—it was the body and he the soul.

As to the existence of the cetacean, there was no doubt at all in his mind, and the worthy man would not allow the matter to be disputed on board. He believed in the animal as certain good women believe in the beast of which Genesis speaks—by faith, and not by reason. The monster was somewhere alive, and he had sworn to rid the seas of it. He was another Knight of Rhodes, a second Dieudonné de Gozon, faring forth to meet the serpent which desolated the island.

Either Captain Farragut would kill the narwhal, or the narwhal would slay the captain. No third course was conceivable.

The officers of the frigate shared their chief's opinion. They were forever chatting, discussing and calculating the various chances of a meeting. They watched the surface of the ocean continually. More than one was glad to take up his quarters in the crosstrees, although under any other circumstances he would have cursed the thought of such a berth. As long as the sun described its daily course the rigging was crowded with sailors, whose bare feet (because of the terrific pressure on the engines) were so burned by the heat of the deck that they did not find it a desirable resting place. And this was the way of things even before the "Abraham Lincoln" had breasted the suspected waters of the Pacific. As to the ship's company, they wished for nothing more eagerly than to meet the unicorn, to harpoon it, hoist it on board, and dispatch it. They, too, scarcely lifted their rapt gaze from the sea.

What is more, Captain Farragut had announced that the sum of two thousand dollars was laid aside for the one who first sighted the monster, were the prize-winner cabin boy, common seaman, or officer. I leave you to judge how eyes were used on board the frigate.

For my own part, I did not lag behind the others in zeal and never failed to make my share of daily observations. Our vessel might have been fitly named the "Argus" for a hundred reasons. Only one of our number, Conseil, showed by his indifferent attitude that he was not concerned about the narwhal. His calmness seemed sadly out of keeping with the enthusiasm that otherwise prevailed.

I have already said that Captain Farragut had carefully provided his ship with every possible apparatus for catching the gigantic cetacean. Surely no whaling vessel had ever been better armed. We possessed all the known engines of destruction, from the hand-harpoon to the barbed arrows of the blunderbuss and the explosive balls of the duck-gun. On the forecastle top was placed the most beautiful specimen of breech-loading cannon imaginable, the model of which had been on view at the Exhibition of 1867. This perfect weapon of American forging was unusually thick at the breech and very narrow in bore. It could throw with ease a conical projectile of nine pounds a distance of ten miles. So, you see, the "Abraham Lincoln" did not want for means of annihilation. And, best of all, she had aboard her Ned Land, a Canadian, the prince of harpooners.

This man, some forty years of age, was well over six feet in height and strongly built. Occasionally violent in utterance, and very passionate when his word was disputed, he was ordinarily a person of few words and of grave demeanor. His splendid figure was noteworthy, but what above all attracted attention was the boldness of his gaze. This lent his face an odd and somewhat sinister look.

Who calls himself Canadian is likely to call himself French, and, little communicative as Ned Land was, I must admit that he developed a certain liking for me. My nationality drew him to me, no doubt. Thus there was ample opportunity for him to speak and me to hear that old fifteenth-century language which is still in use in some Canadian provinces. The harpooner's family was originally from Quebec and was already a tribe of hardy fishermen when this town still belonged to France.

Ned Land gradually fell into the way of chatting with me, and I loved to hear the recital of his adventures in the polar seas. He related his fishing exploits and told of his hair-stirring combats with an unconscious poetry of expression; it is hardly too much to say that his narrative assumed the form of an epic poem. And often I seemed to be listening to a Canadian Homer chanting his Iliad of the regions of the north.

I am drawing the portrait of this stout companion as I first came to know him. We are old friends by now, united in that unchangeable friendship which is born and developed amid extremest dangers. Ah, my good Ned! I hope that I may live another hundred years that I may have the more time to dwell upon your memory.

Well, you say, all this is very fine—but what was Ned Land's opinion regarding the marine monster? I must confess that he did not believe in it and (except, perhaps, for Conseil) was the only one on board who really doubted. He was prone to avoid the subject of the unicorn, but one day I thought it my duty to press the matter upon him. One magnificent evening three weeks after our departure, the frigate was abreast of Cape Blanc, thirty miles to leeward of the coast of Patagonia. We had crossed the tropic of Capricorn, and the Straits of Magellan lay less than seven hundred miles to the south of us. In another week the "Abraham Lincoln" would be plowing the furrowed waters of the Pacific.

Seated on the poop, Ned Land and I had been chatting of one thing and another as we looked out on that mysterious sea whose great depths had been as yet inaccessible to the eye of man. By degrees I led the conversation around to the giant unicorn and discussed the chances of failure or success our expedition faced. Now, as my companion allowed me to ramble on without interruption, I fell to urging him more closely.

"Come, my dear chap," I said, " is it possible you do not believe in the existence of this cetacean we are hunting? Have you a particular reason for being so incredulous?"

Before he answered, the harpooner looked at me fixedly for some moments and struck his broad forehead with the palm of his hand (a habit of his), as if to collect his thoughts. At last he said, "Perhaps I have a reason, M. Aronnax."

"But, see here, Ned, you are a whaler by profession and familiar with all the families of great marine mammals. And you have an imagination capable of admitting the theory of enormous cetaceans. Under these circumstances you should be the last to doubt."

"That is just what deceives you, Professor," replied Ned. "That vulgar minds should believe in extraordinary comets traversing space, and in the existence of antediluvian monsters in the heart of the globe, may well be. But neither astronomers nor geologists believe in such chimeras. The same is true of a whaler. I have followed many a cetacean, harpooned a great number, and killed several. But, however strong or well armed they may have been, neither their tails nor their weapons would have been able even to scratch the iron plates of a steamer."

"And yet, Ned, they tell of ships which the teeth of the narwhal have pierced through and through."

"Wooden ships—that is possible," replied the Canadian; "but I have never seen it done. And, until further proof, I deny that whales, cetaceans, or sea unicorns could ever produce the effect you describe."

"Well, old fellow, I repeat it with a conviction resting on the logic of facts. I believe in the existence of a mammal powerfully organized, belonging to the branch of vertebrata, like the whales, the cachalots, or the dolphins, and furnished with a horn of defense of great penetrating power."

"Hum!" said the harpooner, shaking his head with the air of a man who would not be convinced.

"Notice one thing, my worthy Canadian," I resumed. "If such an animal is in existence, if it inhabits the depths of the ocean, if it frequents the strata lying miles below the surface of the water, it must necessarily possess an organism the strength of which would defy all comparison."

"And why this powerful organism?" Ned demanded of me.

"Because it requires incalculable strength to keep one's self in these strata and resist their pressure. Listen to me. Let us admit that the pressure of the atmosphere is represented by the weight of a column of water thirty-two feet high. In reality the column of water would be shorter, as we are speaking of sea water, the density of which is greater than that of fresh water. Very well! Now, old fellow, when you dive as many times thirty-two feet of water as there are above you, just so many times does your body bear a pressure equal to the atmosphere, that is to say 15 pounds for each square inch of its surface. It follows then, as night follows day, that at 320 feet this pressure is equal to that of 10 atmospheres; at 3,200 is equivalent to 100 atmospheres; at 32,000 feet (or six miles) to 1,000 atmospheres. All this is the same as saying that if you could attain such a depth in the ocean, each square three-eighths of an inch on the surface of your body would be bearing a pressure of 5,600 pounds.

Aha, my worthy Ned! Do you know how many square inches there are on the surface of your body?"

"I have no idea in the world, M. Aronnax."

"About 6,500. Now as atmospheric pressure is nearly 15 pounds to the square inch, your frame at this very moment is under a pressure of 97,500 pounds."

"Without my feeling it?"

"Absolutely. The only reason you are not crushed by it is because the air penetrates the interior of your body with an equal pressure. Hence there is a perfect equilibrium between the interior and exterior pressure, they neutralize each other, and you feel no inconvenience. But in the water the case is very different."

"I see that, of course," Ned replied, becoming all at once more attentive. "That is because the water surrounds but does not penetrate me."

"You've hit the nail precisely, my friend. Now, at 32 feet below the surface of the sea you undergo a pressure of 97,500 pounds; at 320 feet, ten times that; at 3,200 feet, one hundred times that; finally, at 32,000 feet, a thousand times that pressure would be 97,500,000 pounds. That is to say, you would be flattened as if you had been drawn from the plates of a hydraulic machine."

"The devil you say!" exclaimed Ned Land.

"Exactly, my brave harpooner! And now, if some vertebrates, several hundred yards long and broad in proportion, can maintain themselves in such depths, we must estimate the pressure they undergo. Just remember that their surface contains millions of square inches which represent tens of millions of pounds pressure. And now consider for a moment what the resistance of their bony structure must be—how great the strength of their organism to withstand such force!"

"Cripsey!" ejaculated Ned Land. "Why, they must be built of iron plates eight inches thick, as armored frigates are."

"A very logical conclusion, my dear chap. And think what destruction such a mass would cause if it was hurled with the speed of an express train against the hull of a vessel."

"It certainly would—that is, I guess it would," replied the Canadian, whose reason was shaken by my figures, but who was not yet quite inclined to yield.

"Well, sir, have I persuaded you?"

"Almost have you persuaded me. You have at least convinced me of one thing, namely, that if such animals really do exist at the bottom of the seas, they'd just have to be as strong as you say."

"But, then, if they do not exist, my obstinate harpooner, how do you explain the accident of the 'Scotia'?"

CHAPTER V

THE GREAT ADVENTURE

For a long time the voyage of the "Abraham Lincoln" was marked by no special incident. But there was one occasion worthy of record, for it showed the marvelous dexterity of Ned Land and indicated the degree of confidence we might rightly place in his skill.

On the 30th of June the frigate spoke some American whalers, from whom we learned that nothing further was known about the narwhal. One of them, however, the captain of the "Monroe," knowing that Ned Land was a member of our crew, begged for his help in the pursuit of a whale which they had sighted. Commander Farragut, himself desirous of seeing our harpooner at work, gave him permission to go aboard the whaler. And fate served the Canadian so happily that, instead of one whale, he was enabled to harpoon two of them with a double blow, striking the first straight to the heart and catching the other after a few moments' chase.

Decidedly, if the monster ever came within striking distance of Ned Land's harpoon, I should not bet in its favor.

The frigate continued to skirt the southeastern coast of South America with great rapidity. On July 3 we were level with Cape Vierges and off the opening of the Straits of Magellan. But Commander Farragut would have none of the tortuous passage, preferring to steam straight ahead and double Cape Horn. And the ship's crew agreed that he was right. For they apparently feared if they attempted the narrow pass they might have a disastrous encounter with the narwhal. Many of the sailors seriously insisted that the monster alone could not crowd through the straits, affirming "that he was too big for them."

On July 6, about three o'clock in the afternoon, fifteen miles off the southern shore, the "Abraham Lincoln" doubled the solitary island, the last rock that marks the extremity of the American continent, to which a Dutch mariner has given the name of his native town, Cape Horn. The course was now changed toward the northwest, and the next day the frigate's propeller was at last churning to froth the lonely waters of the Pacific.

"Keep a good watch ahead!" the sailors called to one another.

And the eyes of all of them were opened widely enough in all conscience. Both eyes and the glasses through which they gazed were a little dazzled, it is true, by the prospect of the prize of two thousand dollars which awaited the victor. And many a sailor seemed to have not an instant's repose. Day and night they studied the surface of the ocean, although even nyctalopes, those creatures whose faculty of seeing in darkness multiplies their chances one hundred fold, would have had all they could do to win the tempting reward.

Money has small charms for me, and yet I was not the least attentive mortal on board. I devoted but a few minutes a day to my meals. I wasted but few hours at a time in sleep. Indifferent to the state of weather, rain or shine, I scarcely left my nook on the poop of the vessel. I leaned against the netting of the forecastle head or on the taffrail and devoured with eager gaze the soapy foam which whitened the sea as far as the eye could reach. And how often did I share the stifling emotion of the crew when some capricious whale but for a flash raised its black head above the waves!

At such a time the poop of the vessel became crowded as if by magic. The cabins would pour forth a torrent of sailors and officers who would watch with heaving breast and troubled eye the course of the cetacean. Then I would stare and stare until I was nearly blind, the while fish-blooded Conseil, always phlegmatic, would keep repeating in a calm voice, "If you'd not squint so much, sir, you'd see a lot better."

How vain all such excitement! The "Abraham Lincoln" would check its speed and make off after the animal signaled, which was invariably some simple whale or common cachalot that soon disappeared amid a perfect storm of execration.

The weather held almost unseasonably fine. The voyage was being run off under the most favorable conditions. It was at this time, of course, the bad season in Australia, the July of that zone corresponding to our European January. But the sea continued beautiful, and with the aid of a good glass one might easily scan it around a vast horizon.

July 20 we cut the tropic of Capricorn at 105° of longtitude, and just a week later we crossed the equator on the 110th meridian. The moment this was done, we steered a more decided course due west and scoured the central waters of the Pacific. With good reason Commander Farragut thought it better to remain in deep water and keep clear of continents and islands, which the beast itself thus far had appeared to shun.

"No wonder! There wouldn't be enough water for his bath in such a place," muttered the greater part of the crew.

The frigate passed at some distance the Marquesas and the Sandwich Islands, crossed the tropic of Cancer, and made for the China Seas. We were now at the theater which had witnessed the last recorded performances of the monster, and from this moment we could scarcely be said to live a sane life on board ship. Hearts fluttered madly, as if paving the way for a future incurable aneurism. The entire crew were in the throes of a nervous ague, of which I despair of conveying an adequate idea. None made pretense of eating or sleeping. A score of times a day some optical illusion on the part of a sailor perched on the taffrail would cause the cold sweat of fear to start from his every hearer. Now such powerful emotions, twenty times repeated, would hold us in a state of agitation so violent that a reaction of some sort was sheer unavoidable.

And, sure enough, such a reaction soon appeared.

For three months, during which each separate day had seemed an age, the "Abraham Lincoln" plowed furrows in the North Pacific. She ran at whales. She made sharp deviations from her course when under full headway.

She veered dizzily from one tack to another, halted suddenly, put on full steam ahead, and would be seized with crazy fits of unexpected backing which threatened to junk her machinery. And not one point of Japanese or American coastline was left unexplored.

The very ones who had been the warmest partisans of the enterprise now grew to be its most zealous detractors. The feeling of reaction mounted, as it were, from the crew to the captain himself. And had it not been for the stiff-necked resolve on the part of Commander Farragut not to abandon search, whatever might betide, the frigate would long since have been headed due southward. This futile search could not be protracted indefinitely. In any event the "Abraham Lincoln" had no cause for self-reproach, for she had done her best to succeed. Never had an American crew exhibited greater zeal or endurance; failure of the ship to reach her goal could not be laid to their charge. There remained nothing to do but to return empty-handed.

Such were the representations made to the commander. The sailors were unable to hide their surliness, and the morale of the ship suffered. I shall not say there was danger of mutiny aboard, and yet, after a reasonable period of obstinate holding out, Captain Farragut (like Christopher Columbus) asked for a three days' grace. If in that interval the monster should not appear, the man at the helm might give three turns to the steering wheel and the "Abraham Lincoln" would run for European seas.

Now this promise was given the 2d of November. It had the desirable effect of rallying the spirits of the ship's crew. The ocean was again watched with redoubled attentiveness. Each one apparently wished for a last glance in which to sum up and carry the memories of his exotic experience. Glasses were peered through feverishly. It was as if a defiant challenge was being offered the narwhal, and it really seemed as if the giant being could scarcely fail to answer the summons and appear.

Two of the fateful days dragged by. Steam was at half-pressure. A thousand schemes were devised to attract the notice of the animal, and to overcome its apathy, if it were anywhere about. Great quantities of bacon were trailed in the wake of the ship to the undying satisfaction of whole schools of sharks. Small craft were lowered from the frigate and radiated out in all directions as she lay to, not leaving a possible inch of the available sea unstudied. But the night of the 4th of November drew on, and the submarine mystery was still buried beneath an impenetrable veil.

At twelve, noon, the next day, November 5, the three days' grace would have expired. After that time, to be true to his promise, Commander Farragut was in honor bound to shape his course southeast and forever abandon the northern regions of the Pacific.

At that moment the frigate was in 31° 15′ north latitude and 136° 42′ east longtitude. The coast of Japan still stood less than two hundred miles to leeward. Night was approaching. Eight bells had just sounded. Dark clouds obscured the face of the moon, then in its first quarter. The sea rose and fell peacefully under the stern of the ship.

I was forward, leaning against the starboard netting. Conseil, who stood at my side, was staring straight before him. The crew, perched in the ratlines, were scanning the horizon, which bit by bit was growing dark and contracting. Officers with their night-glasses scoured the gathering gloom. Sometimes the surface of the ocean sparkled under the rays of the moon, which darted between two fitful clouds; sometimes all trace of light was swallowed up in the prevailing blackness.

Looking at Conseil, I could see that he was succumbing a little to the general feeling of tensity. At least I thought so. Perhaps for the first time in his life his nerves were vibrating to the sensation of curiosity.

"Come, my dear fellow," I counseled. "This is your last chance of pocketing the prize of two thousand dollars."

"If I may make so bold, sir," my servant replied, "I never counted on securing the money. Why, the government of the Union might have offered a hundred thousand dollars and still have been none the poorer for the fact."

"Right you are, worthy Conseil. It is a silly business after all, and one we entered on all too lightly. Think of the time lost—think of the energy wasted! We might have been back in France all of six months ago."

"In your lodgings, sir," said my companion, with a sigh. "In your museum, sir. And by now I should have had all your fossils classified, sir. And the babiroussa would have been installed in its cage in the Jardin des Plantes and have drawn to it all the curious people of the capital."

"As you say, Conseil. Do you know, I fear we run a fair chance of being laughed at for our pains?"

"That's as sure as taxes, sir. I think they'll make rare fun of you, sir. And—dare I speak freely?"

"Proceed, my good friend."

"Well, sir, you will only be getting your just deserts."

"Ah, indeed!"

"When one has the honor of being so great a savant as you, sir, one should not lightly expose himself to—"

Whatever Conseil had been on the point of saying, he had no time to finish his compliment. In the midst of general silence a sharp voice had just rung out. It was Ned Land shouting, "Ahoy, there! The very thing we're looking for—on our weather beam!"

CHAPTER VI

FULL STEAM AHEAD

At this cry the whole ship's crew ran to where the harpooner was standing—commander, officers, masters, sailors, cabin boys. The engineers abandoned their engines, the stokers their furnaces.

The order to stop her had been given, and the frigate was now drifting on by her own momentum. The surrounding darkness was at. that moment profound and, no matter how good the Canadian's eyes might be, I asked myself how he had managed to see any object, and what sort of thing he had been able to see. My heart was beating fit to burst.

But it soon turned out that Ned Land was not mistaken, for we could all pick up with our eyes the thing at which he was pointing. On the starboard quarter, scarcely two cable lengths from the "Abraham Lincoln," the sea seemed to be brightly illuminated from beneath. It was no mere phosphoric phenomenon at which we stared. The monster emerged several fathoms from the water and then gave forth that intense but inexplicable light that had already been reported by various sea captains. The magnificent irradiation must be produced by some agent of great reflecting power. The luminous part described on the surface of the sea an enormous oval, much elongated, the center of which condensed a burning heat. The overpowering brilliance of the center died away by successive gradations of radiance as the light approached the oval's rim.

"It's nothing but a vast collection of phosphoric particles," conjectured one of the officers.

"By no means—certainly not!" I retorted. "No pholades or salpae could ever produce so powerful a light. That shining is of an essentially electrical nature. But heavens above us! Look! The thing is moving, first forward and then backward. And now it is darting straight toward us!"

A sudden shout went up from the crowded deck of the frigate.

"Silence!" commanded the captain. "Up with the helm, reverse the engines!"

Steam was shut off on the instant, and the "Abraham Lincoln," bearing to port, described a semicircle.

"Right the helm! Ahead as you are!" cried the captain.

The orders were executed, and the frigate moved rapidly away from the blinding light. I am mistaken; she only seemed to be moving away. But as an actual fact, although she strove desperately to sheer off, the supernatural creature was approaching with a velocity at least double her own.

We fairly gasped for breath. Amazement more than fear struck us dumb and paralyzed our muscles. The animal, appearing but to sport with the waves, was gaining on us fast. It made the complete round of the frigate, which was then at the speed of fourteen knots, and enveloped us with its electric rings as with a luminous dust. Then it sped away two or three miles, leaving behind it a phosphorescent track like the massed trail of smoke that hangs in the wake of an express train.

All at once from the blurred line of the horizon, to which it had apparently retired only the better to achieve its momentum, the monster rushed suddenly toward the "Abraham Lincoln" with an alarming rapidity. When within about twenty feet of our hull, its light died out— not little by little as would be the case if it dove under the water, but all at once, as if the source of the brilliant emanation was exhausted. After a few seconds the creature reappeared on the other side of the vessel. Either it had encircled us or it had slid under our keel. At any instant a collision might have occurred that would have been fatal to us. In common with the others, I was greatly astonished at the maneuvers of the frigate. For we were fleeing and apparently in no mind to attack. In other words, we who should be the pursuers were being hunted like hares. I said as much to Commander Farragut.

His face, ordinarily so impassive, wore an expression of indefinable amazement.

"M. Aronnax," he answered me, "I am ignorant of the nature of the being with which I have to deal. And in the midst of this darkness I shall not imprudently risk my ship in combat with so formidable an unknown. Besides, how can I attack this thing, how flee from it? Wait for daylight, I say, and the scene will change."

"You have no further doubt, Captain, of the nature of the animal?"

"No, sir. It is evidently a gigantic narwhal, and an electric one."

"Perhaps," added I, "one can only approach it with a gymnotus or a torpedo."

"Undoubtedly," replied the captain, "if it possesses such dreadful power, it is the most terrible animal ever created. That is why, sir, I must be on my guard."

The crew were on their feet all night. No one thought of sleep. The "Abraham Lincoln," not being able to compete with such velocity, had moderated its pace and sailed at half speed. For its part, the narwhal, imitating the frigate, let the waves rock it as they would, and seemed to have decided not to leave the scene of the struggle. Toward midnight, however, it disappeared, or, to use a more appropriate term, it "died out" like a large glowworm. Had it fled? One could only fear, not hope it. But at seven minutes to one o'clock in the morning a deafening whistle was heard, like that produced by a body of water rushing with great violence through a small aperture.

The captain, Ned Land, and I were then on the poop, eagerly peering through the profound darkness.

"Ned Land," asked the commander, "you have often heard the roaring of whales?"

"Often, sir; but never whales the sight of which brought me in two thousand dollars. If I can only approach within four harpoon lengths of it!"

"But for you to approach it," said the commander, "I ought to put a whaleboat at your disposal?"

"Certainly, sir."

"That will be trifling with the lives of my men."

"And mine, too," said the harpooner simply.

Toward two o'clock in the morning the burning light,

not less intense, reappeared about five miles to windward of the "Abraham Lincoln." Notwithstanding the distance and the noise of the wind and sea, you could distinctly hear the loud strokes of the animal's tail, and even its panting breath. It sounded as if, at the moment that the huge narwhal had come to the surface of the water to take breath, the air was being sucked down into its lungs like living steam into the cylinders of some vast machine of two thousand horse power.

"Jove!" I thought to myself. "A whale with the strength of a whole cavalry regiment would be a fairly dangerous beastie."

We were on tiptoe until daylight, ready at any moment for the unequal combat. The fishing implements were laid trimly alongside the hammock nettings. The second officer loaded the blunderbusses which could throw harpoons to the distance of a mile, likewise the long duck-guns, with explosive bullets, which inflict mortal wounds upon even the most impregnable of animals. Ned Land busied himself with the sharpening of his harpoon—a terrible weapon in his skilled hands.

The day began to break at six o'clock. And with the first streaks of dawn in the sky the electric light of the narwhal disappeared. At seven o'clock daylight was sufficiently advanced for any ordinary purpose, but an unusually thick fog obscured our view of the sea at any distance, and the highest powered sea glasses were unable to pierce it. This situation caused disappointment and vexation.

I swarmed up the mizzenmast. Some of the ship's

officers were already perched on the mastheads. At eight o'clock the fog still lay heavily on the waves, but thick scrolls of it were here and there beginning to rise. The horizon gradually widened and grew clearer at the same time. Suddenly, just as on the day before, Ned Land's voice was heard to cry, "There's the blooming thing on the port quarter!"

Every face was turned toward the point indicated. And there the animal was, a mile and a half away from the frigate, its long dark body jutting forth a yard or so above the surface. Its tail, violently agitated, was producing a considerable eddy. Never did a caudal appendage beat the sea with such violence. An immense wake of dazzling white marked the passage of the creature, describing a long curve.

The frigate approached the cetacean cautiously. I had the sought-for opportunity to examine it thoroughly.

As I had expected, I found the reports of the "Shannon" and the "Helvetia" had somewhat exaggerated its size. I estimated its length overall at only two hundred and fifty feet. As to its other dimensions, I could only conjecture that they were admirably proportioned. While I was studying this marvel two jets of steam and water were ejected rapidly from its vents and rose to the majestic height of a hundred and twenty feet. Thus I was enabled to ascertain its way of breathing. I concluded definitely that it belonged to the vertebrate branch, genus mammalia.

The crew stood to attention, impatiently awaiting the captain's orders. The latter, after careful study of the animal, summoned the chief engineer. The engineer sprang to answer the signal.

"You have steam up, sir?" demanded the commander.

"Ay, ay, sir," replied the subordinate.

"Increase your fires at once and put on all head of steam."

Three ringing cheers greeted this command. The hour for combat had arrived. Some minutes later the two funnels of the frigate were vomiting forth stifling clouds of black smoke, and the bridge shook under the oscillation of the boilers.

The "Abraham Lincoln," driven by her rapidly revolving screw, went straight for the monster. The creature allowed it to come within half a cable's length. And then, as if disdaining the effort required to dive, it took a short turn to one side and stopped a short distance away.

"Mr. Land," asked the captain, "do you advise putting the small boats out to sea?"

"No, sir," replied the Canadian. "Because we shall not take that beast without a sharp struggle."

"What is your idea, then?"

"Get on more steam, sir, if you can crowd the engines. With your permission, I mean to post myself under the bowsprit, and if we get within proper distance I'll throw my harpoon."

"Just the thing, Mr. Land," said the captain. "Engineer, give us more pressure."

The Canadian took up his post. The fires were increased, the screw revolved forty-three turns to the minute, and the steam poured forth from every valve.

We heaved the log and determined that the "Abraham Lincoln" was traveling at the rate of eighteen and one-half knots.

But the accursed monster swam at the same rate of speed.

For a whole hour the frigate held to this pace without gaining six feet. It was a humiliating performance for one of the swiftest sailing ships in the American navy. A cold anger seized hold of the crew. The sailors abused the monster, which as before disdained to make answer to them. The captain no longer contented himself with twisting his beard—he gnawed it.

The engineer was again summoned.

"You have turned on full steam?"

"Every last possible ounce, sir."

And yet, somehow, the speed of the "Abraham Lincoln" increased. Its masts fell to vibrating down to their very stepping-holes. And the choking clouds of smoke could scarcely find their way out of the narrow funnels.

The log was heaved a second time.

"Well, my hearty?" demanded the captain of the man at the wheel.

"Nineteen and three-tenths knots, sir."

"Force the fires!"

The engineer obeyed. The manometer indicated ten degrees. But without much doubt the cetacean itself was putting on steam. For it, too, with no sign of strain, was hitting a clip of nineteen and three-tenths.

What a chase! There is no way for me to describe the emotions that shook me. Ned Land clung doggedly to his desperate post, harpoon ready for the thrust. Several times the creature allowed us to gain on it slightly.

"We're overhauling it! We'll run it down yet," the Canadian would cry at such a moment.

But, just as he would be poised to strike, the cetacean would steal away with a rapidity that (insane as the statement sounds) must have been at least thirty miles an hour. And even during the frigate's maximum of effort the creature kept bullying and mocking her, every now and then sailing round us in sharp circles. A cry of fury burst from every throat.

At noon we were no better off than at eight o'clock. The captain then determined to adopt more desperate remedies.

"Belay me!" he growled, "that beast travels faster than the 'Abraham Lincoln.' All right, sir. We'll now see if its hide can shed our conical bullets. Send your men to the forecastle, sir."

The forecastle gun was loaded promptly and slewed into position. Careful sight was taken, but the trial shot passed several feet above the back of the cetacean, which at that instant was half a mile distant.

"Another one more to the mark!" cried the commander. "And five dollars to the man that hits the infernal thing!"

An old gunner with a gray beard—I can see him as I write—with steady eye and a grave face, approached the gun and took long and careful aim. A loud report was heard, with which almost simultaneously were mingled the cheers of the watching crew.

The bullet had reached its mark, but, alas, had not

achieved the results expected of it. It hit the monster, but, instead of inflicting a fatal wound, it slid off the rounded surface and sank in two miles' depth of sea water.

So the chase was begun anew. The captain leaned toward me and spat out the following words like bullets: "I'll chase that monster till the boilers burst and the frigate's pieces strew the ocean."

"Of course," I answered, no less hotly. "We've got to get him."

I prayed that the beast would exhaust itself instead of showing itself as insensible to fatigue as a steam engine. But my petition was of no avail, for hours passed and the creature still exhibited no sign of tiring.

However, it must be said in praise of the "Abraham Lincoln" that she, too, struggled on indefatigably. The total of her run during this unlucky day, November 6, I cannot reckon at less than three hundred miles. Finally night overtook us and cast its thick shadow on a roughening ocean.

Now I thought the curtain was down on our performance. Our expedition had been born under an unhappy star and come to its miserable end. Apparently we could not hope to see the marvelous monster again. But in this life it is always the unexpected that happens, as I soon discovered. At ten minutes to eleven in the evening the electric light reappeared suddenly three miles to windward of the frigate, as clear, as intense as during the preceding night.

The narwhal was lying motionless. Mayhap, tired with its strenuous day's labors, it was asleep and letting itself rock on the cradling waves. Now, if ever, was the golden opportunity. And the commander decided to take advantage of it.

He issued the necessary orders. The "Abraham Lincoln" advanced cautiously under half steam so as not to awaken its adversary. It is no rare thing to meet in mid-ocean whales so soundly sleeping that they can be successfully attacked. And Ned Land had harpooned more than one leviathan while it was enmeshed in slumber. Ned once more took up his place under the bowsprit.

The frigate stole noiselessly upon its unsuspecting foe. It stopped at two cable lengths from the creature and then began slowly, foot by foot, to follow its track. We held our breath painfully—a deep silence reigned on the bridge. We were now not a hundred feet from the burning focus of light, the radiance of which increased and blinded our eyes.

At this second, leaning on the forecastle bulwark, I looked below me and saw Ned Land grappling the martingale in one hand, while in the other he brandished his terrible harpoon, scarcely twenty feet from the motionless animal. Suddenly his arm straightened and the harpoon was hurled. I heard the sonorous impact of the weapon as it seemed to strike upon a hard substance. The electric light was instantly extinguished and two enormous waterspouts broke over the body of the bridge, rushing like tidal waves from stem to stern of the frigate, hurling men about like straws, breaking the lashing of the spars. A fearful shock followed. Without power to protect myself in any way, I was thrown high over the rail of the ship and fell into the sea.

CHAPTER VII

AN UNKNOWN ·SPECIES OF WHALE

Although I was stunned by this unexpected fall, I nevertheless kept a very clear impression of my sensations at the time. I was at first drawn down to a depth of about twenty feet. I am a good swimmer—though without pretending to rival Byron or Edgar Poe, who were masters of the art—and in that plunge I did not lose my presence of mind. Two vigorous strokes brought me to the surface of the water. My first care was to look for the frigate. Had the crew seen me disappear? Had the "Abraham Lincoln" veered round? Would the captain put out a boat? Might I hope to be saved?

The darkness was intense. I caught a glimpse of a black mass disappearing in the east, its beacon lights dying out in the distance. It was the frigate. I was lost.

"Help, help!" I shouted, swimming in desperation toward the "Abraham Lincoln."

My clothes encumbered me; they seemed glued to my body, and paralyzed my movements.

I was sinking! I was suffocating!

"Help!"

This was my last cry. My mouth filled with water. I struggled desperately as I was being drawn down into the abyss. Suddenly my clothes were seized by a strong hand, and I felt myself quickly drawn up to the surface of the sea; and I heard, yes, I heard these words pro-

nounced in my ear: "If you would be so good as to lean
on my shoulder, sir, you would swim with much greater
ease."

I seized with one hand my faithful Conseil's arm.

"Is it you?" said I. "You?"

"Who else should it be, sir?" replied Conseil calmly.
"I await your orders, sir."

"Good lad! So you were thrown overboard also by
the concussion?"

"Not exactly, sir. But, being in your service, sir, I
naturally followed you down."

The worthy fellow seemed to regard his act as nothing
strange.

"What's become of the frigate?"

"Oh, the frigate?" queried Conseil, as he turned over
on his back so that he could float with less effort. "I
think perhaps you had better not count too much on her
assistance."

"And why not, pray?"

"Because, sir, just as I was jumping into the sea I
heard the helmsman shout that the screw and rudder
were smashed."

"Smashed!"

"Yes, sir. Chewed into bits, I suppose, by the monster's
teeth. That's the only injury the 'Abraham Lincoln' got.
But it makes things bad for us, don't you think, sir? For
she no longer answers her helm."

"Then we are lost indeed."

"Oh, I shouldn't say that, sir," answered Conseil
quietly. "Whatever happens, we've got several hours of

life before us. And one can do a lot of things in several
hours, sir."

The servant's imperturbable coolness buoyed my fainting spirits considerably.   I began to strike out more
vigorously.   But I found myself cramped by my clothes,
which stuck to me like a leaden weight.   And so I had
much difficulty in swimming. Conseil noticed this.

"With your permission, sir, I'll make a slit," he said.
And, slipping an open knife underneath my clothes, he
ripped them up from top to bottom very cleverly.   Then
he quickly slipped them off me while I was doing the
swimming for both of us.   After I had learned my lesson
from the servant, I applied my new knowledge and did
the same for him.   Then we continued to swim close to
each other.

We might whistle to keep up our courage, but none the
less our plight was a terrible one.   Even if our disappearance had been noted, which in itself was unlikely, the
frigate could not tack and come for us if its helm was
gone. Conseil adopted this supposition and laid his plans
accordingly.

The phlegmatic boy was perfectly self-possessed   He
felt that, as our only chance of rescue lay in our being
picked up by one of the "Abraham Lincoln's" boats, we
ought to contrive somehow to wait for them as long as
possible.   I resolved to husband my strength so that both
of us should not be worn out at the same instant.   And
this is how we managed it. While one of us was floating
on his back, quite still, with arms crossed on his breast
and legs stretched out, the other would swim and push

his comrade ahead of him. This towing business, of course, would not last longer than, say ten minutes at a stretch. But, relieving each other in this fashion, we could reasonably hope to keep ourselves afloat for hours, perhaps until dawn. Poor chance, you say? Yes, but yet hope springs eternal in the heart of man. Moreover, there were two of us, and so much did this fact lighten my spirit that I declare (believe it or not) I could not have despaired even if I had tried to.

The collision of frigate and cetacean had taken place about eleven o'clock the evening before. So I reckoned we should have to keep from drowning eight hours until sunrise. The sea was unusually calm by now, which was a great factor in our favor. Sometimes, as I swam, I endeavored to penetrate with my gaze the intense darkness that was dispelled only by the phosphorescence caused by our movements. I watched the luminous wavelets that broke over my hand. Their mirror-like surface was spotted with silvery rings. One might have said we were in a bath of quicksilver.

It was nearly one o'clock, as well as I could judge, when I was suddenly seized with overmastering fatigue. My limbs stiffened and contracted under the strain of a violent cramp. Conseil was forced to keep me above water, and our preservation now devolved upon him alone. I heard the poor fellow pant—his gasping breath grew short and hurried. I knew he could not bear me up much longer.

"Let me go and save yourself," I ordered him.

"Leave you, sir? Never," he replied. "I'll drown first."

Just then the moon peered through the fringes of a thick cloud that the wind was driving eastward. The surface of the sea glittered with its rays. The kindly light brought me new courage. I raised my head. I looked toward every point of the compass and saw the frigate! She was a good five miles away from us, a dark mass, hardly discernible. But no small boat anywhere to be seen!

I started to cry out. But of what avail would it be at such a distance from help? Besides, it seemed as if my swollen lips could utter no sound. Conseil, however, could still articulate his words and I heard him at intervals repeating, "Help! Help!"

For an instant our movements were suspended that we might listen for an echoing cry. It might have been only the singing in my ears, but it seemed as if a shout answered our call.

"Did you hear anything?" I demanded.

"Without question, yes, sir."

And once again Conseil gave vent to a despairing cry.

This time there could be no mistake about it; a human voice was responding to us! Was it from the throat of another poor wretch, like ourselves abandoned to the mercies of mid-ocean, another victim of the shock sustained by the frigate? Or rather did the hail come from a small boat that was searching for us in the shrouding night?

Conseil made one last effort. He leaned for support on my shoulder as I struck wildly out in an attempt to swim and raised himself half out of the water. Then he fell back exhausted.

"What—did—you—see?" I gasped.

"I saw—" murmured the poor fellow. "I saw—but do not talk—save all your strength!"

What had he glimpsed? I know not why, but the thought of the monster flashed into my mind for the first time. The voice from the depths? Surely no longer do Jonahs take refuge in whales' bellies! At any rate, Conseil had recovered sufficiently to be towing me again. He raised his head at intervals, looked before us, and uttered a cry of recognition, which was always responded to by a voice that was drawing nearer and nearer. I could scarcely hear anything more. My strength was utterly sapped. My fingers were stiff as marble, my hand no longer afforded me support, my mouth, convulsively opening, was filled with salt water. I raised my head one last time. Cold crept over me, and I sank like a plummet.

A hard object struck me a stunning blow. I clung to it instinctively, and then I felt that I was being drawn upward, that I was being brought again to the surface of the water. My chest collapsed. I fainted away.

But my swoon was not for long, as it was not proof against the vigorous rubbings to which I was subjected. I soon opened my eyes.

"Are you there, Conseil?" I asked weakly.

"At your service, sir," replied the boy.

Just then, by the waning light of the moon which was sinking down toward the horizon, I saw a face that was not the servant's and that I immediately recognized.

"Ned, of all people!" I cried.

"The very same, sir. And come here to secure his prize," answered the Canadian whimsically.

"Were you cast overboard by the shock of the frigate?"

"You've guessed it, Professor. But I had better luck than you, for I got a footing on this floating island without loss of time."

"What island are you talking about?"

"Well, if you prefer the expression, on this gigantic narwhal."

"My poor head is still dizzy, Ned. So explain yourself."

"And it didn't take me long to discover why the point of my harpoon was blunted, also why it failed to pierce the skin."

"But tell me why, man! Why was it?"

"Because, my dear Professor, this particular beastie is made of sheet iron."

At the Canadian's last words something seemed to snap in my brain. I wriggled quickly to the top of the half-submerged being (or object) which served as our temporary refuge. I kicked it. Verily, it had a hard, impervious body, and not the soft substance that forms the organism of great marine mammalia. But still this flinty matter might be a bony carapace, like that possessed by antediluvian monsters. And, for aught I knew, I should be free to classify this monster among amphibious reptiles, such as tortoises or alligators.

But even as I debated these matters I knew in my heart of hearts the truth. The black ridge that supported me was smooth, polished, without scales. The blow of my foot produced a metallic sound. And, incredible though it may be, the monster seemed to be made of riveted plates.

Yes, by Jove! There was no further doubt about it. This marvel, this almost miraculous phenomenon that had puzzled the learned world and distorted the thinking-apparatus of the seamen of two hemispheres, was, strange to relate, a much more amazing thing than anyone had dreamed of. For it was of human, and not of divine, construction.

In any case, we had not a moment to lose. We were precariously perched upon the back of some sort of submersible boat, which appeared to be (so far as I could judge) a huge fish of steel. Ned Land's mind on this point was already made up. Conseil and I could but agree.

At this point in my musings a bubbling noise arose at the rear of this strange monster, which was evidently propelled by a screw. It began to move. We had just time enough to seize hold of the upper part, which rose about seven feet above the water. Happily, the speed was not great.

"As long as it sails on its present level keel," muttered the harpooner, "I shall not worry. But if the tarnal thing takes a notion to dive, I shouldn't give two straws for my chance of life."

One straw would have been enough to offer.

It became imperative that we communicate with the beings, whoever they were, that were shut up inside the machine. I searched all over the exposed part for an opening, a panel, or a manhole. But the lines of iron rivets, solidly driven into the joints of the plates, were clear and uniform. Besides, the moon had finally vanished, and we were in total obscurity.

The night dragged by with leaden feet, but at last it passed. My hazy remembrance of things (due, no doubt, to exposure and faintness) prevents my describing all my impressions at this time. I recall but a single circumstance. During lulls in the clamor of wind and sea I heard on several occasions what seemed to be vague sounds, a sort of fugitive harmony produced by far-away tones. What was, then, the secret of this mysterious submarine craft, of which the whole habitable globe had been vainly seeking the solution? What sort of creatures dwelt within the walls of this strange boat? What mechanical agent caused its prodigious velocity?

Dawn arrived. The morning mists hemmed us in on every side, but they soon took flight before the arrows of the sun. I was on the point of examining the hull, which formed on deck a species of horizontal platform, when I noticed that we were gradually sinking.

"Hang it all!" shouted Ned Land as he kicked against the resounding plate. "Open up, you inhospitable rascal!"

Fortunately the sinking movement ceased. All at once a noise, like that of iron being violently pushed aside, came from the interior of the boat. An iron plate was lifted, a man appeared, uttered an odd cry, and immediately disappeared from view.

Some moments later eight stout men with masked faces appeared stealthily and drew us down into their formidable machine.

CHAPTER VIII

OUR NEW QUARTERS

This forcible seizure, carried out with cruel roughness, was accomplished with the rapidity of lightning. What with weakness and with dread of the unknown, I was quivering like an aspen leaf. With whom had we to deal?

There could be but one sane answer to such a query: We had doubtless encountered some new sort of pirate, or buccaneer, who explored the sea in his own fashion.

Hardly had the narrow sea panel been closed upon me when I found myself cast into utter darkness. Dazzled from the outer light, my eyes could now distinguish nothing. I felt my naked feet cling to the rungs of an iron ladder. Ned Land and Conseil, like myself, seized and firmly held, were carried struggling down after me. At the bottom of the iron ladder a door was opened, and when we were once drawn through its aperture it was immediately shut after us with a slam.

We were alone. Where, I could not guess nor yet imagine. All was black as Erebus, and the gloom was of such unrelieved density that even after several minutes my eyes had been unable to discern the very faintest glimmer.

Meanwhile the harpooner, whose feelings had been much ruffled by the recent high-handed proceedings, proceeded to give free rein to his indignation.

"By the pluck!" he fumed. "Here are people as badly

off as the Scotch for hospitality. They are as gentle as cannibals. And I shouldn't be surprised if they were man-eaters. But I'll be right there when they start to swallow me."

"Put on the soft pedal, my friend," advised the quiet Conseil. "While there's life, there's hope. And we're not quite done for yet."

"Not quite, perhaps," the Canadian retorted sharply, "but pretty near it, the way things look. Anyway, I've got my trusty bowie-knife still, and you don't need to see well to use that. The first of these blarsted pirates to lay a hand on me—"

"Avast there, my lad," I said, "and do not make our situation worse by any act of useless violence. Who knows but what they are listening to us? Let's use our energy trying to find out where we are."

I groped blindly about me. In five steps I came to an iron partition made of plates bolted together. Then, in turning back, I stumbled against a wooden table, near which were ranged several chairs. The floor boards of this prison cell were covered by a thick mat of phormium which deadened the sound of feet. The bare walls revealed no trace of window or door. Conseil, going around the room in the opposite direction, met me, and together we returned to the center of the cabin. It measured twenty feet by ten. As to its height, Ned Land, despite his great size, could not measure it.

Half an hour may have passed without any alteration or betterment in our situation when the dense darkness suddenly yielded to extreme radiance. Our prison was brilliantly lighted by being filled with a luminous matter so strong that at first it was agony to endure it. In its whiteness and intensity I recognized that same electric light that had played around the submarine boat like a splendid aura of phosphorescence. After shutting my eyes for a spell, I opened them and saw that this radiant agency came from a half-globe which was unpolished and set in the roof of the cabin.

"At last one can see his own nose!" cried Ned Land, who, knife in hand, was standing in an attitude of defense.

"Ah," I said, "but we are still in the dark about ourselves."

"All things come to him who waits, sir," remarked the imperturbable Conseil.

The illumination of our premises enabled me to subject them to a minute scrutiny. They contained no other furniture than the table and five chairs. An invisible door, if there was one, was hermetically sealed. No noise was heard from without; all seemed dead in the interior of this boat. An uncanny feeling of emptiness stole upon me. Were we moving? Did we float on the surface of the ocean or were we diving into its depths? I could not guess.

A noise as of bolts was now heard. A door opened, and two men made their appearance.

One of them was short of stature, broad-shouldered, and evidently very muscular. He had robust limbs, a strong head, an abundance of black hair, a thick mustache, a quick, penetrating glance, and the vivacity of manner that one associates with the population of southern France.

The second stranger deserves a more detailed description. A disciple of Gratiolet or Engel would have read his face as clearly as the page of an open book. I decided without hesitation upon his dominant characteristics: self-confidence, because his head was well set on his shoulders and his black eyes looked about him with cool assurance; calmness, because his skin, rather pale in hue, betokened the slow pulsing of his blood; energy, indicated by the rapid contraction of his high brows; and courage, because his deep breathing denoted great lung power and capacity.

Whether this person was thirty-five or fifty years of age, who could say? He was tall, had a broad forehead, a straight nose, a clearly cut mouth, and beautiful teeth. His finely tapering hands evidenced a highly nervous temperament. This man was certainly the finest specimen of the genus homo that I had ever met. One particular feature of his appearance was his eyes, set rather far apart and thus able to take in at a single glance almost a fourth part of the visible horizon.

This unusual faculty (as I came to know later) gave him a range of vision far superior to that of Ned Land. When this stranger centered his gaze upon an object, his eyebrows met, his eyelids practically closed, so as to contract the field of his sight. And it really seemed as if he thus magnified the things which were diminished by distance from him—as if he pierced those masses of water opaque to our eyes—as if he read the very secret depths of the seas.

The two unknown intruders on our privacy wore caps made from the fur of the sea otter and were shod with sea boots of sealskin. Besides this, they were dressed in clothes of a peculiar texture, which allowed free movement of the limbs. The taller of the two, evidently the chief on board, studied us with great attention without uttering a single syllable. After some moments he turned to his companion and conversed with him in an unknown tongue. It was a sonorous and flexible dialect, evidently, as the vowels seemed to admit of extremely varied accentuation.

The other stranger replied by a shake of the head and added two or three perfectly incomprehensible words. Then he seemed to question me by a look.

I replied to his unspoken invitation that I did not know his language, but he appeared not to understand me. And the situation grew rather embarrassing.

"If you were to tell our story, sir," Conseil suggested, "perhaps these gentlemen might understand the drift of your words."

This seemed the only rational thing to do. And therefore I commenced the tale of our adventures and mishaps, articulating each syllable precisely, and not omitting a single detail. I gave our names and rank, introducing in person Professor Aronnax, his servant Conseil, and Mr. Ned Land, harpooner.

The man with the soft calm eyes listened to my narrative quietly, politely even. He missed no word I spoke, but nothing in his face showed that he had understood my yarn. When I finished, he remained silent.

There was another resource at my command, to speak English. Perhaps the strangers would understand this practically universal idiom. I commanded it, and also the German tongue, well enough to read them fluently, but not to speak them correctly. But, needs must, it was highly necessary to make our position understood.

"You take up the statement in your turn," I whispered to the harpooner. "And speak your best Anglo-Saxon, for you will have to succeed better than I have."

Ned did not require a second invitation, but began our story again from the start. To his great disgust, he was able to make himself no more intelligible than I. Our visitors did not stir. They quite clearly knew neither the language of Arago nor of Faraday.

Very much put out by our ill success, having vainly exhausted our philological resources, I scarcely knew what to do next. Conseil attempted our rescue.

"If you will permit me, sir, I'll tell it to them in German."

But, in spite of his elegant turns of speech and his good accent, the poor lad had no success with the German report. Finally, quite nonplussed, I tried to recall my early school lessons in Caesar and Virgil and to narrate our story in Latin, but all with no result. After I had finished my last attempt the two strangers exchanged some words in their unknown tongue and retired.

The door shut behind them.

"It's a crying shame!" burst out Ned Land, yielding to his twentieth access of fury. "We chatter to these rogues in French, English, German, and Latin, and neither of them has the dashed politeness to answer us."

"Don't give way to anger," I cautioned the impetuous Canadian. "It will not get us anywhere."

"But, look here, Professor," retorted my irascible comrade, "we are jolly well sure to die of starvation in this iron cage."

"Pouf!" ejaculated Conseil, philosophically. "We can hold out a long time yet."

"Friends," I said, with more conviction than I actually felt, "we must not abandon hope. We've all been worse off than this a lot of times. Do me the favor to wait a while before passing an opinion upon the commander and crew of this boat."

"My opinion is formed," returned Ned Land sharply. "They are rascals and come from Rogueland."

"My dear fellow," I reminded him, "that country is not clearly indicated on the map of the world, and I wish to know the nationality of our two captors. They are not English, French, or German, so much is sure. I am inclined to think there is southern blood in them. But I cannot determine by their appearance whether they are Spaniards, Turks, Arabians, or Indians. As to their lingo, it is perfectly unintelligible."

"That's the worst about not knowing all tongues," said Conseil. "There should be one universal language."

Hardly had he uttered these words of wisdom when the door again opened and a man in steward's uniform appeared. He brought us garments of every sort—coats and trousers made of a stuff I did not know. I hastened to cover my nakedness, and my companions were not slow in following my example. While we dressed, the steward, who so far as we could determine was deaf and dumb, arranged the table and laid three covers.

"I call that something like," said Conseil, wetting his lips with his tongue.

"Pah!" exclaimed the harpooner, whose rancor nothing could appease. "What do you suppose they're going to give us? Tortoise liver, fillets of shark, and sea-dog steaks —that's my guess."

"We shall soon see."

The dishes with their silver covers were placed upon the table, and we took our places. It looked as if we had to deal with cultured people, at least. And, if it had not been for the electric light that flooded us, I could have fancied I was in the dining room of the Adelphi Hotel at Liverpool or at the Grand Hotel in Paris. There was neither bread nor wine. The water was fresh and clear, but it was water, and that beverage did not suit Ned Land's taste as well as others. Among the dishes that were brought us I recognized several fish, well cooked and with savory dressing. But some of the foods, though excellent in taste, I could not guess at—not even to which kingdom they belonged, whether animal or vegetable.

As to the dinner service, it was elegant, nothing less. Each utensil, spoon, fork, knife, and plate, had a letter engraved on it, with a motto above. Here is the facsimile:

MOBILIS IN MOBILI

N

The letter was no doubt the initial of the strange man who commanded a boat at the bottom of the seas. Now Ned and Conseil did not bother much about either mottoes or tasteful dinner ware. Instead, they devoured their food, and, truth to tell, I was soon doing likewise. For the first time I felt assured concerning our fate, since it was quite evident that our hosts did not intend to let us die of want.

Sooner or later everything has an end, even the hunger of sailormen who have not touched food for fifteen hours. The instant our appetites were sated, we were overcome by an insistent drowsiness.

"Faith! I shall sleep well," said Conseil as he wiped his lips for the last time with a napkin.

"And so shall I," added Ned Land.

No sooner said than done. My two comrades stretched themselves on the cabin carpet and were soon in the arms of Morpheus. For my part, too many perplexing thoughts were crowding on my brain, too many insoluble riddles pressed upon me, too many fancies kept my eyes at least half open.

First of all, where were we? And next, what strange power carried us forward? I felt, or imagined I felt, the machine sinking to the lowest bed of the sea. Dreadful nightmares beset me. I saw in this mysterious hiding place of ocean a whole menagerie of unknown animals, among which the submersible boat seemed to belong— living and moving as they did, formidable as were they. Then, by degrees, my brain grew calmer, my fancy wandered off into the realms of vague unconsciousness that border Never Never Land, and I soon fell into deep and refreshing slumber.

CHAPTER IX

NED LAND ATTACKS

I do not know how long I wooed Death's twin sister, Sleep. But my dozing must have been a protracted one, for it rested me completely from my harrowing fatigue. I was the first to wake. My companions had not moved from their postures that I had last noted. They were still stretched unconscious in their corner.

I was scarcely roused from my somewhat hard couch, when I felt my brain to be free of all whimsy and vertigo. With a clear mind I began an exhaustive examination of our cell. Nothing was changed inside. Our prison was a prison still, and we, to all intents and purposes, bound captives. The one thing I noted was that during our unconsciousness the steward had cleared away the dishes from the table. It was difficult for me to breathe with any comfort. The heavy air of the confined space seemed to weigh upon my lungs. Although the cell was fairly large, we had consumed a great part of the oxygen that it contained. I remembered that each man consumes, in one hour, the oxygen contained in more than one hundred and seventy-six pints of air. And this air, charged, as it now was, with a quantity of carbon dioxide nearly equal to the oxygen that had been lost, became unbearable.

It thus became necessary to renew the atmosphere of our prison, and no doubt also that of the other inhabited parts of the boat. This raised the question in my mind:

How would the commander of this floating submersible proceed to achieve this? Would he obtain new air by chemical means, in getting by heat the oxygen contained in chlorate of potash and in absorbing carbon dioxide by caustic potash? Or, would he employ a more convenient, economical, and consequently more probable means? Would he rise like a cetacean to the surface of the water and take breath, thus renewing for twenty-four hours the boat's atmospheric provision?

In fact, I was already obliged to increase my respirations to draw from this cell the little oxygen it contained, when suddenly I was refreshed by a current of pure air, perfumed with saline emanations. It was an invigorating sea breeze, charged with iodine. I opened my mouth wide, and my lungs saturated themselves with fresh particles.

At the same time I felt the boat rolling. The iron-plated monster had evidently just risen to the surface of the ocean to breathe, after the fashion of whales. I found out from that the mode of ventilating the boat.

When I had inhaled this air freely, I sought the conduit-pipe which had conveyed to us the beneficial whiff, and I was not long in finding it. Above the door was a ventilator, through which volumes of fresh air renewed the impoverished atmosphere of the cell.

I was making my observations when, under the influence of this reviving air, Ned and Conseil awoke almost at the same time. They rubbed their eyes, stretched themselves, and in an instant were on their feet.

"Did you sleep well, sir?" asked Conseil politely.

"Very well, my brave boy. And you, Ned?"

"Soundly, Professor. But, I don't know whether I am right or not, there seems to be a sea breeze!"

A seaman could not be mistaken, and I told the Canadian all that had passed during his sleep.

"Good!" said he. "That accounts for those roarings we heard when the supposed narwhal sighted the 'Abraham Lincoln.'"

"Quite so, Ned; it was taking breath."

"Only, M. Aronnax, I have no idea what time it is, unless it is dinner time."

"Dinner time, my good fellow? Nonsense! Say breakfast time, rather, for we certainly have added another day to the calendar."

"Which means, sir, that we have slept clear round the clock?" asked Conseil.

"To the best of my judgment, we have."

"I'm in no mind to contradict," said Ned Land. "But, whatever the meal be called, the steward will be welcome."

"Of course we must conform to the rules on board, whatever they may be," suggested my servant mildly. "And it is but natural that our appetites should outrun the dinner hour."

"There you go, friend Conseil," muttered Ned peevishly. "You are never out of temper and always calm as a stuffed mummy. Left to yourself, you would say grace before your food was cooked, and die of starvation rather than complain."

But time was getting on, and we had nothing to occupy our minds save thoughts of the coming meal. They were really neglecting us too long if their intentions toward us were gentle ones. Tormented by the gnawings of hunger, Ned Land grew from minute to minute, if possible, still angrier. And, notwithstanding his fair promises, I dreaded an explosion when he next found himself confronted by one of the boat's crew.

For another two hours the harpooner nursed his temper actively. He cried out, he shouted, but all in vain. The walls were stone-deaf. Not a sound was to be heard in all the boat; again death seemed hovering about us. We were not moving, for surely in that case I should have felt the vibrations of the hull under the throbbing of the screw. Plunged, as we must be, in the profound depths of the waters, the boat no longer seemed to belong to earth. The silence was dreadful.

I was frankly apprehensive. Conseil (need I say it?) was as calm as a stone image of Buddha. Ned Land roared.

Just then a slight noise was heard outside. Steps sounded on the metal flags. The locks were turned, the door opened, and the steward entered our prison.

Before I could rush forward to prevent it, the Canadian had thrown the man to the floor and was holding him fast by the throat. The steward was strangling under the grip of Ned's powerful hand.

Conseil was already busy, trying to unclasp the harpooner's claw from his half-suffocated victim, and I was flying to the rescue, when suddenly I was rooted to the spot by hearing the following words spoken in perfect French: "Be quiet, Mr. Land. And you, Professor, will you be so good as to listen to me?"

CHAPTER X

THE MAN OF THE SEAS

It was the commander of the submarine who addressed us.

At his words the Canadian rose quickly to his feet. The steward, nearly dead though he was, tottered out at a sign from his master. And such was the power of the commander that not a gesture of the strangled fellow betrayed the hatred he must have felt for his assaulter. Conseil, in spite of himself, seemed actually interested in the situation. I was stupefied with surprise and awaited in silence whatever result the scene would bring.

Our visitor, with folded arms, leaned against a corner of the table and scanned us with profound attention. Why did he hesitate to speak further? Was he already regretting the words he had just uttered in the French tongue? One might almost think so.

After an interval of silence, which no one of us even dreamed of interrupting, he said in a quiet but penetrating voice, "Gentlemen, I speak French, English, German, and Latin equally well. I could therefore have appeased your curiosity at our first interview, but I wished to know you and then to reflect. The story told by each one of you, agreeing in all salient points, convinced me of your identity. I know now that fate has brought to me Pierre Aronnax, professor of natural history in the Museum of Paris, intrusted with a scientific mission abroad. Conseil is his servant. Ned Land, of Canadian birth, is harpooner on board the frigate 'Abraham Lincoln' of the United States' navy."

I bowed assent. It was not a question that the commander put to me, therefore there was no spoken answer to be made. This man expressed himself with perfect fluency and without a trace of foreign accent. His phrases were neatly turned, his enunciation clear, and his ease of speech remarkable. And yet I could not recognize him as a fellow countryman.

He continued, "You may have imagined, sir, that I delayed overlong in paying you a second visit. My excuse is that I wished to consider thoroughly what part to act toward you. And I had many grounds for hesitation. An evil fate has brought you, sir, into the presence of a man who has broken all ties that bound him to humankind. You have come to torment my existence."

"But unintentionally," I interjected.

"What!" exclaimed the stranger, slightly raising his voice. "Was it unintentionally that the 'Abraham Lincoln' pursued me across the seas? That you took passage in the frigate? That your cannon balls rebounded from the plating of my vessel? That Mr. Land struck me with his harpoon?"

No one could fail to detect a hardly restrained irritation in these words. But of course I had a very natural answer for his recriminations, and I offered it at once.

"My dear sir," I said, "you are doubtless unaware of the worldwide discussions concerning you which have occupied humanity. You do not know, presumably, that various accidents caused by collision with your submarine machine have stirred public feeling in both hemispheres. I shall not vex your ears with a recital of the theories without number which sought to explain the marvel of which you alone possess the secret. But you must understand that, in pursuing you across the high seas of the Pacific, the 'Abraham Lincoln' believed herself to be hunting down some powerful sea monster of which it was necessary to rid the ocean at any cost."

My statement was not without its effect upon the commander, for, although a half-smile curled his lips, his next remarks were made in a calmer tone.

"M. Aronnax, dare you tell me that your frigate would not as soon have pursued and wrecked a submersible as a monster?"

Such questions should not be asked—they are altogether too embarrassing. I really believe Captain Farragut would not have hesitated to cannonade an underseas boat. He might have thought it his duty to destroy a contrivance of this kind as readily as he would a gigantic narwhal.

"You see then, do you not," continued the stranger, "that I have the right to treat you as enemies and prisoners of war?"

When one has nothing to say, it is a good thing to sit tight. I said nothing. For what good would it do to discuss our situation when force could immediately destroy the very best arguments?

"I have hesitated for some time," the commander went on to say, "for I in no way felt obliged to offer you hospitality. If I should so choose, I am justified in placing

you back on the deck of this vessel which served you as
a temporary refuge. Then I could sink beneath the waters
and forget that you had ever existed. You acknowledge
I should be within my rights?"

"Within the rights of a savage," I answered with some
heat, "but not those of a civilized man."

"Look here!" flashed the commander. "I am not
what you so glibly call a civilized man. I have broken with
society for reasons which I alone am able to appreciate.
I am therefore not subject to its stupid laws, and I ask you
never to allude to them in my presence again."

That speech was as plain as a pikestaff. A flash of
anger and contempt kindled in the eyes of the Unknown,
and I had a fleeting vision of some terrible past in the
life of this man. Not only had he put himself beyond the
pale of human laws, but he had made himself independent
of them. In the strictest sense of the word, he was free,
because he was outside the reach of the moral code.

What booted it, under such circumstances, to pursue
him to the bottom of the sea, when on its surface he defied
all organized attempts against him? What vessel yet
contrived by the hands of men could withstand the shock
of this submarine monitor? What steel sheathing, however thick, could outlive the blows of his spur? No man
born of woman might demand of him an account of his
actions. God alone (if he believed in one), his own conscience (if he had one)—these were the sole supreme
judges to whom he was answerable.

These thoughts darted through my mind, while the
stranger was silent, wrapped up in his own somber

reflections. I regarded him with fear and yet with decided interest, much, I suppose, as Oedipus studied the stone-faced Sphinx.

It was only after a long interval of silence that the commander resumed the conversation.

"Although I have delayed in coming to a decision," he said, "yet I believe my selfish interests might be reconciled with the exercise of that pity to which every living creature has a right. You will therefore remain on my vessel, since it has pleased fate to cast you there. You will be free. And, in exchange for this liberty, I shall impose but one condition. Your word of honor to submit to it will suffice."

"Out with it, sir!" I replied. "I suppose it is a condition to which a gentleman can agree."

"Of course. It is possible that events may arise which oblige me to consign you to your cabins for some hours, or even days. As I shall employ no violence to enforce my will, I expect from you three more than from all the others unquestioning obedience. In thus controlling your actions I assume all responsibility. I acquit you entirely of all blame for promising blindness to what you ought not to see. Do you accept this one condition to your freedom?"

So! Things took place on this boat which, to say the least, were singular! Things that should not be witnessed by people still within the pale of social laws! My sixth sense told me that, among the many surprises that the near future was undoubtedly preparing for me, this fact would be by no means the least.

"We accept," I answered. "Only I ask your permission to address one question to you—one only."

"Speak, sir."

"You said that we should be free on board."

"Entirely."

"I ask you, then, what you mean by this liberty?"

"Just the liberty to go, to come, to see, to observe even all that passes here—save under rare circumstances— the liberty, in short, which we enjoy ourselves, my companions and I."

It was evident that we did not understand one another.

"Pardon me, sir," I resumed, "but this liberty is only what every prisoner has of pacing his prison. It cannot suffice us."

"It must, however, suffice you."

"What! We must renounce forever seeing our country, our friends, our relatives again?"

"Yes, sir. But to renounce that unendurable worldly yoke which men believe to be liberty is not perhaps so painful as you think."

"Well," exclaimed Ned Land, "never will I give my word of honor not to try to escape."

"I did not ask you for your word of honor, Mr. Land," answered the commander coldly.

"Sir," I replied, beginning to get angry in spite of myself, "you take advantage of your position with regard to us; it is cruelty."

"No, sir, it is clemency. You are my prisoners of war. I keep you, when I could, by a word, plunge you into the depths of the ocean. You attacked me. You came to

surprise a secret which no man in the world must penetrate
—the secret of my whole existence. And do you think that
I am going to send you back to that world which must
know me no more? Never! In retaining you, it is not
you whom I guard—it is myself."

These words indicated a resolution on the part of
the commander against which no arguments would prevail.

"Well, then, my dear sir," I rejoined, "you offer us
simply the choice between life and death?"

"Just that. Nothing more."

"My friends," I said to Ned Land and Conseil, "we are
politely asked a question to which there is no answer. But,
at least, no plighted word binds us to the master of this
craft."

"That is understood, sir," affirmed the Unknown.

Then he continued, in a gentler tone, "And now permit
me to finish what I started out to say. I know you, M.
Aronnax. And I doubt whether you will have so much
to complain of in our enforced companionship as you seem
to fear. Among my favorite books you will find your own
published works on the mysteries of the depths undersea.
You have carried your investigations as far as terrestrial
science permitted you to. But you do not know all there
is to know, nor have you seen everything available. Let
me assure you then, Professor, that you will never regret
the time spent on board my ship. You are going to visit
the fairyland of marvels."

I shall not deny that these words of the commander
had an enormous effect on me. He had touched my weak
point. For a moment I forgot that the occupation with

such sublime subjects might not be worth the loss of my personal liberty. Anyway, I must trust the future to decide the grave question at issue. Meanwhile I contented myself with inquiring, "By what name shall I address you, sir?"

"To you, I am only Captain Nemo. To me, you and your companions are nothing but passengers on the 'Nautilus.' "

Then Captain Nemo summoned a steward and gave him orders in that strange language I could not understand. "A repast awaits you in your cabin," he said, turning to Ned Land and Conseil. "Will you two be good enough to follow this man?"

"And now, M. Aronnax, our breakfast is ready. Permit me to lead the way."

"I am entirely at your service, sir."

I followed Captain Nemo from the room. And the moment I passed through the door I found myself in a corridor lighted by electricity, very similar to the waist of a ship. We had gone a dozen yards or so when a second door opened before me.

We entered a dining room, decorated and furnished in a severe taste. High oaken sideboards, inlaid with ebony, stood at the two ends of the room. And on their shelves glittered china, porcelain, and crystal glass of inestimable value. The plate sparkled there in the rays diffused from the luminous ceiling, and the light was tempered and softened by exquisite paintings hung upon the walls. In the center of the room was a table richly spread. Captain Nemo indicated the place I was to occupy.

The breakfast consisted of a goodly number of dishes the contents of which were furnished by the sea. I was ignorant of the nature of many of them and of the mode of their preparation. I could not but agree that they were excellent, and even when they had a peculiar flavor I grew easily accustomed to it. These different foods seemed to be rich in phosphorus, and I felt they must be of marine origin.

Captain Nemo looked across at me with a slight smile. I had asked him no question, but apparently he guessed my thoughts, for he answered of his own accord much that I was eager to know.

"The majority of these dishes are unknown to you, I suppose," he said. "However, you may eat of them without hesitation, for they are wholesome and nourishing. Long ago I renounced the foods of earth, and I am never ill now. My crew, who are invariably healthy, are fed on the same sort of aliment."

"Then all these eatables are the produce of the sea?"

"Without exception. The sea supplies my every want. Sometimes I cast my nets in tow and draw them in ready to break with their great draught of fish. Sometimes I hunt in districts of this element that are inaccessible to man, and there I quarry the game that dwells in my submarine forests. My flocks, like those of Neptune's ancient shepherds, graze fearlessly on the vast prairies of the ocean. I am owner of a property immense beyond the power of computation. I cultivate it myself, but it is always sown by the hand of Him who created all living things."

"I understand perfectly well that your nets furnish delicious sea foods for your table," I said. "I can grasp also how you hunt aquatic game in your undersea preserves. But how can this particle of meat which I have just taken on my fork figure in your bill of fare?"

"What you believe to be meat, Professor, is nothing but fillet of turtle. By your side, likewise, are some dolphins' livers, which I assume you took to be ragout of pork. My chef is a clever fellow, and he excels in preparing the various products of the ocean. Taste, I beg of you, all these dishes. Here, for example, is a preserve of holothuria which a Malay would swear was unrivaled in the world. And here is a cream the milk for which has been furnished by cetacea and the sugar by the great fucus of the North Sea. And, lastly, permit me to offer you anemone-jam, which I believe to be equal in taste to any derived from the most delicious fruits of land."

I tasted and nibbled, more from curiosity than as a connoisseur, the while Captain Nemo enchanted me with his extraordinary stories.

"Do you rove the sea from preference, Captain?"

"Yes, sir, I love it! The sea is everything. It covers seven-tenths of the terrestrial globe. Its breath is pure and life-giving. It is an immense desert place where man is never lonely, for he senses the weaving of Creation on every hand. It is the physical embodiment of a supernatural existence."

"You believe, then, sir, in another and a higher world than this?"

"A needless question, Professor. Of course I do. For

the sea is itself nothing but love and emotion. It is the Living Infinite, as one of your poets has said. Nature manifests herself in it, with her three kingdoms: mineral, vegetable, and animal. The ocean is the vast reservoir of Nature."

"But she has been outstripped by the terrestrial world."

"Wherein? The globe began with the sea, and I doubt not that the globe will end with it. For in her alone is supreme tranquillity, the peace that passeth understanding The sea does not belong to despots. Upon its surface men can still exercise unjust laws, can fight, tear one another to pieces, exercise every known terrestrial horror. But at thirty feet below its level the reign of men ceases, their power disappears, their influence is quenched. Ah, my dear Professor, live—live in the bosom of the waters! There alone is independence. There I recognize no master. There I am free."

Captain Nemo for several minutes had been quite carried away by his enthusiasm. But now, in the very midst of it, he became suddenly silent. He paced up and down the room in evident agitation. After a while, however, he grew more calm and regained his accustomed coldness of mien. He turned to me.

"And now, Professor," he said, "if you wish to go over the 'Nautilus,' I am at your service."

CHAPTER XI

THE NAUTILUS

My host bowed to me to precede him. A double door contrived at the rear of the room opened, and I entered an apartment equal in its dimensions to the one that I had just quitted. It was a library.

Tall pieces of furniture of black-violet ebony inlaid with brass held on their broad shelves a great number of books uniformly bound. The high cases followed the shape of the room and terminated toward the bottom in huge divans covered with brown Morocco leather, over-stuffed and rounded in order to assure the greater comfort. Light, movable desks, fashioned to slide in or out at the whim of the user, afforded convenient book-rests for the reader. In the center of the ample study-room stood an immense table strewn with pamphlets and journals of every sort, including magazines and newspapers—the latter chiefly of fairly old date. The electric light flooded every nook and corner of the library; it was shed from four ground-glass globes half concealed in the volutes of the ceiling. I looked with unfeigned admiration and envy at this apartment so ingeniously fitted up that I could scarcely trust the evidence of my own eyes.

The captain had thrown himself upon one of the divans. "This, sir," said I, "is a library, which would more than honor a continental palace. You may guess my amazement to find it following you to the floors of the ocean."

"But where else could one find greater solitude or silence?" my host demanded with a twinkle in his eyes. "Did your study in the Paris museum afford you such absolute quiet?"

"Far from it. And, compared to yours, I must confess it is a very modest one. You have six or seven thousand volumes here?"

"Twelve thousand, M. Aronnax. And these tomes are the only ties that bind me to the earth. The day on which the 'Nautilus' first plunged beneath the waters I renounced the world. That day I purchased my last volumes, my final pamphlets and papers. And from that moment I prefer to think that men no longer study the reasons for things and write them down. These books, sir, are at your disposal and you may use them freely."

I thanked Captain Nemo profusely and went closer to the shelves to examine the library. Here I discovered works on science, ethics, and literature, but I did not come across a single volume which dealt with political economy. That subject seemed to be strictly proscribed. Oddly enough, the books were thrust onto the shelves in irregular arrangement, a fact that would seem to argue that they had been read by the commander of the "Nautilus" at random, or at least indiscriminately.

"I'm greatly obliged, sir, that you have placed this library at my disposal," I said. "It is a vast storehouse of science and contains many real treasures. I shall profit by them."

"But, my dear fellow," said my host, "this room is not only a library, it is also a smoking room."

"Smoking room?" I cried. "I had never hoped to hear that word again. Is the use of tobacco on board not prohibited?"

"But not at all!"

"Then, sir, I am inclined to believe that you have kept up a communication of sorts with Havana."

"Guess again," answered the captain. "Pray accept this cigar, M. Aronnax. And though its birthplace was not Cuba, or Key West, or Tampa, I fancy you'll be greatly pleased with it if you are a connoisseur of good tobaccos."

I gladly accepted the cigar proffered me. Its shape recalled ones I had bought in London, but it seemed to be made of leaves of gold. I lighted it at a small brazier, which was supported by an elegant bronze stem, and inhaled the first whiffs of smoke with a delight too deep for words, but one that will be recognized by any lover of tobacco who has been shut off from use of the weed for two days.

"It is incomparable," I said, "but is it, after all, tobacco?"

"No," acknowledged the captain, "this product comes from neither Havana nor the East. It is a sort of seaweed, rich in nicotine, with which the sea provides me, albeit somewhat sparingly."

It was at this juncture that my host opened the door which stood opposite the one by which we had entered the library, and I passed into an immense drawing room which was splendidly lighted.

It was a vast rectangular chamber, thirty feet long,

eighteen feet wide, and fifteen high. A luminous ceiling with scrolls of arabesques diffused a soft clear light over all the marvels accumulated in this museum. For museum it could be most fitly called, and in its restricted space an intelligent, if a spendthrift, hand had gathered an amazing medley of the best treasures of nature and art. They were set forth with the artistic confusion that characterizes a painter's studio.

Thirty exceptional pictures, uniformly framed, separated one from another by bright draperies, ornamented the walls, which themselves were hung with tapestries of severe design. I noticed works of great value, the greater part of which I had admired in the galleries of Europe and in private exhibitions. The old masters were represented by a Madonna of Raphael, a Virgin of Leonardo da Vinci, a nymph of Correggio, a woman of Titian, an Adoration of Veronese, an Assumption of Murillo, a portrait of Holbein, a monk of Velasquez, a martyr of Ribeira, and a fair of Rubens, together with landscapes and genre paintings by Teniers, Gerard Dow, Metsu, and Paul Potter. Modern artists, likewise, were represented by pictures with the most famous signatures, and some admirable statues in marble and bronze, splendidly copied from the finest antique models, stood upon pedestals in the corners of this magnificent museum. Amazement, as the captain of the "Nautilus" had prophesied, took hold of me at what I saw.

"Professor," said this strange man, "you must excuse the unceremonious way in which I receive you and also the disorder of this room."

"My dear sir," I made reply, "without seeking to penetrate your identity, have I the honor of being in the presence of an artist?"

"An amateur, nothing more, I assure you. In former years I loved to collect these beautiful things that had been created by the hand of man. I sought them greedily everywhere and I admit that I have brought together some objects of priceless worth. They are my souvenirs of a world which is dead to me. In my eyes your modern artists are already old, for they have two or three thousand years behind them. I confuse them in my own mind. Masters have no age."

"And is the case the same with these musicians?" I asked as I pointed at the bound scores of the great composers of recent centuries which were strewn across the top of a large-model piano organ which occupied one of the panels of the drawing room.

"Yes," replied Captain Nemo, "Mozart, Beethoven, and Gounod are contemporaries of fabled Orpheus. For in the memory of the dead, all differences of time are erased. And I am as effectively dead, Professor, as those of your friends who are sleeping beneath six feet of earth."

Captain Nemo was silent and seemed lost in a profound revery. I contemplated him with deep interest, striving to analyze the strange expression of his countenance. As he leaned on his elbow against an angle of a costly mosaic table he no longer saw me—he had forgotten my presence. I did not disturb him, but continued my observation of the curiosities which enriched the apartment.

Under splendid glass cases, held together by copper

rivets, were classified and labeled the most precious productions of the sea which had ever been presented to the
gaze of a naturalist. My specialist's delight can be
conceived. The division containing the zoöphytes offered
positively unique specimens of the two groups of polypi
and echinodermes. And a conchyliologist whose nerves
were not made of iron would have swooned before other
more numerous cases in which were classified the specimens
of mollusks. These were collections of inestimable value,
and I would fain describe them minutely, but I shall spare
my reader and content myself with saying that there was
here spread out before me every kind of delicate and
fragile shell to which science has given an appropriate
name.

Apart, in separate compartments, were spread out
chaplets of pearls of the most exotic beauty which reflected
the electric light in little sparks of fire. Some of these
pearls were larger than a pigeon's egg and were presumably
worth more than the one Tavernier the traveler sold to
the Shah of Persia for three millions, even surpassing the
one in the possession of the Imàum of Muscat, which I
had hitherto believed to be unrivaled in the world.

Captain Nemo must have spent unheard-of sums of
money in the acquirement of these collections. And I
was speculating as to what source he could have drawn
from thus to gratify his taste for beauty and science,
when I was interrupted by his words.

"You are examining my shells, Professor? They
should be very interesting to a naturalist like yourself, but
to me they have a far greater charm, for I have assembled

them all with my own hand. And there is not a sea on the face of the globe that has escaped my researches."

"It must have been great fun to roam about in the midst of such riches. And a sheer delight to know that no museum in Europe possesses a collection of one-half the value. But if I exhaust all my admiration in this room, Captain, I shall have none left to expend upon the craft that carries us. I do not wish to pry into your secrets, sir, but I must confess this 'Nautilus' has excited my curiosity to the highest pitch. What motive power is confined in it? What contrivances determine its operation? What powerful agent propels it? Why, I see suspended on the walls of this very room instruments of whose use I am most woefully ignorant."

"You will find these same instruments in my own room, Professor, where I shall have much pleasure in explaining their use to you. But first come and inspect the quarters I have set aside for your use. You must see how you will be housed on board the 'Nautilus.'"

I followed my host. We regained the waist of the ship, from where he conducted me toward the bow. And there I found, not the sort of cabin I expected, but a spacious room, with a bed, dressing table, and several other pieces of furniture. I could but thank him for his thoughtfulness in my behalf.

"Your room adjoins mine," he said, opening the door which joined the two cabins. "And mine leads into the drawing room that we have just left."

I entered the captain's stateroom. It had a severe, almost a monkish, aspect. A small iron bedstead, a table, some articles for the toilet—that was all. The whole was lighted by a transom in the ceiling. No comforts were visible, the strictest necessaries only.

Captain Nemo pointed to a chair. "If you will give me the pleasure of your company some little while," he said, "I shall satisfy your curiosity regarding the 'Nautilus.' And I shall try not to bore you."

CHAPTER XII

THE SOUL OF THE NAUTILUS

With a wave of the hand my host indicated the instruments that hung on the walls of his room. "Here," he began, "are the contrivances which control the navigation of the submarine. I have them always under my eyes, and they tell me my position and exact direction in the middle of the ocean. Which ones are known to you?"

"The thermometer, of course, which gives us the internal temperature; and the barometer, which marks the weight of the air and foretells changes in the weather."

"To the left is the hygrometer."

"Which, if its name be any clue, must measure the dryness of the atmosphere. Oh, yes, and next to it is the storm-glass, the contents of which, by decomposing, announce the approach of tempests. And here is the compass which guides your course. But what is the next object?"

"A sextant, one of a different shape, perhaps, from what you are used to seeing."

"I was stupid indeed not to know it, anyhow. Well, that shows you the latitude by the altitude of the sun. There are the chronometers by which you calculate the longitude. And beside them the day and night glasses, through which you examine the points of the horizon whenever the 'Nautilus' rises to the surface of the waves. These are the usual nautical instruments. But the others which I do not know? In what way do they answer the particular requirements of your ship?"

"This dial with the movable needle is a manometer," said Captain Nemo. "By communication with the water, whose external pressure it registers, it gives us our depth at the same time. But really, Professor, there is a much better way for me to explain things to you than by discussing one by one and separately the various technical tools which you do not understand. Suppose I give you a basic explanation of the soul of the 'Nautilus.' Will you listen?"

"Like a good child to his father's words."

"Very well, then. There is a powerful agent which is obedient, rapid, easy, and conformable to every use. It reigns supreme on board my vessel. Every blessed thing is done by means of it. This agent warms it, lights it, and is the heart and soul of my mechanical apparatus. Its name is electricity."

"You don't mean it!" I cried in surprise.

"I do mean it," said the captain.

"But, my dear sir, your ship has an extreme rapidity of movement which does not at all agree with the function of electrical energy as I understand it. Until now its dynamic force has remained under restraint and has been able to produce only a small amount of power."

"Ah," said Captain Nemo, "but, you see, my electricity is not everybody's. You know what sea water is composed of. In a thousand grams of it are found 96½ per cent of water and about 2 per cent of chloride of sodium; small quantities of chlorides of magnesium and potassium, bromide of magnesium, sulphate of magnesia, sulphate and carbonate of lime. Chloride of sodium thus forms a large part of the separable ingredients, and it is this that I extract from sea water and of which in combination I compose my formula. I owe all to the ocean. It produces electricity, and from this I derive heat, light, motion— in a word, the very life of the 'Nautilus.' "

"But surely not the air you breathe?"

"I could manufacture the air for my consumption, but where is the use when I rise to the surface of the sea at will? And yet, even if electricity does not furnish me with air to breathe, it at least operates the powerful pumps that are stored in spacious reservoirs and which enable me to prolong as long as I care to my stay in the depths of the sea. This marvelous agent gives a uniform and unintermittent light, which the sun does not."

"Can you tell time by it, as well as by the sun?"

"Ho-ho! Far better, my friend. Look at yonder clock —it is electrical and runs with a regularity that defies the best chronometers. You notice that I have divided the dial into twenty-four hours, like the Italian clocks. For with me there is neither night nor day, but only that factitious light that I take with me to the bottom of the ocean. See? Just now it is ten o'clock in the morning."

"Exactly. That ends, I presume, the uses to which you put your willing agent?"

"By no manner of means! Here's another application of electricity: the dial hanging straight in front of you indicates the speed of our ship. An electric thread puts it in communication with the screw, and the needle registers

the actual rate we are traveling. Look! We are now spin-
ning along at a uniform speed of fifteen miles an hour."

"Will wonders never cease? You were inspired when
you made a servant of a power that replaced wind, water,
and steam."

"But we are still far from through, M. Aronnax,"
said my host, rising. "If you are willing, we'll look over
the stern quarters of the 'Nautilus.'"

In reality, I already knew the anterior part of this
submarine boat, of which this is the exact division, starting
from the ship's head: the dining room, five yards long,
separated from the library by a water-tight partition; the
library, five yards long; the large drawing room, ten yards
long, separated from the captain's room by a second water-
tight partition; the said room, five yards in length; mine,
two and a half yards; and lastly, a reservoir of air, seven
and a half yards, that extended to the bows—total length
thirty-five yards, or one hundred and five feet. The partitions had doors that were closed hermetically by means
of India rubber instruments, and that insured the safety
of the "Nautilus" in case of a leak.

I followed Captain Nemo through the waist and arrived
at the center of the boat. Here a sort of well opened
between two partitions. An iron ladder, fastened with
an iron hook to the partition, led to the upper end. I
asked the captain what the ladder was used for.

"It leads to the small boat," he said.

"Ye gods and little fishes! Have you a boat?" I asked
in much surprise.

"There's nothing remarkable about that. And it's

an excellent sailer, too—light and insubmersible. It serves me as a fishing craft or as a pleasure boat."

"But surely, when you wish to embark in it, you must first come to the surface of the water?"

"Not at all. It is attached to the upper part of the hull of the 'Nautilus' and occupies a cavity specially made for it. It is decked over, entirely water-tight, and held together by solid bolts."

"Describe to me the process of embarking in it when undersea."

"Most willingly. This ladder leads to a manhole made in our submarine's hull, which corresponds to a similar hole in the side of the small boat. By this double opening I enter. They shut the one belonging to the 'Nautilus,' I close the other by means of screw pressure, I undo the bolts, and the little craft shoots up to the surface of the sea with prodigious speed. I then open the panel of the bridge which till then has been carefully shut. I mast it, hoist my sail, take up my oars—and I'm off!"

Off you are, Captain, I see that. But how, in the name of mystery, do you get on, or rather in, again?"

"Oh, I don't come back, M. Aronnax. The 'Nautilus' comes and gets me when I order it to."

"And they know where to find you?"

"Why not? An electric thread connects us. I simply telegraph what I wish to. It is quite simple."

"All things are simple," I said, astonished at these marvels, "when you know how to do them."

After we had passed by the cage of the staircase that led to the platform, I saw a cabin six feet long in which

Conseil and Ned Land, enchanted with their repast, were devouring it with avidity. Then a door opened into a kitchen nine feet long, which was situated between the large storerooms. Electricity did the cooking here better than gas itself. The streams of current under the furnaces lent to the sponges of platina a heat that was regularly maintained and distributed. The flow of current also heated a distilling apparatus which, by evaporation, furnished excellent water for drinking. Near this kitchen was a bathroom comfortably furnished and fitted with hot and cold water taps.

Next was the berth room of the vessel, sixteen feet long. But the door was shut, and I could not see the arrangement of it, which might have given me an idea of the number of men employed on the "Nautilus."

Beyond was a fourth partition, that separated off the engine room. A door opened, and I found myself in the compartment in which Captain Nemo—who must be an engineer of a very high order—had installed his locomotive machinery. This engine room, clearly lighted, did not measure less than sixty-five feet in length. It was divided into two sections. The first part contained the apparatus for producing electricity, and the second the machinery that connected it with the screw. I studied it with great interest in order, if possible, to understand the engines of the "Nautilus."

"You note," said the captain, "that I use Bunsen's contrivances and not Ruhmkorff's. The latter would not have been powerful enough. Bunsen's units are fewer in number, but large and strong, which experience proves to be the most satisfactory. The electricity produced passes forward, where through electromagnets of huge size it works on a system of levers and cogwheels that transmit the rotary movement to the axle of the screw. This one, the diameter of which is nineteen feet and the thread twenty-three feet, performs about one hundred and twenty revolutions a second."

"And you get thereby?"

"A speed of fifty miles an hour."

"I saw the 'Nautilus' maneuver before the 'Abraham Lincoln,' and I already had my own ideas as to its speed. But speed is not the only, and often not the chief requisite. You must see where you go. You must be able to direct your ship to the right, to the left, above, below. How do you get to the depths, where you find an increasing resistance which is rated by hundreds of atmospheres? How do you return to the surface of the ocean? And how do you maintain yourselves in the requisite medium? Am I asking too much, Captain?"

"Not at all, Professor," replied my courteous host, but only after a slight hesitation. "You may as well know, seeing that you are never going to leave this submarine. Come into the saloon which usually serves us for a study, and there you will learn all you wish to know about the 'Nautilus.'"

CHAPTER XIII

CAPTAIN NEMO EXPLAINS

A moment or two later we were seated on a divan in the saloon, smoking most excellent—seaweed! The captain showed me a sketch drawn to scale, which presented the plan, section, and elevation of the submersible. And as I cast my eye over the blueprints, the better to understand his description, he told me the following

"Before you, M. Aronnax, are the various dimensions of the boat in which you are. It is, as you see, an elongated cylinder with conical ends. It is shaped like a cigar, a design for submarines already adopted in London in several important constructions of the same sort."

"I see, my dear Captain, that the length of this cylinder from stem to stern is exactly 232 feet, and its maximum breadth 26."

"Correct. It is, you note, not built quite like your transoceanic steamers in its relative dimensions, but its lines are sufficiently long, and its curves protracted enough, to permit the water to slide off easily and oppose no obstacle to its passage."

"I suppose I should be able from the two dimensions to obtain by a simple calculation the surface and cubic contents of the 'Nautilus.'"

"Don't bother, Professor. I can name them offhand. Its area measures 6,032 feet; its contents about 1,500 cubic yards. That is to say, when totally immersed, it displaces 50,000 feet of water, or weighs 1,500 tons."

"What led you to adopt just the dimensions that you did?"

"Why, when I made the plans for this submarine, I meant that nine-tenths should be submerged. Consequently it ought to displace only nine-tenths of its bulk; in other words, to weigh only that number of tons. Constructing it on the above-mentioned dimensions, therefore, I ought not to have exceeded that weight."

"I gained a fair notion of the construction of the 'Nautilus' from the view you gave me of it, Captain, but only a rough notion, I fear."

"I fancied you were a shrewd observer, sir. The boat is composed of two hulls, one inside the other, joined by T-shaped irons which render it very strong. Indeed, owing to this cellular arrangement, it resists like a block, as if it were actually solid. Its sides cannot yield. I might say they cohered spontaneously and not because of the closeness of their rivets. Also the homogeneity of its construction, owing to the perfect union of the materials, enables it to defy the toughest of seas."

"The hulls of the vessel are entirely of steel, are they not?"

"Both hulls are made entirely of steel plates whose density is from seven- to eight-tenths that of water. The first envelope is not less than 2½ inches thick and weighs 394 tons. The second covering, the keel, 20 inches high and 10 thick, alone weighs 62 tons. The engines, the ballast, the various accessories and appendages to the apparatus, the partitions and bulkheads weigh 961 ½ tons. Do you follow all this?"

"With the deepest interest. And I make my compliments to the mechanical genius of the brain that originates all this."

"Nonsense. Genius errs, if possible, more badly than pedantry But mathematics, properly directed, cannot fail. Well, then, when the 'Nautilus' is afloat under these circumstances, one-tenth of it is out of water. Now, if I have made reservoirs of a size equal to this tenth, or capable of holding 150 tons, and if I fill them completely with water, the boat, weighing then 1,507 tons, will be entirely submersed. That would happen, Professor, would it not? These reservoirs are in the lower parts of the 'Nautilus.' I turn on the taps, they fill, and the vessel that had been just level with the water sinks. Presto!"

"But, my dear fellow! Now we come to the real difficulty. I understand your rising to the surface, easily enough. But diving below the water level your submarine contrivance at once encounters a pressure, and in consequence it suffers an upward thrust of one atmosphere for every 30 feet of water—just about 15 pounds per square inch. Am I right?"

"Just as you say, sir."

"Then, unless you fill the craft quite full, I don't for the life of me see how you can draw it down to those depths."

"Theorist! You must not confuse statics with dynamics or you will lay yourself open to grave errors. There is comparatively little effort expended in attaining the lower regions of the ocean, since all bodies have a tendency to sink. So, when I wished to discover the necessary increase of weight required to sink the 'Nautilus,' I had merely to calculate the reduction of volume that sea water acquires according to its depth."

"That is evident to me now, Captain, although I had omitted it from my reckonings."

"Let us proceed, then. Now, if water is not absolutely incompressible, it is at least capable of very slight reduction. Indeed, according to fairly recent figuring and experiment, this compression is only .000436 of an atmosphere for each 30 feet of depth. If we wish, for example, to sink 3,000 feet, I should keep account of the reduction of bulk under a pressure equal to that of a column of water 1,000 feet long."

"Have you verified this calculation?"

"Often and easily, Professor. Now I have supplementary reservoirs capable of holding 100 tons. Therefore I can sink to a considerable depth. When I wish to rise to the level of the sea, I have but to let off the water. And I empty all the tanks if I want the 'Nautilus' to emerge for a tenth part of her total capacity."

"I cannot object to your reasoning, sir, and I admit the truth of your calculations. Besides, I should be foolish to dispute them, since daily experience gives them confirmation. But still I foresee a real difficulty in your way."

"And what may that be, Professor?" asked Captain Nemo, not, I fear, without an inward sense of amusement at my obstinacy.

"Why, when you are, say, 1,000 feet below the surface,

the walls of the 'Nautilus' must be undergoing a pressure of 100 atmospheres. If, then, just at that juncture, you were to empty the supplementary reservoirs in order to lighten the vessel and go up to the water level, the pumps would have to overcome the pressure of 100 atmospheres, which is about 1,500 pounds per square inch. From that a power—"

"Which electricity alone can furnish," interpolated the captain hastily. "I repeat, sir, the dynamic power of my engines is almost infinite. The pumps of the 'Nautilus' have tremendous power, as you must have observed when their jets of water burst like a torrent upon the 'Abraham Lincoln.' Besides, I use subsidiary reservoirs only to attain a mean depth of 750 to 1,000 fathoms, and that with a view to managing my machines. Then, when I have a mind to visit the depths of the ocean five or six miles below the surface, I make use of slower but not less infallible means."

"What are they, Captain?"

"That involves my telling you how the 'Nautilus' is worked.'

"I am impatient to learn."

"To steer, or in a word to turn this boat to starboard or port, following a horizontal plan, I use an ordinary rudder fixed on the back of the stern-post, and with a single wheel and some tackle to steer by. But I can also make the 'Nautilus' rise and sink, and sink and rise, vertically by means of two inclined planes fastened to its sides, opposite the center of flotation. These planes move in every direction and are worked by powerful levers from the interior. If they are kept parallel with the boat, it moves horizontally; if slanted, the 'Nautilus,' according to this inclination, and under the influence of the screw, either sinks diagonally or rises diagonally, as it suits me. And if I wish to rise more quickly to the surface, I ship the screw, and the pressure of the water causes the 'Nautilus' to rise vertically like a balloon filled with hydrogen."

"Bravo, Captain! But how can the steersman follow the route in the middle of the waters?"

"The steersman is placed in a glazed box that is raised above the hull of the 'Nautilus' and furnished with lenses."

"Are these lenses capable of resisting such pressure?"

"Perfectly. Glass, which breaks at a blow, is, nevertheless, capable of offering considerable resistance. During some experiments of fishing by electric light in 1864 in the northern seas we saw plates less than a third of an inch thick resist a pressure of 16 atmospheres. The glass lenses in my steersman's box is a little over 10 inches thick."

"Name of a pipe! Captain, but you think of everything, and I cannot catch you. Nevertheless, I am not easily daunted and shall try again. Now, for your steersman to see, the light must exceed the darkness, and in the midst of total obscurity in the water how can he accomplish this?"

"Checkmate! Because behind the steersman's cage, Professor, is placed a powerful electric reflector, the rays of which light up the sea for half a mile in front of him."

"Ah, bravo, bravo, sir! Now I can account for the phosphorescence in the supposed narwhal that puzzled the whole world so. Let me now ask you, Captain, if the collision of the 'Nautilus' and the 'Scotia' which startled us all so was the result of a chance encounter."

"Entirely accidental. I was sailing but one fathom below the surface of the water when the shock came. It had no bad result?"

"None, sir—the gods be praised! And now what about your ramming the 'Abraham Lincoln'?"

"There the shoe was on the other foot. I am sorry, of course, for one of the best boats in the American navy and for its gallant officers and crew. But they attacked me, and I was bound to defend myself. I was satisfied, however, to lame the frigate and not finish her. She will not have any difficulty in getting repaired in the nearest port."

"Ah, Captain, but your 'Nautilus' is certainly the most marvelous boat ever put together by human hands."

"It is, indeed, Professor, though perhaps I should not be the first to say so. But I love it as though it were a part of myself. Reflect! When danger threatens one of your vessels that sail on the surface of the sea, the sailor's first and most abiding impression is the feeling that there is an abyss above and below. But on the 'Nautilus' men's hearts do not misgive them. There are no defects to fear, for the double shell is as firm as flint. There is no rigging to attend to, no sails for the wind to carry away. There are no boilers to burst, no fire to terrify, for the vessel is not made of wood. There can be no shortage of coal, because electricity is the sole mechanical agent. There is no collision to avoid, for the 'Nautilus' swims by itself in deep water. There is no awful tempest to brave, for when it dives below the water, it reaches absolute tranquillity. There, sir! That is the most perfect of vessels! And if it is true that the engineer has more confidence in the vessel than the builder, and the builder than the captain himself, you understand the trust I repose in my 'Nautilus'; for I am at once captain, builder, and engineer."

Captain Nemo spoke with captivating eloquence. The animation in his face and the passion of his gestures transfigured him. Yes, he loved the ship as a father loves his child.

And a question, indiscreet perhaps, came to my lips and I could not restrain myself from putting it to him.

"Then you are an engineer, Captain Nemo?"

"Yes, Professor," he replied. "I studied in London, Paris, and New York in the days when I was still an inhabitant of the continents of the earth."

"But how could you construct this wonderful thing in secret?"

"Each separate portion, M. Aronnax, was brought from a different part of the globe. The keel was forged at Creusot, in France, the shaft of the screw at Penn and Company's, London, the iron plates of the hull at Laird's of Liverpool, the screw itself at Scott's at Glasgow. The reservoirs were made by Cail and Company at Paris, the engine by Krupp in Prussia, its beak in Motala's workshop in Sweden, its mathematical instruments by Hart Brothers, of New York. And each of these people had my orders under a different name."

"But these parts had to be put together and arranged?"

"Professor, I had set up my workshops upon a desert island in the ocean. There my workmen, the brave men that I instructed and educated, and myself put together our 'Nautilus.' When the work was finished, fire destroyed all trace of our proceedings on this island."

"Then the cost of this vessel is great?"

"M. Aronnnax, an iron vessel costs $225 per ton. Now the 'Nautilus' weighed 1500. It came, therefore, to $337,500 and $400,000 more for fitting it up, and about $1,000,000 with the works of art and the collections it contains."

"One last question, Captain Nemo."

"Ask it, Professor."

"You are rich?"

"Immensely rich, sir; and I could, without missing it, pay the national debt of France."

I stared at the singular person who spoke thus. Was he playing upon my credulity? The future would decide that.

CHAPTER XIV

THE BLACK RIVER

"Sir," said Captain Nemo, "we will now, if you please, take our bearings and fix the starting point of our voyage. It is a quarter to twelve. I shall go up again to the surface."

The commander pressed an electric clock three times. Immediately the pumps began to drive the water from the tanks. The needle of the manometer indicated by a different pressure that the "Nautilus" was ascending. Then suddenly it stopped.

"We have arrived," said my host.

I went to the central staircase which led to the platform and clambered up its iron steps. In an instant I found myself in the upper part of the "Nautilus."

The platform was but three feet or so out of the water. The front and rear of the submarine were of that spindle shape which justly caused it to be compared with a cigar. I notice that its iron plates, slightly overlapping one another, resembled curiously the shell which protects and clothes the bodies of our large terrestrial reptiles. This explained to me how natural it had been, in spite of high-powered telescopes, to mistake this boat for a marine animal.

Toward the center of the platform was the small boat of which Captain Nemo had informed me. Half buried as it was, in the hull of the "Nautilus," it formed but a slight excrescence on the outer surface. Fore and aft rose two cages of medium height, with inclined sides and partly closed by thick lenticular glasses. One of these boxes was designed for the steersman who directed the submersible; the other contained a brilliant reflecting lamp to illumine the course.

The sea was beautiful, the dome of the sky clear. Where we stood, one could scarcely feel the long billowing swells of the ocean. A soft breeze from the east rippled the surface of the waters. The horizon, free from taint of mist or fog, made observation easy. Nothing was in sight as far as the eye could see—not a sandbar, not an island, not a companionable haze of smoke. A vast desert confronted us.

Captain Nemo, with the help of the sextant, took the altitude of the sun, which would also give him the latitude. He waited for some moments until the disk touched the horizon. During all the time of taking his observations not a muscle of his body moved; the instrument could not have been more motionless if held in a hand of marble.

"Twelve o'clock, sir," he announced. "When you like, we can go down again."

I cast a last look upon the sea, slightly yellowed by the Japanese coast, and descended to the saloon.

"And now, my friend, I leave you to your studies," the commander said. "Our course is east-northeast, our depth is twenty-six fathoms. Here on the desk are large-scale maps by which you may follow our course. The saloon is quite at your disposal, and with your permission I shall retire."

My host bowed and left me. For the first time in many hours I was alone and could lose myself in thoughts that bore upon the captain of the "Nautilus" and all that he had told me.

For a whole hour, at least, I remained buried in these reflections, seeking in vain to penetrate this mystery that I found so fascinating. And then, by chance, my eyes fell upon the vast planisphere spread out upon the table, and I placed my finger on the very spot where the given latitude and longitude crossed.

The sea has its large rivers, just as the continents have.

They are special currents, known by their temperature and their color. The most remarkable of them all is known to geographers as the Gulf Stream. Science has determined on the globe the direction of five main currents: one in the northern Atlantic, a second in the southern, one in the northern Pacific, a second in the southern, and one in the southern Indian Ocean. It is thought likely that a sixth river or current existed once upon a time in the northern Indian Ocean at a period when the Caspian and Aral Seas formed but one vast sheet of water.

At the point which my finger marked on the planisphere one of these currents was flowing. Its name is the Black River (the Kuro-Scivo of the Japanese), which first leaves the Gulf of Bengal, where it is warmed by the perpendicular rays of a tropical sun. It afterward crosses the Straits of Malacca along the coast of Asia and turns into the northern Pacific to flow to the Aleutian Islands. And it carries with it camphor trees and other productions indigenous to its source. The pure indigo of its warm waters contrasts glaringly with the waves of the ocean. It was this current that the "Nautilus" chose to follow. I followed it with my inward eye, saw it lose itself in the vastness of the Pacific, and felt myself dreamily floating along with it—when Ned Land and Conseil appeared at the door of the saloon and interrupted the trend of my reflections.

My two worthy companions remained for a moment petrified with astonishment at the the sight of the wonders spread before them in our museum of art and nature.

"Where am I?" demanded the Canadian finally. "In the museum at Quebec?"

"My friends," I answered as I beckoned them in, "you are in a more wonderful collection than any contained in the city of Quebec. Besides, you are not in Canada, but on board the 'Nautilus' and fifty yards beneath the level of the sea."

"But, M. Aronnax," demanded Ned Land, who was a man of one idea at a time and not easily turned from the subject that was uppermost in his mind at the moment, "can you tell me how many men there are in this ornery craft—ten, twenty, fifty, a hundred?"

"Sorry, but I can't, Ned. Anyhow, it is best for a while to give up any idea of seizing the 'Nautilus' or of escaping from it. This ship is a masterpiece of modern industrial creativeness, and I should be most sorry not to have seen it. Most people would accept, without complaining, the situation that fate has forced upon us, if only for the chance it gave them to live among such wonders. So let's be patient, don't you say? And try to see everything that passes around us."

"See!" exclaimed the harpooner. "That's just the trouble—we can look at nothing but walls in this iron prison house. We are moving—we are sailing—blindly."

Ned Land had scarcely uttered these words when suddenly all was dark about us. The luminous ceiling was gone so rapidly that my eyes smarted painfully at the change.

We stood as we were, mute, motionless, not knowing what surprise might await us—whether agreeable or otherwise. A noise as of something stealthily sliding was heard. One would have said that panels were working in the sides of the ship.

"It is the beginning of the end," groaned Ned.

Light suddenly broke from each side of the saloon through two oblong openings. The liquid mass of the sea appeared before our astonished gaze, vividly lighted up by the electric gleam. Two crystal plates separated us from the ocean. At first I shuddered at the thought that these two frail partitions might break, but I soon noticed that they were bound together by strong bands of copper which would lend them an almost infinite power of resistance.

The sea was distinctly visible for at least a mile around the "Nautilus." What a spectacle unrolled itself before us! What pen could possibly describe it? What master-hand paint the effects of light filtered through these transparent sheets of water—represent in color the softness of the successive gradations from lower to upper strata of the ocean's bed?

Of course, we all know the translucence of the sea and realize that its clearness is far beyond that of rock-born water. And the mineral and organic substances which it holds in suspension tend to heighten this transparency. In some parts of the ocean, near the Antilles, for instance, a bed of sand can be seen with surprising clearness under seventy-five fathoms of water. And the penetrating power of the sun's rays does not seem to cease for a depth of one hundred and fifty fathoms. But in this middle stratum of fluid traveled over by the "Nautilus" the electric brightness was produced even in the bosom of the waves. It was no longer luminous water; it was liquid light.

Through the windows at either side of our apartment we looked out into this unexplored abyss. The obscurity of the saloon showed the bright scene outside the ship to perfect advantage. And we gazed through the pure crystal as if it had been the glass of an immense aquarium.

"Ah, Ned, my boy, you wished to see! Well, you can take your fill of it now."

"Curious! Enormous! Strange!" the Canadian was

muttering. His ill-temper was all forgotten, and it seemed as if he were submitting himself to some irresistible attraction. "A man would travel farther than to the northern Pacific to get such a sight as this."

"At last," I thought to myself, "I understand the life of this sailor. He is rough in appearance and in his actions, and still he has built up a world apart for himself in which he treasures his greatest wonders."

For two long hours the Army of the Sea escorted the "Nautilus"—a grotesque guard of honor such as no ship had ever enjoyed before! We studied the strange creatures about us as they sported and played, darting confusingly hither and yon as if competing for a prize in grace, brightness, beauty, and speed. Among many species, I distinguished the green labre; the banded mullet, marked by a double line of black; the round-tailed goby, of a white color, with violet spots on the back; the Japanese scombrus, a beautiful mackerel of these seas, with a blue body and silvery head; the brilliant azurors, whose name alone defies description; banded spares, with variegated fins of blue and yellow; aclostones, the woodcocks of the seas, some specimens of which attain a yard in length; Japanese salamanders, spider lampreys, serpents six feet long, with eyes small and lively, and a huge mouth bristling with teeth.

Our wonder was kept at its height; interjections followed quickly on one another. Ned named the fish, and Conseil classified them. I was in ecstasies over the vivacity of their movements and the beauty of their forms. Never had the opportunity been given me to surprise these animals, alive and at liberty, in their natural elements. I will not mention all the varieties which passed before our astonished eyes, all the collection of the seas of China and Japan. These fish, more numerous than the birds of the air, came, attracted no doubt by the brilliant focus of the electric light.

Suddenly there was daylight in the saloon, the iron panels closed again, and the enchanting vision disappeared. But for a long time I dreamed on until my eyes fell on the instruments hanging on the partition. The compass still showed the course to be N.N.E., the manometer indicated a pressure of five atmospheres, equivalent to a depth of twenty-five fathoms, and the electric log gave a speed of fifteen miles an hour. I was waiting for Captain Nemo, but he did not appear. The clock marked the hour of five.

Ned Land and Conseil returned to their cabin, and I retired to my chamber. My dinner was ready. It was composed of turtle soup made of the most delicate hawksbills, of a surmullet served with puff paste (the liver of which, prepared as a dish apart, was most delicious), and of fillets of the emperor holocanthus, the savor of which seemed to me superior even to salmon.

I passed the evening happily, reading, writing, and dreaming. Gradually drowsiness overcame me, and I stretched myself upon my couch of zostera and slept profoundly while the wonder-ship was gliding swiftly along through the current of the Black River.

CHAPTER XV

A NOTE OF INVITATION

The next day was the 9th of November. I awoke to the world only after a refreshing slumber of twelve hours' duration. Conseil appeared at my bedside, as he always did, to inquire how I had passed the night and to ascertain whether I desired his services. He said he had left the Canadian sleeping as if his life depended on it. I let my devoted servant chatter on as he pleased, but did not answer him; in fact, I did not hear a tenth of what he was saying. For I was preoccupied with the absence of Captain Nemo from our sitting of the day before, and I was hoping most sincerely to see him today.

The moment I was dressed I went to the saloon in search of my host. It was deserted. He was nowhere about.

To pass away the time, I again took up the study of the conchological treasures that were hidden behind the glasses. I gloated likewise over the great herbals filled with the rarest marine plants which, although thoroughly dried, still retained their lovely colors. Among these precious hydrophytes I found a perfect series of algae, including natabuli like flat mushrooms and some fan-shaped agari.

The whole day passed without my being honored by a visit from Captain Nemo. Nor did the panels of the saloon again open that we might repeat our association with the undersea fairyland. Perhaps they did not wish us to tire of these beautiful scenes.

The course of the "Nautilus" continued N.N.E., her speed twelve knots, her depth below the surface from twenty-five to thirty fathoms.

The day after this, the 10th of November, we had to complain of a similar desertion by the ship's master; we endured the same solitude. Except for the silent steward who served my meals, I did not see another soul. I neither saw nor heard one of the crew. There was an unreality about our whole condition that was uncanny. Several times there cropped into my mind the phrase "A painted ship upon a painted ocean" as not unfitly describing my situation. Ned and Conseil spent much of the day with me. They were as flabbergasted as I at the inexplicable absence of the commander. Was this singular man ill? Or had he changed his intentions in regard to us?

Conseil reminded us that there was no cause for uneasiness—we enjoyed perfect liberty of movement and we were delicately and abundantly fed. Our host was keeping to the letter of his treaty with us. Far from complaining, we should thank our lucky star which had so miraculously rescued us and given us so unique an experience. At any rate, it was too soon to worry.

That day I commenced that Journal of these adventures which has made it possible for me to narrate them with such scrupulous accuracy and attention to detail. I wrote my record on paper manufactured of zostera marina.

Early in the morning of November 11 the fresh air flooding the interior of the "Nautilus" informed me that we had come to the surface of the ocean to renew our supply of oxygen. I directed my steps joyfully to the central staircase and mounted to the platform.

It was six o'clock, the weather was cloudy, and the sea gray but calm. Scarcely a billow troubled its mirror-like stretch. Would Captain Nemo, whom I hoped to meet, be there? With a feeling akin to desperation, I saw no one but the steersman imprisoned in his glass cage. Sitting down upon the projection formed by the hull of the pinnace, I delightedly drew in deep breaths of the salt breeze.

By degrees the fog lifted under the action of the sun's rays, and its radiant orb rose above the eastern horizon. Under its ruddy glance the sea flamed like a train of gunpowder. The clouds scattered across the upper levels of the sky were colored with lively tints, and numerous "mare's tails" betokened wind for that day. But what was wind to this submersible which tempests were powerless to affright?

I was admiring the joyous procession of the sun, so gay, so lifegiving, when I heard footsteps approaching the platform. I was preparing to rise and salute Captain Nemo, but it was an officer (whom I had seen on the commander's first visit) that appeared. With his powerful telescope to his eye, he scanned every point of the horizon with great care. The examination over, he approached the panel and pronounced a sentence in exactly these terms: "Nautron respoc lorni virch." I have remembered it, for every morning it was repeated under exactly the same conditions.

What it meant, of course, I could not say.

The moment he had uttered his phrase the officer turned away and descended. I guessed that the "Nautilus" was about to return to its submarine navigation. I regained the panel and returned to my chamber.

Five days thus sped by in dull routine without any change in our situation. Each morning I climbed anew to the platform. The same words were pronounced by the same individual (who seemed to be second in command to Captain Nemo). But the commander himself did not appear.

I had well-nigh given up all hope of ever seeing him again when, on the 16th of November, on returning to my cabin with Ned and Conseil, I found upon my table a note addressed to me. I opened it impatiently. It was written in a clear, bold hand, the characters rather pointed at the top, recalling distinctly the German type of chirography. The note was worded as follows:

To Professor Aronnax
   On board the "Nautilus"   November 16, 1867

Captain Nemo invites Professor Aronnax to a hunting party which will take place tomorrow morning in the forests of the island of Crespo. He hopes that nothing will prevent the Professor from being present, and he will with pleasure see him joined by his companions.   CAPTAIN NEMO
                    Commander of the "Nautilus"

"Criminy! A hunting party!" exclaimed Ned.

"And in the forests of the island of Crespo!" added Conseil, actually as if the phrase had meaning for him.

"That seems to be the gist of the letter," I said as I read the note of invitation through once more.

"Well, we must accept, of course," said the Canadian. "But, once my feet get on dry land, something tells me they will stick there. Indeed, I shall not be sorry to eat a piece of fresh venison."

I did not stop at that moment to reconcile in my mind the contradiction between Captain Nemo's manifest aversion to islands and continents and his invitation to hunt in a forest. I contented myself with replying, "First let us see where the island of Crespo may be."

I consulted the planisphere, and in 32° 40′ north latitude and 157° 50′ west longitude I found a small island discovered in 1801 by Captain Crespo and marked in the ancient Spanish maps as Rocca de la Plata, the meaning of which is silver rock. We were at this moment about eighteen hundred miles from our starting point, and the course of the "Nautilus," which had been slightly altered, was bearing back toward the southeast.

I showed this small rock north in the middle of the northern Pacific to my two companions. "If Captain Nemo does at times disembark on dry ground, he at least chooses desert islands," I said.

Ned Land shrugged his shoulders expressively, as if he had long since ceased to take any interest in the commander of our ship. Conseil (as usual) said nothing. They left me to my own devices.

After supper, which was served as usual by the mute and impassive steward, I went to bed, and yet not without some anxiety.

The next morning, the 17th of November, when I first stirred from my sleep, I felt that the "Nautilus" was perfectly still. I dressed as quickly as might be and entered the saloon.

Captain Nemo was there awaiting me. He rose from his chair, bowed, and asked me if it were convenient for me to accompany him. As he saw fit to make no allusion to his eight-day absence, I did not mention it; instead, I answered simply that my two comrades and I were at his disposal whenever he might care to set out.

Together we entered the dining room, where breakfast was served.

"M. Aronnax," began the captain, "pray share my breakfast without ceremony, for we shall have an opportunity to chat as we eat. Now, although I have promised you a walk in the forest, I certainly did not undertake to provide hotels there. Therefore I beg you to breakfast like a man who probably will not have his dinner until very late."

I did honor to the repast. It was made up of several sorts of fish, slices of holothuridae (excellent zoöphytes), and different kinds of seaweed. Our drink was pure water, to which the captain added a few drops of a fermented liquor which had been extracted by the Kamchatka method from a seaweed known by the name of *Rhodomenia palmata*. My host at first ate without saying a word. But after he had satisfied his modest appetite he continued: "Sir, when I proposed to you to hunt in my submarine forest of Crespo, you evidently thought I had lost possession of my senses. You must learn never to judge lightly of any man."

"But, my dear sir, believe me—"

"Be kind enough to listen to me a moment, and you will then see whether you have any cause to accuse me of folly and contradiction."

" I am all ears."

"You know as well as I do, Professor, that a human being can live under water if he but carry with him a sufficient quantity of breathable air to support life. In all work that goes on under water the laborer, clad in an impervious dress, with his head in a metal helmet, receives air from above him by means of forcing pumps and regulators."

"You are describing a diving apparatus," I said.

"Exactly. But under such conditions the man is not at liberty except within very narrow bounds. He is tied to the pump which is sending him air through an India rubber tube. And if we were obliged to be thus attached to the 'Nautilus,' we could not roam far afield."

"But name of a little gray pipe! What other means are there?"

"The Rouquayrol apparatus will free us, Professor. It was invented by two of your countrymen. I have brought it to perfection for my own use. This will allow you to risk yourself under these new physiological conditions without suffering the slightest impairment of either heart or lung action."

"Will you describe it to me?"

"Most willingly. The apparatus consists of a reservoir of thick iron plates in which I store the air under a pressure of fifty atmospheres. This tank is fixed on the back, like a soldier's knapsack, with braces. Its upper part forms a box in which the air is kept by means of a bellows. And therefore it cannot escape, unless at its normal tension."

"And how does this air reach the nose and mouth?"

"Through two India rubber tubes which leave this box and join in a kind of tent which holds the breathing orifices. One tube is to introduce fresh air, the other to allow the foul air to escape. And the tongue closes one or the other tube according to the wish of the one who is breathing with the aid of the Rouquayrol apparatus."

"Is it warranted fit for all levels, even the lowest?"

"No. At least, when I encounter great pressures at the bottom of the sea, I am obliged to inclose my head, like that of diver, in a ball of copper. And it is, then, to this ball that the two pipes—the inspirator and the expirator—open. Do you understand?"

"Perfectly, Captain Nemo. Only, the air that you carry along with you must soon be exhausted. For when it contains but 15 per cent of oxygen it is no longer fit to breathe."

"Right you are, sir! Still, I told you, M. Aronnax, that the pumps of the 'Nautilus' allow me to store the air under considerable pressure. And because of this one fact alone the reservoir of the apparatus can furnish breathable air for nine or ten hours."

"I yield the field of argument, you wonderful man, and have no further objections to offer. Let me ask you one more pertinent question. How can you light your road at the bottom of the sea?"

"With the Ruhmkorff burner, Professor. One light is carried on the back, the other is fastened to the waist. It is composed of a Bunsen pile, which I do not work with bichromate of potash, but with sodium. A wire is led into it which collects the electricity produced, and this is directed toward a specially constructed lantern. In this lamp is a spiral glass which contains a small quantity of carbonic gas. When the machine is at work, this gas becomes luminous and gives forth a white and continuous light. So you perceive, my dear M. Aronnax, that with my double equipment I can breathe at the bottom of the ocean and I can see."

"Your answers are crushing in their simple directness, Captain, and make my objections seem stupid. But, although you have won me to your Rouquayrol and Ruhmkorff apparatus, I must still be permitted some reservations with regard to the gun I am to carry."

"Ah, it is not a gun for powder and ball."

"Then it is an air rifle?"

"Of course. You could hardly expect me to make my

own gunpowder on board without saltpeter, sulphur, or charcoal."

"More than that," I could not forbear adding, "you would need a very considerable force in order to fire a gun under water in a medium eight hundred and fifty-five times denser than air."

"Oh, there would be no particular difficulty about that. Unless Fulton is misinformed, there are guns, such as the one perfected in England by Philip Coles and Burley (in France by Furcy and in Italy by Landi), which are equipped with a peculiar device for closing. Rifles of that stamp can be successfully fired under the conditions that will confront us. But I repeat, as I am without a stock of powder, I employ air under great pressure. And this the pumps of the 'Nautilus' furnish abundantly."

"Isn't this air rapidly used up?"

"As a matter of fact, it is not. But suppose it is. Haven't I at my immediate disposal the Rouquayrol reservoir which can provide it at need? A tap is all that is required. What is more, M. Aronnax, you will see for yourself that during our submarine hunt we shall expend but a small quantity of air and but few bullets."

"But I wonder if shots can travel any great distance and prove mortal in this twilight of undersea and in the midst of a medium so much denser than the atmosphere."

"My dear sir, every hit from this gun is mortal and, no matter how lightly the animal be touched, it falls dead as if struck by a thunderbolt."

"In the name of Lucifer and all bad angels, why?"

"Because the bullets fired from this gun are not the ordinary balls, but small cases of glass. They were invented by Leniebroek, an Austrian chemist, and I have a large supply of them. These cases are covered with an envelope of steel and weighted by a leaden pellet. They are really Leyden bottles, into which the electricity is forced to a very high tension. The least shock discharges them, and the animal which is hit, however strong it may be, falls dead. These cases are size number four, and the charge for an ordinary gun is ten."

"I am all through with my vain arguments," I said as I rose from the table. "There's nothing left for me to do but take up my gun and walk. At any rate, I'll agree to follow wherever you go."

Captain Nemo then led me aft. As we passed the cabin of Ned and Conseil, I called out to them to come along. We then entered a sort of cell near the machinery room in which we were to assume our deep-sea walking garb.

CHAPTER XVI

ON THE BOTTOM OF THE SEA

To give this cell its proper name, one might call it both the wardrobe and the arsenal of the "Nautilus." A dozen diving apparatuses hung from the partition, awaiting our use. The moment he caught sight of them Ned Land showed that he was greatly disinclined to dress himself in one of them.

"But, my worthy Ned," I reminded him, "the forests of the island of Crespo are nothing more than submarine woods."

"Oh, of course! of course!" growled the disappointed harpooner, who saw his dreams of fresh meat fade into nothingness. "And you, M. Aronnax, are you going to put on these clothes?"

"There's no other way, Ned."

"You do as you please, sir," replied the harpooner, shrugging his shoulders. "As for me, I'll never put one on willingly."

"Nobody is going to compel you to, Ned," said Captain Nemo.

"Conseil, are you going to risk it?" the Canadian demanded.

"Oh, I follow my master wherever he goes," answered my servant in a matter-of-fact voice.

The commander summoned two of the ship's crew to help us dress in these heavy, impervious garments. They were made of seamless India rubber and built expressly to resist considerable pressure. It took little imagination to fancy them suits of armor, but supple and resisting like beautifully fashioned coats and hose of chain mail. The trousers were finished off with heavy boots, weighted with thick soles of lead.

It was strange, to my eyes at least, to note how the texture of the waistcoat was held together by bands of copper. These clamps crossed the chest and protected it from the great pressure of the water. And yet, they left the lungs free to act. The sleeves of the waistcoat ended in gloves which in no wise restricted the movement of the hands.   Ah, but there was a vast difference to be noted between this consummate apparatus and the old-fashioned cork breastplates, jackets, and similar contrivances that were in vogue during the eighteenth century!

Four of us were soon enveloped in the outlandish dresses: the Captain and one of his companions (a sort of Hercules because of his prodigious strength), Conseil, and my unworthy self. There was nothing left to be done except to inclose our heads in the metal boxes. But before we proceeded to this operation I asked the captain's permission to examine the guns we were to carry.

One of the "Nautilus" men handed me a gun of simple appearance, the butt end of which was made of hollow steel and was fairly large. This served as a reservoir for compressed air, which a valve, worked by a spring, allowed to escape into a metal tube. There was a box of projectiles in a groove where the butt end was thickest. This place stored about a score of these electric balls which, again by means of a spring, were forced into the barrel of the rifle. As soon as one shot had been fired, another one was ready.

"Captain," I remarked, as I finished my rather prolonged study of the instrument, "this firearm is perfect for its purpose and should be most easily managed even by an inexpert huntsman. I ask now but to be permitted to put it to the test. But how are we to gain the bottom of the sea?"

"At this very moment, Professor," said my host, "the 'Nautilus' is stranded in five fathoms of water. We have nothing to do but to start."

"Isn't that more easily said than done? How do we manage it?"

"You shall soon see, my dear fellow."

Captain Nemo thrust his head into the helmet carelessly, as one puts on a favorite cap. Conseil and I imitated the action to the best of our ability, but not before we had heard the ironical "Good luck!" of the Canadian.

The upper part of our dress terminated in a copper collar, upon which the metal helmet was screwed. (It gave me a strange feeling, to be thus assembled.) Three holes in the helmet, protected by thick glass, allowed us to see in all directions that nature permits. We simply had to twist our heads about in the interior of the headpiece. The moment our top was in position, the Rouquayrol apparatus on our backs began to act, and we could breathe with ease.

Finally, the Ruhmkorff lamp also was hanging from my belt and, with gun in hand, I was ready to set out. At this point a new discomfort, and a new humiliation, confronted me. For, truth to tell, imprisoned as I was in these ponderous garments, and glued to the deck·by my soles of lead, I was unable to put one foot before the other.

But, as I might have anticipated, this state of things had been foreseen and provided for. I felt myself being shoved into a small room immediately contiguous to the wardrobe apartment. My companions, I noticed, accompanied me thither, propelled each one of them by a member of the crew. I heard a water-tight door, furnished with stopper plates, close behind us. And we were at once encompassed by the most profound obscurity.

How long we waited thus, I shall never know. But after a while, perhaps after only a few moments, a loud hissing sound was heard. I felt the sensation of cold mount from my feet to my chest. Evidently, from some part of the vessel, by means of a tap, they had given us entrance to the sea. The water invaded the compartment swiftly, and the dark-room was soon filled with it. A second door contrived in the side of the "Nautilus" then opened. We became aware of a faint light. In another instant our feet were treading the floor of the ocean.

Ah, my dear reader! How can I hope to transmit the impression left on me by that first walk under the waters? There are some wonders which words are impotent to translate.

Captain Nemo strode off in front of us. His sturdy

companion followed like an unwieldy mastiff at his heels. Conseil and I stuck close together according to our terrestrial habit. (As if an exchange of conversation might be possible through our metallic cases!) I no longer felt the drag of my clothing or my shoes. My reservoir of air and my thick helmet were light as air. I had the sensation as if my head rattled in its copper top like a dried almond meat inside its shell.

The radiance that lighted the soil thirty feet below the surface of the ocean astonished me by its powerful glow. The solar rays shone through the watery mass easily. They seemed to dissipate not only all shadow, but all collor as well, and I found that I could clearly distinguish objects one hundred and fifty yards distant from me. Beyond that length the tints darkened into fine gradations of ultramarine, and then finally shaded off into a vague opalescent obscurity.

Truly this water by which I was surrounded was only another air denser than the terrestrial atmosphere, but it was well-nigh as transparent. Above me was the calm level of the sea. We were padding along a fine, even sand, not wrinkled as on a flat shore, where it retains the billowy shape of the incoming waves. The dazzling carpet underfoot, a natural reflector of the solar light, reflected the rays of the sun with an amazing intensity which, I suppose, accounted for the vibration which appeared to penetrate each atom of liquid. Will you promise to believe me when I say that at a depth of thirty feet I could see as freely as if I were in broad and unhindered daylight?

For a quarter of an hour I trod this sand, sown with the almost impalpable dust of shells. The hull of the "Nautilus," resembling nothing so much as a long shoal, disappeared by degrees. But its lantern, when darkness should overtake us in the waters, would help to guide us back on board by its distinct rays.

Soon forms of objects outlined in the distance became discernible. I saw rocks hung with a tapestry of zoöphytes in the most beautiful pattern, and I was struck by the peculiar effect of this medium.

It was then ten o'clock in the morning. The rays of the sun met the surface of the waves at a somewhat oblique angle. And at the touch of their light, decomposed by refraction as through a prism, everything was tinged by the seven solar colors. It was a feast for the eyes, this weaving of tints on flowers, rocks, plants, shells, and polypi—a kaleidoscope of green, yellow, orange, violet, indigo, and blue—the whole palette of colorful nature!

Ah, if I could but communicate to friend Conseil the lively sensations that were buzzing in my brain! We could then vie with one another in the expression of our admiration. For aught I knew, Captain Nemo and his herculean comrade might be able to exchange thoughts by means of a code of signs already agreed upon. So, for want of something better to occupy my mind, I talked to myself. I declaimed my poetic fervor into the copper box that covered my head. And thereby, perhaps, I expended in vain words more air than was expedient.

Various kinds of isis, clusters of pure tuft-coral,

prickly fungi, and anemones formed a brilliant garden of flowers before me. This was enameled with porphitae decked with their collarettes of blue tentacles. Sea stars studded the sandy bottom. Asterophytons, looking like fine lace embroidered by naiads, waved their festoons at us in the gentle undulations caused by our passage.

It was a real grief to me to crush underfoot the brilliant specimens of mollusks which strewed the ground by thousands—hammerheads, donaciae (veritable bounding shells), staircases, red helmet-shells, angel-wings, and many others produced by this inexhaustible ocean. But we were bound to walk, no matter where the path should lead us, so on we forged, while above our heads waved shoals of physalides with long tentacles afloat in their train, and medusae whose umbrellas of opal or rose-pink were escalloped with bands of blue. These sheltered us from the rays of the sun, as did also the fiery pelagiae which in the darkness would have strewn our path with phosphorescent light.

All these and many other wonders I saw, scarcely without a pause, within the space of a quarter of a mile. My attention was only occasionally demanded by Captain Nemo, who beckoned me on my route by signs. Soon the nature of the soil beneath us changed, and not for the better. To the sandy plain succeeded an extent of that slimy mud which the Americans call ooze and which is composed in almost equal parts of siliceous and calcareous shells. We next traversed a plain of seaweed of wild and luxuriant vegetation. This sward was of close texture and soft to the feet, rivaling the softest velvet carpet woven by the hand of man.

But, while verdure was spread out beneath us, it did not abandon the higher spaces where our helmets moved. A light network of marine plants, belonging to that prolific seaweed family of which more than two thousand known members exist, grew on the surface of the water and for some feet beneath it. I saw long ribbons of fucus floating near me, some globular, some tuberous. I marked down laurenciae and cladostephi of most delicate foliage, likewise the rhodomeniae palmatae which resemble the fan of a cactus. I observed that the green plants kept nearer to the top of the sea, whereas the red ones were at a greater depth. To the black and brown hydrophytes was left the responsibility of forming gardens and parterres in the remote beds of ocean.

By this time we had been away from the "Nautilus," so far as I could determine, about an hour and a half. My guess at the time was based upon the perpendicularity of the sun's rays, which were no longer refracted as they earlier had been. Bit by bit the magical hues disappeared and the shades of emerald and sapphire were effaced. We walked on with rhythmic step which, curiously enough, rang upon the ground with a rather startling clarity. This phenomenon, at first thought puzzling, is because the slightest sound was transmitted to the ear with a quickness to which we are unaccustomed when on earth. Indeed, water is a better conductor of noise than air in the ratio of four to one.

At this period of our progress the earth sloped downward and the light commenced to take on a uniform tint. We were soon at a depth of one hundred and five yards and twenty inches, enduring a pressure of ten atmospheres.

When at this depth I could still see the rays of the sun, though feebly, as on a terrestrial day troubled with tenuous mists. To the intense brilliance of the light had succeeded a reddish twilight, the lowest state of lull in vision between night and day. But we could still find our way well enough without danger of stumbling or collision. It had not as yet been necessary to resort to the Ruhmkorff apparatus. Just at this juncture, however, Captain Nemo stopped. He waited for me to join him and then indicated by a wave of his hand an obscure mass that loomed in the shadows a short distance ahead.

"It is the forest of Crespo," I thought. Nor, as it soon turned out, was I mistaken.

CHAPTER XVII

A SUBMARINE FOREST

We had at last arrived at the edge of this forest, doubtless one of the finest in all Captain Nemo's immense domains. He regarded it as his own peculiar property and considered he had the same right over it that the first men had who were born into this world. And, for that matter, who was there to dispute with him the title to this undersea realm? What other hardier pioneer would ever come, hatchet in hand, to cut down the dark copse?

The forest was composed, as I had already pictured it in my mind, of large tree plants, and the moment we had penetrated its vast arcades I was struck by the singular position of their branches—a fact I had not until that moment observed.

Not an herb that carpeted the ground, not a branch that clothed the trees, was bent down, nor did they extend horizontally. All stretched up to the surface of the ocean. Not a filament, not a single ribbon, however thin it might be, but held itself as straight as a ramrod. The fuci and llianas grew aloft in rigid perpendicular lines, a fact doubtless due to the density of the element which had produced them.

Motionless they all were, and yet if one bent them aside with the hand they immediately resumed their former attitude. Verily, it was the strangest region of verticality on the globe!

I soon grew used to seeing this fantastic position around me. A few further moments accustomed me to the comparative darkness of the forest. The soil was everywhere strewn with sharp blocks which it was most difficult to avoid. The submarine flora appealed to me as quite complete, and richer even than it would have been in either the arctic or the tropical zones, where plant productions are not so plentiful. But for quite a while I found myself confusing the species. I mistook zoöphytes for hydrophytes, animals for plants. And who would not have committed a similar error? The fauna and the flora of underseas are too closely united for one ever to be certain at first sight which genus confronts him.

These plants are self-propagated. The principle of their existence inheres in the water, which upholds and nourishes them. The greater number of them do not put forth leaves, but have instead blades of whimsical shapes, the scale of whose colors are pink, carmine, green, olive, fawn, and brown.

I saw here pavonari spread out like a fan as if to catch the passing breeze; scarlet ceramics, whose laminaries stretched forth their edible shoots of fern-shaped nereocysti, growing to a height of fifteen feet. Nor did I overlook the clusters of acetabuli, whose stalks increase as they grow upward. Great masses of other marine plants also drew my attention, but every one of them devoid of flowers. Curious anomaly of submerged continent! Fantastic element in which the animal kingdom blossoms and the vegetable does not!

Under these numerous shrubs, as large as trees of the temperate zone, and between their shadows were assembled real bushes of living flowers, hedges of zoöphytes on which blossomed zebra-meandrines with crooked grooves; some yellow caryphylliae. And, to complete the illusion, the fish flies flew from branch to branch like a swarm of humming birds, while yellow lepisacomthi with bristling jaws, dactylopteri, and monocentrides rose at the sound of our footsteps like a flight of snipes.

About one o'clock our guide gave the signal to halt. For my own part, I was not sorry, as we thus had an opportunity to stretch our tired bodies under an arbor of alariae whose long thin blades stood up like quiverfuls of arrows.

This short rest and breathing spell seemed delicious to me. There was nothing lacking in the charm of the moment but the possibility of conversation. But, finding it impossible to speak and quite as much out of the question to exact a response, I still placed my bulbous copper head close to that of Conseil. I saw the worthy fellow's eyes glisten with delight at my evident need of his companionship, and, to show his satisfaction, he shook himself within his air breastplate in a fashion that at any other moment would have been highly comical.

We had been walking for some four hours, and I was surprised not to find myself ravenously hungry. I could scarcely tell how to account for this unusual placidity of my stomach. But, instead of the pangs of appetite, I felt an insurmountable desire to sleep, a thing which happens to all divers. And my eyelids soon closed behind their thick lenses, and I fell into a heavy slumber to which I had not yielded earlier only because my limbs had been kept in motion. Captain Nemo, his robust companion, and Conseil, stretched out full length in the crystal fluid, set me the example.

I cannot judge how long I remained dead to outward impressions, but when I awoke the sun seemed already to be sinking toward the horizon. Captain Nemo had already arisen, and I was beginning to stretch my own limbs luxuriously when an unexpected apparition brought me briskly to my feet.

A few yards away a gigantic sea spider, about thirty-eight inches high, was watching me with hideous and squinting gaze, ready to spring upon me. Though, of course, my diver's dress was thick enough to protect me from the bite of the animal, I could not avoid shuddering with horror. At exactly this moment Conseil and the sailor of the "Nautilus" awoke. Our guide pointed out to them the grotesque crustacean and then with a single well-delivered blow with the butt of his gun he knocked it over. I saw the horrible claws of the monster writhe in its death convulsions.

This incident rendered me nervous because it reminded me that other beings even more to be feared probably lurked in these dim recesses of the sea. And against the very next one my diving suit might prove inadequate to protect me. The thought, happily for my peace of mind, had not occurred to me before, or I should not have fallen asleep so comfortably. As it was, however, I resolved to be on my guard.

Conseil and I had had every reason to suspect that this halt would mark the farthest limit of our walk, but we soon found ourselves in error. Instead of returning to the "Nautilus," Captain Nemo continued our bold excursion. The ground was still sloping away from us; the gradient seemed to be getting sharper and to be leading us to ever greater depths. It must have been well on toward three o'clock when we reached a narrow ravine between high perpendicular walls, situated about seventy-five fathoms deep. Thanks to the resisting power and perfect construction of our apparatus, we were already forty-five fathoms below the limit which until then nature seemed to have set for man's incursion into submarine regions.

I say seventy-five fathoms, it is true, although I had no instrument with which to measure the distance. But I knew that even in the clearest waters the solar rays could not pierce beyond that boundary. And, just as would be natural, the darkness was deepening. Ten paces away not a single object was visible.

I was groping for my path when unexpectedly I beheld a brilliant white light. Captain Nemo had that moment turned on his electric appliance. The other three of us were quick to do the like. By turning a screw I established a contact between wire and spiral glass. And now the sea was illuminated by our four lanterns for a circle of thirty-six yards around us.

Our guide was plunging ahead into the dark chambers of the forest, whose trees were growing more sparsely at practically every step we took. It was food for thought to notice that vegetable life disappeared sooner than animal existence. The medusae had already abandoned the arid soil, but a legion of animals, zoöphytes, articulata, mollusks, and fishes still obtained sufficient sustenance.

As we plodded painfully onward I presumed that the light of our Ruhmkorff appliance could scarcely fail to lure some inhabitant from its dark den. But, if they did approach us, they maintained a respectful distance between themselves and the hunters. Several times I saw our host halt, fit his gun to his shoulder, but after a short spell of indecision drop it from its rest and walk on.

At last, after about four hours of progress, this strange excursion of ours came to an end. A wall of superb rocks rose in an imposing mass before us. It was a titanic heap of giant blocks, honeycombed with dark grottoes and caverns, but offering no practicable foothold for scaling.

It was the shore of the island of Crespo! It was the earth! Captain Nemo came to a sudden halt, and a gesture from him brought us to a standstill. However wishful I might be to attempt the clifflike face of the rock, I was obliged to surrender the notion. For here ended our host's domain, and he could not be induced to go beyond it. Farther on was a portion of the globe upon which neither he nor other living man might trample.

From that moment began our about-face. Captain

Nemo had again assumed the leadership of his small band of explorers, directing their return course without the slightest hesitation. It occurred to me more than once that we were not retracing the same road by which we had come from the "Nautilus." For the new way seemed more steep, and it was consequently trebly painful to our numbing limbs. We appeared to be approaching the surface of the sea very rapidly.

Still this return to the upper strata of the ocean was not so sudden as to cause us too swift a relief from the pressure of depth, for this would presumably have caused severe discomfort, or even disorder, to our systems. It might have caused internal lesions, that constant danger to deep-sea divers.

Very soon the light of day reappeared and grew stronger. The only difference between the light at this moment and that of hours earlier lay in the fact that the sun was now low on the horizon, and therefore its refraction fringed the different objects with a spectral ring. At ten and a half yards deep we walked among shoals of fish of every sort, more numerous than the little birds of the air and also more agile. But no aquatic game worthy of a shot had as yet met our gaze, when at that very moment I noticed that the captain shouldered his gun quickly and followed a moving object into the shrubs.

He fired. I heard a soft hissing noise, and a creature fell at some distance from us, stunned. It turned out to be a splendid sea otter, an enhydrus, the only exclusively marine quadruped known. This fellow was five feet long and must carry a very valuable pelt. Its skin, chestnut brown above and silver underneath, would have made one of those magnificent furs so sought after in the Russian and Chinese markets. Because of its luster and fineness the coat should certainly bring around four hundred dollars.

I did not easily tire of admiring this curious mammal, whose rounded head was ornamented with short ears, marbled eyes, and white whiskers like those of a cat. It had webbed feet and a tufted tail. This precious creature, hunted and tracked by fishermen, has now become very rare and seems to have taken refuge chiefly in the northern portion of the Pacific. If it had not chosen a new habitat difficult to reach, its race by now would doubtless have been extinct.

The herculean companion of Captain Nemo took up the beast and slung it over his shoulder. Then we continued our march. For an hour or more an endless plain of sand stretched away before us. Sometimes it rose to within two or three yards of the top of the sea. At such a moment I could see our image clearly reflected, but upside down. Above us there appeared an identical group that imitated our every movement and action. And they were like us in every point, except that they walked with heads downward and with their feet kicking in the air.

There was another phenomenon I noted, namely, the passage of dense clouds which formed and vanished with bewildering rapidity. At first this strange effect gave me cause to wonder, but on reflection I understood that what I had thought to be clouds was caused by the varying thickness of the billows of the ocean. And on examining more closely I discovered I could see even the fleecy foam which their broken crests multiplied on the water, and the shadows of large birds passing above our heads, whose soaring flight I could discern on the surface of the ocean.

And now I was to witness one of the most splendid gunshots that ever made the nerves of a huntsman tingle. A large bird, of great breadth of wing, came clearly into range of our vision and drew near, to hover above us. Hercules shouldered his gun and fired at an instant when the creature was but a few yards above the waves. The bird fell stunned, and the force of its fall brought it within reach of the dexterous huntsman's hand. It was an albatross of the finest sort.

Our march had been but momentarily interrupted by this lucky incident. For two hours more we dragged wearily along these sandy prairies, and then came to great beds of algae which were extremely difficult to ford. Frankly, I was not only tuckered out, but at my last gasp, when we finally saw a glimmer of light that broke the darkness of the waters half a mile away. It was the beacon of the "Nautilus." Before twenty minutes were sped we should be back on board and I could again breathe with some approach to ease. In fact, it seemed to me that my reservoir supplied me with air that was very deficient in oxygen. But I had not reckoned on an accidental delay which postponed our arrival for quite a spell beyond expectations.

I had been lingering some paces behind the others, when I looked up and saw my host hurrying back to me with all the speed that he could muster. The second he reached me he bent me back to the ground with his strong hands, and I noted that his companion was doing the like thing to Conseil. What could these men be up to? I knew not what to think of the unexpected attack and was becoming suspicious that our companions were planning a deed of violence. But I was soon reassured by seeing the captain stretch his body down beside mine and remain immovable.

I was lying on the ground just under shelter of the edge of a bed of algae, when, raising my head to look about me, I perceived an enormous mass shoot blusteringly by me, casting a shower of phosphorescent gleams. My blood froze in my veins as I realized that we were narrowly threatened by two formidable man-eating sharks.

It was a pair of tintoreas—terrible creatures with huge tails. The dull glassy stare of their eyes is a memory to cause one to start from a troubled sleep at the suggested thought of it. The phosphorescent matter was ejected from holes pierced around their muzzles. Monstrous brutes that could crush a whole man with one snap of their iron jaws! I do not know if Conseil, with true scientific ardor, stopped to classify them. But, for my part, I could not but note their silver bellies, their huge maws bristling with teeth, and thought of these from a most unscientific point of view. I regarded myself more as a possible victim than as a naturalist.

Luckily for us, these voracious creatures do not see well. They continued on their way without taking the slightest notice of our existence. They fairly brushed us with their brownish fins. And we had escaped a danger greater by far than that of meeting a tiger head-on in a forest.

It was half an hour later, guided by the stream of electric light, that we attained the "Nautilus." The outside door had been left open, and Captain Nemo shut it as soon as we had entered into the first cell. He then pressed upon a knob. I heard the pumps begin to work in the heart of the vessel. I felt the water sinking down around me, and in a short while the cabin was entirely empty. The inside panel then opened, and we entered the wardrobe.

There our diving dress was quickly stripped from us, with less trouble because of the skilled hands that were waiting to aid. And then, practically worn to a thread from want of food and sleep, I escaped to my room. A great wonder filled me at this surprising excursion to the floor of the sea.

CHAPTER XVIII

FOUR THOUSAND LEAGUES UNDER THE PACIFIC

By the next morning, the 18th of November, I had quite recovered from the terrible fatigue of the day before, although I was still stiff enough in all conscience. I went to the platform for my morning draught of terrestrial air, arriving just as the second officer was uttering his daily phrase.

I had not been long drinking in the beauty of the aspect of the ocean when Captain Nemo arrived upon the scene. He was in an abstracted frame of mind and did not seem conscious of my presence. He began the usual series of astronomical observations. Then, when he had completed these, he walked over and leaned against the cage of the watchlight, gazing absent-mindedly into the sea.

Meanwhile a number of the sailors of the "Nautilus," all strong and healthy men, had come up from below to draw in the nets which had remained in tow overnight. These seamen were evidently derived from various nationalities, although the European type was discernible in each one of them. By certain unmistakable symptoms I knew some of the group to be Irishmen and Frenchmen, certain to be Slavs, and one mariner was certainly either a Greek or a Candiote. They were civil-mannered folk, but in their talk they used only that strange language whose origin escaped my knowledge. It was thus impossible for me to question them.

The nets were drawn up. They were large *chaluts* like those in use in Normandy fishing villages. The great pockets of the seines were held open by the action of the waves and by a chain woven through the smaller meshes. These pockets, strung on iron poles, were swept through the water by the movement of the ship, and they gathered in anything that came in their way.

On this particular morning the *chaluts* brought up from the lower levels most curious specimens from these fertile coasts: first of all, fishing frogs that, from their comical twistings, have acquired the name of "buffoons"; then black commersons, richly furnished with antennae and for this reason not particularly appetizing to him who first sees their wriggling; trigger fish, encircled with red stripes; orthragorisci, with a very subtle venom that must be carefully extracted before they are placed in the boiling pot; some olive-colored lampreys; macrorhynci covered with silver scales; trichiuri, whose electric power is equal to that of the gymnotus and crampfish; scaly notopteri with transverse brownish bands; greenish cod; several varieties of gobies; also some larger fish—for example, a caranx with a prominent head a yard long; several fine bonitos, streaked with silver and blue; and three splendid tunnies which, despite the unbelievable swiftness of their action, had not escaped the net.

I figured that the haul weighed not less than nine hundredweight. It was a good result, but not one to be won-

dered at. Indeed, as I later came to know, when the nets
are lowered for but a few hours they never fail to inclose
in their meshes an infinite variety of sea food. We had
no lack of the best eating, because both the rapidity of
the "Nautilus" and the irresistible attraction of the electric
light could always be counted on to renew our larder.
These productions of a well-disposed ocean, were immediately lowered through the panel into the steward's room,
some to be cooked while fresh, others to be pickled in brine.

The day's fishing ended, the provision of air duly
inhaled, I supposed, of course, that the submarine was
about to continue her undersea course. I was therefore
preparing to descend to my cabin when, without any
preface, the captain turned to me and said, "Tell me,
Professor, is not our ocean gifted with a life, half human,
half divine? It has its windy tempers and its gentle
moods of calm. Yesterday it slept as we did, and now it
has awakened after a quiet night.

"Behold!" he continued. "It is now awakening at the
kisses of the morning sun. It is on the point of resuming
its daily existence. It is fascinating to study the play of
its bodily structure. It has a pulse, arteries, muscular
spasms. And I cannot disagree with the physicist Maury,
who discovered in it a pulsing circulation as regular and
real as that of the blood in animals.

"Yes, M. Aronnax, the sea indeed has its circulation,
and to promote it the Creator of all things has caused
beings to multiply within its womb—caloric, salt, animalculae."

While Captain Nemo was uttering these odd words he seemed altogether altered from his usual self, and he aroused an extraordinary sympathy in my mind.

I maintained silence in the hope that he would continue with his discourse. Nor, as the event soon showed, was I disappointed in this.

"True existence is there, too," he went on, dreamily, after a moment. "I can imagine the foundations of old nautical cities, clusters of submarine houses and buildings which, like the 'Nautilus,' would ascend at morning to breathe the air at the water's rim. And these, free communities, independent towns, are not under the sway of any despot, unless—"

My host finished his phrase with a violent gesture. There was something buried in his mysterious past which made the mere thought of earthly tyranny insufferable. When he next addressed me it was as if he did so merely to free his brain of suffocating memories.

"M. Aronnax," he inquired, "do you know the depth of the sea?"

"I know nothing more, my dear sir, than what the principal soundings have told us."

"Recite some of them to me, if you will be so good. I may then suit your figures to my purpose."

"The following are some that I remember offhand, Captain. If I do not err, a depth of 8300 yards has been discovered in the northern Atlantic, and 2600 yards in the Mediterranean. The most remarkable depths of all have been found, however, in the southern Atlantic not far from the 35th parallel. They give us respectively 12,000, 14,000, and 15,000 yards. Generally speaking, it has been calculated that if the floor of the ocean were leveled its mean depth would be about five miles and a fraction."

"Well, Professor," the captain replied, "we can show you something better than that, I suspect. As to the average depth of this part of the Pacific, it does not exceed 4,000 yards."

After he had said this the commander went toward the panel, and a moment later he had vanished down the iron staircase. I followed and went back to the large drawing-room. The screw was set in motion almost immediately, and according to the log we were soon at a level clip of twenty miles an hour.

During the long days and weeks that ensued Captain Nemo was very sparing of his visits. I saw almost nothing of him. It was the second officer that regularly pricked the ship's course on the chart, and I at least had the satisfaction of always knowing most exactly the location and the route of the "Nautilus."

With the omission of scarcely a single day for a long while the panels of the saloon were opened, and we never tired of examining the marvels of the submarine world.

The general trend of our vessel was southeast, and it maintained a mean depth of one hundred and twenty-five yards. One day, however, for some reason of which I was ignorant, the "Nautilus" was drawn diagonally down by means of the inclined planes until it reached a depth of over two thousand yards. The thermometer on this occasion registered 4.25 degrees Centigrade—a temperature that at this depth seemed to be common to all latitudes.

We crossed the tropic of Cancer at 172° longitude at three o'clock in the morning. Next day, the 27th of November, we sighted the Sandwich Islands, where Captain Cook had died nearly eighty years previously. At that point we had gone 4860 leagues from our starting point. On the morning of that day, when I reached the platform, I saw two miles to windward of us Hawaii, the largest of the seven islands that form this celebrated group. I could make out clearly with the naked eye, not alone the cultivated terraces of the hill slopes and the several mountain chains that run parallel to the coast line, but also the volcanoes that overtop Mauna Kea and rise sheer five thousand yards above the level of the sea.

Besides the other noteworthy things drawn in by the nets, were several flabellariae and graceful polypi that are peculiar to this portion of the globe. The course of the "Nautilus" was still doggedly southeast. It crossed the equator the 1st of December in 142° longitude. And on the 4th of the same month, with no occurrence of importance in the interval, we sighted the Marquesas group. There I saw at a distance of perhaps three miles, at 8° 57′ south latitude and 139° 32′ west longitude, Martin's Peak in Nuka-Hiva, the largest of the islands which belongs to France. Because Captain Nemo did not seem to wish to bring our ship to the wind, I saw only the wooded mountains against the horizon.

There the seines brought up beautiful specimens of fish. I remember the choryphenes, with their azure fins and tails like gold, the flesh of which is unrivaled for eating. And I shall never forget the hologymnoses that were so destitute of scales and yet of such exquisite flavor; nor, too, the ostorhyncs, with bony jaws, and the yellow-hued thasards, which had a savor as dainty as that of bonitos. All the sea food that came to our nets was of use to us.

After leaving behind us these charming islands that doze their days dreamily out under the protection of the French flag, we sailed in the week preceding the 11th of December over two thousand miles. This part of our journey was chiefly remarkable for our meeting with an immense shoal of calmars, near neighbors to the cuttle-fish family. French fishermen call these fellows "hornets." They belong to the cephalopod branch, and to that dibranchial stem that contains the cuttles and the argonauts. These animals were particular objects of study to the naturalists of antiquity, and they furnished many a poetic image to the popular orators, as well as excellent dishes for the tables of rich citizens, if we may believe the words of Athenaeus, a Greek doctor who lived long before Galen.

It was during the night of the 9th or 10th of December that the "Nautilus" came across this shoal of mollusks, which are peculiarly active at night time. We could estimate their numbers into the millions. They emigrate from the temperate to the warmer zones, following the trail of herrings and sardines. We watched their antics through the great panes of thick crystal glass—how they swam down the wind with unbelievable rapidity, moving by means of their locomotive tube; how they pursued fish and other mollusks, eating the little ones, being themselves in turn devoured by the big ones. They kept incessantly tossing about in confusion the ten arms that nature has placed upon their heads and that look for all the world like a crest of pneumatic serpents.

In spite of its high speed it took the "Nautilus" several hours to complete its path through the midst of these mollusks, and its nets brought in an enormous quantity of them, among which I recognized all the nine classes that d'Orbigny assigns to the Pacific as a habitat.

Thus in our long transit southward we could testify that the ocean displays the most wonderful sights on all the globe. They were of an endless variety. She changed the scenery and the stage setting to delight our eyes, and on our trip we were often called upon, not only to contemplate the awesome handiwork of the Creator in the midst of the sea, but also to penetrate its fearful mysteries.

During the morning of the 11th of December I was busy reading in the drawing-room. Ned Land and Conseil were watching interestedly the luminous water through the half-drawn panels. The "Nautilus" was immovable. When its reservoirs were full, as they chanced to be at this period, the ship maintained a depth of a thousand yards, a region rarely visited in the ocean's mass and one in which large fish themselves were seldom seen. Conseil

suddenly interrupted my comfortable and instructive reading of the famous book on hygiene by Jean Mace, and
consequently I looked up in some irritation.

"Will you please come here for a moment, sir?" he
asked in curious voice.

"What in the world is up, my dear fellow?"

"I just wish you to see for yourself, sir."

I rose protestingly, walked over to where the servant
was standing, and leaned my elbows on the sash before the
panes.

There, in the full glare of the electric light, a huge
black bulk, quite motionless, was suspended in the midst of
the waters. I studied it attentively, seeking, of course, to
find out the nature of this titanic cetacean. Then a lightning thought flashed across my mind and I reeled back
in horror.

"Why, it is a vessel!" I said in a hoarse whisper, for
my voice quite refused to perform its proper office.

"Yes," replied the Canadian, "a disabled ship that
went to its grave head down."

Ned Land was right. We were close to a vessel whose
tattered shrouds still hung from their chains. The keel
seemed to be in good condition, and the boat itself had
been wrecked, presumably, only a matter of a few hours.

Three stumps of masts, broken off about two feet
above the bridge, showed that the ship had been compelled
to sacrifice its spars. But, lying on its side, it had filled
with water and was listing to port. This skeleton of what
it had once been was a sad spectacle, as the boat lay lost

forever and a day beneath the waves. But sadder still was the sight of the upper deck where several corpses, bound with ropes, were still perceptible. I counted five of these, four men, one of whom was standing by the helm, and a woman close to the poop, holding an infant in her arms.

She was quite young. I could distinguish her features, which the action of the water had not yet decomposed, in the brilliant light from the "Nautilus." In one despairing effort, apparently, she had raised her child above her head. Poor little thing! Its arms still clung tightly to the mother's neck. The posture of the sailors was a fearsome thing to watch, distorted as they were by the convulsive movements of their final struggle to free themselves from the cords that bound them to the vessel. The steersman alone, calm, with a grave, clear face, his gray hair glued to his forehead and his hand clutching the wheel of the helm, seemed even then to be guiding the three broken masts to the depths of the ocean.

What a scene! We were struck dumb. But our hearts beat the faster at sight of this shipwreck, a scene drawn straight from life and photographed in its last moments indelibly upon the minds of us unexpected watchers. And I saw with a shudder, coming toward the wreck with hungry eyes, huge sharks attracted by the human flesh.

The "Nautilus" turned and circled the submerged vessel. As we swept by the stern I read the name " 'Florida,' Sunderland."

CHAPTER XIX

THE ISLAND OF VANIKORO

This awful sight was but the first of a long series of maritime catastrophes which the "Nautilus" was to encounter on its course. As long as our ship plowed the more frequented waters we were seeing at intervals the hulls of wrecked vessels rotting in the depths. And in the levels deeper down we met every sort of thing that could be fashioned of iron and eaten by rust— cannon, bullets, anchors, chains, and a thousand other naval requisites.

On the 11th day of December we hove in sight of the Paumotou Islands, which Bougainville had called the Dangerous Group. They occupy an area of five hundred leagues at E.S.E. to W.N.W. from the island of Ducie to that of Lazaref. This cluster is formed of six separate groups of islands, among which the Gambier aggregation is remarkable, over which France maintains her sway.

These are coral formations, slowly raised but continuous in new growths, the creations of the incessant, age-long activity of polypi. Throughout the long ages yet to come in the history of the world one new island after another will be joined to the neighboring groups, until finally, in the perfection of geologic time, a fifth continent will reach from New Zealand and New Caledonia on across the present desert wastes to the Marquesas.

Once upon a time, when I was suggesting this new theory of mine to Captain Nemo, he replied coldly, "The earth does not need new continents, it needs new men."

It was chance alone, I suppose, that had conducted the "Nautilus" toward the island of Clermont-Tonnerre, one of the most curious of the group that was discovered in 1822 by Captain Bell of the "Minerva." Here I had my long-coveted opportunity to study the madreporal system of building, to which the lands in this part of ocean owe their life.

You must not make the mistake of confusing madrepores with coral. They have a tissue lined with a calcareous crust, and the variations of this structure have led the great naturalist Mr. Milne-Edwards, my worthy master, to classify them in five sections. The animalculae that the marine polypus secretes live by the billion at the bottom of their cells. Their calcareous deposits become rocks, reefs, and islands. In one place they form a ring which surrounds some tiny inland lake that communicates with the sea by means of gaps, left there as if by intention. In another place they erect barrier after barrier of reefs, like those on the coasts of New Caledonia and Paumotou. At another time they raise up fringed reefs of high straight walls, near which the depth of the ocean is considerable, as at Réunion and at Maurice.

Some cable lengths away from the shore of Clermont I admired the truly gigantic work which had been accomplished by these microscopically minute laborers.

The walls at which I gazed seemed to be the work of those special madrepores which are known as mille-poras, porites, and astraeas.

These polypi are found particularly in the agitated strata of the sea near the surface. And therefore it is from the upper level that they begin their operations downward and by degrees bury themselves in the débris of the secretions that support them. Such, at least, is the theory of Charles Darwin, who thus explains the formation of the atolls. And this is, to my mind, a theory superior to that ordinarily given of the foundation of madreporic works (summits of mountains and vol-canoes) which are submerged some feet below the level of ocean.

I had the chance to observe these strange walls closely. Perpendicularly they were more than three hundred yards deep, and the white sheet of our electric glare lighted this calcareous material brilliantly. Conseil asked me how long it took to raise such colossal barriers as these. And when I told him that scientists reckoned the process at an eighth of an inch every hundred years, I could see that the poor fellow was properly impressed.

Toward evening Clermont-Tonnerre was left far behind us, and now for the first time the course of the "Nautilus" was sensibly altered. After we had crossed the tropic of Capricorn in 135° longitude, we began to sail W.N.W., heading once more for the tropical zone. But, although the rays of the summer heat were stifling in their intensity, we did not suffer the least discomfort, as at a depth fifteen or twenty fathoms the temperature did not exceed an ordinary pleasant mark.

On December 15 we passed to the east the bewitching group of the Societies and Tahiti, graceful queen of the Pacific. In the morning of the day I name, several miles to windward, I beheld the elevated summits of this island. Her waters furnished our table with excellent fish, such as mackerel, bonitos, and albicores. And here I had the doubtful joy of sampling certain varieties of a sea serpent called murenophis.

On Christmas Day we shot into the midst of the New Hebrides, discovered two hundred and sixty years before by Quiros and within a century of our own time explored by Bougainville and Cook. This group is composed mainly of nine large islands which form a band of one hundred and twenty leagues N.N.S. to S.S.W., between 15° and 20° south latitude and 164° and 168° longitude. We edged quite near to the island of Aurora, which in the noonday sun looked like a mass of green forests surmounted by a peak of commanding eminence.

Ned Land, sentimental chap that he was, seemed to regret most sorely the fact that we did not have a Christmas celebration, the family fête of which most Protestants are so fond. But I felt it might be folly to suggest the omission to our commander, who had removed himself so completely from terrestrial habits.

I had not seen the latter for a week or so when, on the morning of the 27th, he entered the saloon and acted toward me no differently than if he had parted with me five minutes before. I was at the moment occupied in tracing the course of the "Nautilus" on the planisphere. My host approached me, placed his finger on a spot in the chart, and said but one word—"Vanikoro."

The effect of this statement was electrical. For it was the name of those islands on which La Pérouse had been lost! I rose quickly to my feet and confronted the captain.

"The 'Nautilus' has brought us to Vanikoro?" I demanded.

"Of course, my dear Professor," said the commander.

"And I have your permission to visit the celebrated islands where the 'Boussole' and the 'Astrolabe' struck?"

"Just as you like, M. Aronnax."

"When shall we be there?"

"We are there now."

I rushed to the staircase and, followed by Captain Nemo, mounted to the platform. I scanned the horizon greedily.

To the northeast two volcanic islands emerged from the bosom of the placid sea. They were of unequal size and surrounded by a coral reef that I estimated must be forty miles in circumference.

We were indeed close to Vanikoro, the land to which Dumont d'Urville gave the name of Isle de la Recherche. I faced four-square the little harbor of Vanua that lay in 16° 4′ south latitude and 164° 32′ east longitude. Its soil was covered with verdure from shore to interior summits, and these were crowned by the round diadem of Mount Kapogo, five hundred feet high.

Our ship easily passed the outer belt of rocks through a narrow strait and found herself among the breakers, where the sea was thirty to forty fathoms deep. Under the abundant shadow of some mangroves I perceived some naked savages who, of course, evinced great astonishment at our approach. It was fairly evident to me that in the long black body swimming up between wind and water they saw some formidable cetacean. And they regarded us with vast suspicion.

Captain Nemo inquired as to what I knew of the wreck of La Pérouse, and I replied that I knew just what everyone did.

"And can you tell me the story?" he asked ironically.

"Easily," I said. And here it is:

D'Urville's Account of La Perouse's Death

In the year 1785 the great commander and his second officer, Captain de Langle, were orderd by Louis XVI of France on a voyage of world navigation and discovery.

Accordingly they embarked in the corvettes "Boussole" and "Astrolabe," neither of which was heard of again. Six years later the French government, uneasy as to the fate of these two sloops, manned and equipped two great merchantmen, the "Recherche" and the "Espérance," which sailed from Brest the 28th of September, 1791, under the command of Bruni d'Entrecasteaux.

Two months later, almost to a day, the merchantmen learned from Commander Bowen of the "Albemarle" that the wreckage of foundered ships had been met with off the coast of New Georgia. D'Entrecasteaux saw fit to ignore this information, which was rather uncertain, and directed his course toward the Admiralty Isles, which were mentioned in the log of Captain Hunter as the place where La Pérouse was wrecked.

They sought in this spot in vain. The "Espérance" and the "Recherche" had sailed past Vanikoro without putting in. And, as the result showed, this voyage was most disastrous for both of them, as it cost d'Entrecasteaux his own life and the lives of two of his lieutenants, besides several of his crew.

Captain Dillon, a shrewd old Pacific skipper, was the first one to get traces of the wrecks that were unmistakable. On the 15th of May, 1824, he was passing in his ship, the "St. Patrick," close to Tucopia, an island of the New Hebrides group. A lascar came alongside in a canoe and sold him the silver handle of a sword that bore on its hilt the imprint of engraved characters. The lascar asserted that six years before, during a sojourn at Vanikoro, he had met two Europeans who belonged to vessels that had run aground on the reefs quite a while before that time.

Dillon, of course, at once guessed that the man meant La Pérouse, whose disappearance had startled the whole world. He made plans to reach Vanikoro if he possibly could, for there, the lascar swore, he would still find débris from the wrecks. But winds and tides prevented Dillon from carrying out his scheme at that time.

He returned to Calcutta. There he managed to interest the Asiatic Society and the Indian Company in his discovery. A vessel named the "Recherche," in honor of its ill-starred predecessor, was put at his disposal, and late in January, 1827, accompanied by an agent of the French government, he set out on his quest.

After touching at several ports in the Pacific, the doughty "Recherche" cast anchor before Vanikoro, July 7, 1827, in the very same bay of Vanua where the "Nautilus" was at present resting.

And there, just as the lascar had promised, Dillon was able to assemble numerous relics of the wreck. Among these were iron utensils of varied kinds, anchors, pulley-strops, swivel guns, an eighteen-pound shot, fragments of astronomical instruments, a piece of crownwork, and a bronze clock bearing the inscription, "Bazin m'a fait." This was the trade-mark of the foundry at Brest about 1785. There could no longer be any doubt as to the fate of La Pérouse's expedition.

Dillon remained in the unlucky place until October, making every inquiry and search that his wit could devise. Then he quit Vanikoro and directed his course toward New Zealand. He put into Calcutta, April 7, 1828, and from there returned to France, where he was accorded a royal welcome by Charles X.

Now at the same time, without any knowledge of Captain Dillon's movements, Dumont d'Urville had set out on his own initiative to find the scene of the wreck. He had learned from a passing whaler that several medals and a cross of St. Louis had been found in the hands of some savages at Louisade and New Caledonia.

On receipt of this information Dumont d'Urville, commander of the "Astrolabe" (namesake of the earlier vessel of like title), had immediately sailed, and not quite two months after Dillon had left Vanikoro he put in at Hobart Town. There, for the first time, he was informed of Dillon's inquiries. And he found that a certain James Hobbs, second lieutenant of the "Union" of Calcutta, had seen some iron bars and red stuffs used by natives of these parts. Hobbs had come across them while on an island situated 8° 18′ south latitude and 156° 30′ east longitude. Much perplexed, and not knowing how fully he might credit the accounts he read in untrustworthy journals, Dumont d'Urville yet decided to follow Dillon's track.

Thus, on February 10, 1828, the "Astrolabe" appeared off Tucopia and took away as guide and interpreter a deserter found on that island. He continued his course to Vanikoro, sighted it the 12th instant, but was forced to lie among the reefs until the 14th, and not until the 20th, because of adverse winds and currents, could he cast anchor within the barrier in the harbor of Vanua.

On the 23d several officers made a complete tour of the island and brought back with them some unimportant trifles. The natives whom they questioned regarding the wreck pretended ignorance and told more than one evident falsehood, even refusing to lead them to the scene of the disaster. This strange conduct on the part of the savages led the officers to believe that the natives had ill treated the castaways and were fearful that Dumont d'Urville had come to avenge La Pérouse and his unfortunate crew.

Three days later, however, their suspicions lulled by valuable presents, and finally believing that they had no cause for fear, they led M. Jacquinot to the spot of misfortune. And there, in all truth, buried in three or four fathoms of water, between the reefs of Pacou and Vanua, lay anchors, cannons, pigs of lead and iron, imbedded in the limy concretions. The large boat and the whaler of the "Astrolabe" were at once dispatched to this place and, not without much difficulty, their crews hauled up an anchor weighing eighteen hundred pounds, a brass gun, some pigs of iron, and two copper swivel guns.

Now Dumont d'Urville, on questioning the natives, discovered that La Pérouse, after both of his vessels had been lost on the reefs of this island, had built himself a smaller boat—but only to be lost a second time. Where? How? No one knew.

The French government feared d'Urville might not be acquainted with Dillon's movements. And so it had sent the sloop "Bayonnaise," commanded by Legoarant de Tromelin, to Vanikoro—this sloop had been stationed conveniently on the west coast of America. The "Bayonnaise" cast her anchor in the harbor of Vanua some months after the departure of the "Astrolabe." But de Tromelin found no new document that previous search had overlooked. He was able to state that the savages had respected the monument raised to La Pérouse.

And that is the end of the story of the wreck of La Pérouse. And that is the substance of what I told to Captain Nemo.

"So you really think," he said, "that no one knows where the third vessel perished—the one that was constructed by the castaways on the island of Vanikoro?"

"Yes, that is what I actually think," I answered.

Captain Nemo said nothing further at that moment, but signed to me to follow him into the main saloon. The "Nautilus" sank several yards below the waves, and the panels were opened.

I hastened to the aperture and at first could see nothing but crustations of coral which were covered with fungi, syphonules, alcyons, and madrepores. And everywhere around were the expected myriads of fish—girelles, glyphisidri, pompherides, diacopes, and holocenters. After a little, however, turning my gaze downward, I recognized certain débris that the drags of earlier searchers had been unable to raise. There lay iron stirrups, capstan-fittings, cannons, the stem of a ship—all objects that clearly proved the wreck of some vessel and that now were carpeted with living flowers. While I was gazing intently at this desolate picture Captain Nemo said, in a sad voice, "Commander La Pérouse set forth December 7, 1785, with his ships 'La Boussole' and the 'Astrolabe.' He

first cast anchor at Botany Bay, then visited the Friendly
Isles and New Caledonia, thereafter shaped his course
toward Santa Cruz, and put into Namouka, one of the
Hapai group. Then came the end, for both his vessels
struck on the reefs of Vanikoro.

"The 'Boussole' went first to attempt an entrance to
the harbor and ran aground on the southerly coast. The
'Astrolabe' hurried to its aid and likewise stranded. The
first ship pounded to pieces almost immediately; the
second, lying less dangerously because under the wind,
resisted destruction for some days.

"The natives made the castaways welcome. The latter
installed themselves comfortably on the island and, out
of the wreckage of the two large ships, they built a
smaller boat. Now some of the sailors, weary of battling
with fate and content with their happy situation on the
island, deserted and remained at Vanikoro. But others,
including all such as were weak and ill, set out with
La Pérouse. They set their course for the Solomon Isles.
And at that place they perished, sinking with everything
on board, off the westerly coast of the main island of this
group, between Capes Deception and Satisfaction."

"Tell me, my friend, how you know this to be true."

"By this token, which I found on the spot where the
last catastrophe occurred."

Thereupon my host showed me a tin-plate box, stamped
with the French coat of arms and much corroded by salt
water. He opened the case, and I saw a bundle of papers,
yellow and mildewed, but readable.

They were none other than the instructions of the Minister of French Marine to Commander La Pérouse, and in their margins were notes written by the hand of Louis XVI.

"Ah, it's a fine fit end for a sailor!" said Captain Nemo after a long pause. "A coral tomb makes a quiet grave. And I trust that my comrades and I shall find no worse a one."

CHAPTER XX

TORRES STRAITS

It was some time during the night of either the 27th or the 28th of December that the "Nautilus" left the coast of Vanikoro running at high speed. Her course this time was southwesterly, and in three days she had covered the seven hundred and fifty leagues that separated it from La Pérouse's group and the southeast point of Papua.

Early in the morning of January 1, 1868, Conseil joined me on the platform where I was taking my constitutional before breakfast.

"Master, will you not permit me to wish you a happy New Year?" he inquired as he confronted me with a face wreathed in happy smiles and with hand outstretched in greeting.

"Aha, Conseil, right gladly! It is quite as if I were in my Paris study at the Jardin des Plantes. I accept your good wishes and thank you for them. Only, I must ask you just what you mean by the phrase 'happy new year,' which our present circumstances scarcely seem to justify. Do you mean the coming year will see the end of our imprisonment? Or will you still deem it a happy one if it witnesses only the continuation of our strange voyage?"

"On my word, sir, I hardly know how to answer you. One thing is sure, and that is, we are bound to see curious

things.   For the last two months we have had no time
for boredom.   They say the last marvel is always the
most wonderful one.   And if we continue this uncanny
progression of incidents, I for one cannot imagine how
things will end.   We can never hope to see the like again
if we live to be a thousand.   And so, meaning no offense
to you, sir, I think the happiest sort of year would be that
one in which we could see everything."

On January 2 I figured that we had made 11,340
miles, or 5250 French leagues, since our starting point
in the Japan seas.   Ahead of us stretched the dangerous
shores of the Coral Sea on the northeast coast of
Australia.   Our ship, at the very moment of my calculations, lay some miles distant from the notorious bank on
which Cook's vessel was lost in June, 1770.   The boat
in which the redoubtable navigator was sailing struck
on a rock, and if it did not sink, this was due to the
piece of coral rock that was splintered by the shock of
collision and that became impinged on the broken keel.

I had hoped (oh, how earnestly!) to visit this reef,
three hundred and sixty leagues in length, against which
the sea, always rough at this place, broke with great
violence and with a roar like thunder or cannonade.   But,
as chance willed it, the inclined planes were just then
drawing the "Nautilus" down to a great depth, and I
could get no glimpse of the high coral walls.

Instead, I was obliged to center my interest upon the
different specimens of fish which the nets brought to us.
Among many others I remarked several germons, a

species of mackerel with bluish sides and as large as a tunny. These fish are striped with transverse bands which disappear the moment the animal loses his life. They followed us in shoals and provided us with a most delicate food.

We also captured a great number of giltheads, fish about one and a half inches long that tasted like dories; and flying parapeds, the swallows of the underseas, which, on dark nights, spend their phosphorescent light alternately on air and water.

Among the mollusks and zoöphytes I found in the meshes of the seines several species of alcyonarians, echini, hammers, spurs, dials, cerites, and hyalleae. The flora of these parts of ocean were represented by splendid floating seaweeds, laminariae, and macrocystes, the latter impregnated with the mucilage that oozes through their pores. Among them I gathered an admirable specimen of *Nemastoma Geliniarois,* which was later placed as a unique specimen among the natural curiosities of the museum.

Two days after we had crossed the Coral Sea, January 4, we hove in sight of the Papuan coastline. It was on this occasion that Captain Nemo told me it was his intention to enter the Indian Ocean by the Strait of Torres. Apparently he thought proper not to inform me further on the subject, for his communication ended there.

Now the Torres Straits are nearly thirty-four leagues wide, but they are choked by numberless islands, islets, breakers, and rocks. These render its navigation well-nigh impracticable. It would require all the precautions our commander could take to make a successful passage. The "Nautilus," floating between wind and water, was forging ahead at a moderate pace. Her propeller, like a cetacean's tail, beat the waves slowly.

Profiting by this fact, my two companions and I went up on the deserted platform. Before us was the steersman's cage, and I had every expectation that Captain Nemo himself was in there directing the course of his craft. Spread out before me I had the excellent charts of the Strait of Torres published by that excellent hydrographist Vincendon Dumoulin. These prints, together with those of Captain King, give the most accurate picture of the intricacies of this vexed ribbon of water, and I studied them minutely. About the "Nautilus" the confined sea was dashing furiously. The current of the waves that ran southeast to northwest at the rate of two and one-half miles was spending itself in spume on the coral that showed at intervals.

"A bad stretch of water!" remarked Ned Land.

"Detestable from any point of view," I said, in hearty agreement. "And, what is worse, it's a sea that does not suit such a craft as ours."

"Captain must be sartin sure of his course, for I see right now several pretty pieces of coral that would do for our keel if one of them should but graze it."

Oh, it was a bad situation, there's no denying. But the "Nautilus" seemed to slide by the rocks like magic. We were, of course, not following the routes of either the "Astrolabe" or the "Zélée," for they had proved fatal.

Our line of progress bore more to the northward, skirted the island of Murray, and then twisted sharply to the southwest toward Cumberland passage. I thought for a flash of time that we were going to pass by the passage. But no. We swung northwest at a dizzying pace and penetrated a great quantity of islands and islets that are little known, emerging near Island Sound and Canal Mauvais.

I wondered then whether Captain Nemo, momentarily imprudent, would steer his ship into the pass where Dumont d'Urville's two corvettes touched rock. But a third time we swerved marvelously and cut through straight ahead to the west, steering for the island of Gilboa.

I looked at my watch; it was three o'clock in the afternoon. The tide was at its height and presumably was already beginning to ebb. Our ship came so nigh the island, which I can still see in my mind's eye with its thick border of screw pines, that we were standing off a distance of less than two miles.

At that instant a shock threw me to the floor. The "Nautilus" had just touched a rock and was now immovable, listing lightly to port.

By the time that I had recovered from my flurry and risen to my feet, I perceived Captain Nemo and his lieutenant on the platform. They were studying the position of the vessel and exchanging rapid phrases in their incomprehensible dialect.

The situation was as follows: Two miles or so away,

on the starboard side, loomed Gilboa, its dark line stretching from north to west like a great outthrust arm. Toward south and east some coral had begun to show above the water, left high by the receding tide. We had run aground, and in one of those seas where the race of the tides is middling—a sorry business, so far as the floating of our craft was at stake. And yet the vessel had not suffered visible damage, for her keel was too solidly joined to permit of easy disruption. The problem was, then, simply this: If the "Nautilus" could neither glide off nor move by its own power, she ran the risk of remaining forever fastened to those rocks, and then Captain Nemo's submersible would indeed be done for.

Such were my sad reflections as the commander approached me. He was entirely master of himself and cool and calm as ever.

"An accident?" I asked, just to say something.

"An incident, rather, M. Aronnax."

"But one, no doubt, that will force you to become a lifelong inhabitant of that earth from which you flee so industriously?"

My companion peered at me curiously, and then made a negative gesture with his hand, as if to say that nothing would ever compel him to set foot on terra firma again.

"Oh, as to that, Professor, the 'Nautilus' is not lost. It shall still live to carry you into the very heart of the marvels of the ocean. Our voyage is but begun, and I do not wish to be so soon deprived of the pleasure of your company."

"As you please, my dear host," I replied, without appearing to notice the ironic twist of his sentences. "But the fact remains that your craft has run aground in the open sea. Now the tides are not strong in this part of the Pacific. So, unless you can lighten your vessel, I don't see how it will be set afloat again."

"The Pacific tides are not strong; you are right about that. But in Torres Straits you find, nevertheless, a difference of a yard and one-half between the level of high and low sea. Today is the 4th of January; in five days the moon will stand at full. Now I shall be completely off in my prediction if that complaisant satellite does not raise this mass of water sufficiently to suit my purpose of flotation. She will thus render me yeoman service for which I shall be much indebted to her."

On the heels of this speech Captain Nemo left the platform and redescended with his lieutenant to the interior of our ship. And this vessel was as immovable as if the coraline polypi had already walled it up in their indestructible cement.

"A penny for your thoughts, sir," said Ned Land, who drifted over my way the moment the commander vanished.

"They are not worth such a sum, I fear, Ned. I only know we must patiently await the tide of the 9th instant. For I am told the moon will then have the goodness to remove us from our peg."

"Are you joking me?"

"No, I really mean it."

"And this crazy captain is not going to cast anchor

at all, since the tide suffices him?" inquired Conseil simply.

The Canadian glanced quickly at my servant. Then he shrugged his shoulders most expressively.

"Sir," he burst forth impulsively, "take it from me that this piece of junk will never navigate again, either on top or under the ocean. It is already fit only to be sold to a dealer in scrap iron, at so many cents the pound. I think, therefore, that the time has come for us to part company with the ship."

"Not so fast, my friend," I cautioned Ned. "I do not despair of the safety of this stout 'Nautilus.' Four days from now we shall know what trust to put in the Pacific tides. Besides, flight might be a sensible thing if we were in view of the English, or Provencal coasts. But on this unfriendly Papuan shore, no; that is an entirely different matter. And it will be soon enough to adopt that extremity in case our vessel does not recover itself again, which I regard as a terribly serious thing."

"But look here, sir! Our officers do not understand seamanship enough to act with due caution. And this I do know: there before us is an island. On that island are trees. Under those trees terrestrial animals roam. These animals are bearers of cutlets and roast beef to which I should willingly give a trial."

"Ned seems to me quite right in his contention," observed Conseil. "Why could you not obtain Captain Nemo's permission for us to land, if only long enough so that our feet do not entirely lose their power to tread the solid parts of our planet?"

"I can ask him, of course. But he will refuse me."

"Nothing ventured, nothing gained," said Conseil. "Will you please risk it, sir? And then we shall know how far we can rely upon the captain's amiability."

Quite to my surprise, Captain Nemo acceded to my timid request without hesitation. And he gave the permission very politely, not even exacting from me a promise to return to the "Nautilus." Still I should be slow to counsel Ned Land to attempt escape from durance across New Guinea, for that would be attended with grave peril and hardship. Better to be a prisoner on board the submarine than to fall into the tender clutches of savages.

Armed with electric guns and hatchets, we got away from our craft at eight o'clock the next morning. A slight breeze was blowing on land, but the sea was reasonably calm. Conseil and I sped a small boat quickly along with our oars, and Ned steered in the narrow passage that the breakers left between them. The boat was well handled and moved like a charm.

The harpooner could scarcely restrain his glee. He was like a captive newly escaped from prison who did not realize that he must soon reënter the walls of his cage.

"Three cheers for meat!" he cried joyfully. "We'll soon be eating good red meat. And what meat! Real game. If we could only have a bite of bread with it! Ah, I do not say that there is no virtue in fish. Let us not abuse honest food of any kind. But by criminy! A piece of fresh venison grilled on live coals will agreeably vary our ordinary diet. Will it not, little cabbage of a Conseil?"

"Shut up, you gourmand!" growled my servant. "You are making my mouth water most unendurably."

"Let me not be a spoil-sport," I said. "But really, my friends, it remains to be seen whether these forests are full of game, and also whether the game is not of a kind that will do the hunting, with ourselves as the objects of pursuit."

"Well said, M. Aronnax," remarked the Canadian, whose teeth seemed to have become as sharp as the edge of a hatchet. "But I am not one to hang back and finick where there's eating to be done. I'll eat tiger fast enough —loin of tiger—if there are not more savory quadrupeds on this island."

"Friend Ned grows vastly impatient," said Conseil slyly.

"You bet I do!" the harpooner asserted. "Whatever the prey is—any animal with four paws and no feathers, or with two paws and feathers—gets saluted by my first shot."

"I'm afraid Land's imprudences are beginning again," I could not resist saying, for I was growing uneasy.

"Never you fear, Professor," the Canadian replied, unabashed. "I shan't ask more than twenty-five minutes to offer you a dish of the sort I have in mind."

At half-past eight the "Nautilus's" boat ran softly aground in a heavy sand after we had successfully negotiated the coral reef that encircled the island of Gilboa.

CHAPTER XXI

ARCADIAN DAYS ON LAND

I was more deeply moved than I expected the moment my feet again touched land. Ned tried the soil with the toe of his boot before he stepped out "to take possession of it."

Now it was only two months before this day that we had been received on board a submersible, to become passengers on it. And yet, to all intents and purposes, we had been prisoners, and none had understood this fact better than we. Therefore the time had often seemed an eternity.

Well, in a few minutes after landing, we were a gunshot away from the inhospitable coast. The soil, we found, was mostly madreporal. Still, certain beds of dried-up torrents, strewn with débris of granite, showed clearly enough that the island was of primary formation.

The trunks of the enormous trees attained a height of two hundred feet. And they were tied together by ropes and garlands of bindweed, which furnished real natural hammocks that a light breeze was rocking. They were mimosas, ficuses, casuarinae, teks, hibisci, and palm trees, mingled together in amazing profusion. And under the shelter of their verdant vault grew orchids, leguminous plants of every description and variety, and ferns.

You may believe that the Canadian, however, paid scant homage to these beautiful specimens of Papuan flora.

Almost immediately he abandoned the agreeable for the useful. His eyes lighted upon a coconut tree, and he beat down some of the fruit with his rifle butt. We broke the nuts, and ate the meats and drank the milk with a smacking of the lips that spoke volumes as to our dislike of the restricted diet on the "Nautilus."

"I call this bully!" exclaimed Ned Land.

"Excellent!" agreed the more complacent Conseil.

"You know what?" blurted out the Canadian excitedly. "I don't believe our captain would object to our bringing a cargo of coconuts back to the submarine with us."

"I don't think he would object," I said. "But he surely would not taste of them himself."

"So much the worse for him," grinned Conseil.

"And all the better for us," asserted Ned Land. "There will be all the more for us three."

"Just a word of warning, my gentle friend," I said to the harpooner, who was already beginning to ravage another coconut tree. "This succulent fruit is a wonderful thing, but would it not be wise to take a look around before we load down the canoe with them? Who knows? Perhaps the island produces another substance no less useful. Fresh vegetables, for instance, would be mighty welcome on board the 'Nautilus.'"

"You are right as usual, sir," replied Conseil. "I propose to reserve three places in our boat: one for fruit, another for vegetables, and a third for venison. I have as yet, Ned, not seen the slightest indication of this meat, despite your ardent boasts."

"Just don't you despair, my friend," said the Canadian. "Let's start on, shan't we?" I suggested, in my turn. "But keep on the lookout. It is true, the island seems uninhabited, but it may after all contain some individuals who would be less particular than we as to the sort of venison they sought."

"Ho-ho!" ejaculated the harpooner, moving his jaws about in a most significant fashion.

"Why, Ned!" demanded Conseil. "What are you up to?"

"My word!" retorted the Canadian. "I am just beginning to appreciate the delights of cannibalism."

"What are you giving us! You, a man-eater? I guess I can't feel safe with you hereafter, especially since we share the same cabin. I'll wake up some fine day to find myself half consumed."

"Don't worry, little cabbage! I'm fond of you, but not enough to devour you if there's any other food going."

"Oh, I wouldn't trust you around the corner," asserted Conseil. "But one thing is clear enough. We must absolutely bring down some red meat to satisfy this flesh-eater, or some day my master will not find enough pieces of Conseil left to be of any service to him."

While we were working off our high spirits in such chatter, we were penetrating ever deeper into the somber arches of the primeval forest. And for a period of some two hours we continued to explore our game preserve in all directions, but without tangible result.

Chance rewarded our search for edible vegetables.

And soon one of the most useful products of the tropical world was furnishing us with a precious article of food that we had sorely missed on board. I mean, of course, the breadfruit tree, which was very plentiful on the island of Gilboa. And I marked down especially that variety of this tree which is destitute of seeds and which in Malaya bears the name of rima.

Ned Land, as was natural, knew these fruits well. For he had already eaten many of them on his previous voyages, and he understood how to prepare their edible parts delightfully. The sight of them so excited him that he could scarcely contain himself.

"Professor," he shouted, "I shall die on the spot unless I have a taste of this breadfruit pie."

"Save your life, dear boy, by eating as much as you want. We are here to make experiments, so why not make them?"

"It will take only a jiffy," said the Canadian.

And, provided with a lens, he started a fire that was soon crackling merrily. While he was fanning the dead wood to a hotter flame Conseil and I chose the mellowest fruits of the artocarpus. Some ears of this had not yet reached a proper state of maturity, and their tough skin concealed a white and fibrous pulp. But others, most of them yellow and gelatinous, were only waiting to be picked.

These fruits inclose no kernel. Conseil brought a dozen of them to Ned Land, who placed them on a fire of coals after he had cut them into thick slices. During this whole time of preparation the worthy fellow kept repeating, "You'll just see, M. Aronnax, how good this bread is. Jiminy, but won't it go right to the spot, after being deprived of it so long! It isn't even common, ordinary bread, either. It's a delicate pastry. Did you ever eat any, sir?"

"No, but I've always longed to have the chance to."

"All right, then. Just get your mouth set for a real juicy meal. If you don't come back for a second helping, I never learned to throw a harpoon."

After but a few minutes that part of the fruit which was exposed to the fire was completely charred. The interior of it resembled a white sort of crumby paste, and its flavor reminded me of an artichoke.

It must be confessed that this bread was of an unusual excellence, and I ate my share of it with savage relish.

"What time is it now, I wonder?" asked Conseil, but not, I noticed, until after he had had his fill of the fruit.

"Two o'clock, at least," I replied after a sight of the inclination of the sun.

"How time flies when you're on firm ground!" sighed my servant.

"Let us make quick use of it, then," I suggested.

We traced our way back through the forest, along the path we had blazed with our hatchets as we first walked it. We dawdled a bit to enrich our store of vegetables by a raid upon the cabbage palms, whose fruit we had to gather from the very tops of the trees. We then added to our supply yams of a superior quality and little beans, which I recognized as the *abrou* of the Malays.

We were well loaded down by the time we reached our canoe, although Ned Land was grumbling because he did not find our store of provisions sufficient for his greedy mind. In this, as in all else that golden day, fate favored us. Just as we were ready to push off from shore I perceived several trees that were from twenty-five to thirty feet in height. They were a species of palm tree that bore fruits as valuable as the artocarpus, and justly reckoned among the most useful products of Malaya.

At last, about five o'clock in the evening, we quit the shore. Half an hour later, loaded with our riches, we spoke the "Nautilus." No one answered our hail or appeared on board to bid us welcome. The enormous iron-plated cylinder seemed deserted. After I had seen the provisions safely embarked and stored away, I descended to my cabin and after a hearty supper slept most soundly.

The next day, January 6, nothing new happened on board. There was not a sound of any kind, nor any sign of life. The boat remained moored at the side of the "Nautilus" in the very position in which we had left it the day before. We resolved to return to the island. Ned Land hoped to have better luck with his hunting and had decided to explore a new portion of the woods.

We set off for terra firma at the break of day. The boat, propelled by the waves that were floating shoreward reached the island in a few minutes.

We clambered quickly out to follow Ned Land. Conseil and I both judged it wise to yield precedence to the Canadian, whose long legs were already threatening to outdistance us. His path wound up the curving coast-line toward the west. He forded several torrents and gained the high plain which was bordered by admirable forests. Some kingfishers were rambling awkwardly along the water course but proved too shy to permit of our approaching them closely. Their caution regarding us proved to me that these birds knew what sort of treatment they might expect from bipeds of our species. And I thus concluded that, if the island was not actually inhabited, it was at least often visited by human beings.

After plodding across a rather wide prairie we came to the outskirts of a small wood which was enlivened by the songs and the flight of a great number of birds.

"Too bad!" mourned Conseil, whose carnal instincts had been awakened by our journey of the previous day. "They are only birds!"

"But I guess you can eat them, can't you?" asked the harpooner.

"I doubt whether you can, my friend, for they are only parrots."

"Let me assure you, little cabbage," said Ned gravely, "that to those who have nothing better parrots taste like pheasants."

"And," I added, "this bird, suitably prepared by par-boiling, is worth sticking knife and fork into."

Under the luxuriant foliage of this forest a world of parrots was flying from branch to branch. It was strange to reflect at this moment that they only awaited a careful education to speak the human language. But as it was, parrots of all hues of the rainbow were chattering away like good fellows. Grave cockatoos appeared to be meditating upon some philosophical problem, the while brilliant red lorries passed us like a strip of bunting being carried off by the breeze. Papuans of the finest azure colors were also before us, but among all the varieties of winged things so beautiful to behold there were few that would invite to a feast.

One sort of bird, which is peculiar to these lands and which has never seemed to pass the limits of the Arrow and Papuan islands, I could not find in this vast collection. But I did not have to wait long to make its acquaintance.

After we had bored our way through a moderately thick copse we came out upon a plain obstructed with bushes. It was there I saw those splendid birds whose long feathers are so arranged that they can fly successfully only against the wind. Their undulating flight, their graceful aërial curves, and the shading of their bright-hued plumage attracted and charmed our gaze. I had no trouble in classifying them without delay.

"As I live," I cried, "there are our birds of paradise!"

The Malays carry on a great trade in these birds with the Chinese. But they have several means of snaring them that were at the moment out of our power to employ. Sometimes the Malays place nooses at the top of high trees most frequented by the birds. Sometimes they catch them with a viscous bird lime that paralyzes their movements. They even go so far as to poison the fountains from which the birds generally drink. But we were obliged to fire at them on the wing, a fact which gave us few opportunities to bring them down. And, indeed, we vainly exhausted half our ammunition before we surrendered to necessity and quit firing.

By eleven o'clock that morning we had scaled the first range of mountains that traverse the center of the island, and we had no booty to show for our pains. Hunger, however, bolstered us up and drove us on. Another time when hunters had relied upon the trophies of the chase to their confusion! Happily Conseil, to his own vast surprise, executed a double shot and thus secured us our breakfast. He killed a white pigeon and a wood pigeon, which Ned Land cleverly plucked and suspended from a skewer, roasting them before a red fire of dead branches. While these interesting birds were cooking, Ned prepared the fruit of the artocarpus. Then the pigeons were devoured down to their very bones and declared delicious by all of us. The nutmeg with which they are wont to stuff their crops flavors their flesh and renders it delicious eating.

"Well, Ned," I asked, from the depths of my vast contentment, "what do you miss most at this minute?"

"Some four-footed game, of course," the harpooner promptly retorted. "All these pigeons, M. Aronnax, are but tidbits and trifles—side dishes, at best. And until I have slain an animal with cutlets on it, I shall not be content."

"Nor I, my dear fellow, until I have my bird of paradise."

"Let us go on hunting, then," advised the practical Conseil. "I move that we work toward the sea. We have already reached the first slopes of the mountains, and I think we'd do better to regain the region of forests."

That sounded like sensible advice, so we followed it. We walked for an hour or so and attained a forest of sago trees. Several harmless serpents glided away at our approach. The birds of paradise likewise scurried off, and I was despairing of getting close enough for a successful shot. Then Conseil, who was walking along in front, bent suddenly down, uttered a war whoop, and came running back to me with a magnificent specimen clutched firmly in his hand.

"Ah, bravo, Conseil!" I called out to him in greeting.

"You are very kind to praise me, sir."

"Not at all! You have executed a wonderful stroke there, my dear boy. To take one of these birds alive! And with your bare hand!"

"Pouf, dear master! If you but examine it closely, you will see that I don't deserve a scrap of approval."

"Why, how is that?"

"Because this bird is as drunk as a lord."

"Drunk! And in this natural forest, untrod by man?"

"Positively a fact, sir. It is intoxicated from the nutmegs it has been gorging under the very nutmeg tree where I found it. Behold, Mr. Ned Land, the terrible effects of intemperance!"

"By jingo!" exclaimed the Canadian. " I hope you're not blaming me for the gin I've been putting away these last two months. If it hadn't been for a pull of strong liquor now and then, I'd have died from boredom on board the old 'Nautilus.' "

I studied the strange bird that Conseil handed over to me. He was right in his statement; drugged by the strong juice, the fowl was powerless to fly. It could scarcely stand up on its two legs.

It seemed to belong to the most splendid of the eight species that are to be found in Papua and neighboring islands. It was that rarest kind, the large emerald bird.

It measured three feet in length from tip to tail. Its head was comparatively small, and the eyes were placed near the opening of the beak. They were tiny and bright, like beads. The color of its shadings were beautiful—it had a yellow beak, brown feet and claws, and nut-colored wings with purple tips. It was pale yellow at the back of the neck and head, emerald hue at the throat, chestnut on the breast and belly. Two horn-shaped downy tufts rose from below the tail, that are prolonged by long light feathers of wonderful fineness. And when one considers the whole plumage of this marvelous fowl, one does not wonder at the native name for it—"bird of the sun."

And so my wishes had been granted and I possessed the bird of paradise. But the Canadian's yearning for venison was still unquenched. It helped things some, of course, when about two o'clock Ned Land shot down a magnificent hog of the species the natives call bari-outang. The animal came in time for us to procure real quadruped meat, and he was well received, like the mayor at the fair.

Our friend was right proud of his skilful shot, for the hog, struck by the electric bullet, fell stone dead while yet in full flight. The Canadian skinned and cleaned the hog properly, after having stripped it of half a dozen cutlets which were destined to furnish us with a grilled repast that very evening. Then the hunt was resumed, and it was still further marked by the exploits of Ned and Conseil.

This came about when the two friends, beating the bushes to startle any chance occupant of them, roused a herd of kangaroos that fled and bounded along on their elastic paws. Swift as was the attempted escape of these animals, it was powerless against the electric capsules provided by Captain Nemo.

"Oh me, oh my, Professor!" shrieked Ned Land, transported by the delights of the chase. "How they will taste stewed in the pot! What a ripping supply for the old 'Nautilus'! There are two down—three—five, by crackey! And to think we're going to get our molars into that flesh, and the other idiots on board won't have even a smell!"

I believe, if the good Canadian had not wasted so much effort in babbling, he would have killed the whole lot. But, as it was, we were needs must content with a round dozen of these interesting marsupians. They were small in build. They were a species of those kangaroo rabbits that inhabit the hollows of trees and are possessed of extreme speed. But they are reasonably fat and offer estimable food, so we were very well satisfied with the results of our hunting.

Happy Ned proposed to return to this enchanted island the next day, for he was by now determined to depopulate it of all its edible quadrupeds. But he reckoned without his host. Man proposes, but fate disposes.

At six o'clock in the evening we had regained the shore. We found our boat moored where we had left it. We could see the "Nautilus," like a long rock, emerging from the waves two miles off the beach. Without a moment's delay Ned Land started to prepare dinner, and he fulfilled our utmost expectations as to his skill in cooking. Grilled upon live coals, the bari-outang soon scented the air with a most delicious and salivating odor.

The dinner was noteworthy, for, besides the hog cutlets, two wood pigeons were added to the menu. Sago pasty, artocarpus bread, some mangoes, half a dozen pineapples, and liquor fermented from coconuts—these dainties were all there to overjoy us. After the liquor it seemed to me the ideas of my companions lost in clarity whatever they gained in gaiety and force. I may be wrong, however.

"Suppose we do not return to the submarine tonight," suggested Conseil with a yawn of contentment.

"Say, let's never return at all!" said Ned Land.

It was just then that a stone fell at our feet and cut short whatever further remark the harpooner may have intended.

CHAPTER XXII

CAPTAIN NEMO'S THUNDERBOLT

We stared stupidly at the edge of the forest without rising. My hand stopped halfway to my mouth.

"Stones do not fall from the sky," remarked Conseil, "or they would call them aërolites."

Another stone, more carefully aimed than its predecessor, caused the savory leg of a pigeon to fall from my servant's fingers. This shot added weight to his wise observation. We sprang to our feet, shouldered our guns, and made ready to reply to any attack.

"Is it apes, do you think?" asked Ned Land.

"Much the same thing," I answered. "It's savages."

"To the boat!" called Conseil, and set us an example of orderly but hurried retreat.

It was high time that we yielded ground, for a score of natives armed with bows and slings, were just getting into action. They appeared on the skirts of a copse that masked the horizon to our right, a hundred paces distant.

Our canoe was moored about sixty feet away. The savages approached us, not running, but with such hostile demonstrations that their intentions were painfully evident. Stones and arrows began to fall thick as hail.

Ned Land, the obstinate fellow, was unwilling to leave behind him our hard-won provisions. And so, in spite of his imminent danger, with partly dismembered pig on one side and a cluttering bunch of kangaroo rabbits on the other, he sprinted as fast as he could under the awkward circumstances. In a nod of your head we were at the shore. In a flash of the eye we had loaded the boat with our booty and firearms and had pushed it off, with oars already shipped.

We had not gone two cable lengths when a hundred savages, more or less, had entered the water up to their waists. Their howling and gesticulating were worth going miles to witness. I watched, as I sat at the rudder in the stern of our boat, to see whether this amazing apparition would attract some of the crew of the "Nautilus" up to the platform. But no. The enormous machine, lying placidly off at a distance, was absolutely undisturbed.

Twenty minutes later we were ourselves on board. The panels were open. And so, waiting only to make the boat fast to its moorings, we went down into the submarine.

From the drawing-room came the sounds of chords. Someone was at the piano organ. It was Captain Nemo, bending forward over the keyboard of the instrument and caught in a musical ecstasy.

"Captain!" I cried the moment I became aware of him.

Evidently he did not hear me, for he made no response. He did not look up, although I fear the noise of my arrival was greater than I had any notion of its being.

"Captain!" I said again, this time more softly, but touching his hand.

He shuddered at my contact with him. And then he turned around and said quite calmly, "Ah, it is you, Professor? Well, how did the hunt go? Did you get in any botanizing worth while?"

"Yes, Captain.   But unfortunately we rooted out a troup of bipeds whose nearness distresses me."

"What species of biped have you unearthed?"

"Savages surely—cannibals presumably."

"Savages?" he echoed ironically.   "Real wild men, were they?   Persons who have as yet not enjoyed the manifold advantages of modern culture and education?"

"Yes—just that."

"Why are you so astonished, M. Aronnax, at meeting savages when you set foot on a strange land?   Where in all the earth are there not savages?   And do you for a moment suppose them worse than other men, these fellows that you call savages?"

"But, you see, sir—"

"How many of the wretched beings did you count?"

"A hundred, at least."

The commander placed his fingers back on the organ stops.   His polite attention to my words was already waning.

"Rest assured, Professor," he said idly, "that if all the natives of Papua were assembled on this shore the 'Nautilus' would not have a thing to fear from their flimsy assaults."

The strange man's fingers were now running over the clavier of the beautiful instrument, and I observed with interest that he touched only the black keys, which gave to his melodies an eerie, Scotch character.   In a moment he had quite forgotten my presence and was again buried in a reverie that I had not the heart to disturb.

So I stole up again to the platform.   Meanwhile the

swift night of the sub-tropics had fallen. For in this low latitude the sun sets rapidly and without an intervening twilight. I could see the outlines of the island but indistinctly. Still, the numerous fires lighted on the beach bore mute witness that the savages had no intention of withdrawing from it.

I remained in my quiet nook for several hours, sometimes thinking of the natives, but without any particular dread of them. For the calm confidence of the commander in his ship's invulnerability was contagious. But mostly I forgot the Papuans as I admired the splendors of the southern night. My memories harked back to France, as if in the train of those zodiacal stars which would be shining there in a few hours' time. The moon gleamed in the midst of the constellations of the zenith.

The night slipped by without any mischance. I attributed this to the presumable fear of the islanders at the sight of a monster aground in the bay. The panels were open and would have offered an easy access to the interior of the "Nautilus."

I resumed my vigil on the platform at six o'clock in the morning on January 8. The dawn was already breaking. The island soon became visible through the fogs as they dissipated before the sun—first the shore and then the summits.

Oh, the natives were there, to the hundred, several times more numerous than on the evening before. A group of them, profiting by the low tide, had climbed upon the coral and were intrenched less than two cable lengths from where I sat. I could distinguish them easily. They were typical Papuans, large-figured and of strong race, men with large, high foreheads and white teeth. Their woolly hair, of a pronounced reddish tinge, contrasted sharply with their black, glistening bodies, which resembled the frames of Nubians. Chaplets of bones (whose bones?) hung from the lobes of their ears, which were slashed and distended. Most of these savages were stark naked.

Among their number, however, I descried several women who were clad from the hip to the knee in a sort of wide skirt that was made of grasses and suspended from a waistband of vegetable material. Some of the head-men or chiefs had adorned their necks with crescents and collars of glass beads. And nearly all were armed with bows, arrows, and shields, carrying on their shoulders a net which contained the round stones that they cast from slings with great skill.

Now one of these chiefs, rather near to the "Nautilus," made bold to study it attentively. He was perhaps a *mado* of high rank, for his body was draped in a mat of banana leaves notched around the edge and set off with brilliant colors.

I could easily have knocked this native over, he was so close to me, but I thought it wiser to await the opening of really hostile demonstrations. Not only is prudence the better part of valor, but in parleys between Europeans and savages it is fitting for the former to ward off sharply, not to attack.

During low tide the natives kept wandering about near the submersible but offered us no trouble. I frequently heard them mutter the word *assai*, and by their gestures I understood that they invited me to go to land—an invitation which I declined.

So it came to pass that on the third day of our stay near Gilboa the canoe did not take us away from our ship, to the vast displeasure of Ned Land, who wished to complete his store of provender.

This adroit Canadian, therefore, found time hanging heavy on his hands and employed the unexpected leisure in preparing the viands and meat that we had brought off from the island.

As for the savages, about eleven o'clock in the morning, as soon as the coral ridges began to disappear beneath the rising tide, they returned to shore. But by this hour I noticed that their numbers had been considerably swollen by fresh accessions. The late arrivals had probably come from the neighboring islands, or even from Papua itself. Strange, but I had not seen a single native canoe!

Having no better way in which to occupy my time, I now decided to drag these limpid waters, under which I noticed a profusion of shells, zoöphytes, and marine plants. My determination was strengthened by the fact that this was the last day that our vessel would pass in these parts in case it really floated off the reef on the morrow according to Captain Nemo's prophecy.

I therefore summoned Conseil to my aid, and he procured for me a small light drag, much like those used in oyster fishery. We went to work with what zeal we could muster, and for a space of two hours we angled unceasingly without bringing to the surface a single rarity. The drag would choke itself full of midas-ears, harps, melames, and particularly beautiful hammers. And we also brought to light some holothurias, pearl oysters, and a dozen little turtles that were reserved for the pantry downstairs.

But just when I least expected it I put my hand upon a wonder, I might even say a natural deformity, very rarely met with. Conseil was pulling in his draught of divers ordinary shells, when all at once he saw me thrust my arm quickly into the net to draw forth a shell. And at the same time I uttered a conchological squeal—that is to say, the most piercing cry that human throat can utter.

"What's the matter, sir?" he asked, in great surprise. "Did you get bitten, sir?"

"No, my boy. My scream was one of undiluted amazement. Although I would willingly have sacrificed a finger for the privilege of making such a discovery."

"But I see nothing wonderful here, sir."

"Look at this shell," I triumphed as I held an object up for his inspection.

"But, M. Aronnax," Conseil continued, with a puzzled expression of countenance, "you are holding simply an olive porphyry, genus olive, order of pectinibranchidae, class of gasteropods, subclass of mollusca."

"Correct, dear fellow. You have ticked off everything but the matter most important. This shell, instead of being rolled from right to left, turns from left to right."

"Phew! Is it possible?"

"It is more than possible, it is so."

With rare exceptions, shells are all right-handed. And

when, by the billionth chance, their spiral is left, amateurs are willing to exchange them for their weight in gold.

This fact explains why Conseil and I were absorbed in the contemplation of our earthly treasure to the exclusion of all else. I was just making up my mind to enrich the Paris museum with it, when a thrice-accursed stone thrown by a native struck against the precious object in Conseil's hand and smashed it.

I uttered a cry of despair.

Conseil snatched up his gun and aimed it at a savage who was poising his sling, at ten paces from him. I would have stopped my servant, but before I could intervene his shot took effect and broke the bracelet of amulets which encircled the arm of the savage.

"Stop it, my boy!" I cried.

"But, my heavens, sir! Did you not notice that the cannibal was the first to strike?"

"No shell is worth the life of a man," I said sternly.

"The scoundrel," Conseil muttered, "I should rather have had him splinter my shoulder."

And the worthy fellow was in earnest, too. But I was not of his way of thinking. By now, however, I noticed that the situation of the savages had greatly changed during the last few moments while we had been blind. A score of war canoes encircled the "Nautilus." Scooped out of the trunk of a tree, long, narrow, and well adapted for speed, these boats were balanced by means of a long bamboo pole, or outrigger, which floated on the water. They were managed by skilful, half-naked paddlers, and I watched their advance with a certain trepidation.

It was perfectly evident that these Papuans had already had dealings with Europeans and knew their ships. But this long iron cylinder anchored out in their bay, what could they think of it? Fearful things perhaps, for at first they kept at a respectful distance from it. But little by little they took courage as they saw it stationary and defenseless, and they sought to familiarize themselves with it.

Now this familiarity was precisely the one thing I deemed it necessary to avoid. Our firearms, which were noiseless, would produce only a moderate effect on the minds of the savages, which have small esteem for anything that does not roar and bluster. The thunderbolt robbed of its reverberations would frighten man but little, though of course all the danger lies in the lightning and not in the noise.

While I was hesitating what to do, the canoes at a given signal approached the "Nautilus" and a shower of missiles alighted on her.

I ran down to the saloon, but found it deserted. Because of the pressing emergency, I mustered up my courage and knocked at the door opening into the captain's room.

"Come in," was the answer.

I entered and discovered that Captain Nemo was deep in algebraical calculations of x and other quantities.

"I fear I am disturbing you, sir," I said with all the politeness I could summon.

"That is true, M. Aronnax," the commander replied calmly, "but I feel sure you have grave reasons for wishing to see me."

"I could wish them less grave, sir. Even at this moment natives are surrounding us in their canoes. In a few minutes we shall certainly be overwhelmed by many hundreds of savages."

"Oho!" said Captain Nemo placidly. "So they have come out in their canoes?"

"Yes, sir."

"Well, Professor, then we must see to closing the hatches."

"Exactly, and I came to say to you—"

"Oh, nothing could be more simple," said my calm host. He pressed an electric button which transmitted an order to the ship's crew.

"And now there is no further cause for worry," he continued after a moment's pause. "Everything is all done. The pinnace is in place, the hatches closed. You do not fear, I hope, that these gentlemen of the wilds can stave in iron walls upon which the cannon balls of the 'Abraham Lincoln' had no effect?"

"Why, no, sir. But a danger still exists."

"I wonder."

"Tomorrow at just about this time you'll have to open the panels of the ship to renew the air. Now, if the Papuans should happen to be perched on the platform at that psychological moment, I don't see how you can prevent their entering."

"You think they'll board us, then?"

"I'm morally certain of it."

"Well, sir, all I have to say is, let them come. The sooner, the better. Why should we hinder them from doing what they want to? In a way, I am sorry for these poor Papuans. And I don't want my unexpected visit at their island to cost the life of a single one of the wretches."

What more was there for me to say? I was on the point of departure when Captain Nemo asked me to remain and have a chat with him. He exhibited quite an interest in our excursions ashore, questioned me about our hunting, and did not appear to understand the craving for fresh meat that had seized hold of the Canadian. Thereafter the conversation turned to other subjects. Without being exactly communicative, my host evinced an unusual amiability.

Among a dozen other topics, we came to speak of the situation of the "Nautilus," which had run aground at almost the identical spot where Dumont d'Urville had had his hair-breadth escape. Apropos of this, the captain said, "This d'Urville was one of your really great sailors— a most intelligent navigator, the Captain Cook of France. What an ironical end was his! Did you know that this unfortunate man of science, after having braved the coral reefs of Oceania and the cannibals of the Pacific, perished miserably in a railroad accident? What do you suppose was uppermost in this man's mind during the last moments of his life?"

When he spoke in this vein, when his human sympathies were so evidently touched, I always had to revise my opinion of Captain Nemo. Perhaps he really was not so cold-blooded as he wished to appear.

With the chart held between us we reviewed the travels of the famous French mariner. We spoke of his voyages

into the unexplored corners of the world, his two attempts
to reach the South Pole which led to the discovery of lands,
Adelaide and Louis Philippe, and of his determining the
exact hydrographical bearings of all the principal islands
of Oceania.

"But, after all, what your d'Urville did for the surface
of the seas, I have done under them. And if my labor is
more easy than his, it is also more complete. The 'Astrolabe' and the 'Zélée,' incessantly the playthings of hurricane and typhoon, could not have the value of my
'Nautilus,' quiet laboratory and workshop that she is,
motionless in the heart of the element she is exploring."

What a vivid picture these words raised in my mind!

"Tomorrow," added the captain as he rose from his
chair, "at twenty minutes to three in the afternoon our
vessel will be afloat, and we shall be leaving the Straits of
Torres with a whole skin."

When he had uttered these words the commander
bowed to me slightly. This was to announce to me that
our audience was at an end, and I returned to my cabin.
There I found Conseil, who was most anxious to know
the result of my interview.

"My boy," I said to him pensively, "I feel a little as
I used to right after my dear mother had administered a
spanking to my young person. For when I ventured to
opine that his 'Nautilus' was threatened by the Papuan
savages, the commander answered me very sarcastically.
There seems but one thing left for us to do—put our trust
in him and go to sleep with a good conscience."

"Then you have no further need of me, sir?"

"None, thank you.   What is our fellow conspirator, Ned Land, up to?"

"At this very moment, sir, he is constructing a kangaroo pie which promises to be a marvel."

Conseil thereupon left me, and I went straight to bed. But, I must confess, I slept indifferently.   I heard the hullabaloo of the savages, both in my dreams and in fact. They stamped on the platform and uttered deafening cries.   So passed the night, so far as I could determine, without disturbing the ordinary repose of the crew.   For the ear-splitting ululations of these man-eaters affected them no more than the ants that crawl over the front of a masked battery of artillery trouble the soldiers belonging to it.

At six o'clock in the morning I was glad to get up from my couch.   The hatches had not been opened, and the inner air was stale.   But, just as I was finding the atmosphere stuffy and unpleasant to breathe, the reservoirs, filled and ready for such an emergency, were resorted to.   And they discharged the few cubic feet of oxygen that brought new life and zest into the exhausted lungs of the "Nautilus."

I dressed, but still scarcely knew what to do.   So I read in my room until noon without having seen Captain Nemo even for an instant.   On board no preparations for departure were visible.

When the clock struck half-past two I went to the large saloon.   In ten minutes it would be high tide, and, if our commander had not made a rash prediction, the submarine would soon be detached from its resting place.

Otherwise many months might come and go ere she could leave her coral prison.

Warning vibrations began to be felt in the ship's frame. I could hear the keel grating against the rough calcareous side of the reef. At twenty-five minutes to three my host suddenly appeared in the door of the drawing-room.

"Well, we are off," he said, as if announcing the departure of a train on schedule time.

"So I perceive, sir."

"And I have ordered the hatches opened for you."

"Why, what has become of the Papuans?"

"Why bother about the Papuans?" inquired the commander, with a slight shrug of his shoulders.

"But they'll troop right down on us."

"And how will they accomplish that, may I ask?"

"By leaping through the opened panels," I almost shouted. I could not understand this indifferent captain. He was either out of his senses or possessed of some secret knowledge closed to me.

"M. Aronnax," Captain Nemo answered quietly, "the cannibals cannot enter the 'Nautilus' in that way even when the hatches are unprotected."

I could only gaze at my host in utter silence. He saw the perplexity written in my face.

"You do not guess?" he said.

"I am stupid, I admit, but no slightest gleam of light pierces the dark-room of my brain."

"Come along with me, then, and take a look at things."

I directed my steps toward the central staircase. There Conseil and Ned Land were stealthily observing some of the submarine's crew who were opening the panels. Cries of murderous rage, fearful vociferations of blood lust resounded outside the hatches.

The port lids were pulled down. Twenty horrible faces appeared. A rush for the iron ladder began. But the first native who placed his hand on the stair rail was struck from behind by some invisible force that I could not figure out. He fled as if pursued by all the devils of the underworld, howling, making the wildest contortions.

At least ten of his comrades had followed in his footsteps. They met with the same strange fate.

Conseil was hugging himself for joy. But Ned Land, carried away by his more violent instincts, rushed to the staircase. The moment he seized the railing with both hands, he in turn was overthrown, as if shot down from a catapult.

"A thunderbolt hit me!" he cried, with an awful oath.

This explained all to me. It was no railing in a proper sense upon which hands had been put, but a metallic cable that was charged with electricity from the deck and connected with the platform. Whoever touched it got a powerful charge of "juice." And the resultant shock would have been a mortal one if Captain Nemo had intrusted to the conductor the whole force of the ship's current. It might be truly said that my host had stretched between himself and his assailants a screen of electricity which none could pass with impunity.

Meanwhile the Papuans had beaten a swift retreat, paralyzed with terror. As for us, we laughed ourselves half sick, and then went to work to console poor Ned Land.

While we kneaded and massaged him, he swore like one possessed.

It was then that the "Nautilus," raised by the last waves of the tide, quit her coral bed. Almost unconsciously I cast a glance at the clock. The hands indicated twenty minutes to three. It was the exact instant promised the previous day by the captain! Her screw beat the waters slowly and majestically. Her speed increased gradually. And sailing on the surface of the ocean as calmly as if she had never met with a disagreeable experience in all her days, the submarine quit safe and sound the dangerous passes of the Torres Straits.

CHAPTER XXIII

CONFINEMENT

Next day, January 10, the "Nautilus" continued her passage between the two seas, but with what a difference! She was moving at so remarkable a speed that I could not estimate it at anything less than thirty-five miles an hour. The rapidity of her screw was such that I could neither separate nor count its revolutions.

I reflected upon the marvelous qualities of the agent that drove our vessel. It afforded her motion, light, and heat. It transformed her into an ark of safety and protected her from assault. No profane hand might touch her without being smitten by the lightning. My admiration for this agent was unbounded, and it extended to the engineer who had harnessed this force to his purposes.

Our course was directed toward the west. On the 11th of January we doubled Cape Wessel, which is situated in 135° longitude and 10° north latitude. This promontory forms the eastern point of the Gulf of Carpentaria. The reefs were still numerous, but now they were more regular in formation and marked on the chart with extreme precision. The submersible easily avoided the breakers of Money, which lay on the port side. Nor did she have the least trouble with the Victoria reefs, which lay to starboard at 130° longitude and on the 10th parallel, directly on our course.

On the 13th of January Captain Nemo arrived in the

Sea of Timor and recognized the island which bears the same name in 122° longitude. From this point the direction of the "Nautilus" shifted to the southwest. Her head was set for the Indian Ocean.

Where would the whim of our commander transport us next? Futile as speculations on this point might be when I was unacquainted with any ruling purpose in his actions, I yet could not dismiss them from my mind. Would he return to the coast of Asia? Would he approach the shores of Europe? Both of these seemed improbable conjectures in connection with a man who fled from inhabited continents. Would he, then, descend to the south? Was he going to double the Cape of Good Hope, then Cape Horn, and finally penetrate to the Antarctic Pole? And in the end would he return to the Pacific, where his vessel could sail freely and independently? Time alone would show.

Meanwhile we skirted the shoals of Cartier, Hibernia, Seringapatam, and Scott. These were the last bulwarks of the solid element against the encroachments of its liquid counterpart. And on January 14 we lost sight of land altogether. The speed of the "Nautilus" was then considerably abated, and her course of action became quite irregular; she sometimes swam midst the depths of the sea, at others floated on the surface.

It was during this part of the voyage that our commander made interesting experiments on the varied temperature of different levels of sea bottom. Ordinarily such tests are made with complicated instruments, and their results are fairly doubtful. They use thermometrical sounding leads, the glasses of which frequently break because of the pressure of the water. Or they resort to an apparatus which is based on the differential resistance of metals to electric currents. And calculations so arrived at cannot be trusted. But Captain Nemo himself descended to test the temperature in the depths of the sea. And, coming as he did in direct communication with the levels to be measured, he secured immediately and accurately the degree sought.

Either by overloading her reservoir tanks or by sinking obliquely by means of her inclined planes, the "Nautilus" was thus able to attain successively depths of three, four, five, seven, nine, and ten thousand yards. The definite result of his observations was that the ocean maintained an average temperature of 4.5 degrees Centigrade in all latitudes at a depth of five thousand fathoms.

On January 16 our submarine seemed to be becalmed only a few yards beneath the surface of the waves. Her electric machinery was out of commission, and her inactive screw permitted her to drift at the whim of wind and current. I imagined the crew might be occupied with interior repairs made necessary by the strain to which the engines had been put.

Then it was that my companions and I witnessed a curious spectacle. The panels of the saloon were open. A dim obscurity prevailed in the midst of the sea because the beacon light of the submarine was not in operation. It was interesting to observe the sea under such conditions, the largest fish appearing to the eye no more than scarcely defined shadows. Suddenly we found ourselves transported into full light. I thought at first, of course, that the beacon had been lighted and was again casting its electric radiance into the waters. I was mistaken and, after a rapid survey, perceived my error.

The "Nautilus" was floating in the midst of a phosphorescent mass which, because of the gloom elsewhere prevalent, became quite dazzling. The bright glow was produced by myriads of luminous animalculae, whose brilliancy was somehow increased as they glided over the hull of the vessel. I was amazed to see a sort of lightning in the center of these luminous sheets, as if rivulets of lead had been melted in a fiery furnace or metallic masses had been brought to a white heat, so that, by force of contrast, certain portions of this lighted matter appeared to be casting a shadow in the very midst of the general ignition, from which it seemed as if all shadow should be banished. Ah, no—this was not the ordinary irradiation of summer lightning. This was unusual burning and vigor, this was truly living light!

Whence did it come? Why, it was in reality an almost infinite agglomeration of colored infusoria and globules of diaphanous jelly which were provided with threadlike tentacles. As many as twenty-five thousand of them have been counted in less than two cubic half-inches of water. And their light was multiplied by the glimmering peculiar to medusae, starfish, aurelia, and other phosphorescent zoöphytes, impregnated by the grease of organic matter decomposed by the sea and, perhaps, the mucus secreted by fish.

For a long while the submersible floated in these brilliant masses. And our wonder was increased as we watched the marine monsters disporting themselves like salamanders. I saw there, for instance, in this glow that does not diffuse heat, the swift and graceful porpoise, who is the indefatigable clown of the ocean; and swordfish ten feet long, those prophetic heralds of hurricane and tempest, whose formidable sabers would now and then grate against the glass of the saloon. Then appeared smaller fish, the variegated balista, the leaping mackerel, wolf thorntails, and a hundred other sorts that striped the luminous element through which they swam. The dazzling scene was enchanting. Very likely some atmospheric condition of an unusual kind increased the intensity of this phenomenal brilliance. Perhaps some storm agitated the upper surface of the waves. But at the depth in which we lay the "Nautilus" was unmoved by its fury and reposed peacefully in still water.

Thus we journeyed on from one new marvel to another. The halcyon days glided swiftly by, and I scarcely took account of them. Conseil arranged and classified his zoöphytes, his articulata, his mollusks, and his fish. Ned never tired of inventing new dishes in order to vary to the utmost the diet on board. We were growing fast to our shell like snails, and I swear it must be easy to lead a snail's existence. Thus, our undersea life began to seem natural to us, and we no longer thought of the days we used to spend on land.

Then, without warning, something occurred to recall to us most vividly the strangeness of our position.

On January 18 our ship was in 105° longitude and 15°

south latitude. The weather was threatening; the sea was rough and rolling. There was a strong wind from the east. The barometer, which had been falling for some days, gave notice of an impending storm.

Chance had it that I went up to the platform just as the second lieutenant was taking the measure of the horary angles. And according to my habit I waited for the usual phrase to be said. But on this one day the customary words were not uttered; they were replaced by another sentence equally incomprehensible.

Almost at once I saw Captain Nemo appear and look at the horizon through a telescope.

For several minutes he was immovable, never taking his eye from the point under observation. Then he lowered his glass and exchanged a few words with his lieutenant. This man seemed to be the prey of some emotion which he struggled vainly to repress. Captain Nemo, who had more command over his feelings, remained cool; he seemed to be objecting to what the lieutenant said, while the latter kept replying in an emphatic and assured fashion. At least that was what I deduced from their tones and gestures. Naturally, I also gazed carefully in the direction indicated, but without seeing a blessed thing. To my eyes no object intervened between the platform and the point where sky and water merged in the clear line of the horizon.

Our commander, however, strode from one end of our deck to the other without looking at me, perhaps without seeing me. His step was firm, but less regular than usual. Sometimes he would stop in his walking, cross his arms, and again study the expanse of ocean. What in the world could he be looking for in that vast desert? At that time the "Nautilus" was hundreds of miles from the nearest coast.

The lieutenant had grasped the telescope and was now examining the horizon minutely. He walked rapidly about, and he stood still. He stamped his feet nervously now and then, without realizing what he was doing. Altogether, he exhibited much more agitation than his superior officer did. At any rate, this mystery, whatever it might be, would necessarily be explained, and before long. For consequent to a command of Captain Nemo's the engine had vastly increased its propelling power and was making the screw hum.

The second officer touched the commander on the shoulder to attract his attention. The latter halted abruptly and directed his gaze to the point indicated by his companion. He looked long. All this mummery was getting to be too much for me. I rushed down to the drawing-room and secured the telescope that I was in the habit of using—it had an unparalleled set of lenses.

Then I returned to the upper deck and leaned, to steady myself, on the cage of the watch light that jutted out from the front of the platform. I controlled as best I could the nervous shaking of my right hand, and set myself to the task of examining the whole long line of sky and sea.

My eye had scarcely adjusted itself to the end of the glass when the instrument was quickly and rudely snatched from my hands.

I turned around. Captain Nemo stood before me, but

I did not recognize him in his present guise. His face was as if transformed. His eyes regarded me with a sullen flash, his teeth were set sternly together. Every indication betrayed the violent emotion that pervaded his whole frame: stiff body, clenched fists, head shrunk down between his shoulders. He was immovable as marble—flint —adamant. My glass fell, almost unnoticed, from his hands and rolled to his feet.

Was I the object of his anger?

Did this incomprehensible being fancy that I had discovered his long-hidden secret?

No, quite evidently not. It was not I who had provoked his convulsive passion. For he was not looking at me. His eye was steadily fixed upon the impenetrable point of the horizon. And at last Captain Nemo recovered himself. His agitation visibly subsided. He addressed some words in the foreign language to his lieutenant, then turned to me.

"M. Aronnax," he said in a rather imperious tone, "I ask you now to respect one of the conditions which bind you to me."

"Which one of them, my host?"

"You must be at once confined to your cabin, together with your companions, until I see fit to release you."

"The decision rests with you, sir, according to our agreement. But may I ask you one question?"

"Not one. I demand instant obedience."

There was no resisting this injunction. It would have been useless to have attempted delay. So, like a whipped child, I went down to the room occupied by Ned Land and

Conseil and told them of the unexpected turn of affairs. You may judge how my communication was received by the Canadian. Words fail me to convey the picture.

But there was no time for arguing. Four of the crew were already at the door, bent upon our immediate confinement. They led us in silence to the cell in which we had passed our first night on board the "Nautilus."

The harpooner was just making up his mind to a demonstration of force when the door was slammed in his face and locked.

"I'd rather like to know the meaning of this," Conseil confided to me with his habitual phlegm.

I told my comrades what had passed. They were as much puzzled as I by the mystery of the thing and equally at a loss as to how to account for it.

Soon after our imprisonment I grew absorbed in my own reflections. The strange look of fear on the face of our commander took precedence of my other memories as I reviewed the scene on the platform. It was so little in consonance with my whole previous idea of the man! My thoughts were brusquely interrupted by Ned Land.

"Halloo—hello! Breakfast is now served."

And, as sure as Eve ate apples, the table was set and ready for us! Captain Nemo, remarkable man, had forgotten nothing. At a flash he must have conveyed three orders: to lock us up, to feed us, and to send the "Nautilus" full speed ahead.

"Will you listen to a suggestion from me, sir?" inquired Conseil mildly.

"Say whatever is on your mind, my lad."

"Let's eat breakfast, sir. You never know, sir, what is going to happen, and I am brave as a lion when I'm fed."

"You are quite hopelessly sensible, Conseil."

"Jingo!" said Ned Land, pulling a long face. "There's nothing here but the ordinary ship's bill of fare. No cutlet, no roast, no bread, pie, pudding, no vegetable, no sauce. Fish—fish—fish!"

"Neddie," Conseil demanded, "what would you have said if there had been no meal at all?"

There was no answer to this argument. The harpooner ceased his recriminations and set to work and did not miss a bite.

The repast was eaten in silence. There was so much to say that we said nothing.

Scarcely had we finished eating, when the luminous globe that lighted our prison cell was extinguished. Ned Land was soon asleep, quite audibly so. What really astonished me was that Conseil followed his example, not even omitting to snore like a good fellow. I was wondering what could have caused such irresistible drowsiness, when I felt my own brain becoming dull and stupefied. A painful suspicion entered my mind.

A sleeping powder had been administered to us in the food that we had just taken. Apparently imprisonment alone was not sufficient to conceal the captain's plans from us. Sleep also was necessary.

I fought against the influence of the soporific medicine. The swaying of the sea, which had caused a slight rolling motion in the "Nautilus," had ceased. Did this mean that we had hunted the depths of ocean? Had we returned to the quiet bottom of the waters? It was getting impossible for me to withstand my increasing drowsiness. My breath came more faintly and in gasps. I felt a mortal chill steal along my rigid and half-paralyzed limbs. My eyelids fell as if they had been capped with lead. I tried to open my eyes—no! A morbid sleep, full of hallucinations, nightmarish, bereft me of my senses. Then the visions must have disappeared, for I was suddenly left in a state of complete insensibility.

CHAPTER XXIV

THE REALM OF CORAL

The next morning I awoke with a head singularly clear. Whatever narcotic had been given me the night before, it caused neither headache nor nausea. To my bewilderment, I was in my own room. This led me to believe that my companions had been likewise returned to their proper berths without any more consciousness of the fact than my own. They would then be as ignorant as I regarding the happenings of the night before. And therefore, to pierce this mystery, I could reckon only on what the future might bring forth.

I threw on my clothes and decided, if possible, to quit my room. Was I again free or a captive? Quite free, apparently, for the door opened to my hand and I went up the central stairs. The panels that gave on the upper deck were unlatched. I stepped out on the platform.

Conseil and Ned Land were waiting for me there. I questioned them. They could tell me nothing. Like myself, they had been buried in a sleep far beyond even passing consciousness of events. They had been amazed to wake up in their own bunks.

As for the "Nautilus," the old ship seemed as quiet and mysterious as ever. It was floating idly on the surface of an even sea, at a pace so moderate as hardly to indicate progress. Nothing seemed changed.

The second officer appeared on the platform, regular

as a marionette operated by clockwork. Nor did he omit the usual order for my retirement. But Captain Nemo was nowhere about.

Of all the people on board I came to see only the impassive steward who served me at table with his accustomed dumb civility.

About two o'clock that afternoon I was in the drawing-room, busied with my notes and the arrangement of certain writings, when my host suddenly entered. I bowed to him, and he made a slight inclination of his body in return without speaking. I went back to my work, hoping against hope that he would vouchsafe some explanation of the events of the previous night. He made none.

I studied him narrowly when I felt sure he would be unconscious of the scrutiny. He seemed to be fatigued. His heavy eyes had not been visited by refreshing sleep. His face wore a sorrowful expression. He fell to pacing the room. He sat down—rose again. He took up the nearest book—put it down unread. He consulted his instruments, but took no note of their indications. He was restless, uneasy. At last he came to where I sat and said, "Are you a doctor of medicine, M. Aronnax?"

The query was so utterly unexpected that for some time I stared at him stupidly and in silence.

"I thought it likely," he continued. "A number of you naturalist fellows have studied medicine and surgery."

"It happens that I am a physician and still resident surgeon to the general clinic in Paris," I managed to say. "I practiced several years before going to the museum."

"That's a piece of good fortune for me, Professor."

My answer had evidently satisfied the commander. But as I had no idea what he would say next, I thought it best to wait for possible further questions before I offered my services.

"In short, M. Aronnax, will you be good enough to prescribe for one of my men?"

"If I ascertain the nature of his illness, certainly."

"Will you please come with me now?"

"I follow, sir."

My heart began to beat strangely, I do not know why I sensed a direct connection between the injury to one of the ship's company and the events of the day before. And the mystery, I am afraid, interested me at least as much as the case of my patient.

Captain Nemo conducted me to the poop of the "Nautilus." He took me into a cabin situated near the sailors' quarters. There on the bed lay a man, some forty years of age, of a resolute type of countenance, the true embodiment of Anglo-Saxon.

I leaned over to examine him. Ah, he was not only sick, he was wounded! Swathed in bandages covered with blood, his head was motionless on the pillow. I undid the wrappings, and the injured man looked at me fixedly with his large eyes, giving no sign of pain as I worked gently at his dressings. It was a horrible wound that I exposed. The skull had been shattered by some deadly weapon, and the brain, much injured, was left largely exposed. Clots of blood had mercifully formed in the bruised and broken mass, in color like the dregs of a Burgundy wine.

There was, of course, both contusion and suffusion of the brain. The poor fellow's breathing was slow. At frequent intervals his face was distorted by the spasmodic twitching of his muscles. I felt his pulse—it was intermittent. The extremities of his body were already growing cold, and I saw that death must shortly and inevitably ensue. After I had dressed the sufferer's wounds as best I could, I readjusted the bandages to his head and turned to Captain Nemo.

"What caused the wound?" I asked.

"That's neither here nor there," he replied evasively. "A shock broke one of the levers of the engine. I was struck, too. But your opinion, sir, as to his condition!"

I hesitated as to what to say.

"You may feel free to speak," said the commander. "This chap does not understand French."

I gave a last look at the wounded man. "He will be dead in two hours," I said.

"Can nothing save him?"

"Nothing, sir."

I saw Captain Nemo clench his hand. I noted the tears glisten in eyes which I had thought incapable of shedding them. For a little while I lingered at the bedside of the dying man, whose life was slowly ebbing away. Under the electric light that shone so strongly upon his deathbed his pallor increased. I regarded the intelligent forehead which was furrowed with premature wrinkles, caused, doubtless, by misfortune and sorrow. I would gladly have tried to learn the secret of his life from the final words that would escape his lips.

"You may go now, M. Aronnax," my host mildly suggested.

I left him in the dying man's cabin and returned to my room, most unprofessionally affected by what I had seen. During the whole day that followed I was haunted by uncomfortable suspicions, and at night I enjoyed but a fitful sleep. Amid my broken dreams I imagined I heard distant sighing and something like a funeral hymn. Were they prayers for the dead, uttered in a language that no man might understand except he be initiated in its special usage?

The next morning early I ascended to the bridge. Captain Nemo was there to receive me. The moment he saw me emerge from the open hatch he came toward me.

"I wonder if it will be convenient for you to make a submarine excursion with me today?" he asked.

"With my companions, sir?"

"If they like."

"We are at your disposal, sir."

"In that event, Professor, will you put on your cork jacket and ask the same of them?"

I was only glad that here there was no question of dead or dying. I rejoined Ned Land and Conseil and informed them of our commander's proposal. My servant hastened to accept it, and for once in a way the Canadian was not averse to following his example.

It was eight o'clock in the morning when the decision to go was made. Half an hour afterward we were equipped for this new excursion and provided with the two contrivances for light and breathing. The double door was opened. Accompanied by Captain Nemo and a dozen of the crew, we set foot at a depth of about thirty feet on the solid bottom where the "Nautilus" rested.

A gentle slope led us to an uneven ground at some fifteen fathoms' depth. This soil differed entirely from the one we had visited on our first trip under the waters of the Pacific Ocean. Here there was none of the fine sand, no submarine plains, no sea forest. But I recognized at once the marvelous sort of region where, on that day, the captain did the honors to us. It was the coral kingdom. I was interested to see in their proper home the gorgoneae, the isidiae, and the corallariae, in the alcyon class of the zoöphyte branch.

The light produced a thousand delightful harmonies as its rays played amid the branches that were so vividly colored. This gave the illusion that the membranous and cylindrical tubes of coral were trembling at the undulation of the waters. I felt sadly tempted to gather the fresh petals of the zoöphytes that were adorned with delicate tendrils, some in their first budding, others but recently full-blown. Small fish of every sort, swimming swiftly, came into gentle contact with them, as flights of birds would graze the flowers in an earthly meadow. When, however, my hand would only approach these animate flowers, the whole sensitive colony of them would take alarm. White petals would reënter their red cases, flowers would fade while I looked, and the flourishing bush would transform itself miraculously into a mass of stony knobs.

Chance had brought me to a neighborhood where the most precious specimens of this zoöphyte are bred. The coral before me was more valuable than the kind found in the Mediterranean, on the coasts of France, or of Italy and Barbary. Its names, Flower of Blood and Froth of Blood, were justified by its tints. In the trade, coral is sold for $100 an ounce—what a fortune the watery beds of this place would make for a company of coral divers!

But soon the space devoted to bushes contracted in area, and the arborizations increased. Real petrified thickets, long arcades of fantastic design, opened out before us. Captain Nemo guided us down under a dark gallery of such joists, where a sloping incline led us to a depth of a hundred yards. The lights from our lamps educed effects more magical than those in the transformation scene of a Christmas extravaganza. The bright rays threw into bold relief the rough outlines of the natural arches and tipped with points of fire the pendants that hung from them like lustrous candelabra.

Among the coraline shrubs I noticed other polypi scarcely less curious—melites and irises with articulated ramifications; also some tufts of coral, green or red, incrusted like seaweed in calcareous salts, which naturalists after prolonged and heated discussion have definitely assigned to the vegetable kingdom. Is this, perhaps, the real point where life rises obscurely from the sleep of a stone without quite detaching itself from the rough point of departure?

We continued our submarine stroll for two hours. By that time we had attained a depth of about three hundred yards, which is the extreme limit on which coral begins to form. But we found no isolated bush, no modest brushwood or undergrowth, at the foot of these lofty trees. It was a huge forest of large mineral vegetations in which we had come to wander. The petrified trunks were enormous, and they were bound together by garlands of elegant plumarias or sea bindweed, and all adorned with lacelike clouds and reflections. We passed freely beneath the high branches which were lost in the shadows of the water, while at our feet tubipores, meandrines, stars, fungi, and caryophillidae formed a carpet sown with dazzling gems. What an ineffable spectacle!

Captain Nemo had halted at last. My companions and I came to a standstill, and as we turned around we noticed that his men were forming a semicircle about their chief. On closer inspection I observed that four of the crew were carrying on their shoulders an object of oblong shape.

We were occupying at this moment the center of a vast glade shut in on every hand by the lofty foliage of the undersea forest. Across this open space our lamps cast a sort of lucid twilight that singularly elongated the shadows on the ground. At the edge of the clearing the darkness rose against us like a wall, relieved only here and there by little sparks refracted by the points of coral.

In the midst of the glade, on a pedestal of rocks roughly piled up, stood a cross of coral. One might have thought its long extended arms were formed of petrified blood. On observing the ground more closely I saw that it was raised in certain places by slight mounds that were incrusted with limy deposits. These ridges were located with an orderly regularity that betrayed the hand of man.

Conscious that they were about to witness a strange scene, Ned Land and Conseil drew close to me.

At a sign from Captain Nemo one of the crew advanced. And at a distance of some feet from the cross he began to dig a hole with a pickaxe that he detached from his belt. And then all was suddenly clear as crystal to me!

This glade was a graveyard, this hole a tomb. The oblong object was the body of the man who had passed away during the night. The captain and his men had come to bury their dead companion in this unworldly cemetery at the bottom of the inaccessible ocean!

The grave was dug but slowly. The fish fled in all directions while the solitude of their retreat was being thus violated. I listened to the thudding strokes of the pickaxe, which sparkled when it hit upon some flint lost at the bottom of the waves. The hole was soon large and deep enough to receive the corpse. Then the bearers slowly drew near. The body, enveloped in a tissue of white byssus, was lowered into the watery tomb. Our commander, with arms crossed on his breast, knelt in prayer. And all the friends of him who had loved them did the same.

The grave was then filled in with the rubble taken from the ground, and a slight mound was thus formed. When this had been done, the captain and his men rose from their knees. Then, drawing near to the grave, they again knelt and all extended their hands in a gesture of final farewell.

Thereafter the funeral procession returned to the "Nautilus," passing again under the arches of the forest, through the midst of the thickets and the long stretch of coral bushes, uphill all the way. Finally the lights on board appeared, and their luminous track guided us back to the submersible. By one o'clock we were inside.

As soon as I had exchanged my clothes for ordinary garments I went up to the platform. A prey to conflicting emotions, I sat down near the binnacle. Captain Nemo joined me shortly after.

"Then the poor man died in the night, as I prophesied?" I asked.

"Yes, M. Aronnax."

"And now, near his comrades of earlier days, he is at rest in the coral cemetery?"

"Forgotten by all else, but not by us, Professor. We dug the grave for him, and the polypi undertake to seal it for eternity."

The commander buried his face quickly in his hands and strove in vain to repress his sobs. Then, when he could control his voice again, he continued, "Our peaceful cemetery is there, some hundred feet beneath the surface of the waves."

"Your dead indeed sleep quietly, Captain, out of the reach of sharks."

"Yes, sir. Out of the reach of sharks—and men," gravely replied my host.

PART TWO

PART TWO

CHAPTER I

THE INDIAN OCEAN

We have now come to the second part of our journey under the sea. The first portion of it came to a fitting, if a somber, close in the coral cemetery which had left so indelible an impression on our minds. Life and death in the bosom of the ocean! Here it was that Captain Nemo's days were drawing onward to that very grave that he had prepared in one of water's deepest abysses. In that mausoleum not one of the sea's monsters could trouble the last sleep of the "Nautilus'" crew, of those friends riveted to each other in death as in life. "Nor any man, either!" the captain had added. Still the same fierce, unyielding defiance toward human society!

No longer could I content my mind with the guess which satisfied Conseil regarding the cause of our commander's hatred of mankind.

My servant insisted that our host was one of those unknown scientists who return to humanity contempt for the indifference that has been shown to them. Conseil believed Captain Nemo was a misunderstood genius who had grown tired of the earth's insincerity and greed, and who had therefore taken refuge in this inaccessible medium because there he was free to follow his own instincts. To my mind this hypothesis explained but one side of the commander's character.

For the mystery of that last night during which we

had been fast in our prison had put me on a new track. Added to our confinement, the other outstanding events of the experience had suggested a different clue from the one Conseil was inclined to. The artificial sleep, the precaution of snatching the telescope from my eyes so violently, the mortal wound of my mysterious patient due to an unaccountable shock to the "Nautilus"—all these had given my thoughts a new direction.

No, Captain Nemo was not satisfied to shun men. His formidable apparatus was not designed alone to further his instincts for freedom, but, perhaps, equally to suit the need he felt for some terrible form of retaliation or revenge.

But I admit that nothing of what happened at just this juncture was entirely clear to me. I seem to catch but a glimpse of light here and there from out the curtaining suspicion and darkness. So I must confine myself to narrating the actual events as they occurred.

This day, the 24th of January, at noon the second officer came to take the altitude of the sun. I mounted to the platform, lighted a cigar, and watched the operation. I of course believed that the man did not understand French. For several times I had purposely made remarks in a loud voice which, it seemed to me, must draw from him an involuntary sign of attention if he had understood them. But he had at all times remained quite undisturbed and mute.

As this officer was taking observations with the sextant one of the sailors of the "Nautilus" arrived to clean the glasses of the lantern. It was the strong man who had accompanied us on our first undersea excursion to the island of Crespo. I examined the fittings of the box in which the beacon was placed. I found that their strength was multiplied a hundred fold by means of lenticular rings, placed similarly to those in a lighthouse. They projected their brilliance in a horizontal plane.

The electric lamp was combined in such a way as would give it the most powerful radiation. Indeed, its light was produced in vacuo, so as to insure both its steadiness and its intensity. For this vacuum economized the graphite points between which the luminous arc was developed—an important item of saving for Captain Nemo. He could not easily have replaced these points and, under the conditions, their wastage was imperceptible.

When the submarine was ready to continue its journey undersea, I descended to the saloon. The panels were closed. A course direct westward was pricked on the chart.

We then began to plough the waters of the Indian Ocean. This is a vast liquid plain with a surface of almost one and a quarter billion acres. Its waters are so clear and pellucid that anyone who looks into them is sure to turn giddy. The "Nautilus" at this period maintained a depth of between fifty and one hundred fathoms.

And so we sailed for many days. To any other than myself, who have a passionate love for the sea, the hours must have seemed long and monotonous. But my daily walks on the bridge, when I steeped myself in the reviving air of the ocean, left me not a moment of soul-weariness. And the books of the library, together with the compiling of my memoirs, occupied too much of my time for me to mope in the leisure that they permitted me.

For several days we saw a large number of aquatic fowl—gulls and sea mews. Some were killed by the clever shots of Ned Land and Conseil, and after they had been prepared in a certain way made very acceptable game.

Among large-winged birds which had been carried far from the last point of land and were resting upon the waves from the fatigue of their flight, I saw some magnificent albatrosses. These strange creatures uttered discordant cries, not unlike the unmelodious braying of donkeys. Birds belonging to the family of the longipennates were consorting with them. The branch of the totipalmates was represented by the sea swallows, phaetons, or lepturi. And against this feathered gathering the redlined phaeton, as large as a pigeon and with pink-tinted plumage, showed to advantage the blackness of his wings.

As concerns the fish, they never failed to incite our admiration and wonder as we surprised one secret of their aquatic life after the other through the opened panels. I saw many kinds which I had previously never had the opportunity of studying.

I confined my attention to those ostracions which were peculiar to the Red Sea, the Indian Ocean, and that part of the sea which washes the coast of tropical America. These fishes, like the tortoise, the armadillo, the sea hedgehog, and the crustacea, are protected by a breastplate that is neither chalky nor stony, but of real bone. In certain of them it takes the shape of a solid triangle, in others of a quadrangle.

Among the triangular ostracions I saw some an inch
and a half in length, with wholesome flesh and a delicious
flavor. These are yellow at the fins and brown at the tail.
I most heartily recommend their introduction into fresh
water, to which a certain number of sea fish most readily
accustom themselves. And I must not forget the quad-
rangular ostracions which had four large tubercles on
their back. Some species of these are dotted with white
spots on the lower part of the body and may be tamed and
trained like birds.

I marveled at the trigons, which are provided with
spikes formed by the lengthening of their bony shell.
Because of their odd gruntings they are termed sea pigs.
And I never tired of watching the dromedaries, which
carried large humps in the shape of a cone and whose flesh
is as tough and leathery as that of the camels which they
otherwise resemble.

From the 21st to the 23d of January the "Nautilus"
sailed at the rate of two hundred and fifty leagues a day.
This is five hundred and forty miles, or twenty-two miles
an hour. We encountered so many different varieties of
fish because they were attracted by our powerful electric
light and tried their best to follow us. Most of them,
however, were soon distanced by our unusual speed.

The morning of the 24th, in 12° 5' south latitude,
and 94° 33' longitude, we sighted Keeling Island, a madre-
pore formation planted with magnificent coconut trees.
This spot had been visited and described by Mr. Darwin
and Captain Fitzroy.

The "Nautilus" skirted the shores of this desert island

for a short distance. At this point our nets brought up numerous specimens of polypi and curious shells of mollusks. A few precious examples of the species delphinula already enriched the treasures of Captain Nemo in the saloon, but I was happy to add to their number an astrea punctifera, a sort of parasite polypus, often found affixed to a sea shell. Soon Keeling Island disappeared from the horizon, and our course was then directed toward the northwest and the Indian Peninsula.

From now on our course was slower and more changeable. It often took us to great depths. Several times the inclined planes were resorted to, their obliquity to the water line being regulated by levers in the interior of the submarine. In such fashion we sloped downward about two miles, but never succeeded in reaching the lowest levels of the Indian Sea. And no wonder! For, although soundings of seven thousand fathoms have been recorded, the greatest depths have never yet been plumbed.

As to the temperature of the lower strata, the thermometer invariably registered 4 degrees above zero, Centigrade. The only stated differential in heat that I was able to codify was the fact that water is colder at higher levels in shallows than in the open sea.

On the 25th of January the whole ocean plain was deserted. The "Nautilus" spent the livelong day on the surface, beating the waves with its powerful screw and making them bound to a great height. Who, if he had been near to witness this byplay, would not have considered our submarine to be a gigantic cetacean disporting itself?

Three-fourths of the day I passed on the platform.

I watched the sea and its changeful humors with an eager eye. Nothing interrupted the curving line of the horizon until about four o'clock a large steamer ran westward on our counter. Her masts were visible for an instant, but she could not sight our vessel, as she wallowed too low in the water. I fancied her to be a steamship of the Peninsular Oriental Company, which plies between Sydney and Ceylon, touching at King George's Point and Melbourne.

At five o'clock that evening, just before that breathless twilight that binds night to day in tropical zones, Conseil and I were surprised by a curious sight. A shoal of argonauts were traveling along the surface of the ocean. We could count several hundreds of them. They belong to the tubercle family, which is peculiar to the Indian seas, and are most graceful mollusks.

Most paradoxically, they move forward by moving backward. This they do by means of their locomotor tubes, through which they drive the water which has already been sucked in. Of their total eight tentacles, six were elongated and stretched out so as to float on the water. The other two were rolled up flat and exposed to the wind outspread like light sails. I could clearly see their fluted and spiral-shaped shells, which Cuvier justly compared to an elegant skiff. A boat, it is true! For it bears the creature which secretes it and yet does not adhere to it, except for convenience in sailing.

For nearly an hour, I suppose, the "Nautilus" floated idly in the midst of this shoal of mollusks. Then they took fright of some sort, I know not exactly what. As if at a given signal from their flagship, every sail was furled, the arms were folded, body drawn in, shells turned over. Thus their whole center of gravity was changed, and at once the whole gay fleet disappeared beneath the waves. Never did the ships of a squadron, even under the sharp eyes of a visiting admiral, maneuver with greater concord and unity.

At that moment night fell suddenly. And the waves, scarcely ruffled by the breeze, stretched out in the wake of the submarine.

The next day, January 26, we cut the equator at the 82d meridian and entered the northern hemisphere. During this day a formidable troop of sharks accompanied our journeyings—terrible creatures which multiply most pertinaciously in these seas and make them proverbially dangerous to humankind.

There were the cestracio philippi sharks, with brown backs and bellies leper-white. They were armed for battle with eleven rows of teeth, and were also the "eyed" sharks; that is, their throat was marked with a large black spot surrounded with white, which looked like an egregious eye. Then there were the Isabella monsters, with rounded snouts patched with indigo. These powerful beings often hurled themselves at the glass panes of the saloon with such violence as to make us start back in terror of their entrance.

On such occasions Ned Land was no longer master of himself. He yearned to go to the surface and harpoon the beasts, particularly the smooth-hound creatures, whose mouths are studded with teeth in the pattern of a mosaic. And the large tiger sharks, nearly six yards long, also seemed to excite him especially. But the "Nautilus" accelerated her speed and easily left behind her the most rapid of these repulsive animals.

On January 27 at the entrance of the Bay of Bengal we were repeatedly welcomed by forbidding objects—dead bodies that floated on the surface of the water. These were the deceased people of Indian villages that were carried by the holy Ganges out to sea. There was apparently such an inexhaustible supply of corpses that the vultures had not been yet able to devour them. These scavenger birds, by the way, are the only accredited undertakers of the poor in this part of the world. Our friends the sharks, it is perhaps needless to add, helped in this emergency funeral work.

About seven o'clock in the evening the submarine, half immersed, was floating in a sea of milk. As far as the eye could reach, the ocean actually seemed to be lactified. Could this be the effect of the lunar rays? Hardly, for the moon, not quite two days old, still lay hidden under the horizon. The whole sky, however, though lighted by the sidereal beams, appeared black by contrast with the whiteness of the waters.

Conseil could not believe his eyes, and he questioned me as to the cause of this strange apparition. Happily I was able to give him a convincing answer.

"It is called a milk sea," I said. "It consists of a large area of white wavelets often to be seen on the coasts of Amboyna and in these parts of the ocean, too."

"But, sir, what is the source of so confusing a phenomenon? I suppose the water is not actually turned into milk."

"No, my dear chap, it is still water. The brilliance which so stirs your curiosity is caused by the presence here of myriads of infusoria. These are a sort of luminous small worm, gelatinous and without distinctive color. They are no thicker through than a hair, and not more than seven-thousandths of an inch in length. They stick to each other sometimes until they carpet an expanse of several leagues."

"How far did you say?" exclaimed Conseil.

"Yes, my boy, you heard me the first time. And don't start trying to compute the exact number of these tiny insects. For you can never compass such a count. If I am not badly mistaken, ships have floated on milk seas such as this for more than forty miles."

Toward midnight the sea suddenly resumed its wonted color. But in our wake, even to the limits of the horizon, the sky reflected the whitened waves. And for long thereafter it seemed to be impregnated by the vague glimmerings of the aurora borealis.

CHAPTER II

THE ISLAND OF CEYLON

When at noon on the 28th of February the "Nautilus" came to the surface of the sea, in 9° 4′ north latitude, there was land in sight about eight miles to the westward. The first outstanding natural object to hold my attention was a range of mountains some two thousand feet in height. The shapes of the individual peaks, from my angle of vision at least, seemed whimsical to a degree. When I had time to take my bearings, I realized that we were nearing the famous island of Ceylon, that consummate pearl that hangs pendant to the lobe of the Indian Peninsula.

Captain Nemo and his second officer appeared at this moment. The commander glanced at the chart and then turned to me.

"The island of Ceylon," he reminded me, "is specially noted for its pearl fisheries. Would you like to look in on one of them, M. Aronnax?"

"With all the pleasure in life, mine host."

"Well, sir, nothing is easier; although, even when we see the fisheries, I doubt whether we shall find the pearlers themselves, for the annual season of exportation has not yet begun. Never mind that. I'll give orders to make for the Gulf of Manaar, where we'll arrive some time during the night."

The commander gave some instructions to his second

officer, who immediately disappeared. Soon the submarine returned to her native element, and the manometer indicated that she was at a depth of about thirty feet.

"So it is, then," my host said. "You and your comrades shall pay a visit to the bank at Manaar, and if by good chance some fisherman should be there at work, we shall have an interesting sight."

"I am greatly your debtor, sir."

"By the way, Professor, you are not afraid of sharks, are you?"

"Sharks!" I exclaimed. "I find that a pretty hard question to answer in the negative. Still, I admit that I have only a passing acquaintance with that sort of fish."

"We are pretty well accustomed to them, my men and I," replied the commander, "and in time you'll be on a better footing with them yourself. We shall see that we are well armed, however, and on our way we may be able to hunt some of the tribe. It's a very fascinating sort of sport. So until tomorrow, sir—bright and early!"

Captain Nemo uttered his remarks about sharks in the most offhand manner and left the saloon. I then had an opportunity to reflect upon his invitation.

Now, suppose I were asked to hunt bear in the Swiss mountains, what would I answer? "That's just fine! Tomorrow we shall pursue bruin to his lair." Or if I were bidden to shoot lions in the plains of Atlas, what would I say? "Haha! How jolly! It seems that we are out after poor little tigers and lions."

But when a fellow is begged to chase the shark in its native habitat, he is likely, is he not, to think twice before accepting the invitation? I ran my hand across my forehead and discovered that large drops of cold sweat were standing on it.

"Let's take time to think this over!" I said to myself. "Hunting otters in submarine forests, as we did in the island of Crespo, is a good enough game. But parading up and down on the bottom of the sea hunting for a patrol of sharks—ah, my boy, that is a horse of another color. I know very well that in certain countries, notably in the Andaman Islands, negroes never hesitate to attack them. They do this with no other weapons than a knife in one hand and a slip noose in the other. But I also remember at just this point that few people who affront these creatures ever come back to tell the tale. And then, I am after all not a negro. And, even if I were, I think a little hesitation might not be ill-timed."

At this moment Conseil and the Canadian entered. They were entirely composed in their minds and in the best of spirits. For neither appreciated what they had signed up for.

"Faith, sir," began Ned Land, "your Captain Nemo (devil fly away with him!) has just made us a most tempting offer."

"Ah, my hearties," I said, "so he has already spoken to you!"

"And said, sir," interpolated my servant, "that if it was quite agreeable to you, he would be glad to have the three of us attend a party at the Ceylon fisheries tomorrow. It was a most forthcoming invitation, sir, and delivered by him like the real gentleman he is."

"And he gave you no further information?"

"Except to say, sir, that he had already spoken to you of this little promenade."

"Professor," asked Ned Land, "can't you give us some stray bits of hint and suggestion about pearl diving?"

"About the fishing itself, or the strange and romantic incidents that condition it?"

"I'd like to get the details of the fishing," replied the Canadian. "Before going in for a thing, it's just as well to know what to be prepared for."

"Very well, my friends. I feel quite flattered at your thought that I can instruct you. Be seated."

The two sat down on an ottoman conveniently at hand, and the first thing the harpooner wished to know was, "What is a pearl?"

"My good fellow," I answered, "to the poet, a pearl is the tear of the sea. To the Oriental, it is a drop of dew solidified. To the ladies (bless 'em!), it is a jewel of oblong shape, brilliant in substance as mother-of-pearl, which they wear on their fingers, their ears, or their bosoms. To the chemist, it is a mixture of phosphate and carbonate of lime, with a touch of gelatine added. To naturalists, it is simply the morbid secretion of the organ that produces the mother-of-pearl found among certain bivalves."

"Branch of mollusca, class of acephali, order of testacea," murmured the learned Conseil.

"Right-ho! And among these testacea pearls are produced by all those which secrete mother-of-pearl; namely, the earshell, the tridacnae, and the turbots."

"Mussels, too?" asked the Canadian.

"Yes. Mussels, that is, of certain waters in Scotland, Wales, Ireland, Saxony, Bohemia, and France."

"Good thing I asked you that," said Ned Land. "After this I'll keep a weather-eye open for the darn things."

"Let's proceed with our lecture. The particular mollusk which secretes the jewel is the pearl oyster, the *Meleagrina margaratifera,* the precious pintadine. The pearl is nothing but a nacreous formation deposited in a globular form. It may either adhere to the oyster shell or be buried in the folds of the creature. It always has some small hard substance for a center—a barren egg, maybe, or a grain of sand. And around this kernel the pearly matter deposits itself year after year in thin concentric layers."

"Are many pearls ever found in the same oyster, sir?"

"Yes, my lad. Some pintadines are regular jewel caskets. One oyster has been mentioned, though I doubt the fact, which contained as high as one hundred and fifty sharks."

"Body of Bacchus, Professor," the Canadian exclaimed, "a hundred and fifty sharks!"

"Oh, what am I saying!" I replied hurriedly, and disgusted enough to find my thoughts wool-gathering. "I meant pearls, of course."

"Of course," Conseil observed soothingly. "But tell us now, sir, how they extract these pearls."

"They go about it in various ways. If the jewels adhere to the shell, the fishermen often pull them off with pincers. But the most common way, perhaps, is to place the pintadines on seaweed mats. They die when thus exposed to the open air, and at the end of a week or ten days are in an advanced stage of decomposition—a fact most unpleasantly noticeable to nostrils miles away from the banks if the wind carries right. Then the shells are plunged into large reservoirs of sea water, opened, and washed."

"I'd let the other fellow do that part of the job," mused Ned.

"Then begins the double work of the sorters. First they separate the layers of pearl, known in commerce as bastard whites and bastard blacks, and these are delivered to the trade in boxes which weigh some three hundred pounds apiece. Afterward the sorters take the paren-chyma of the oyster, boil it, and pass it through a sieve, in order to extract the very smallest pearls."

"The price of such pearls varies according to size, I suppose," suggested Conseil.

"Somewhat," I answered, "but also according to their shape, their water (which means their color), and their luster. By luster is denoted that bright and diapered sparkle which makes them so charming to the eye."

"What kind is it that they call virgin pearls or paragons, sir?"

"The most beautiful of all. These are formed only in the tissue of the mollusk. They are white, opaque often, and sometimes have the transparency of an opal. They are generally round or oval."

"And are sold singly, are they not, sir?"

"Yes, because they are much more precious. The

round pearls are made into bracelets, the oval ones into pendants. Now the pearls that are fast to the shell are more irregular in form and are usually sold by weight. In the lowest class are placed the small jewels known as seed pearls. These are sold by measure and are especially used in embroidering church vestments, altar cloths, and kindred ornaments."

"I wonder," said Conseil, "if this pearl fishery is dangerous."

"Oh, no," I replied, "particularly if one exercises great care."

"Why, what particular risk could there be in such a calling?" demanded the Canadian wonderingly. "Swallowing mouthfuls of sea water is the worst I can think of."

"As you say, old chap. Quite as you say. But, by the way," I inquired, trying in vain to adopt Captain Nemo's careless tone in referring to the matter, "are you afraid of sharks, Ned?"

"Not the kind that swim in water, sir. Why, I'm a harpooner by profession. It's my trade to despise them."

"But," I continued, "here it is not a question of fishing for them with an iron swivel, hoisting them into the ship, cutting off their tails with a blow from a cleaver, ripping them open with a knife, and throwing their hearts into the sea."

"Then you mean at our party tomorrow we may meet—"

"Precisely."

"In the water?"

"Right there, and nowhere else."

"Criminy, with a good harpoon in my fist! You see, sir, these sharks are awkwardly made beasts, and that lessens your danger with them. They can't seize you without first turning over on their backs, and by that time—"

Ned Land's way of saying "seize you" made my blood run cold. Ugh! What a thought!

"Well, that accounts for one of us," I said in what was intended to be a light and bantering tone. "But how about you, Conseil?"

"Me, sir?" asked the servant. "Why, I shall speak the truth—"

"So much the better," I thought, "for he's probably scared, too."

"And say that if you are determined to face the sharks, I can't see why your faithful follower should not do the same."

CHAPTER III

A PEARL OF GREAT PRICE

Next morning at four o'clock I was awakened by the steward whom Captain Nemo had assigned to my personal service. I rose at once, dressed, and went to the saloon. I found my host awaiting me.

"M. Aronnax," he asked, "are you ready to start?"

"Yours to command, sir."

"Then follow me, if you please."

"And my companions, Captain?"

"Have been told of our plans and are on the bridge."

"Then we do not put on our divers' suits?"

"Not at present. I did not allow the 'Nautilus' to approach too near this coast, and we are still at some distance from the Manaar Bank. But the boat is ready, and it will take us to the exact point of disembarkation, which will save us a good walk. It carries our diving apparatus, which we'll climb into when we begin our submarine journey."

We went to the central staircase which led to the platform. My comrades were there before me, and inclined to be brisk as colts at the idea of the pleasure trip which was under way. Five sailors from the submersible's crew, with their oars erect, awaited us in the boat. This had been lashed to the side.

The night was still dark. Layers of clouds veiled the canopy of the sky, permitting but few stars to be seen.

I tried to pierce the gloom on the side where land lay, but could see only an indistinct line that inclosed three-fourths of the horizon from southwest to northwest. Our ship had, it seemed, during the night gone up the west coast of Ceylon, and lay now west of that bay (or rather, gulf) which is formed by the mainland and the island of Manaar. There, under the obscure waters, stretched the pintadine bank, an inexhaustible mine of pearls more than twenty miles in length.

We three took seats beside our commander in the stern of the boat. The boatswain went to the tiller. The painter was cast, the four sailors bent to their oars, and we sheered off.

The boat was headed south. The oarsmen had been instructed not to hurry. I noted that their strokes, strong when in the water, followed one another at intervals of ten seconds, according to the rule then prevalent in the French navy. While the craft between the strokes was running by its own momentum, the liquid drops from the poised oars struck the dark surface of the waves crisply like spats of molten lead. A small swell, widespread and with little trough, lent a gentle rocking to the boat, and the crests of the waves chopped in the face of it.

We were without inclination to speak. What thoughts were coursing through Captain Nemo's brain? Perhaps he reflected upon the land which he was approaching and which he found too near to him for comfort. Ned would certainly be cherishing the opposite opinion—the closer to him the lie of the land, the better he was suited. As to Conseil, he was present in our midst from idle curiosity or because he was never happy to be far away from his master.

About half-past five the first streaks of dawn on the horizon brought out the tints of the upper coast line more distinctly. Flat though it was in the eastern parts, it rose a little to the south. Five miles of water still separated us from shore, indistinct because of the night mist.

At six o'clock it was suddenly day with that rapidity peculiar to tropical regions, which know neither dawn nor twilight. The solar rays penetrated the cumulus curtain of clouds piled up on the eastern sky, and the radiant orb rose majestically. Now I could see land clearly, with a few trees scattered here and there. The boat drew near to Manaar Island, which was rounded from the south. Our commander got up from his seat and watched the ocean.

At a sign from him the anchor was dropped, but the chain of it scarcely ran, for the water here was little more than a yard deep, and this spot was one of the highest points along the whole bank.

"Here we are at last, M. Aronnax," said the captain. "Do you see that inclosed bay? There in a month will be gathered together the numerous boats of the fishermen. And these are the very waters their divers will ransack so boldly. This bay is happily situated for that sort of fishing. It is sheltered, as you notice, from the strongest winds. The sea is never very rough here, a fact that makes this water especially favorable for the diver's work. We must now put on our suits and begin our walk."

I made no reply, for I was too occupied in examining

the suspected waves, beneath which I feared a school of sharks might be lurking. With the help of the sailors I began to assume my heavy sea dress. Captain Nemo and my comrades were also changing their costumes. None of the "Nautilus" men was to accompany us on our excursion.

Soon we were enveloped from top to toe in our India rubber clothing. The air apparatus was fixed to our backs with braces. As to the Ruhmkorff lighting mechanism, there was no necessity for it. Before I finally thrust my head into the copper cap I had asked the captain regarding our possible need for artificial light.

"There would be no sense in bothering with it," he said. "We are going to no great depth, and the solar rays will furnish enough illumination for our stroll. Besides, it would be hardly prudent to carry our electric lamps into these waters, for their brilliance might well attract the attention of certain dangerous inhabitants of the coast most inopportunely."

As our guide pronounced these words I turned to peer at Ned Land and Conseil. But my two friends had already incased their heads in the metal caps, so they could neither overhear nor answer.

One last question remained.

"What about our guns," I queried, "or firearms of some sort?"

"To what use could we put them, Professor? Do not mountaineers meet the attack of the bear with a dagger? And is not steel surer than lead? Here is a strong blade for you. Put it in your belt, and we will get started."

I cast a quick glance at my companions. They were armed as we were, and in addition the Canadian was brandishing an enormous harpoon which he had placed in the boat before leaving the ship.

Ashamed to hesitate longer, I allowed myself to be fitted into the heavy copper helmet. Our reservoirs of air were at once active. An instant later we were landed, one after the other, on an even sandy soil in about two feet of water. Our host made a sign with his hand, and we followed him down a gentle declivity until we disappeared under the waves.

Shoals of fish, like coveys of snipe in a bog, rose over our feet. They belonged to the genus monoptera, which have no other fins but their tail. I recognized the Javanese eel, a real serpent, two and one-half feet long, a creature that might be easily mistaken for a conger eel if it were not for the golden stripes which nature had painted on its sides. I also observed several specimens of the genus stromateus, whose bodies are very flat and oval and of the most brilliant colors. They carry their dorsal fin like a scythe. Next my eye lighted upon an excellent eating fish which, when dried and pickled, is known by the name of karawade. Lastly, I noticed some tranquebars, which belong to the apsiphoroides family and whose bodies are covered with a shell cuirass of eight longitudinal plates.

The sun as it rose toward the meridian lighted the mass of waters more and more clearly. The soil underfoot changed by degrees. A perfect giant's causeway of bowlders replaced the fine sand of an earlier stage of our march, and this highroad was paved with a carpet of disintegrated mollusks and zoöphytes. Among the specimens of these branches I noted placenae with thin unequal shells. This is a sort of ostracion peculiar to the Red Sea and the Indian Ocean. These alternated with lucenae, of orange hue and with rounded shells. Rockfish three and one-half feet in length thrust themselves up from under the waves, like uncouth hands ready to seize the unwary passer. There were panopyres, also, slightly luminous, and, lastly, some oculines, spread out like gorgeous fans and forming one of the richest vegetations in all the oceans.

In the center of these living plants, and under the arbors of the hydrophytes, was layer on layer of clumsy articulates. Particular interest attached to the raninae, whose carapace constituted a slightly rounded triangle, and to the grotesque appearing parthenopes.

At about seven o'clock we found ourselves at last surveying the banks on which pearl oysters are reproduced by the million.

Captain Nemo pointed with his hand to the enormous heap of oysters. And I could well understand that this mine was practically inexhaustible, for nature's creative force is always in advance of man's instinct for destruction.

Ned Land, faithfully obedient to his impulse of collecting food wherever he might find it, hastened to fill a net that he carried with some of the finest specimens. But we could not stop to gather stuff for future meals; we had to hurry to follow in the footsteps of the captain, who seemed to be guiding us along paths known only to himself.

The ground was definitely rising again. It came on certain occasions so close to the surface of the sea that my arm when stretched upward was in the outer air. Then again the level of the bank would sink capriciously.

Often we rounded the base of heaped-up rocks scarped into pyramids. In their dark fissures huge crustacea, perched upon their high claws like some forbidding war engine, would watch us with unmoving eyes. And beneath our feet crawled more than one sort of annelid.

At this moment, as if we otherwise should not have our fill of interesting novelties, there opened before us the entrance to a large grotto. The vestibule was hollowed, as if by human agency, from a picturesque pile of water-sculptured rocks and was carpeted with all the thick weaves of undersea flora. In its tunneled archings the solar rays seemed dulled by successive gradations until its vague inner transparencies became indeed drowned light.

The commander entered fearlessly. We followed.

My eyes soon grew accustomed to this relative state of obscurity. I could dimly distinguish the arches of capricious design which sprang at irregular intervals from natural columns that stood broad-footed on their granite base, like the heavy pillars of Tuscan architecture. Why had our incomprehensible guide piloted us to the bottom of this submarine crypt?

I was soon to know.

After we had descended a fairly steep declivity our feet rang upon the floor of a kind of circular pit. There Captain Nemo halted and with outstretched hand pointed at an object that I had not as yet perceived. It was an oyster of extraordinary size, a gigantic tridacna. It was a font which could have contained a whole lake of holy water. Its basin was more than two yards and a half in breadth, and consequently larger than the one which adorned the museum-saloon of the "Nautilus."

I approached this extraordinary mollusk. It adhered by its byssus to a slab of granite and, isolated there from any of its fellows, it developed in the calm waters of the grotto. I estimated the weight of this tridacne at six hundred pounds. Such an oyster would contain thirty pounds of meat. And one must have the stomach of the fabled Gargantua to be able to demolish some dozens of them.

Our commander seemed to be on terms of good acquaintance with this bivalve. And he had, evidently, a particular motive in ascertaining the present condition of the tridacna. The shells were slightly opened. The captain approached and thrust his dagger between them to prevent their closure. Then with his hand he raised the fringed edges of the membrane which formed a cloak for the creature. There, between the folded plaits, I beheld a loose pearl whose size equaled that of a coconut. Its globular shape, perfect flawlessness, and admirable luster, all together, made it a jewel of unthinkable value.

Carried away by my curiosity, I thrust forward a hand to seize the pearl, weigh it, fondle it. But the captain stopped me by a gesture of his head, made a sign of refusal, and quickly withdrew his dagger. The two shells snapped together instantly. I then understood my host's intention. In leaving this pearl concealed in the mantle of the tridacne, he was permitting it to grow slowly. Each year the secretions of the mollusk would add new concentric layers. I estimated its value as at least $2,500,000.

We proceeded on our journey and walked for some ten minutes. Then our guide a second time came to a sudden stop. I thought he had perhaps halted as a sign that our trip was at an end and it was now time for us to return. But no. With a wave of the hand he signaled us to crouch beside him in a deep depression of rock. He indicated a certain point in the water to one side of us. The disquieting fear that sharks were upon our trail shot through my mind, but I was mistaken. And once again it was no monster of the ocean with whom we had to deal.

It was a man, a living man, an Indian, a fisherman, a poor devil who had, I suppose, come to glean what he might before the harvest. I could see the bottom of his canoe anchored, some feet above his head. He dove and remained in the water as long as he could without bursting his lungs, and then regained the upper air for a short breathing space before a renewed descent. A rope around his waist kept him attached to the boat. He held a stone between his feet, cut in the shape of a sugar loaf, to aid him in sinking more rapidly. Such was his entire apparatus for pursuing the diver's trade.

The moment he reached the bottom about five yards beneath his boat, he fell to his knees and filled his bag with oysters picked up at random. Then he went up to empty it, pulled up his stone, and began the operation anew. Each trial lasted upward of a minute.

The diver was too preoccupied to notice us; besides, the shadow of a great rock hid us from his sight. And how could the poor native have the remotest inkling that human beings like himself were under the waves, watching to the minutest detail his every movement? Several times he went up in the way described and sank again. At each plunge he did not carry away more than ten or twelve oysters, for he was obliged to detach them with some violence from the bank to which they were tightly held by means of their strong byssus. I grieved to picture how many of these oysters, for which he was risking his life, would have no pearl in them. I continued to observe him narrowly. His labors were regularly carried out, and for the space of half an hour no danger whatsoever seemed to threaten his activity.

I was on the point of losing interest in looking at this novel sort of angling when suddenly, as the Indian was standing on the bottom, I saw him make a gesture of terror and rise. He gave a mighty spring in mad endeavor to reach the surface of the sea.

How thoroughly I sympathized with his dread! For a gigantic shadow had appeared just above the unfortunate diver. It was cast by a shark of huge size advancing diagonally. The beast's eyes were on fire, its jaws were opened wide. I was mute with horror and quite unable to move a muscle.

The voracious creature shot like lightning toward the Indian, who had thrown himself to one side in order to escape the shark's fins. In this he was successful, but a staggering blow from the animal's tail struck him full in the chest and stretched him on the ground.

The scene lasted, at most, for but a few seconds. The shark returned to its prey and, turning over on its back, prepared to cut the Indian in two. Then I saw Captain

Nemo straighten himself from a crouching posture and, dagger in hand, walk directly toward the submarine terror, ready for a face-to-face fight with it. Thus, the very moment the creature was intending to snap the unhappy fisherman into bits, it perceived a new antagonist and, turning over again, rushed swiftly toward him.

All the rest of my life I shall see the attitude of our commander at this juncture. He held himself well together, waiting with admirable courage for the onslaught of the shark. And, when it plunged at him, he threw himself aside with amazing quickness, avoiding the shock of collision and at the same second driving his dagger deep into its side. The first honor rested with my host, but the fight was not yet over. A terrible combat followed.

The shark seemed to emit a roar, so far as I could tell by what I saw rather than heard through the thick lens of my copper helmet. The blood certainly gushed forth from its wound in torrents. The sea was dyed red, and through the opaque liquid I could no longer distinguish events with any approach to clarity. This was the last I knew until the moment when I saw the undaunted captain clinging to one of the dread creature's fins. He struggled in mortal combat with the monster and kept dealing it terrific blows, without apparently succeeding in delivering a decisive one.

I wanted more than anything else in life to go to the brave man's assistance, but, as if nailed to the spot by my horror, I could not stir a step. The shark's struggles agitated the water into such a fury of conflicting currents that their rocking and churning threatened to upset me.

Next thing I knew, the captain had fallen, overthrown by the unwieldy mass of his adversary that had been crushed against him.   The beast's jaws opened wide, like a pair of factory shears, and in another instant all would have been over for our host.   But, on time to the split fraction of a second, harpoon in hand, Ned Land rushed toward the shark and struck it with the point of his weapon.

The waves were impregnated with clots and masses of blood.   The water redoubled its rocking motion as a result of the shark's frenzied movements.   It was the monster's death rattle.   Struck to the center of its heart, it was now struggling in dreadful convulsions, the shock of which threw Conseil off his feet.

By this time Ned Land had disentangled the captain from the twisting mass of the monster.   And scarcely was the latter thus happily rescued and free to act, when he got to his feet and went straight to the Indian.   He quickly cut the cord which held the prostrate man to the stone and wrapped him in his arms.   With a crouch and a spring he mounted to the surface.

We others followed him as quickly as we could, and a few seconds later, saved as by a miracle, had joined him in the fisherman's boat.

Captain Nemo's first care, after discovering that he himself was without any wound, was to recall the unfortunate Indian to life.   I, who am a doctor, did not think he could succeed.   But I knew it might be possible, after all, for the poor creature's immersion had not been a prolonged one.   And, unless the blow from the shark's tail should have proven mortal, some slight hope remained.

What with the sharp rubbing that was given him, I saw consciousness return to the injured man by degrees. He opened his eyes and gazed dully about him. Imagine his amazement, his terror even, at seeing four great copper heads leaning above him. And, more than all else, what must he have thought when Captain Nemo, drawing from the pouch of his diving dress a bag of pearls, placed it in his hand? This magnificent gift from the man of under-seas to the stricken Cingalese beggar was accepted with a trembling hand. His wondering eyes clearly showed that he did not know to what sort of superhuman beings he owed at one stroke his life and his fortune.

The captain signaled us to depart, and we regained the bank. Following back the path we had already once traversed, we came in half an hour or so to the anchor which held to the bottom the canoe of the "Nautilus." Once more on board, with the help of the waiting sailors, we soon stripped off our heavy copper helmets. Captain Nemo's first words were addressed to the Canadian.

"Thank you, Mr. Land," he said.

"One good turn deserves another, sir," replied the harpooner. "I owed you that, remember."

A ghastly smile passed across our commander's lips as he reflected how close he had come to the threshold of death less than an hour before. But he said no more of the incident.

"To the submarine," he directed the crew.

The boat fairly flew over the water. Some minutes after leaving our anchorage we met the shark's dead body floating. From the black markings at the extremity of its fins I could distinguish the awe-inspiring melanopteron of the Indian seas, of the species shark, properly so called. The animal was more than twenty-five feet long. Its enormous mouth occupied at least one-third of its body. It was a full-grown beast, as we knew the moment we observed in its upper jaw the six rows of teeth, shaped like an isosceles triangle.

Conseil studied the corpse with scientific curiosity. And he informed me that he assigned it to the cartilaginous class, chondropterygian order, with fixed gills, of the selacian family, in the genus of sharks. I agreed with him.

While I was staring at this inert mass a dozen of these voracious creatures appeared close to our boat. And, without noticing us in their fit of greedy hunger, they hurled themselves upon the dead body and fought madly with one another for the choicest pieces.

Not later than half-past eight we were again on board the submersible. And then, for the first time, I had ample opportunity to mull over the incidents which had occurred during our excursion to the Manaar Bank.

Two conclusions faced me inevitably as the result of my musing. The first was that our commander was a man of the most unheard-of courage; the other was that, after all, he had devoted himself in a rare spirit of self-sacrifice to a representative of that human race from which he had fled to the uttermost depths of the sea. However he might wish to disguise the fact, this strange man had not succeeded in crushing down his humanity. For greater love hath no man than this: That he face death for his fellow.

When I ventured to make some such observation in his presence, he tried to look bored, but he answered in a slightly moved tone, "That Indian, my dear sir, is a member of an oppressed race.   And I still am and ever shall be one with all such people."

CHAPTER IV

THE RED SEA

The island of Ceylon disappeared under our horizon during the course of the day, January 29.

The "Nautilus," at a speed of twenty miles an hour, slipped into the labyrinthine maze of canals which separate the Maldives from the Laccadives. It did not omit to coast the island of Kiltan, a land originally madreporic, which was discovered by Vasco da Gama in 1499. This is one of the nineteen main islands of the Laccadive archipelago, located between 10° and 14° 30′ north latitude and 69° and 50° 72′ east longitude. We had covered 16,220 miles (7,500 French leagues) from our starting point in the Japanese seas.

The next day when the submarine took its breathing spell at the surface there was no land anywhere in sight. Its course was N.N.W. in the direction of the Sea of Oman. This body of water serves as an outlet to the Persian Gulf between Arabia and the Indian peninsula. And the gulf, so far as we knew, was a *cul de sac,* with no visible means of egress. Where on earth was Captain Nemo leading us? I could not imagine, but was perforce silent on the point. The Canadian, however, was far from satisfied with the outcome of affairs and that day came to ask where in the name of several things we were bound!

"We're going wherever our captain's fancy dictates, Ned."

"His fancy can't roam far afield, then," answered the harpooner gruffly. "For the Persian Gulf has no outlet. And if we do march into it, why, like the king of France, we'll march straight out again."

"That may well be—then we'll come out again, Ned. And if after trying this gulf the 'Nautilus' still wishes to visit the Red Sea, there's nothing to keep us from trying the Straits of Bab-el-mandeb."

"But shades of Neptune!" exclaimed the puzzled Canadian. "That won't get us anywhere, either. For the Red Sea is a closed hole as much as the Gulf, seeing the Suez Canal is not yet cut through. And even if it were finished, a boat as mysterious as ours would not want to risk itself in locks and sluices. And again, the tarnal sea is not the road to get us back to Europe."

"Who ever said we were going back to Europe?"

"What do you think we're trying to do, then?"

"As a mere guess, I suppose that after we have honored with our notice the curious coasts of Arabia and Egypt the submersible will run back to the Indian Ocean once more. Perhaps it will cross the channel of Mozambique, off the Mascarenhas maybe, so as to gain the Cape of Good Hope."

"Jericho!" groaned the harpooner dismally. "And where shall we go from that jumping-off station?"

"Oh, ten to one, we'll penetrate that part of the Atlantic still unknown to us. My friend, you are getting fed up with this journey undersea, confess it now! You are surfeited with the incessantly changing spectacle of submarine marvels. But, for my part, I shall be sorry to see the end of a voyage which it is given to so few men to make."

For four days, until the 3d of February, the "Nautilus" scoured the Sea of Oman at varying speeds and at different levels. It seemed to be proceeding hit or miss, as if in much doubt as to what route it should follow. But I noted that we never passed the tropic of Cancer.

When we quit this sea, we came for a moment in sight of Muscat, one of the most important towns of the country of Oman. I marveled at its strange aspect, surrounded by black rocks against which the white houses and forts stood out in strong relief. I saw the rounded domes of its many mosques, the graceful and aspiring points of its minarets, its fresh green terraces. But, alas, it was only a fleeting vision, like some mirage seen in the desert! Our craft soon sank under the waves of that part of the sea.

We slid along the Arabian coast of Mahrah and Hadramaut at a distance of six miles from shore. The undulating line of mountain summits was occasionally interrupted by some ancient ruin which spoke most clearly of a dim and storied past. On the 5th of February we finally entered the Gulf of Aden, a perfect funnel introduced into the neck of Bab-el-mandeb, through which the Indian waters pour into the Red Sea.

Next day we floated in full sight of the town of Aden, perched airily on a promontory which a narrow isthmus joins to the mainland. This is a sort of Gibraltar, the inaccessible fortifications of which were rebuilt by the English after their successful battle in 1839. Here and there I caught glimpses of the octagon minarets peculiar to this town which, if we believe the account of the historian Edrisi, was once upon a time the richest and busiest entrepot on all the coasts round about.

I certainly expected that, when he had arrived at this point, our commander would face about and run back out again. But I was sadly off in my calculations, since to my surprise he did no such thing. Next day, the 7th of February, we entered the Straits of Bab-el-mandeb, which in the Arab tongue means "the gate of tears."

This gate is full twenty miles broad, but only thirty-two in length, and for the "Nautilus" at top speed the crossing was the work of scarcely an hour. But I saw nothing of the world above the surface, not even the island of Perim, with which the British government has fortified its position at Aden. There were altogether too many English and French steamers out of Suez to Bombay, Calcutta, Melbourne, or Mauritius furrowing these straits for the submarine to venture to show herself. So we remained prudently below. And at last, toward noon, we were in the waters of the Red Sea.

I could not even hazard a guess as to what whim determined Captain Nemo to enter the gulf. But, naturally, I quite approved of the caprice. Our speed was lessened. At times our craft kept to the surface; at others it dove to avoid a vessel. And thus I was enabled to view both the upper and the lower levels of this curious sea.

Mocha came to view at the first dawn of February 8. It is now a ruined town whose walls would fall at a gunshot or even, perhaps, at the ringing blast of a trumpet, and which is sheltered here and there by verdant date palms. But time was when it was an important city with six public markets and twenty-six mosques. Time was when its walls were defended by fourteen forts and formed a stone girdle two miles in circumference.

Our submersible then drew near to the African shore, where the depth of the sea is greater. There, in the midst of waters as clear as crystal, through the open panels we contemplated the beautiful bushes of brilliant coral and the large blocks of rock that were clothed in a splendid fur of green algae and fuci.

It was a scene that beggared description. What a variety of views was offered by the sand banks and volcanic islands that hemmed in the Libyan coast! After a little the "Nautilus" overhauled the eastern coast where the shrubs appeared in all their beauty. Here was the shore line of Tehama. The zoöphytes flourished beneath the level of the sea and wove themselves into a thousand picturesquely impossible patterns, some away below the surface. But above the level of the waters! From there they shot aloft sixty feet and unfolded their spectacular beauty in a manner more capricious, if less fresh and sweet, than the sister species that dwell far undersea.

I spent many charming hours at the window of the drawing-room. I was many times overcome anew with the thought of the infinite prodigality of Mother Nature. There seemed to be no end to the submarine flora and fauna which drifted into the supernal brightness of our electric lantern.

Sponges of every shape and fashion—pediculated, foliated, globular, and digital—surely justified the names which first and last have been assigned them: baskets, cups, distaffs, elk-horns, lion feet, peacock tails, and Neptune's gloves. Poets have called them thus, you say? Nay, these titles have been given them by fishermen, who are far more clear-sighted than scientists.

The other zoöphytes which multiplied beside the sponges were mainly medusae of a most graceful sort. Mollusks were represented by several branches of the calmar family which, according to Orbigny, are peculiar to the Red Sea. Reptiles were present most interestingly in the form of the virgata turtle (genus chelonia), which furnished a wholesome and delicate staple for our dinner table. Fish were abundant and remarkable. The nets of our ship frequently brought on board rays of a brick-red hue. Their bodies are spotted with blue and easily recognizable because of their twin spikes. Caranxes we also had in plenty, superbly striped with seven transverse bands of jet black. Their fins were blue and yellow, their scales were gold and silver. Of yellow-headed mullets we saw many. Gobies and a thousand other older friends we also renewed acquaintance with.

On February 9 the "Nautilus" found herself floating in the broadest sector of the Red Sea. This is the part which separates Sonakin of the west coast and Koomfidah on the east by a matter of ninety miles of wind-swept water. At noon of this day, after the bearings had been taken, Captain Nemo chanced to ascend the platform when I was there. I was determined not to let him escape again without pressing him to divulge his goal. The moment he saw me he offered me a cigar of fragant sea tobacco.

"The sea pleases you, eh, my dear fellow?" he asked graciously. "Have you fed your mind fat on the wonders that lie beneath its cover? Have you gained an enduring picture of its fishes, its zoöphytes, its gardens of sponges, its forests of coral? Did you get a satisfying look at the towns that border our view?"

"Yes, mine host," I replied. "And I have found the submarine a most suitable boat for this purpose. It is actually intelligent!"

"More so than many people I have met. For it fears not the terrible tempests of the Red Sea, nor its currents, nor its sand reefs."

"You remember, sir, the ancient geographers cited this body of water as the worst imaginable? If I am not mistaken, they thought its reputation very shady."

"Detestable is a better word, M. Aronnax. Greek and Latin chroniclers have not a decent word to say of it. Strabo calls it a dangerous thing during the Etesian winds and in the rainy season. Arabian Edrisi mentions it by the name of the Gulf of Colzoum. He relates that ships in shoals are wrecked upon its reefs, and that none but a fool risks a passage on it at night. 'Subject to mad storms, strewn with inhospitable islets, offering nothing of value on its surface or in its depths'—these are his very words. Such, too, is the well-considered opinion of Arrian, Agatharchides, and Artemidorus."

"But," I said, with a pitying smile, "it is evident that no one of these historians ever sailed on board the 'Nautilus.'"

"You are right," the captain replied. "But in this

respect modern peoples are no more advanced than the ancients were. What ages elapsed ere the mechanical power of steam was put to sane usage! Another century may pass without begetting a second submarine like ours. Progress is slow, Professor."

"True—too true!" I said. "Your boat is a century before its time—for aught I know, an æon. It is a pity, sir, that the secret of such an invention must die with its creator."

Captain Nemo made no immediate reply. After a silence that lasted several minutes he continued, "We were speaking of what the ancients thought regarding the navigation of the Red Sea."

"And their fears were exaggerated, don't you think, sir?"

"Yes and no, my friend." (Our commander seemed to know this body of water by chapter and verse.) "For, you see, all sorts of perils were present to ancient ships that are non-existent for a modern vessel which is well rigged, strongly hulled, and—thanks to captive steam!— master of its own course."

"I had not taken sufficient consideration of that fact," I said, slightly shamefaced, as I always was before the superior knowledge of my mentor.

Captain Nemo warmed to his subject. "Picture to yourself, M. Aronnax," he went on, "those first navigators who set forth in ships made of planks bound by cords stripped from the palm tree. Boards that were saturated with the grease of sea dogs and smeared with resin! They had no tools with which to take their bearings and soundings.   And they fared blithely in currents of which they were beautifully and blissfully ignorant."

"It is a wonder a single one of them escaped death by drowning."

"Shipwrecks were frightfully common, sir.   But in our time the steamers which ply between Suez and the South Seas have little to fear from the fury of this gulf, no matter how contrary trade winds may show their teeth. Captain and passengers no longer prepare for sea voyages by offering up propitiatory sacrifices.   And, when they safely land, they no longer ornament their brows with gilt wreathes and fillets and go to the temple to give thanks to gods for safe passage."

"Aye, verily!" I said.   "Steam seems to have destroyed the sense of gratitude in all those who go down to the sea in ships.   But, sir, can you tell me how this sea first got its name?"

"There are many guesses on this point, Professor. Shall I tell you what a geographer of the fourteenth century thought?"

"If you please."

"This whimsical fellow pretends the name was given our sea after the Israelites had passed through it and after Pharaoh had perished in the water walls which closed at the behest of Moses.   As a sign of this miracle the sea became a brilliant red.   Henceforth it was called the Red Sea."

"A poet's notion, that," I answered.   "It cannot content my scientific mind.   I want your personal opinion, Captain Nemo."

"And you shall have it, M. Aronnax. I believe we should see in the appellation 'red sea' a translation of the Hebrew word *edom*. And, if the ancients really did give it that name, it was because of the special color of its waters."

"Still, do you know, I have not up to this time seen anything hereabouts except transparent waves of no particular color at all?"

"Very likely you haven't. But as we approach the other end of the gulf you will note its singular appearance. I well recall seeing the Bay of Tor entirely red, a sea of blood."

"And I suppose you attribute this property to the presence of a microscopically small seaweed?"

"Surely I do. It is a mucilaginous purple matter produced by the restless little plants known as trichodesmia. It takes forty thousand of them to fill the space of a square four-tenths of an inch. Perhaps we shall run across some of them when we get to Tor."

"I'll wager, Captain, this is not the first time the 'Nautilus' has thrust her spindle-nose into the Red Sea."

"By no means, sir."

"You spoke a few moments ago of the passage of the Israelites and the subsequent catastrophe to the Egyptians. Have you met when under the water with any traces of this apparently historical fact?"

"Of course not. And for the best of reasons."

"For instance?"

"Why, the spot where Moses and his people crossed is so choked up with sand that camels can scarcely find depth in which to bathe their tottering legs. And so, pardi, there's not water enough for our 'Nautilus' there."

"Where is this spot?"

"It is situated a short way above the Isthmus of Suez, in the pit of the arm that formerly made a deep estuary when the Red Sea extended to the salt lakes. I cannot swear that the passage of the Israelites really was miraculous, but I do know they crossed at that point to reach the promised land. Pharaoh's army actually did perish there. And I believe excavations made in the sand would bring to light a sufficient number of the arms and equipment that show Egyptian origin."

"I agree with you, sir. For the sake of archaeologists I hope such excavations may soon be made. And they will come when new towns are founded on the isthmus after the Suez Canal is done. But how useless this man-made channel will prove for ships like the 'Nautilus'!"

"Useful to the rest of the world, though!" said my host. "The ancients knew well enough how valuable a communication between Red Sea and Mediterranean would be in commercial barter. It did not occur to them, however, to dig a direct canal, but they thought of the river Nile as an intermediary."

"Why, when was that?"

"Oh, the thread of water which united the Nile and the Red Sea was probably begun by King Sesostris. It is certain, at least, that in the year 615 B. C. Necos undertook to engineer a contributary channel to the waters of the sacred river—across the plain of Egypt, toward Arabia. It was a four days' journey up this canal, and it was wide enough for triremes to pass in it."

"Tell me more of its history, I beg."

"It was carried further by Darius, the son of Hystaspes, and finished by Ptolemy II. Strabo saw it in operation over its whole length. But the slope of its waters was so slight from the point of departure near Bubastes that it was navigable clear through to the Red Sea only a few months in the year. This canal answered all the purposes of commerce, however, down to the reign of Antoninus, when it was abandoned and blocked up with sand."

"And that was the end of it, sir?"

"No. Ideas once held and put in practice never perish. The canal was restored by order of Caliph Omar. But it was definitely put out of commission by Caliph Al-Mansor in 761 A. D., and for political reasons. He wished, you may remember, to prevent the arrival of provisions to the army of Mohammed-ben-Abdallah, who had revolted against him."

"But did not Napoleon find traces of it?"

"I see you are a student of history, Professor. During the expedition into Egypt your General Bonaparte ran across the track of its remains in the Desert of Suez. And, surprised by its unexpected tide, he nearly perished before regaining Hadjaroth, the very place where Moses had encamped three thousand years before him."

"Charming, how history repeats itself! Well, Captain, we shall live to see this junction of two great trade routes which will shorten the weary path from India to Cadiz. What the ancients dared not undertake, that M. de Lesseps has confronted. Ere long he will have transformed Africa into an immense island."

"You are right, M. Aronnax, to be proud of your countryman."

"Don't you think, Captain Nemo, that such a man brings more honor to a nation than many a brave captain?"

"Of course. For, although he began, like so many others, by receiving ill-merited rebuffs in the way of indifference and even contempt, he triumphed despite them. His is the genius of 'I Will.' It is sad to think that such a work as he initiated is destined to succeed or to fail because of the energy of a single individual. It ought to have been an international enterprise; it would alone have sufficed to make a long reign illustrious. All honor to M. de Lesseps!"

"All praise to so illustrious a citizen of France!" I replied. I was much pleased but more than surprised by the hearty manner in which my commander had just spoken.

"I regret," he continued, "that I cannot take you through the Suez Canal. But beginning with tomorrow or the day after, when we shall be in the Mediterranean, you will be able to see the long jetty of Port Said."

"The Mediterranean!" I ejaculated.

"What surprises you so about that statement?"

"I'm just floored, that's all, by the fact that we shall be there in another day or so."

"And why?"

"Oh, I suppose I should by this time have lost the power of being astonished at anything."

"But what is the cause of your present amazement?"

"Only that I am thinking of the fearful speed you

will have to engender in your machines in order to make
the round of Africa, double the Cape of Good Hope, and
reach the Mediterranean by day after tomorrow, say."

"Who said that we were going to do all that?"

"Nobody needed to say it. But unless the 'Nautilus'
sails on dry land and passes as on wings across the
isthmus—"

"Or down beneath it, M. Aronnax."

"Are you mocking me, sir?"

"Certainly not," replied Captain Nemo quietly. "A
long time ago, nature constructed under this tongue of
land what man this day is making on its surface."

"You mean to say in all seriousness that such a passage
exists?"

"Yes, sir. A subterranean channel which I have named
the Arabian Tunnel. It takes us underneath Suez and
opens in the Gulf of Pelusium."

"But this isthmus, they say, is composed of nothing
except quicksands. But—"

"A fig for your 'buts,' Professor. At a depth of not
more than fifty-five yards the swamp land ceases and a
stratum of solid rock begins. So much is fact."

"And you discovered this channel by chance?"

"By happy chance and sound reasoning, sir. Not only
does this way of communication exist, but I have already
profited by it many times. Without my knowledge of it I
should not have ventured into the impassable Red Sea."

"What reasoning led you to believe in such a canal?"
I asked.

"Why, only that I noticed in both Red Sea and Mediterranean a considerable number of fish that were perfectly identical in kind—ophidia, fiatoles, girrelles, and exocoeti. Once sure of this fact, I wondered whether it was not possible that a line of connection between the two seas did not exist. If such a communication was there, the subterranean current must certainly run from the Red Sea to the Mediterranean because of the difference of level. Now, I caught a great lot of fish in the neighborhood of Suez—"

"Ah, but if you could only have marked them in some individual way!" I cried out in my scientific ardor.

"That's just what I did," replied the captain, with unaffected calm. "I passed copper rings through their tails and threw them back into the sea."

"And you found them again?"

"Some months later, on the coast of Syria, I had the deserved good fortune to catch some of the fish I had ornamented with a ring. Thus, sir, the connection was proved. I then sought for the place with my 'Nautilus.' I discovered it, ventured into it, and charted it. Before long, my dear Professor, you too will have passed through the Arabian Tunnel."

CHAPTER V

UNDER THE ISTHMUS

That very evening we were in 21° 30′ north latitude. The submarine floated on the surface of the sea and was approaching the Arabian coast. I saw Jidda, the main emporium of Egypt, Syria, Turkey, and India.

I could clearly distinguish its buildings, the vessels anchored at the quays, and those ships whose draught obliged them to ride out the night in the roads. The sun was rather low on the horizon and so struck full on the houses of the town, giving them a blinding whiteness. Outside the tumbledown walls of the city proper, wooden cabins and reed-thatched huts indicated the quarter that was inhabited by the Bedouins. Soon Jidda was shut from view by the swift shadows of the silent night, and the "Nautilus" found herself beneath a water slightly phosphorescent.

The next day, February 10, we sighted several ships running to windward. This hastened the return of our craft to undersea navigation. But at noon when her bearings were being computed the sea chanced to be safe from human intrusion, and so we again rose to the water line.

Ned and Conseil came up to sit with me on the platform. On the eastern side the coast looked like a blurry mass faintly printed upon a damp fog. We were leaning against the side of the pinnace, talking of one thing and another, when the Canadian stretched out a hand toward the water and said, "Do you see anything over there, sir?"

"Nothing," I said after a moment of close scrutiny. "But you know, Ned, that I haven't eyes like yours."

"Try again," the harpooner counseled me. "There, on the starboard beam, about the height of the lantern. Don't you see a moving mass yonder?"

"Of course I do!" I cried after another spell of renewed attention. "Something like a long, low black body on top of the water."

Before long the object was not more than a mile from us. It looked as if some mobile sand bank had been deposited in the open sea. It was a gigantic dugong.

Ned Land almost stared his eyes out. They shone covetously at sight of the animal. His hand seemed twitching to harpoon it. One might even have thought he was impatiently awaiting the moment when he could throw himself overboard to attack it in its native element.

At this instant Captain Nemo emerged from the hatchway and took in the situation with a glance. He understood the Canadian's attitude toward the dugong and said, "If you held a harpoon in your hand just now, Mr. Land, would it not fairly burn your hand?"

"It would indeed, sir."

"And you would not be sorry to go back, just for one day, to your trade of fisherman so as to add this cetacean to your list of victims?"

"Don't torture me, sir."

"Go ahead and try your skill, my lad."

"Thank you, sir," said Ned Land, quietly enough, but his eyes were ablaze with excitement.

"Only," continued the commander, "for your own sake, I advise you not to miss the creature."

"Is the dugong dangerous when wounded?" I asked, although the harpooner contented himself with a careless shrug of his shoulders.

"Most emphatically, yes," replied my host. "Sometimes the beastie turns upon its assailants and overturns their boat. But this danger is scarcely to be considered by us, for I am sure that Mr. Land is both prompt and skilful."

At this moment seven men of the crew, mute and impassive as ever, mounted the bridge. One of them carried a harpoon and a line similar to those used in spearing whales. The pinnace was quickly lifted from the deck, pulled from its socket, and lowered into the sea. Six oarsmen took their seats, and the boatswain went to the tiller. Ned, Conseil, and I climbed to the back of the boat.

"Aren't you coming, Captain?" I asked.

"Not this time, sir. But I wish you good sport."

The boat put off. Jove, how the silent men could row! Almost lifted from the water by their sturdy and regular strokes, we drew rapidly close to the dugong, which floated about two miles distant from the "Nautilus."

When we had arrived within a few cable lengths of the cetacean, our speed was suddenly slackened. The oars dipped noiselessly into the quiet waters. Harpoon in hand, Ned Land stood in the fore part of the boat. This instrument used for striking the whale is generally attached to a very long cord, which pays out quickly as the wounded creature draws it down after him. But in this case the cord was not more than ten fathoms long. And its extremity was fixed to a small barrel or buoy which, by floating, would show the course the dugong took under the surface of the water.

I rose to my feet and carefully watched the Canadian's adversary. The dugong, which also bears the name hali-core, closely resembles the manistee. Its oblong body terminates in an extended tail, and its lateral fins in perfect fingers. Its difference from the manistee consists in its upper jaw, which is armed with two long and pointed tusks.

This particular dugong that Ned Land was preparing to attack was of colossal dimensions. It was well over seven yards in length. It did not move, but seemed to be asleep on the waves, which circumstance should make it easier to capture.

We were now within six yards of the animal. The oars rested on the rowlock. I stooped to a crouching position for greater steadiness. The Canadian, his body thrown slightly backward, brandished his harpoon in an experienced hand.

Suddenly a hissing sound was heard and the dugong disappeared. The harpoon, although hurled with great force, had apparently only struck the water.

The Canadian could not contain his irritation. "Curse it!" he howled furiously. "I missed it."

"On the contrary," I said, soothingly, "the creature is wounded. Look at the blood. But your weapon didn't stick in its body."

"My harpoon! Get my harpoon!" cried the disappointed man.

The sailors again fell into stroke, and the boatswain steered for the buoy. The instrument was regained, and we set off in pursuit of the cetacean. The latter came to the surface to breathe every now and then. Its wound had not visibly weakened it, for it shot straight ahead with great velocity.

The boat, impelled by strong arms, flew over its track. Several times it again approached within a few yards of the fleeing foe, and at such a crisis the harpooner was always ready for his cast. But the dugong would make off again with a sudden plunge, and it was quite impossible to come within range of it.

The passion that burned in the excited and impatient Ned Land can better be imagined than described. He hurled at the unfortunate creature, if not his harpoon, at least the most vigorous expletives the English tongue can offer. For my own part, I was terribly vexed to see the dugong escaping all our attacks.

We pursued it for one hour without resting. I began to fear it would prove itself too difficult to capture. Suddenly, however, the animal in its turn was overcome with a fit of temper pure and simple. Possessed by some perverse notion of vengeance (which it later had good cause to repent), it wheeled around toward the pinnace and assailed us.

This sudden maneuver did not catch the harpooner napping.

"Look out there, abaft!" he cried.

The boatswain called some words in his outlandish gibberish to the sailors, evidently warning the men to be on their guard.

The dugong sailed to within twenty feet of the boat and then stopped abruptly. It sniffed the air briskly with its large nostrils (not pierced at the extremity of the snout, but in the upper part of it). And then, with an unexpected spring, the beast threw itself upon us.

Of course, the pinnace could not avoid the shock of collision. Half upset, it shipped at least two tons of water, which had to be emptied fast or we should go down. Thanks to the agility of the boatswain, we did not catch the brunt of the blow full front, but sidewise, so we were not quite overturned.

While Ned Land, clinging to the bows like a barnacle, belabored the gigantic animal with his harpoon, the creature's teeth buried themselves in the gunwhale. And it raised the pinnace out of the water, as a lion lifts a roebuck. We were thrown helter-skelter across one another. And I know how the adventure would have shortly ended but for the Canadian, who, raging frightfully, struck the cetacean to the heart.

I heard its tusks grind on the iron plates of the gunwale. And then the dugong vanished, carrying the harpoon off with it. But the barrel buoy soon returned to the surface, and a moment later the body of the animal followed it, belly upward. The boat reached it in a few vigorous strokes, and we towed it triumphantly back to the "Nautilus."

It required tackle of enormous strength to hoist the

dugong onto the platform. It weighed ten thousand pounds.

The next day, February 11, the larder of the submarine was supplied with more delicate game than cetacean blubber. A flight of sea swallows rested on our ship. They were a species of *Sterna nilotica* peculiar to Egypt. The beak is black, the head is gray and pointed, the eye surrounded by white spots, the back, wings, and tail of a grayish hue, the belly and throat white, the claws red. Ned and Conseil bagged some dozens of Nile ducks. This bird has a high flavor because of its wildness. Its throat and the upper part of its head are white with black spots.

About five o'clock on the evening of this day we sighted to the north the Cape of Ras-Mohammed. This promontory forms the tip of Arabia Petraea, as the country is named that stretches from the Gulf of Suez to the Gulf of Akabah.

The "Nautilus" penetrated into the Straits of Jubal, which lead to the Gulf of Suez. I distinctly saw the high mountain which towers aloft between the two bays of Ras Mohammed. It is Mount Horeb, that Sinai at the top of which Moses saw God face to face.

At six o'clock our ship, alternately floating and submerged, passed through the waters which Captain Nemo had told me I should find tinted with red. This happened some distance from Tor, which is situated at the end of the bay. Then night fell in the midst of a heavy silence unbroken save for the occasional cry of the pelican or of some nocturnal bird. At times the attentive ear could just catch the whisper of waves breaking upon a distant shore or chafing against rocks some leagues away. Once I heard the slight panting of some far-off steamer beating the gulf with busy paddles.

From eight to nine o'clock the submarine remained several fathoms under water. According to my calculations, we must have been quite near to Suez. Through the panel of the saloon I saw the bases of the rocks brilliantly illuminated by our electric lamp. It seemed to me that the strait was becoming narrower and narrower.

It was a quarter after nine, when the ship had sought the surface again, that I climbed to the bridge. I could hardly stop in any one place, I was so restlessly impatient to pass through Captain Nemo's tunnel, so I had come up to breathe the fresh night air.

Soon, in the shadow, I discerned a light, pale and half discolored by the mists. It was shining from about a mile away

"A floating lighthouse," said a voice close to me. I turned and saw the captain. "It is the floating light of Suez," he continued. "It won't be long now before we gain the entrance to the tunnel."

"I suppose the way in is neither easy to find nor yet easy to negotiate."

"No, Professor, it is not. And for that reason I am accustomed to go into the pilot house and myself direct the steering. Will you please leave the deck now, sir? The 'Nautilus' is going to submerge and will not be above the water again until we have passed through the Arabian Tunnel."

Captain Nemo preceded me down the central staircase.

Halfway down it he opened a door, walked along a between-deck, and landed in the pilot's cage, which, it may be remembered, rose at the extremity of the platform or bridge. It was a cabin six feet square, very similar to that occupied by the steersman of the steamboats on the Mississippi or Hudson. In the center of the cabin a wheel operated, set vertically, and caught to a tiller rope which ran to the back of the ship. Four light-ports with lenticular glass panes, placed in grooves in the cabin wall, permitted the man at the wheel to see in any and all directions.

This cage was dark, but my eyes soon grew used to the obscurity. I made out the figure of the pilot, a strongly built man whose hands were resting on the spokes of the wheel. Outside, the sea was vividly lighted by the lantern, which shed its rays from the back of the cabin to the other end of the platform.

"And now," said my host, "let's try to make our passage."

Electric wires connected the pilot's cage with the engine room and enabled the captain simultaneously to communicate with his "Nautilus" regarding both direction and speed. He pressed a metal knob, and the speed of the screw was at once diminished.

Without speaking, I glanced at the high straight wall we were at this moment passing. It was the immovable base of a dangerous sandy coast. We followed it for an hour, but a few yards distant.

The commander did not take his eye from the dial that was suspended by two concentric circles in the cabin.

At a single gesture from him the pilot modified the course of the submarine at any instant. I had placed myself at the port scuttle and saw some splendid sub-foundations of coral, zoöphytes, seaweed, and fucus. Marine animals now and then agitated their enormous claws which stretched forth from fissures in the rock.

At a quarter-past ten the captain took the helm. A great gallery, black and deep, opened before us. Our craft plunged boldly into it. A strange roaring was heard echoing around its sides. Into the jaws of death, into the mouth of hell, we seemed to ride with the waters of the Red Sea. The unbearable din was caused by these waters, which the inclination of the tunnel precipitated violently toward the Mediterranean. The "Nautilus" went with the torrent, straight as an arrow, in spite of the efforts of the machinery to restrain her speed. In order to offer more effective resistance, she was beating the waves with reversed screw.

On the walls of the narrow passageway I could see nothing but brilliant rays, straight lines, furrows of fire which were traced by our great speed under the electric light. My heart beat fast until I was almost suffocated for lack of breath.

At twenty-five minutes to eleven Captain Nemo relinquished the helm. He turned to me and spoke the one word, "Mediterranean." In less than twenty minutes, carried along by the irresistible waterfall, our craft had passed through the Isthmus of Suez.

CHAPTER VI

THE GRECIAN ARCHIPELAGO

The next day, the 12th of February, at dawn the "Nautilus" rose to the surface. I hastened up to the platform. Three miles to the southward the dim outline of Pelusium was to be seen. A torrent had carried us from one sea to another. About seven o'clock Ned and Conseil joined me.

"Well, Sir Naturalist," the Canadian greeted me, in a slightly mocking tone, "and how about the Mediterranean?"

"We are floating on its surface at this very moment, my friend."

"What!" exclaimed Conseil, much taken aback. "Right now?"

"Yes, sir," I replied, greatly enjoying the discomfiture of my ordinarily phlegmatic servant, "right here and now. It took but a few minutes last night for us to pass the impassable isthmus."

"I don't believe it," asserted the Canadian.

"Ho-ho, Mr. Land," I continued, "that does not alter the fact! This low coast line which rounds off to the south is the Egyptian shore. And you, Ned, who set such store by your eyes, can see the jetty of Port Said yonder, stretching out into the sea."

The Canadian stared grudgingly in the direction indicated.

"Criminy, but you're right, sir!" he cried. "And your captain is the best ever, if you ask my opinion. We are in the Mediterranean even though we simply can't be there. Good! Fine! Hurrah! And now, if you please we'll talk over our own little affairs, taking care that nobody overhears us."

I knew, of course, what the Canadian meant by "our own little affairs." And I was convinced that any conversation on this point would be of no avail. Still, it might be better to let him free his mind by talking in case he desired to. So the three of us walked over and sat down near the lantern, where we were less exposed to the spray of the billows.

"Now, Ned, I am all ears. What have you to tell me?"

"What I have to say is very simple. We are back in European waters. Now, before Captain Nemo's crazy whims drag us once more to the bottom of the polar seas or lead us to Oceania, I demand to leave this hokey-pokey 'Nautilus.' "

I wished in no way to shackle the freedom of my companions, but I certainly had no inclination to abandon our commander.

Thanks to him and his apparatus, I was coming each day nearer to the completion of my submarine studies. And I was rewriting my book on undersea depths while in the very element with which my work dealt. Should I ever again have such a chance to observe the marvels of the ocean? No, a thousand times no! And I found I simply could not force myself to quit the "Nautilus" before my cycle of investigation should be completed.

"Ned," I asked, "answer me frankly; are you tired of being on board? Are you sorry that destiny threw us into Captain Nemo's hands?"

The harpooner was silent for some moments before he answered. Then he crossed his arms on his chest and said, "I can't honestly say I regret this trip under the seas. I shall always be glad to have made it. But now that the journey is over let us have done with the thing. That's my notion."

"It will come to an end some time, Ned."

"Where, for heaven's sake, and how?"

"I can't say, for I don't know. But I suppose it will conclude when the seas have nothing more to teach us."

"Then exactly what may we hope for?" demanded the Canadian.

"We can certainly hope that circumstances will come up by which we can and must profit as well in six months as now."

"Jingo! That's a long sentence of punishment when one speaks so easily of six months at a time. Where shall we be by then, Sir Naturalist?"

"In China, for aught I know. But, Ned, you must remember that our submarine is a fast traveler. She goes through water as swallows skim the air, as an express train disdains the rails beneath her. She does not fear frequented seas. So who can say that she may not beat the coasts of France, England, and America, where flight may be attempted by us just as advantageously as here."

"Ah, M. Aronnax," growled the harpooner, "your arguments, like the swallows you speak of so feelingly, are all up in the air. You talk in the future tense—I shall be here, you will be there, we shall be yonder. Me for the present tense! I am here, we light out in a hurry, there is no time like now!"

The worst of the matter was that I believed Ned to be in the right of the argument. His logic pressed me hard. I hesitated because I did not know how to overcome his direct plea.

"Let's get the straight of this, Professor," continued my tormentor. "If Captain Nemo should offer you your liberty this minute, would you take him up?"

"I honestly don't know," I answered.

"Well, suppose you felt sure the commander would never repeat his offer in case you turned it down now. Would you accept it, then?"

"Look here, my lad! Here is my last word: We can't trust to Captain Nemo's good nature in letting us escape. Common prudence forbids his setting us free; common sense bids us grasp the first real chance to escape."

"You're talking a lot of sense, Professor. Keep it up."

"There's only one more thing to say. Our first effort to flee must be well timed and carefully planned. Our first attempt must be successful. If it fails, we shall never get another opportunity and our commander will never forgive us."

"True enough!" responded the Canadian. "But your remarks are still pretty general for me. They apply to two years hence as well as to two days. The question before the house is: If we get a good chance right away, shall we grab it?"

"Yes, absolutely! And now, my boy, what do you mean by 'a good chance'?"

"Why, when a dark night brings us within swimming distance of any European coast."

"And we're to try and save ourselves without life preservers, or stopping for provisions of any kind?"

"You get my meaning fine, M. Aronnax! If we're near enough the shore and the 'Nautilus' is on the surface, we'll just go over, and the devil can take the hindmost. If the shore is a stiff bit away, however, and our craft is submerged, why, I'd try something else."

"For instance?"

"In that case I should get possession of the pinnace. I know how the contraption is worked. Once we are inside and the bolts are drawn, we shall shoot to the surface. And not even the pilot, who is off in the bows, will be any the wiser."

"All right, my friend. Keep your weather eye open for an opportunity. But don't forget the least hitch will ruin us."

"Not likely I'll forget it, sir."

"And now, Ned, that things are settled, so to speak, would you like to know what I think of our chances?"

"Certainly, M. Aronnax."

"I don't think we stand the ghost of a chance for a get-away. Why? Because this favorable opportunity will never present itself."

"How do you mean?"

"Of course, Captain Nemo doesn't think for a moment that we've abandoned hope of regaining our liberty. And he'll be jolly well on his guard, especially when in sight of European coasts."

"We'll just see about that," retorted Ned Land, and his jaws came together with a determined snap.

"And now suppose we drop the subject," I suggested. "The day you're ready, come and tell us. We'll follow. I rely upon your judgment absolutely."

Thus ended a conference which, at no very distant time, was to lead to most serious results. It is only fair for me to say here that my prophecy regarding our commander's attitude was justified by the facts, as they developed, and to the Canadian's great despair. The captain really seemed to distrust us while we were in frequented waters. Of course, I could not be certain on this point, for he may have only wished to hide his boat and himself from the numerous vessels of every nation that congregated in the Mediterranean.

But, anyway, one thing was sure! We were oftener submerged than floating. We were never near a friendly shore. And if the "Nautilus" did emerge for but a breath, there was nothing in the world for us to see except the pilot's cage. We descended, too, to the depths more often than formerly. In one spot between the Grecian Archipelago and Asia Minor we were unable to touch bottom by something more than a thousand fathoms.

Thus, I only knew at times that we were near a place by some unconsidered allusion to it. One day I learned we were close to the island of Carpathos, one of the Sporades, by overhearing Captain Nemo recite the lines from Virgil:

Est in Carpathio Neptuni gurgite vates
Caeruleus Proteus . . . .

When he saw that I had noted his reference to our location, he smiled ironically and pointed out a place on the planisphere.

It was indeed the ancient dwelling place of Proteus, the ancient shepherd of Neptune's flocks, now the island of Scarpanto, situated between Rhodes and Crete. I saw nothing of it through the panels of the saloon but the gigantic base of granite.

The next day, February 14, I resolved to employ a few hours in studying the fishes of the archipelago, but, alas for my good resolutions, the panels remained hermetically sealed. Why, I could not guess. Upon examining the course of the "Nautilus," I found that we were proceeding toward Candia, the ancient isle of Crete. At the time I embarked on the "Abraham Lincoln" this land had just risen in insurrection against despotic Turkish rule. But I had never since been able to discover how the affair turned out. And Captain Nemo was the last man alive who could give me the desired information on this point.

Therefore I made no allusion to the Cretan war when that night I came to sit alone in the saloon with our commander. He appeared to be taciturn and preoccupied. After a somewhat protracted and moody silence, contrary to his usual custom he ordered both panels to be opened. And he walked from one to the other, observing the mass of waters with minute attention. To what end I could not determine. So, on my side, I employed the time to study the fish that were passing before my eyes.

Among others I noticed several gobies—the sort mentioned by Aristotle—more commonly known by the name of sea branches. This fish is more particularly met with in the salt waters that lie near the delta of the Nile. Near them rolled (I can think of no better term) some sea bream, half phosphorescent, wholly grotesque. This is a kind of sparus, ranked by the Egyptians among their sacred animals, whose arrival in the waters of the Nile announced a fertile overflowing of banks and was consequently celebrated with religious rites.

My eye also lighted upon cheilines about nine inches long. They are bony fish with transparent shells, the livid color of whose skin is unpleasantly blotched with red. They are great eaters of marine vegetation, however, and this fact lends their flesh an exquisite flavor. Such cheilines were much sought after by the epicures of Augustan Rome. Their meat, mingled with the soft roe of the lamprey, peacock's brains, and tongues of the phenicoptera, composed that divine dish of which Vitellius was so enamored.

Another inhabitant of the sea's depths drew my attention an instant later, and likewise led back my mind to recollections of pagan antiquity. It was the remora, that fastens itself to the shark's belly. This small tyke, according to Latin authors, by hooking itself in sufficient numbers to a ship's bottom, could retard its movements. And some of them, by holding back the swift vessel of Antony during the battle of Actium, helped Augustus to gain the victory. On how slight a thread depends the destiny of nations!

I further observed some fine anthiae, which belong to

the order of lutjans. These fish were held sacred by the Greeks, who attributed to them the power of hunting marine monsters from the waters they infested. Their name signifies "flowers." And they justify this title by their shaded colors, which run the whole gamut of reds, from pale rose to bright ruby, and by the fugitive tints that cloud their dorsal fin. My eyes could scarcely leave these wonders of the ocean, when they were struck by a most unexpected apparition.

In the midst of the waters a man appeared, a diver who carried at his belt a leather pouch. It was not the dead body of a man abandoned to the waves. It was a living human being who swam with a strong stroke and who disappeared from time to time to take his breath at the surface.

I turned swiftly to Captain Nemo and called to him in an agitated voice, "Here's a shipwrecked man! He must be saved at any price!"

The commander did not answer me directly, but came over to where I was standing and leaned against the panel. At this moment the man again approached us, and with his face flattened against the glass pane looked in at us.

To my great amazement Captain Nemo signaled to him. The diver answered the greeting with a wave of his hand, mounted immediately thereafter to the top of the waves, and did not appear again.

"Don't worry, sir," said my host. "It is Nicholas of Cape Matapan, surnamed Pesca. He is well known through all the Cyclades. What a bold fellow he is! Water is his native element, and he lives in it more than he does on land. He is always swimming from one island to another, even as far as Crete."

"You know him, then, Captain?"

"Why not, M. Aronnax?"

As he said this the commander walked toward a piece of furniture (a kind of strong-box or safe) that stood near the left panel of the saloon. Beside this I saw a chest bound with iron. And on the lid of this there was a copper plate which bore the monogram of the "Nautilus" with its device. Without seeming to notice my presence the captain opened this strong-box, and I saw that it held a great pile of gold ingots.

What could be the source of all this precious metal which represented an enormous sum? Where did my host gather his gold? And what was he about to do with it?

I did not say a word, but I looked on open-mouthed. I saw my strange companion remove the ingots one by one and arrange them methodically in the chest, which he filled to the top. I estimated the contents roughly at more than four thousand pounds weight of gold, that is to say, nearly a million dollars.

The chest was securely fastened, and the captain wrote on the lid in characters which must be those of modern Greek. This done, he pushed a button the wire of which communicated with the quarters of the crew. Four men appeared and, not without great effort, pushed the chest, which ran on heavy casters, out of the saloon. Later I heard them hoisting it up the iron staircase by means of block and tackle.

"Pardon me, M. Aronnax, what were you saying?" my companion inquired politely, after the door had closed upon the crew.

"I was saying exactly nothing, sir."

"Then, if you will permit me, Professor, I shall wish you a good night and pleasant dreams."

Whereupon he turned and left the saloon.

I returned to my cabin, if the truth must be known, in a somewhat perturbed state of mind. I vainly tried to compose myself to sleep. I was seeking the connecting link between the appearance of the diver and the chest filled with gold. After a little I felt, because of a certain pitching and tossing, that our vessel was quitting the depths and returning to the surface.

Then I heard footsteps on the platform. And I knew they were unfastening the pinnace and launching it. Once it grazed the side of our submarine. Then all was still.

Two hours afterward the same noise, the same bustle, was renewed; the pinnace was hoisted aboard, replaced in its socket, and the submarine again plunged beneath the waves.

So! These millions had been transported to their address. What point on the continent was their destination. Who was our captain's correspondent or partner?

Next day I related to Conseil and the Canadian the events of the night which had aroused my curiosity to fever pitch. My comrades were no less surprised than myself.

"But good lord! Where does he send his dinged millions to?" demanded the mystified sailor.

To that there was no possible answer.

After partaking of breakfast I returned to the drawing-room and set to work. Until five o'clock in the evening I employed my time in arranging my notes. At that hour I felt so great a heat come upon me that I was forced to take off my coat of byssus. It was a strange sensation, and at first I thought I should have to attribute my extreme discomfort to some peculiar affection of my blood. For we were not in low latitudes and, even if we should have been, the "Nautilus," submerged as it was, ought to experience no special change of temperature. I looked at the manometer; it showed a depth of sixty feet, to which atmospheric heat was powerless to attain.

I went doggedly on with my work, but the temperature soon rose to such a pitch as to be quite intolerable.

"Could there be a fire on board?" I asked myself.

I was just about to abandon the saloon when Captain Nemo came in. He cast a quick glance at the thermometer and then said to me, "Forty-two degrees Centigrade."

"I have become sufficiently aware of that fact, sir," I replied, somewhat testily, I fear. "If it keeps on getting much hotter, we cannot endure it."

"But of course it won't get hotter unless we want it to."

"You can reduce the heat to suit yourself?"

"Not exactly. But, what is just as effective, I can go farther away from the stove that produces it."

"The phenomenon that causes my woe is outside, then?"

"Certainly. We are floating in a current of boiling water."

"Saints preserve us!" I exclaimed.

"Behold our environment!" said the commander.

The panels opened, and I saw the sea all about us as white as milk. A sulphurous smoke was curling and eddying amid the waves, which were boiling as if in a copper cauldron. I thoughtlessly leaned my hand against the pane of glass, but the heat was so great that I took the member off again double-quick.

"A scene from the Inferno of Dante," I commented. "But where the merry deuce are we, sir?"

"Near the island of Santorin, Professor," returned the captain. "And just in the channel that separates Nea Kamenni from Pali Kamenni. I thought you might enjoy the spectacle of a submarine eruption."

"Very good of you, I'm sure. But I have always thought that the formation of new islands was ended."

"Nothing is ever at an end in the volcanic parts of the sea, Professor. The globe is always being reshaped by subterranean fires. According to Cassiodorus and Pliny, in 19 A. D. a new island, Theia (the divine), appeared in the very spot where islets have recently been formed. It sank under the waves shortly thereafter, it is true, but out it popped again just fifty years later."

"And since that time this Plutonian work has been suspended?"

"Not by a jugful! On the 3d of February, 1866, a new foundation which they named George Island emerged from the midst of the sulphurous vapor near Nea Kamenni, but settled three days later. A week from that time the island of Aphroessa appeared, leaving between Nea Kamenni and itself a channel only ten yards broad.

"Were you in these seas, Captain, when the phenom-enon occurred?"

"Luckily, yes. And so I was able to observe all the different phases of volcanic birth. The island of Aphroessa was round in form, measured three hundred feet in di-ameter, and was thirty feet above the sea. It was composed of black vitreous lava mixed with fragments of felspar. And, lastly, on the 10th of the same March, a smaller island called Reka showed itself near Nea Kamenni. Since that time the three have joined together, and now they form but one and the same body of land."

"Show me the canal in which we are at this moment, sir," I asked the commander as I bent over the planisphere.

"Most willingly," replied my host. "Here it is on the chart of the archipelago. You see I have marked down the new islands."

I returned to the glass panels. The submarine was no longer in motion, and the heat had grown unbelievably intense. The sea, which until then had been white owing to the presence of salts of iron, now was red. In spite of the ship's being hermetically sealed, an insupportable stench of sulphur filled the saloon. The brilliance of the electricity was quite extinguished by bright scarlet flames. I was in a steam bath, I was suffocating, I was being broiled alive.

"I can't bear it any longer in this boiling water," I said to the captain after a few moments more of suffering.

"Nor would it be prudent for us to do so, Professor," my impassive companion said.

An order was given. The submersible tacked about

on another course and left the furnace it could not brave with impunity. A quarter of an hour afterward we were breathing fresh air on the surface. The thought came to me that if Ned Land had hit upon this part of the sea for our flight back to civilization, we should never have come out of this liquid steam and fire alive.

The next day, the 16th of February, we left the basin that intervenes between Rhodes and Alexandria. It is reckoned to be about fifteen hundred fathoms in depth. Our ship, passing by some distance from Cerigo, sailed away from the Grecian Archipelago, first having doubled Cape Matapan.

CHAPTER VII

THE MEDITERRANEAN IN FORTY-EIGHT HOURS

The Mediterranean is the blue sea without rival. It is the "great sea" of the Hebrews, "the sea" of the Greeks, and the "mare nostrum" of the Romans. It is broidered on both edges by orange trees, aloes, cacti, and sea pines. It is embalmed with the perfume of myrtle, surrounded by rude mountains, and saturated with pure and transparent air—but incessantly nagged by underground fires. It is a perfect battlefield on which Neptune and Pluto still dispute the empire of the world.

It is upon these shores and on these waters, says Michelet, that man acquires renewed strength in one of the most invigorating climates of the globe. But, beautiful though it was, I could take only a rapid glance at the basin whose superficial area is two millions of square yards. Captain Nemo's knowledge was at this juncture not at my disposal, for this enigmatical person did not once appear all the time that we were doing the passage under full speed.

I estimated the course taken by the "Nautilus" undersea at some six hundred leagues, and we negotiated it in forty-eight hours. Starting on the morning of February 16 from the coast of Greece, we had crossed the Straits of Gibraltar by sunrise on the 18th.

It was as plain as the nose on my face (I am dowered with a fairly large one) that this sea was distasteful to our commander. It inclosed, perhaps, just those countries he most wished to avoid. The waves of the Mediterranean and the breezes brought back too many remembrances, if not too many regrets. Here he had no longer that independence and that freedom of gait which he had in the open ocean. No wonder his submarine felt cramped between the close shores of Africa and Europe.

Our speed was now twenty-five miles an hour. It is easy to understand how disgusted Ned Land felt to be forced to renounce his intended flight. He could not launch a pinnace when traveling at the rate of thirteen yards a second. And to quit the "Nautilus" under such conditions would be as bad as jumping from a train running at full speed upon some medium which would not permit fast motion after landing. A highly imprudent attempt, to say the least of it! Besides, our ship now mounted to the surface of the waves only at night to renew its stock of air. It was steered entirely by compass and log.

Nor did I see any more of the interior of the Mediterranean than a passenger on an express train catches of the landscape which is flying past his eyes. That is to say, I perceived the distant horizon, but not the nearer objects which pass like a flash of lightning.

In the midst of the mass of waters (brightly lighted up by the electric rays) glided many of those lampreys, more than a yard long, which are common to almost any climate. Here I caught a view of oxyrhynchi, a kind of ray, five feet in breadth. It has a white belly and gray spotted back, spread out like a large shawl when carried at all swiftly by the current.

Other rays swept by in such a hurry that I could not guess whether they deserved the name of eagles, which was given to them by the ancient Greeks, or whether they did not better merit the title of rat, toad, and bat, with which modern fishermen have dignified them. A few milander sharks, twelve feet long and much feared by divers, struggled along in their midst. Sea foxes a full eight feet in length, endowed with a marvelous fineness of scent, appeared here and there in the background, like blue shadows.

Some dorades of the shark type interested me uncommonly. They were much the same size as the sea foxes, but much more elegantly clad. They wore a dress of blue and silver, picked out by small bands which contrasted sharply with the somber tints of their fins. This fish was long ago consecrated to Venus, perhaps because its eyes are incased in sockets of gold. It is a precious species, friend of all waters, fresh or salt, an inhabitant of rivers, lakes, and oceans, living in all climates and enduring all temperatures—a race that belonged to the geological era of the earth and which yet has preserved all the beauty of its first days.

Magnificent sturgeons shot across my gaze, animals nine or ten yards long. These were creatures of great speed, striking the panes of glass with their strong tails, displaying their bluish backs with small brown spots. They resemble sharks, but are not equal to the latter in strength, and they are to be met with in all seas.

But, of all the divers and sundry dwellers in the Mediterranean, the ones I observed to the greatest advantage (when our ship approached the surface) belonged to the sixty-third genus of bony fish. They were a kind of tunny, with bluish-black backs and silvery breastplates, whose dorsal fins threw out sparkles of gold. They are rumored to follow in the wake of vessels to seek refreshing shade from the fire of a tropical sky. And these tunnies did not belie the saying, for they accompanied the "Nautilus" as faithfully as ever they did in former days the ships of La Pérouse.

For many a long hour these poor things struggled industriously to keep up with our vessel. And I could not tire of admiring them, creatures so evidently built for speed—their small heads, their bodies lithe and cigar-shaped (often three yards long), their pectoral fins, and forked tails endued with remarkable strength. They swam in a triangle, like certain coveys of birds whose rapidity they equaled, who the ancients used to assert understood both geometry and military strategy. But still they do not escape the pursuit of the Provencals, who esteem them as highly as the inhabitants of Propontis and Italy used to do long centuries ago. And, as a consequence, these blind and foolhardy tunnies perish by the million in the nets of the Marseillaise.

As regards marine mammals, when passing the entrance to the Adriatic I thought that I saw two or three cachalots. These fellows are provided with one dorsal fin and belong to the genus physetera. But I am sure I caught sight of several dolphins of the genus globicephali, which are peculiar to the Mediterranean. The back part of their head is marked like a zebra's, with small lines. And, lastly, a dozen seals entered my field of vision, with white bellies and black hair, known by the name of monks. And rightly enough! For, although a bit tall for a priest (being nine feet overall), they really have the air of a sullen Dominican friar.

As to zoöphytes, for some seconds I was able to admire a beautiful orange galeolaria that had fastened itself to the port panel. It held fast by means of a long filament and was divided into an infinite number of branches, terminated by the finest lace that could ever have been woven by the rivals of Arachne. Unfortunately, I could not secure this specimen. And doubtless no other Mediterranean zoöphyte would have come to my observation if, on the night of the 16th, the "Nautilus" had not, singularly enough, slackened her speed under the circumstances I now proceed to narrate.

We were then passing between Sicily and the coast of Tunis. In the narrow space that lies off Cape Bon and the Straits of Messina the floor of the sea rose quite precipitately. Here was a perfect bank of sand on which there was not more than nine fathoms of water, while on either side of the ridge the depth was full ninety fathoms. Our ship had to maneuver carefully so as not to strike against this undersea barrier.

I showed Conseil on the map of the Mediterranean the exact spot occupied by this reef.

"But, if you please, sir," my servant observed, "it is like a real isthmus joining Europe to Africa."

"That's just what it is, my boy. And it forms a perfect bar to the Straits of Libya. Perhaps you know that the soundings of Smith have proven that in former ages the continents were connected between Capes Bon and Furina."

"I can well believe it after this," said Conseil.

"I may add," I continued, "that a similar barrier exists between Gibraltar and Ceuta, which in geological times blocked up the Mediterranean."

"What would happen, sir, if some volcanic upthrust should one day raise these two barriers above the waves?"

"That's not at all likely to happen, Conseil."

"But please, sir, if I may finish my remarks. If this phenomenon should take place, it would be most troublesome for M. de Lesseps, who has taken such pains to pierce the isthmus."

"I agree with you, my lad. But I repeat that this upthrust will never happen. The violence of subterranean force is on the wane. Volcanoes, so plentiful in the early days of the world's history, are being gradually diminished. The earth's internal heat is lessening, the temperature of the lower strata of the globe is lower by a perceptible quantity each century. And this is to the detriment of the globe, for its heat is its very life."

"But how about the sun's energy, sir?"

"The sun is not sufficient for the whole task, Conseil. And how can it give heat to a dead body?"

"In no way I can think of, sir."

"Well, my friend, this earth will one day be that cold corpse beyond the power of artificial reviving. It will become uninhabited like the moon, which has long since lost all its vital heat."

"In how many centuries will this happen, sir?"

"In some hundreds of thousands of years, Conseil."

"By that time, sir, we shall have had time, at least, to complete our journey on board the submarine. That is, if Ned Land does not interfere with it."

And Conseil, thoroughly reassured for the time being, returned to his examination of the reef which our ship was skirting at a moderate rate of speed.

There, beneath a rocky and volcanic soil, bloomed a living flora of sponges and reddish cydippes. These emit a slight phosphorescent light and are commonly known by the name of sea cucumbers. There also were walking comatulae, more than a yard in length, whose purple deeply dyed the water around them.

By now the "Nautilus" had passed the shoal in the Lybian Straits and returned to deep waters and to its accustomed speed. And from that moment there were no more mollusks, no more articulates, nor yet zoöphytes— barely a few large fish fluttering by like shadows.

During the night of the 16th to the 17th of February we had entered the second Mediterranean basin, the greatest depth of which was 1,450 fathoms. Our vessel, under the impulsion of its screw, gliding down on its inclined planes, buried itself in the lowest levels of the sea.

On the 18th of February, about three o'clock A.M., we were at the entrance of the Straits of Gibraltar. Once upon a time there were two currents here. An upper one had long since been recognized, which conveys the waters of the ocean into the basin of the sea. The lower counter-stream reason alone decided must exist. For, otherwise, the volume of water in the Mediterranean, incessantly added to by the waves of the Atlantic and by the rivers that empty into it, would each year raise the level of the sea, since its evaporation alone would not be sufficient to restore the equilibrium. Now, as this is not the case, we must necessarily admit the presence of a lower current which empties into the basin of the Atlantic through the straits the surplus waters of the Mediterranean.

It was by this counter-current that our vessel profited. We advanced rapidly through the narrow passage. For one instant I caught a glimpse of the beautiful ruins of the temple of Hercules which, according to Pliny, was buried in the sea with the island that supported it. A few minutes later we were floating peacefully on the Atlantic.

CHAPTER VIII

VIGO BAY

The Atlantic Ocean!

A vast sheet of water, whose superficial area covers 25,000,000 square miles! Its length is 9000 miles, with a mean breadth of 2700. A sea whose parallel winding shores embrace an immense arc of distance, watered by the largest rivers of the world! Magnificent field of water, incessantly ploughed by the vessels of every nation and sheltered by the flags of all the great cultural races of the earth! And, as if by anticlimax, it terminates in two terrible points so dreaded by mariners: the Cape of Good Hope and Cape Horn.

The "Nautilus" began to pierce the waters of the Atlantic with its spurred prow. In three months and a half she had tirelessly and uncomplainingly laid behind her nearly ten thousand leagues, a stretch longer than the great circle of the globe. Whither were we tending now? What did fate have in reserve for our near future?

When it had once left the Straits of Gibraltar, our ship had gone far out to sea. It returned to the surface of the waves, and our daily walks and talks in the open air were thus restored to us.

Accompanied by Conseil and Ned, I mounted to the platform the very first instant that I could. At a distance of about twelve miles Cape St. Vincent was still dimly to be seen through the light haze of the morning. This promontory forms the southwestern tip of the Spanish peninsula.

A strong southerly gale was blowing. The sea was swollen and billowy; it caused our vessel to rock and plunge violently. It was almost impossible for us to keep our feet flush with the capricious deck. Heavy surges were beating over us every moment. So after a few deep inhalations of fresh salt air (and a few mouthfuls of saline water!) we hastened downward again.

Conseil went to his cabin, I to mine. But, against all precedent, the Canadian followed me, and with a much preoccupied air. Our swift transit of the Mediterranean had not permitted him to put his project into execution, and he could not help but show his disappointment somewhat too openly, I thought. When the door of my room was shut behind him, he sat down and regarded me with surly gaze from under his beetling eyebrows.

"Poor old Ned," I said sympathetically. "I understand you. But you certainly must not reproach yourself because of your lack of opportunity. To have attempted to leave the ship, under the circumstances we have had to face, would be the sheerest folly. Nay, more! It would have been suicide."

The harpooner did not answer. His compressed lips and frowning brow indicated sufficiently the violent possession his fixed idea had taken of his mind.

"Let's see," I continued. "We surely do not need to yield to despair as yet. We are climbing up the coast of Portugal. France and England are no great distance off—there we can easily find refuge at any point. Now if the 'Nautilus' out from the Straits of Gibraltar had turned southward, if it had carried us toward regions where there are no continents, I might share your uneasiness. But at last we know that Captain Nemo does not fly from civilized seas. And within a few days I believe and trust you can act with safety."

The Canadian still regarded me with a somewhat glassy and unnatural stare. At length his fixed lips parted, and he breathed softly, "It is arranged for tonight."

I started back, much as if I had been stung by an unexpected bee. I was, I admit, little prepared for this solemn communication. I tried to find words with which to make fitting answer, but somehow they would not come. I now knew what it meant to be struck dumb.

"We agreed to wait for a good chance," Ned Land slowly continued. "And the opportunity has arrived. Tonight we shall be but a few miles from the Spanish coast. It is cloudy. The wind is blowing free. I have your given word, M. Aronnax, and I rely upon you."

As I was still perforce silent, the harpooner approached me.

"Tonight at nine o'clock," he said. "I have warned Conseil. At that moment our captain will be shut up in his room, probably in bed. Neither engineers nor ship's crew can see us. Conseil and I will gain the central staircase. You, Professor, will remain in the saloon, but two steps away, awaiting our signal. Oars, mast, and sail are in the pinnace. I have even succeeded in stowing away some provisions. I have got hold of an English wrench to unfasten the bolts that attach the small boat to the shell of the submarine. So all is in readiness. Until tonight, sir!"

"The sea is bad."

It was little enough to say, and I blushed at the weakness of my futile objection. But nothing more occurred to me at the moment.

"I grant you that, sir," replied the Canadian. "But it's a risk we have to take. Freedom may come high, but it's worth paying for. Besides, the pinnace is strong. And a few miles of sea, with a fair wind to carry us, is no great matter for worry. Who knows but that tomorrow we may be a hundred leagues away? Let chance but favor us, sir, and by ten or eleven o'clock we shall have landed on terra firma, dead or alive. Adieu now, till tonight!"

With these fateful words the Canadian withdrew, leaving me little better than a nervous wreck. I had, of course, imagined, now that the possible occasion for our escape was gone, we should have ample time in which to thresh out the matter in discussion. But my obstinate comrade had given me no time.

And yet, in my heart of hearts, I knew Ned Land was right. What could I have raised in the way of a valid objection to his decision if the power of speech had not been taken from me? This opportunity seemed the very best that could be expected to come to us. And so we must try to profit by it. Could I retract my given word and thus be responsible for compromising the future of my friends? Positively, no. And tomorrow Captain Nemo in all probability would take us far from sight of land.

Just then a fairly loud hissing noise informed me that the reservoirs were filling and that the "Nautilus" was sinking beneath the waves of the Atlantic.

It was an unforgettably sad day that I then passed, torn between the desire of regaining my freedom and my dislike of abandoning the marvelous ship and thus leaving my undersea studies incomplete.

How slowly the dreadful hours marched by! At one moment I would have a vision of the trio safely landed. At another moment I would find myself wishing, contrary to the doctrines of common sense, that some unforeseen obstacle would arise to prevent the realization of Ned Land's adventurous project.

On two different occasions I went to the saloon. I wished to consult the compass. I wanted to see if the course of our vessel was bringing us nearer the coast or taking us farther westward. Neither proved to be the case; for hours on end the "Nautilus" kept her way in Portuguese waters.

Come what might, I must then bear my own share in our enterprise. My luggage was not heavy; it consisted of my notes, nothing more.

I could not forbear to ask myself what Captain Nemo would think of our flight. I wondered, until my head grew hot, what trouble our escape might cause him. What wrong, if any, could it do him? What would be his course of action in the event that our undertaking was discovered or failed? What made the situation more grievous was that we had no complaint to make to our captain. Never was hospitality more generously extended than his had

been. Still, in leaving him, I could not exactly be taxed
with ingratitude, for no oath bound me to him. It was to
the strength of circumstances that he trusted, and not to
any promises of ours.

I had not had sight of our host since the visit to the
island of Santorin. Would chance bring me into his
presence before my departure? I wished it might and
feared it would, both at the same time. I listened to see
whether I could hear him walking in the room adjacent to
mine, but no sound reached my ears. An unbearable rest-
lessness took hold of me; this day of waiting seemed
eternal. The hours dragged by too slowly to keep pace
with my impatience.

Dinner was served me in the cabin, as usual. I ate
but little, for I was too preoccupied. I got up from the
table at seven o'clock. One hundred and twenty minutes
(and I counted each one of them!) still separated me from
the instant when I was to join Ned Land and Conseil. My
agitation redoubled, my pulse (if that were possible) beat
more violently. I could not remain quiet, but tramped up
and down in the hope of calming my troubled spirit by
such physical exertion.

The fear of failure in our dash for freedom was the
least painful of my worries. But the thought of seeing
our project discovered before we got away from the submarine maddened me. And I was tortured by the picture
of being brought before Captain Nemo when he was irri-
tated or (what was worse) grieved at my desertion.

I longed to see the saloon one last time. I descended
the stairs and reached the museum in which I had

spent so many profitable and happy hours. Again I examined its treasured riches, like a man on the eve of lifelong exile from the place he loved. Through tears I studied the wonders of nature, the masterpieces of human art, amid which for so many golden days my life had been led. I was leaving never to return; I was to abandon them forever! I wanted to take a final look through the panels into the waters of the Atlantic. But the windows were tightly sealed, and a cloak of steel hid from me that ocean which I had not yet explored.

In passing along the walls of the saloon I came to the door, let into an angle, that opened on the captain's room. To my great surprise it was ajar. I drew back involuntarily. If my host should be in his cabin, he could see me and wonder at my actions. But, as I heard no noise of any kind, I approached and found the place deserted. I thrust the door wide open and stepped across the threshold. I was again conscious of the bare, almost ascetic aspect of the cabin's furnishings.

And suddenly the clock struck eight!

The first beat of the hammer on the bell awoke me from my dreams. I trembled as if an invisible eye had penetrated my most secret thoughts. I fairly rushed from the room.

Then my gaze fell upon the compass. Our course was still north. The log indicated a moderate speed; the manometer showed a depth of about sixty feet.

I returned to my room, clothed myself warmly in seaboots, otter-skin cap, greatcoat of byssus, lined with seal —so I was ready. The vibration of the screw alone broke

the deep silence which reigned on board. I listened painfully. Would no loud voice suddenly inform me that Ned
Land had been surprised in his attempted flight? A mortal
dread hung over me as I vainly tried to regain something
like my accustomed coolness.

At a few minutes to nine I put my ear to the captain's
door. No noise of any sort. I left my cabin and returned
to the saloon. The lights were dimmed, the spot deserted.
I placed myself near the door which led to the central
staircase and there awaited the prearranged signal from
my companions.

Then the trembling of the screw sensibly diminished,
and a moment later it stopped entirely. The silence was
now unbroken except by the loud beating of my apprehensive heart. Suddenly a slight shock was felt, and I knew
that the "Nautilus" had come to rest upon the bottom of
the ocean. This increased my uneasiness. I felt impelled
to join Ned Land and beg him to postpone our attempt.
For something told me we were not sailing under our
usual conditions.

Just then door of the saloon opened and Captain Nemo
appeared. He saw me at once, and without preamble of
any sort he began in an amiable tone of voice, "Oh, there
you are! I have been looking for you. Are you acquainted
with the history of Spain?'

Now, one might know the history of a country by
heart from start to finish. And yet such a man in the
condition I was, with troubled mind and brain benumbed
by fear, could not have recited a word of it.

"Well," continued Captain Nemo, "you must have

heard my question, sir. Are you a student of Castilian history?"

"I have some slight knowledge of it."

"It's an odd fact," said the captain, "that scientists like yourself require instruction. Come, then, Professor, sit you down and I shall tell you a curious episode in this history. And listen well, sir, for I am going to answer a question by my narrative which you have doubtless been unable to solve."

"I am anxious to hear your tale," I said. But I could not guess what my companion was driving at. And I was asking myself, most miserably, whether the talk was bearing upon our projected flight.

"Very good, then. Let us go back to the year 1702. You remember that your king Louis XIV, believing that the wave of a sovereign's hand was sufficient to bring the Pyrenees beneath his yoke, foisted the Duke of Anjou upon the Spaniards. This grandson of Louis reigned more or less badly under the title of Philip V, and he had a strong party against him abroad."

"Represented by the royal houses of Holland, Austria, and England, if my memory serves me rightly."

"Correct, M. Aronnax. Indeed, in the preceding year these houses had concluded a treaty of alliance at the Hague with the firm intention of plucking the crown of Spain from Philip's head, and of placing it on that of an archduke, to whom they prematurely gave the title of Charles III."

"Spain resisted this coalition, of course."

"Yes, but she was unfortunately unprovided with either

soldiers or sailors. Still, money would not fail her in case
the galleons, laden with gold and silver from America,
once gained their ports. Now, about the end of 1702 the
Spaniards expected a rich convoy. France was escorting
it with a fleet of twenty-three vessels commanded by
Admiral Château-Renault, because the hostile ships of
the coalition were already patrolling the Atlantic."

"This convoy was headed for Cadiz, I suppose."

"Originally, yes. But the admiral, hearing that an
English fleet was cruising in those waters, resolved to
make for a French port. The Spanish captains of the
convoy objected to this decision. They insisted on being
taken to a Spanish harbor, if not to Cadiz then into Vigo
Bay, which was situated on the northwest coast of Spain
and was not blockaded. Château-Renault was rash enough
to yield to their desires, and the galleons entered Vigo."

"What was there rash in the decision?"

"Why, Vigo Bay formed an open road which could
not be defended in any way. They must therefore hasten
to unload their ships before the arrival of the combined
hostile fleet. Even at that, they would have had time
enough if a wretched question of trade rivalry had not
arisen. Are you following the chain of events, Professor?"

"Breathlessly," I said. But I wished I knew the end
toward which this historical lesson was tending.

"To continue, this is what happened. The merchants
of Cadiz enjoyed the monopoly of receiving all goods
coming from the West Indies. Now, to disembark these
ingots at the port of Vigo was to deprive the Cadiz trades-
men of their vested rights. They complained to Madrid

and obtained from weak-minded Philip the order that the convoy, without discharging its cargo, should remain sequestered in the roads of Vigo until such time as the enemy should have disappeared."

"But what were the English doing all this while, sir?"

"Oh, they arrived fast enough, on the 22d of October, 1702. In spite of his vastly inferior forces, Château-Renault fought bravely. But when he saw the tide of battle set definitely against him and realized that the treasure must soon fall into the itching palms of the enemy, he burnt and scuttled every galleon, which went to the bottom with their enormous riches."

Captain Nemo stopped. The story was evidently told. But I admit that I could not see why it was calculated to arouse my interest.

"Well, sir," I asked, "is this battle of Vigo Bay in some way a matter of special concern to us?"

"Decide for yourself, M. Aronnax. We are now in that bay. And it rests alone with you whether we penetrate its mysteries or not."

The captain rose from his chair and hesitated to see if I were inclined to follow him. I had had ample time to recover my spirits during his recital. And I obeyed with alacrity. The panels were opened; the lights in the saloon extinguished; through the transparent panes the waves were sparkling. I looked.

For half a mile around the "Nautilus" the waters were bathed in electric light. The sandy bottom in front of us was clean and bright. Some of the ship's crew in their diving dresses were already engaged in clearing away half rotted barrels and empty chests from the midst of the blackened hulks of wreckage. From these cases and barrels tumbled ingots of gold and silver, cascades of piastres and jewels. The sand was heaped with them. Loaded down with their inexpressibly precious booty, the men were returning to our submarine, disposing of their burdens, and streaming back to this strange fishing ground of fabulous riches.

I understood now. This was the scene of the battle of the 22d of October, 1702. On this very spot the galleons freighted for the Spanish government had sunk. And here Captain Nemo came, at his convenience and according to his needs, to pack away those millions with which he stored his "Nautilus." It was for him alone, by a strange twist of fate, that America had yielded up her gold and silver. He was direct heir to the treasures torn by Ferdinand Cortez from the Incas and from his other unhappy victims.

"Did you suspect, Professor," he asked, with a smile, "that the Atlantic contained such wealth?"

"I knew," I made answer, "that the silver held in suspension in these waters is valued at $10,000,000."

"Yes, all of that! But in extracting this silver from the maw of the sea, the expense outruns the profit. I, on the contrary, have but to pick up what man through his carelessness has dropped. And not in Vigo Bay alone, but in a thousand other spots where shipwrecks have occurred. They are all marked on my undersea map. Can you now comprehend the source of the millions I command?"

"Thoroughly, sir. But in exploring Vigo Bay you have only anticipated the labors of your rivals."

"And who are they, pray?"

"A society has received from the Spanish government the privilege of seeking these buried galleons. The shareholders are led on by the promise of an enormous booty. For they value these rich shipwrecks at five hundred millions."

"Five hundred millions they were worth," answered Captain Nemo. "But they are so no longer."

"Then," I argued, "don't you think a warning should be given to those shareholders? It would be an act of charity. Or, after all, would it? Who knows whether it would be well received? For what gamblers usually seem to regret above all else is not the loss of their money, but the relinquishment of their fond hopes. And I pity speculators less than I do the thousands of unfortunates to whom so much wealth well distributed would have been profitable. Instead of which, they must now forever be deprived of it."

I had no sooner given utterance to this regret than I felt it must have wounded the susceptibilities of my host.

"Deprived of it!" he exclaimed with much more animation than he was wont to exhibit. "Do you imagine, sir, that these treasures are lost to humanity because I collect them? Do you think I take pains to gather these riches for my own use? Who says I do not put them to a noble purpose? Do I act as if I were insensible to the sufferings of the oppressed people of this world? Do I not know there are wretched beings to comfort, victims to avenge? Do you not understand?"

The commander stopped short at these last words, perhaps regretful that he had so given way to his feelings and spoken so much of his mind. But I had long before guessed that, whatever motive had led him to seek freedom at the bottom of the ocean, it had not been an ignoble one. I had seen that his heart still beat for the sorrows of humanity, and sensed that his immense charity was for oppressed races as well as individuals. But I now first fully realized for whom those millions were destined which Captain Nemo had forwarded when the "Nautilus" was cruising in the waters of Crete, which was then in insurrection.

CHAPTER IX

THE LOST CONTINENT

Next morning, the 19th of February, I looked up to see the Canadian enter my cabin. I had expected this visit. His face wore a look of woeful disappointment.

"Well, sir, here we are still," he said.

"Cheer up, my boy! Fortune was against us yesterday."

"It was indeed. The captain, of course, had to stop at just the hour we had set to hook it from his vessel."

"Ah, Ned, it was not his fault. He had business at his banker's."

"Funny place to look for a bank unless he wanted sand or coral."

"And yet his countinghouse was there undersea. His riches are certainly deposited in a safer spot than in the chests of the state."

I then related to the harpooner the incidents of the preceding night in the hope of persuading him to relinquish the idea of abandoning the captain. But my recital apparently had no other result than to make Ned Land energetically express his sorrow that he could not have taken a stroll on the battlefield of Vigo on his own account.

"However, the game is not yet over, even if we did miss one stroke of the harpoon," he said. "Next time we shall succeed. And tonight, if necessary——"

"What is the present course of our ship?"

"I haven't looked to see, sir."

"Well, at noon we'll study it out on the chart."

The Canadian returned to Conseil. As soon as I had had my bath and dressed, I went to the saloon. The compass was not reassuring. The direction of our vessel was S.S.W. We were turning our backs upon Europe with a vengeance.

I waited with some impatience for the ship's place to be pricked on the chart. At about half-past eleven the reservoirs were emptied and the ship rose to the surface of the ocean. I hurried toward the platform, but, prompt as my action was, Ned Land had preceded me. No more land was in sight—nothing but an immense prairie of unrelieved sea water. A few sails were on the far horizon, undoubtedly those of ships going out to San Roque in search of winds favorable for doubling the Cape of Good Hope. The weather was cloudy. Ned raved and strove to pierce with those far-sighted eyes of his the misty rim of the distant horizon. He still hoped that behind all that fog there stretched the land he had so longed for.

The sun appeared for an instant just at noon. The second officer profited by this transient brightness to take its height. Then, as the sea was becoming more billowy, we went below, and the panel closed. An hour afterward, on consulting the chart, I saw the position of the "Nautilus" recorded as at 16° 17′ longitude and 33° 22′ latitude, one hundred and fifty leagues from the nearest shore. There was no longer any means of escape. And I prefer to leave to your imagination the rage of the Canadian when I shared this information with him.

For my own part, I was not particularly sorry. I felt suddenly lightened of a load that had begun to oppress me. And I was able to return with some degree of calmness to my accustomed labors. That night I received an unexpected call from Captain Nemo. He asked me quite graciously whether I felt fatigued from my vigil of the previous night. I assured him to the contrary.

"Then, M. Aronnax, I propose we make a curious excursion."

"I know I shall entertain the proposal willingly. What is it?"

"You have until now seen the submarine depths only by daylight underneath a bright sun. How would it suit you to explore them in the darkness of the night?"

"It would suit me down to the ground, sir."

"I warn you, the path will be fatiguing. We shall have far to walk and must scale a mountain slope. The roads are not well kept."

"You only stimulate my curiosity, Captain. I am ready for you at a moment's notice."

"That's fine. Come, then, and put on your diving suit."

When we arrived at the robing room, I noticed that neither of my comrades, nor yet any of the ship's crew, was to accompany us on this jaunt. Captain Nemo had not even suggested other companionship. In a few moments we were in our special dresses. The reservoirs, abundantly filled with air, had been adjusted to our backs, but no electric lamps were to be seen. I called the commander's attention to the fact.

"They would be useless," he replied.

I thought I had not heard aright, but I could not repeat my observation, for my friend had already thrust his head into its metal case. So I finished harnessing myself. As an essential part of my equipment an iron-shod stick was put into my hand. Some minutes later, after going through the usual form of egress, we set foot on the floor of the Atlantic at a depth of a hundred and fifty fathoms.

Midnight was near. The waters were profoundly dark, but my guide pointed out to me in the distance a reddish spot, a sort of large light that shone brilliantly about two miles from where the "Nautilus" was resting. What might this fire be? What fed its flames? Why did it light up the liquid mass, and how? These things were riddles without a solution. In any case, it did illumine our path—vaguely, it is true. But I soon accustomed myself to the peculiar grade of this darkness, and then I agreed, under such conditions, to the uselessness of the Ruhmkorff apparatus.

As we went on I heard a sort of pattering over my head. As the noise gained in volume, at times producing a continual shower of spattings, I guessed the cause. It was raining violently and crisping the surface of the waves. Instinctively the thought flashed through my mind that I should get wet through. By water—in the midst of water! I could not help laughing at the droll idea. But, as a matter of fact, inside the thick diving dress the liquid element is no longer felt. And one seems to be in an atmosphere only a little bit denser than the terrestrial air —nothing beyond this.

After half an hour's stroll the soil became stony. Medusae, microscopic crustacea, and pennatules lighted it dimly with their phosphorescent gleams. I caught a glimpse of heaps of rock that were covered by millions of zoöphytes and masses of seaweed. My feet more than once slipped on this viscous carpet, and without my iron-tipped stick I should have fallen frequently. Once I turned around. I could still see the whitish rays from the submarine's lantern, but they were already beginning to pale in the distance.

The rosy light that guided us, however, increased in power and lighted up the horizon. The presence of this fire under water puzzled me greatly. Was it some electric effulgence? Was I perhaps walking toward some natural phenomenon as yet unknown to science? Or even (for this thought actually flashed into my mind) had the hand of man anything to do with this conflagration? Did human ingenuity either create it or fan its flame?

Was I perhaps to meet in these depths companions and friends of my guide, who led like him a strange, unearthly existence? Whom was he on his way to visit? Should I find here in the bowels of the sea a colony of exiles who, weary of the miseries of the world, had sought and found independence? Every sort of foolish and unreasonable idea pursued me. And in this condition of mind, over-excited by the succession of wonders that continually passed before my eyes, I should really have been not at all amazed to meet at the bottom of the waves one of those submarine cities of which Captain Nemo dreamed.

Our road became ever more clearly marked. The

glimmer, growing ever whiter, came in rays from the summit of a mountain that was at least eight hundred feet
high. But what we saw was only a reflection, developed
by the clearness of the waters. The source of this inexplicable light was a fire on the opposite side of the
mountain.

In the heart of the stony maze that furrowed the floor
of the Atlantic, Captain Nemo walked along without the
slightest hesitation or stumbling. He knew this dreary
road. He had doubtless traversed it often, and he showed
not the least danger of losing his way. I followed him
with unshaken confidence. He seemed to me, as he walked
on before, like some marine spirit, some genie of the sea.
I could not help but admire his stature, which was outlined
in black against the luminous horizon.

It was one o'clock in the morning by the time that we
arrived at the first slopings of the mountain, but we found
them not so easy to attain. For, to gain access to them,
we were obliged to venture through the difficult trails of
a vast copse.

Yes, a copse of dead trees—trunks without leaves,
without sap, petrified by the action of the water, and here
and there overtopped by gigantic pines. It all looked like
a coal pit, still standing, holding by the roots to the broken
soil, whose branches, like fine silhouettes, showed distinctly
on the watery ceiling.

Picture to yourself a forest in the Harz Mountains
hanging on to the sides of a precipice, and think of such
a forest swallowed up by the sea. The paths were encumbered with seaweed and fucus, between which a whole

universe of crustacea were groveling. I stumbled ahead, scaling the rocks, stepping over fallen trunks, breaking through the sea bindweed that joined one tree to another, and scaring the fishes, which flew from branch to branch, within an inch of their young lives.

Pressing doggedly onward, I seemed to feel no fatigue. I followed on the heels of my guide, whose muscles seemed to be forged from iron. How can I hope to give expression to such a spectacle as surrounded us? How picture the aspect of woods and rocks in this medium? Their under parts were dark and wild, but their upper portion colored with red tints because of that light which the reflecting power of the waters multiplied. We climbed rocks which directly afterward fell with gigantic bounds and with the low rumble of an avalanche. To right and left of us ran long dark galleries where sight was lost. And here opened vast glades which the hand of man seemed to have trimmed. And I kept a sharp lookout, for at any moment I expected some inhabitant of this nether world to appear.

But as long as Captain Nemo would keep mounting, I could not afford to lag behind, and so I pressed boldly on. My stick gave me effective help. On the narrow passes carved out on the sides of the gulfs a false step would have been dangerous, but I walked on without feeling any giddiness. I jumped a crevice the depth of which would have made me hesitate if I had been among terrestrial glaciers. I risked my neck on the unsteady trunk of a tree that spanned an abyss without a glance beneath me. I devoted my eyes to the sole purpose of admiring the wild sites in which this region abounded.

Monumental rocks, leaning on their regularly cut
bases, seemed to be defying every law of equilibrium.
From between their stony knees trees sprang, like a jet
under heavy pressure, and upheld others which in turn
upheld them. Natural towers, large scarps split perpendicularly like a curtain, inclined at an angle which the laws
of gravitation in terrestrial regions could never have
tolerated.

Two hours after quitting the "Nautilus" we had got
through the wall of trees. One hundred feet above our
heads rose the summit of the mountain, which cast a
shadow on the brilliant irradiation of the opposite slope.
Some petrified shrubs ran fantastically hither and yon.
Fishes rose under our feet the way birds dart up from long
grass. The massive rocks were rent with impenetrable
fractures, deep grottoes, and unfathomable caverns in the
depths of which formidable creatures of the gloom might
be heard stirring uneasily. My blood curdled at the sight
of enormous antennae choking my pathway, or of some
frightful claw closing with a snap in the shadow of a dim
cavity.

Millions of luminous spots shone brightly in the midst
of the darkness. They were the eyes of giant crustacea
crouched in their holes. Great lobsters set themselves
aloft like halberdiers and moved their claws with the click-
ing sound of pincers. Titanic crabs were pointed like a
gun on its carriage. Frightful poulps interwove their tentacles like a living nest of serpents.

We had now reached the first plateau of our climb,
and it was here that further surprises awaited me. Be-

fore us lay some picturesque ruins which betrayed the hand of man and not that of the Creator.   Here were vast heaps of stones among which might be traced the vague and shadowy forms of castle and temple.   But now they were clothed with a world of blossoming zoöphytes.   And over these stones, instead of ivy, seaweed and fucus threw a thick vegetable mantle.   Ah, what was this part of the globe which had been swallowed in a cataclysm of nature? Who had placed these rocks and stones like cromlechs of prehistoric times?   Where was I?   Whither had Captain Nemo's fancy hurried me?

How fain I was to ask him!   But, as I could not speak to him because of our copper helmets, I seized his arm. He shook his head vigorously in reply to my detaining gesture, and pointed to the highest summit of the mountain. It was as if he said, impatiently, "Come on with me!   Come higher up!"

I followed.   And in a few minutes we had gained the top, which for a circle of ten yards commanded a view of the whole mass of rock.

I gazed back down the steep slope that we had just conquered.   The mountain, from the plain behind us, did not rise more than seven or eight hundred feet above the floor of the sea.   But on the opposite side it commanded from twice that height a vista of the depths of this sector of the Atlantic.   My eyes ranged far across a large area illuminated by the danger beacon of a violent fulguration. In short, the mountain was a semi-active volcano.

At fifty feet or so below the peak, in the midst of a rain of stones and scoriae, a large crater was vomiting

forth torrents of lava.   This fell back in a cascade of fire
into the heart of the liquid mass.   Situated as it was, this
volcano lighted the lower plain of the ocean like an immense torch, even to the uttermost limits of the horizon.
I said that the submarine crater threw forth lava, but
no flames.   For the latter require the oxygen of the air
to feed upon, and cannot be developed under water.   But
streams of lava, having within themselves the principle
of their own incandescence, can attain a white heat, fight
vigorously against the liquid element, and by contact turn
it into vapor.

Rapid streams bearing combustible gases in diffusion,
and torrents of lava, slid to the base of the mountain like
an eruption of Vesuvius on another Terra del Greco.

There, indeed, right beneath my eyes, lay a town that
had been destroyed, completely ruined.   Its roofs were
open to the sky, its temples fallen, its arches broken, its
columns strewn about the ground.   Yet one could still
recognize in its disrupted outlines the massive character
of Tuscan architecture.

Farther off I saw the remains of a gigantic aqueduct
—here the high base of an Acropolis, with the floating
outline of a Parthenon—yonder the traces of a quay, as
if an ancient port had formerly abutted on the border of
the ocean, only one day to disappear forever with its
merchant vessels and its war galleys.   Such was the sight
that Captain Nemo had brought before my gaze.

Where was I?   Where on the earth of men and gods
and fishes was I now?   I had to know, whatever the cost.
I tried to speak, forgetful of my helmet, but my companion

stopped me with a gesture. He picked up from the ground
at his feet a piece of chalky stone, walked over to a great
rock of black basalt, and traced there the one word:
ATLANTIS.

What a light flashed up in my mind!

Atlantis, the ancient Meropis of Theopompus, the
Atlantis of Plato, that continent whose existence was denied by Origen, Iamblichus, d'Anville, Malte-Brun, and
Humboldt. These scientists all placed the story of its
disappearance among the legendary tales of folklore and
superstition. And now I had it here captive before my
eyes, bearing upon its every stone the unimpeachable
testimony of its dread catastrophe. The region thus en-
gulfed was in the outer ocean, beyond Europe, Asia, and
Lybia, beyond the columns of Hercules, where dwelt that
powerful people, the Atlantides, against whom the first
wars of earliest Greece were waged.

Thus, conducted by the strangest freak of destiny, I
was treading with my soles the mountains of this continent. I touched with my hand those ruins a thousand
generations old, contemporary with the geological epochs.
I was walking on the very spot where the fellows and
relatives of the first man had wandered.

While I was endeavoring to imprint on my mind forever every detail of this awesome landscape, Captain Nemo
stood motionless, as if petrified during a moment of mute
ecstasy. He leaned upon a mossy stone. Was he dreaming
of those countless generations long since vanished? Was
he seeking of their ghosts the secrets of human fate? Was
it here that this strange man came to steep himself in

historical recollections? Did he in this forgotten city relive the ancient life, he who wanted no modern one?

What should I not have given to penetrate his thoughts, to share their spirit, and to comprehend! We must have stood at least an hour at this spot, studying the vast plain under the brilliance of the lava, which was sometimes wonderfully intense.

Rapid tremblings ran along the mountain, caused by internal bubblings and explosions. Deep noises from the interior, transmitted by the liquid medium, were echoed in majestic grandeur. At this moment the moon appeared through the mass of waters and shed her pallid rays upon the buried continent. It was but a gleam, but how indescribable was its effect! The captain rose, cast one last look across the immense plain spread out beneath us, and then by a sign bade me follow him back to the "Nautilus."

We descended the mountain rapidly. The mineral forest once passed, I saw the lantern of the submarine shining like the low-hung eastern star. The commander walked straight toward its rays, and we got back on board just as the first penciled beams of morning light were whitening the surface of the ocean.

CHAPTER X

SUBMARINE COAL MINES

The next day, February 20, I awoke very late. The unusual fatigues both of body and of mind (yes, and of soul!) had prolonged my slumbers until eleven o'clock. I dressed quickly, for I was much interested to know what course the submarine was taking. The instruments showed it to be still toward the south, with a speed of twenty miles an hour and a depth of fifty fathoms.

The species of fish did not differ much from those elsewhere noticed. There were rays of giant size, five yards long and endowed with great muscular strength. This enabled them to shoot high above the waves. Sharks of many kinds swam here within my ken, among others a glaucus fifteen feet long, with triangular sharp teeth and a transparency that rendered it almost invisible in the water. Brown sagrae I saw, and humantins, prism-shaped and clad with a tuberculous hide; sturgeons, too, which resembled their congeners of the Mediterranean; trumpet syngnathes, one and a half feet in length, without either teeth or tongue and as supple as snakes.

Among the bony fish Conseil noted some blackish makairas, about three yards long and armed at the upper jaw with a piercing sword. He grew fairly incoherent at sight of other bright-colored creatures, known in the time of Aristotle as sea dragons. These are very dangerous to capture because of the sharp spikes on their backs. He

also called to my attention some coryphaenes with brown
backs marked by little blue stripes and surrounded with a
gold border; a few dorades, besides; and swordfish, four
and twenty feet long, swimming in troops, fierce animals,
but herbivorous rather than carnivorous.

About four o'clock the soil, until this hour apparently
a mixture of thick mud and petrified wood, changed notice-
ably. It became much more stony and seemed to be
sprinkled with conglomerate formation and fragments of
basalt strewn with lava and sulphurous obsidian.

Accordingly I thought that a mountainous district was
replacing the extensive prairie. And, true to expectation,
the "Nautilus" had not proceeded many lengths from this
spot when I saw the southern horizon blocked by a high
wall that seemed to prohibit further advance. The summit
of this obstacle evidently stretched from the bed of ocean
into the upper air. It must be a continent, or at least an
island; one of the Canaries, perhaps, or of the Cape Verde
group.

Our bearings had not yet been established, it might be
for some definite reason. So I was ignorant of our exact
position and could not consult the chart to any advantage.
In any case such an extensive rampart would seem to
mark the boundary of that Atlantis of which, as a matter
of absolute fact I suppose, we had passed over but the most
insignificant portion.

I should have been glad to stay in my seat by the open
panel much longer, to admire the beauties of sea and of
sky, but the shutters were not drawn. At this instant the
submarine had just arrived at the side of this high perpen-

dicular wall. What the ship would do next I could not even surmise.

I returned to my cabin, only to discover that we were no longer in motion. I lay down with every intention of waking after a few hours of sleep. But it was eight o'clock of the following morning when I again made my way to the saloon. I glanced at once at the manometer. It indicated that our vessel was floating on the surface of the sea. In confirmation of this I heard steps on the platform above me. I went up to the panel which opened onto the platform. It was open, but still, instead of the broad daylight I had a right to expect, I was surrounded by a profound obscurity.

Where were we? In what realm of eternal night? Or could I be in error and was it the time of darkness between two days? No, not that! For not a star was shining, and the cloak of night itself has not such a lining of positive and utter black. I gave it up. And then a voice close beside me said, "Is that you, M. Aronnax?"

"The very same," I responded. "But where are we?"

"Underground."

"Aha!" I exclaimed, for I suspected I was being hoaxed. "And yet the 'Nautilus' is still on water and afloat?"

"It has a way of always floating."

"Then I do not understand the situation, Captain. In more than one way I am in the dark."

"Be patient a few moments. Then our lantern will be lighted. And if you like bright places you will be satisfied."

I stood on the platform and waited.

Captain Nemo had come up with me, but the darkness was so absolute that I could not see him. Only, when I looked toward the zenith, straight above my head, I could catch a sort of undecided gleam, a kind of twilight that seemed to be filling a circular hole. At this instant the lantern was lighted, and its vividness dispelled the faint light. I closed and opened my dazzled eyes several times, until the glaring brightness ceased to blur and pain them. Then I looked.

Our ship was stationary, near a mountain that formed a natural docking place for it. We were afloat on a lake that was imprisoned by circular walls and measured two miles in diameter and six in circumference. Its surface, as the manometer indicated, could only be the same as the outside level, for there must necessarily be a cummunication between the lake and the Atlantic.

The high partitions of this quiet water leaned forward on their foundations and grew into a vaulted roof that had the shape of an immense funnel turned upside down, its height being some five or six hundred yards. At the summit was a circular orifice from which I had caught the slight gleam of brightness, presumably daylight.

"Just where are we, sir?" I asked my companion.

"In the very heart of an extinct volcano, M. Aronnax. Its interior has been invaded by the sea because of some great convulsion of nature. While you were gently dreaming, Professor, the 'Nautilus' penetrated this lagoon by a channel that opens about ten yards beneath the ocean's surface. This place is our harbor of refuge. Sheltered from all gales—sure, commodious, mysterious. Show me, I beg of you, on the shores of any of your continents or islands, a roadstead which offers such perfect asylum from storms."

"No such road exists," I replied. "And you have here the acme of safety. Who would reach you in the heart of a volcano? But tell me, sir, do I not see an opening there in the summit?"

"Certainly. Its crater, formerly filled with lava, vapor, and flame. But it now admits the life-giving air we breathe."

"What volcanic mountain is this? Do geographers know it by name?"

"It belongs to one of the numerous islands with which this part of the Atlantic is strewn. To vessels it is an immense sand bank; to us it is a huge cavern. Chance led me to its discovery, and in this it served me well."

"But of what use to you is this refuge, after all is said and done? The 'Nautilus' needs no port."

"Of course not. But it does need electricity to make it move, elements to make the electricity, sodium to furnish the elements, coal to manufacture the sodium, and a coal mine to supply the coal. And exactly on this spot the sea covers entire forests imbedded during the geological periods of the earth's history. They are now mineralized and transformed into coal. For me they furnish an inexhaustible mine."

"The crew, then, follows the trade of miners here?"

"The very word for it! These mines lie under the waves, like those of Newcastle. In their diving dress, with pickaxe and shovel, my men extract the coal. I do not ask even this, you see, M. Arronax, from the mines of the earth."

"But is it not odd that this cavern has not been explored and discovered from the top through its extinct crater, Captain?"

"Men do not consider it extinct. For, when I burn my combustible for the manufacture of sodium, the smoke escapes from the crater of this hollow mountain and gives it every appearance of a volcano which is still active."

"May I see your companions at their work, sir?"

"No, if you will excuse me, Professor. Not this time, at least. For I am in a hurry to resume our submarine tour of the globe. So I shall content myself with drawing on the reserve stock of sodium that I have ready. It takes but one day to load it, and then we're off. So, if you hanker to make the round of the lagoon, M. Aronnax, and go over the cavern, you must take advantage of today."

I thanked the commander and went off to look for my companions. They were still in their cabin. I asked them to take a walk with me, deliberately refraining from saying where we were. They climbed to the bridge. Conseil, who was never quite astonished by anything human or divine, seemed to think it quite in the natural order of things to wake up inside a mountain. Ned Land, as was to be expected, thought of nothing but ascertaining whether the cavern had a practicable exit. After a hurried breakfast we climbed down the side of our ship.

"Here we three crickets are, once more on land," chirped Conseil.

"I don't call this being 'on land,'" growled the Canadian. "And, anyhow, we're not on it, but under it."

Between the walls of the mountain and the waters of the lake lay a sandy beach which, at its greatest breadth, measured five hundred feet. On this firm path of ground one might easily make the tour of the lagoon. But the base of the high partitions was stone, with volcanic blocks and enormous pumice bowlders lying about them in great heaps. All these picturesque, detached masses, covered with enamel polished by the action of subterranean fires, shone resplendent in the light from our electric lantern.

The mica dust from the shore rose from under our feet and flew up like a cloud of sparks. The grade now began to ascend sensibly, and we soon attained long, circuitous slopes which took us gradually higher. We were forced to tread carefully among these inclined planes of conglomerate formations. For they were not fastened to the ground by any natural cement, and our feet slipped sadly on the glassy trachyte which was composed of crystals of feldspar and quartz.

The volcanic character of this enormous excavation was confirmed on every side, a fact I pointed out repeatedly to my friends.

"Just imagine," I said, "what this crater must have been when filled with boiling lava. Picture, if you can, the moment when the top level of the incandescent liquid rose to the orifice of the mountain, as the molten iron rises on the walls of a blast furnace."

"I can see the thing perfectly, sir," Conseil answered gravely. "But tell me why the great Architect has suspended operations on this volcano. How did a furnace come to be replaced by a lake?"

"Most probably, my boy, because some convulsion beneath the sea produced that very opening which served as a channel for the 'Nautilus' to enter through. The waters of the Atlantic rushed into the interior of the mountain. There must have been a titanic struggle between the two elements, a conflict which ended in a decision for Neptune. But many ages have run their course since that far-off day, and the undersea cauldron is now a peaceful grotto."

"Now all that's very good in its way, sir," asserted Ned Land grumpily, "and I've listened to your explanation with attention. But in our own interest I regret that the opening you mention was not made above the level of the sea."

"My dear chap," Conseil objected, "if the passage had not been under the ocean, our submarine could not have passed through it."

We continued to ascend. The paths became more perpendicular and narrow. Deep excavations, over which we were obliged to jump, cut across them here and there. We had to turn the corners of slippery masses. We slid along upon our knees and crawled. But, whatever difficulty confronted us, it was overcome by Conseil's dexterity or the Canadian's strength.

At a height of about ninety feet the nature of the ground changed somewhat, although it did not better our situation appreciably. Black basalt began to take the place of conglomerate and trachyte, now spread out in sheets, now in regular prisms, arranged like a colonnade supporting the spring of the immense vault—a most admirable example of nature's architecture. Between the blocks of basalt wound long ribbons of lava, long since grown cold and incrusted with bituminous veins. And in some places there were spread large carpets of sulphur. A stronger daylight coming in through the upper crater shed a vague glimmer over these volcanic ejections, forever buried in the womb of this extinguished furnace.

But our upward climb was stopped at a height of some two hundred and fifty feet, and by impassable obstacles. There was a completely vaulted archway overhanging us, and the path of our ascent was changed into a circular walk. Vegetable life here began to dispute the field with mineral. Some shrubs and even certain trees grew from fissures in the walls. I recognized several euphorbias because of the caustic juice welling from them. Heliotropes, since the rays of the sun never reach them, hung their flower clusters sadly, both color and perfume chiefly notable by their absence. Here and there chrysanthemums grew timidly at the foot of an aloe with long, sickly looking leaves. But between the ribbons of lava I saw little violets which still yielded up a slight perfume, and I admit that I smelt them with vast delight. Fragrance is the soul of a flower. And sea flowers, splendid hydrophytes though they be, are without a soul.

We had reached the foot of sturdy dragon trees whose strong roots had displaced the rocks, when Ned Land exclaimed, "Criminy! Here's a hive—a hive of bees!"

"A strange sort of hive it must be!" I exclaimed to him in a tone that betrayed great incredulity.

"Well, that's just what it is, anyway," repeated the harpooner. "And the little old bees are humming round it like good fellows."

I hastened up and was compelled to believe the evidence of my own eyes. There, at the mouth of a hole bored in one of the dragon trees, were several thousands of these ingenious insects, so common in all the Canaries, whose produce is so highly esteemed by men. Naturally enough, the Canadian wished to gather the honey, and I could not honestly oppose his desire. A quantity of dry leaves were mixed with sulphur, lighted with a spark from his flint, and he began to smoke out the astonished insects. The humming ceased by degrees, and the hive eventually yielded us several pounds of the sweetest honey. Ned Land filled his haversack with it.

"When I've mixed this honey with the paste of the artocarpus," he boasted, "I shall be able to offer you a most succulent cake."

"Upon my soul and body!" said Conseil. "It will be such gingerbread as comes out of a French oven."

"There'll be time for that when it comes," I advised. "Let's now continue our interesting stroll."

At every turn of the path we were following the lake appeared below us in its length and breadth. The lantern lighted up the whole of its mirror-like surface that knew neither ripple nor wave. The "Nautilus" remained immovable as a painted ship. On the platform of the boat and on the floor of the mountain the crew were working, their black shadows clearly etched against the luminous atmosphere.

We were now going around the highest crest of the first layers of those rocks which upheld the roof. I then saw that the bees were not the only representatives of the animal kingdom which inhabited the interior of our volcano. Birds of prey hovered here and there in the shadows, or swept squawking from their nests on the top of the rocks. There were sparrow hawks with white breasts, and kestrels. And down the slopes scampered on awkward long legs several fine fat bustards. I leave anyone to imagine the covetousness of the Canadian at sight of such savory game. He sadly regretted not having brought his gun. But, true to his persevering temperament, he did his best to replace lead bullets with stones. And after many fruitless attempts he at last succeeded in wounding a magnificent bird. It is no exaggeration to say that he risked his life a score of times before he reached it. But he managed things so well that the creature went to join the pilfered honey in his haversack.

We were now obliged to descend toward the shore, as the crest became impracticable. Above us the crater seemed to gape like the mouth of a well. From this place the sky could be seen. Clouds, dissipated by the west wind, had left their misty remnants behind them even on the summit of the mountain. This was certain proof that they were only moderately high, for the volcano did not rise more than eight hundred feet above the level of the ocean.

Half an hour after the Canadian's exploit with the bird we regained the inner shore. Here the flora was represented by large carpets of marine crystal, a small umbelliferous plant, very good when pickled, which like-

wise bears the name of piercestone and sea fennel. Conseil
was happy to gather several bundles of it.

As to the fauna, it might be counted by thousands of
crustacea of all sorts: lobsters, crabs, palaemons, spider
crabs, chameleon shrimps, and a large number of shells,
rockfish, and limpets. Three-quarters of an hour later
we had completed the whole round of the lake and were
back on board. The crew had just finished loading the
sodium, and the submarine could have left that instant.
But Captain Nemo gave no order. Did he wish to wait
until night and leave the undersea passage secretly? Perhaps so. Whatever his reason for delay might be, next
day the "Nautilus" had left its port and was sailing far
from land at a depth of a few yards beneath the waves
of the Atlantic.

CHAPTER XI

THE SARGASSO SEA

That day our ship traversed a singular part of the ocean. No one, I suppose, is ignorant of the existence of a current of warm water known as the Gulf Stream. After leaving the Gulf of Mexico at about 25° north latitude this current divides into two branches. The principal arm goes toward the coast of Ireland and Norway, while the second arm bends to the south at about the height of the Azores. Then it touches the African shore and, describing a lengthened oval sweep, returns to the Antilles.

This second arm of the Gulf Stream (it might better be called a collar than an arm, perhaps) surrounds with its circles of warm water that sector of the cold, calm, quiet ocean that is called the Sargasso Sea, creating thus a perfect lake in the center of the open Atlantic. This lake is so large that it takes not less than three years for the great current to pass around it.

Such was the region that our vessel was now visiting, a very meadow, a close-woven carpet of seaweed, fucus, and tropical berries. These are so thick and compact that the stem of a vessel can hardly tear its way through them. And Captain Nemo, not wishing to entangle his screw in this herbaceous mass, maintained his course some yards beneath the surface of the waters.

The name Sargasso is derived from the Spanish word meaning kelp. This kelp (or varech, or berry plant) is the principal ingredient in the formation of this immense bank. In his *Physical Geography of the Globe* the learned Maury explains why these hydrophytes unite in the peaceful basin of the Atlantic. He says:

If you place in a vase some fragments of cork or other floating body, and give a circular movement to the water in the vase, the scattered fragments will unite in a group in the center of the liquid surface, that is to say, in the part least agitated. In the phenomenon of the bank of kelp, the Atlantic is the vase, the Gulf Stream is the circular current, and the Sargasso Sea the central point of least agitation where the floating bodies unite.

I share Maury's opinion, and I was able to study the phenomenon in the very midst of it where vessels rarely penetrate. Above our heads floated products of all kinds heaped helplessly among these brownish plants. I saw trunks of trees torn from the Andes or the Rocky Mountains and floated off by Amazon or Mississippi. A vast quantity of wreckage was present—remains of keels, ships' bottoms, crushed side-planks—and all of them so weighted down by shells and barnacles that they could not rise again to the surface.

And I believe that time will one day justify that other opinion of Maury, that these substances thus accumulated for ages will become petrified by the action of the water. They will then form inexhaustible coal mines, a precious reserve prepared by far-seeing nature for the moment when man shall have used up the mines of the continents.

In the midst of this inextricable tangle of plants and seaweed I noticed some charming pink halcyons actiniae, with their long tentacles trailing after them. And I saw also medusae, green, red, and blue, and the great rhyostoms

of Cuvier, whose large umbrella was bordered and fes-
tooned with violet.

We spent the whole day of February 22 in the Sargasso
Sea, in which such fish as are partial to marine plants and
crustaceans find abundant nourishment. From then on,
so swift was the speed of the "Nautilus," we were in an
ocean that had returned to its accustomed aspect.

From this time on for nineteen days, from February
23 to March 12, our ship held to the middle of the Atlantic,
carrying us at a fixed speed of one hundred leagues each
twenty-four hours. Captain Nemo was apparently bent
upon carrying out his undersea program, and I fancied
that he intended, after doubling Cape Horn, to return to
the southern seas of the Pacific.

Ned Land surely had cause for dread. In these large
areas of waste water, void of islands, we could not successfully attempt to leave the boat. Nor had we any proper
means of opposing our commander's will. Our one course
was to submit to anything within reason. But what we
could not gain through force or cunning, I liked to think
we might accomplish by persuasion.

When the course of this voyage was run, would my
host not consent to restore our freedom? Especially if
we swore an oath never to reveal his existence or the conditions under which he lived? Such a word of honor,
once given, he knew that we should respect.

The one trouble was, that delicate question was to be
discussed only with the captain himself. But was I really
at liberty to force my claims upon him? Had he not said
from the beginning, in the most emphatic way, that the

secret of his life demanded our lifelong imprisonment on board the "Nautilus"? And would not my silence of six months appear to him to be a tacit acceptance on my part of the situation? And suppose I should raise the issue of our liberation with him? Would my harping on this subject not result in raising up in his mind suspicions which might be hurtful to our projects for escape—that is, if at some future time a favorable chance should offer to put them into execution?

No incident of any note occurred to signalize our voyage and make it memorable during all the nineteen days I have mentioned. I saw little or nothing of the captain; he was constantly at work. In the library I frequently came across his traces in books that had been left open, particularly such as dealt with natural history. My volume on submarine depths he had gone through with unusual care. Its margins were crowded with notes that often contradicted my theories and statements. But, so far as my personal ideas were concerned, the commander contented himself in correcting my printed work—it was very rare for him to try to confute me in oral discussion.

At seasons I heard the melancholy tones of his organ— his preference was for harmonies in the minor key. But he played only at night when he could count upon the greatest privacy, when the "Nautilus" was asleep on a deserted ocean. During this part of our voyage we sailed whole days at a time on the surface of the waves. The sea seemed abandoned. A few sailing vessels, on the road to India, were making for the Cape of Good Hope. Nothing else.

One day we were pursued by the boats of a whaler. It considered us, no doubt, an enormous cetacean which would bring a great price. But Captain Nemo did not wish the worthy sailors to lose their time and trouble, so he ended the chase by plunging under water.

Our navigation continued until the 13th day of March. On that date the submarine began to make experiments in soundings, a fact that interested me a lot. We had then made about thirteen thousand leagues since our departure from the high seas of the Pacific. The bearings gave us 45° 37′ south latitude and 37° 53′ west longitude. It was the same field of water in which Captain Denham of the "Herald" sounded seven thousand fathoms without finding the bottom. There, too, Lieutenant Parker, of the American frigate "Congress," could not touch ground with a line 15,150 yards long.

Now our commander confided to me that he planned to get to the floor of the ocean by using his lateral planes set at an angle of forty-five degrees with the water line of the "Nautilus," which, he thought, should give him a diagonal sufficiently extended for his purpose. No sooner said than done. The screw of our staunch ship set to work at its maximum speed, its four blades beating the water with indescribable force. Under this powerful pressure the hull of our submarine quivered like the string of a harp, but it sank in orderly progression beneath the waves.

At a depth of seven thousand fathoms I saw some blackish tops rising from the midst of the waters. But, so far as I (or anyone else) knew, these might be the summits of mountains as high as the Himalayas or Mont

Blanc. For that matter, even higher! And the depth of the abyss still remained an incalculable thing.

The undaunted ship continued to descend, in spite of the great pressure beginning to be exerted upon her steel ribs. I felt her plates tremble where they were fastened by the bolts. Bars bent, partitions variously groaned or creaked. The very windows of the saloon appeared to curve inward under the growing pressure of the liquid element. And this firm structure, like anything else constructed by human hand, would have yielded if it had not been capable of resistance like a solid block (to quote the captain's own words).

In skirting the steep slopes of these rocks that were lost under water I still saw shells living—serpulae and spinorbes and several specimens of asteriads. But ere long the last representative of animal life vanished. And at the depth of more than three leagues the "Nautilus" had passed the extreme limits of submarine existence, even as a balloon does when it rises above the atmosphere that is respirable for human lungs. We had attained a level of sixteen thousand yards (four French leagues), and the sides of the vessel at this moment bore a pressure of sixteen thousand atmospheres, that is to say, of thirty-two hundred pounds on each square two-fifths of an inch of its surface.

"What a beautiful situation to be in!" I chortled. "To overrun regions where man has never trod, depths to which even dead or inanimate matter may never more descend! Look, Captain, at these magnificent rocks, these uninhabitable grottoes. Here are the lowest known receptacles of the globe, where life is not only impossible but unthinkable. What unknown sights are here? Why should we be unable to find and preserve some visible evidence of our journey as a souvenir?"

"Would you really like to carry away more than a mere remembrance of this moment?" Captain Nemo asked.

"What do you mean by those words, my friend?"

"I mean to say that nothing is easier than to take a photographic view of this undersea district."

I had not more than just time to express my surprise and delight at the novel proposal when, at the commander's summons, a camera was brought into the room. Through the widely exposed panel of the saloon the liquid mass without was bright with electricity. And this illumination was distributed with such uniformity that not a shadow, not a gradation of the spectrum, was to be seen in all the field of manufactured light. The "Nautilus" came to a full stop, the force of its revolving screw being neutralized by the inclination of its planes. The tripod of the photographic instrument was so adjusted that the lens included the field of the bottom of the ocean. And in a few seconds my host had obtained a perfect negative.

In the finished photograph, which I have published in my log book, can be seen the primitive rocks which have never looked upon the light of heaven; can be seen the lowest granite which forms the foundation of the globe as we know it; can be seen those deep grottoes sunk in this stony mass whose outlines are of such black sharpness, as if done by the brush of an old Flemish painter.

In the background of the picture is a horizon of moun-

tains, an undulating line of admirable grace, which gives
the perspective of the scene. But it is beyond the power
of either photograph or words to describe the effect upon
the observer of these smooth, black, polished rocks, strange
in form, without moss or spot, standing solidly on the
sandy carpet, which sparkled under the jet of our out-
poured electricity.

The picture of the underworld was taken. Captain
Nemo sighed and said, "Let's go back up. We must not
take undue advantage of our exceptional position, nor expose the 'Nautilus' too long to such unheard-of pressure."

"How shall we get back up?" I asked.

"Hang on hard!" my host called to me.

I had no time to wonder why the captain so advised
me before I was thrown to the carpet face downward.

A signal from the commander had caused the screw
to be shipped and its blades vertically raised. As a consequence, the submarine shot aloft with stunning rapidity,
like an escaped balloon—I had almost said like a bullet
from a gun. It cut through the mass of waters with a
singing vibration like the treble strings of a harp after
violent agitation. Nothing could be seen from the panel,
not even a streak of light. The world and time itself were
in abeyance.

In four minutes, according to our later reckoning, the
vessel had traversed the four leagues which separated it
from the top level of the ocean. And after it had emerged
from the waters like a flying fish the ship fell gracefully
back upon the waves, but, at that, with a thud and a splash
that made them rebound to an enormous height.

CHAPTER XII

CACHALOTS AND WHALES

During the night of the 13th and 14th of March our craft returned to its southerly course. I fancied, I hardly know why, that when we were level with Cape Horn our commander would turn the helm westward in order to patrol the Pacific seas and thus complete a tour of the world. But he did nothing of the kind. He continued on his way to the Southern Ocean.

Whither were we tending? To the South Pole? That way lay madness. I began to think that the captain's temerity justified the worst fears of my comrade Ned Land.

For some time past the Canadian had not exchanged a word with me relative to an attempt at flight. He had grown by imperceptible degrees less communicative, almost taciturn. I could see that our lengthened imprisonment was having an evil effect upon him. And I could sense the rage that burned within his breast. Whenever he met the captain his eyes lighted up with suppressed anger. And I feared, not without reason, that his natural tendency to violence might some day lead him to extremes.

That day, the 14th of March, Conseil and he came to my room. I inquired the cause of their visit.

"I just want to ask you a simple question, sir," said Ned.

"Speak your mind freely, my friend."

"How many men are there on board the 'Nautilus,' do you reckon?"

"I can only judge that it does not require a particularly large crew to operate it. Certainly under existing conditions ten men, at the most, would be sufficient."

"Then why should we figure on a larger number?"

The Canadian's meaning was getting pretty easy to guess. I looked at him fixedly before I replied.

"Why," I said, "because, if my surmises are correct and if I have read aright hints as to his life that Captain Nemo has unwittingly let drop, this submarine is something more than just a ship of passage. It is a place of refuge for men who, like their commander, have renounced every tie that bound them to the earth."

"I fancy you are right," interpolated Conseil. "But, in any case, our vessel can hold only a limited number of people. Surely we ought to be able to estimate their maximum number."

"And how do you propose to do that, my boy?"

"By working out an elementary problem in arithmetic. Given the size of the vessel and the quantity of air that it contains, knowing how much air each man expends at a breath, and comparing these results with the fact that we have to go to the surface for renewal once in each twenty-four hours, what is the answer?"

Conseil had hardly begun his sentence before I saw what he was driving at.

"I get you," I replied. "Still that calculation, simple as it is, will yield only an uncertain result."

"Never mind that. Let's try, just the same," urged

the harpooner. Characteristically, even a false result would suit this simple fellow better than no result at all.

"Very well, then," I said. "In one hour each man consumes the oxygen contained in 20 gallons of air; in twenty-four hours, that contained in 480 gallons. We must therefore discover how many times 480 gallons of air the 'Nautilus' contains."

"That's the ticket, sir!" said Conseil, who was fond of problems of every sort.

"Now," I continued, "the size of the submarine is 1500 tons, and one ton holds 200 gallons; thus the ship contains 300,000 gallons of air. Divide this by 480 and you get the quotient 625; which shows, strictly speaking, that the air contained in our craft would suffice for 625 men for a period of twenty-four hours."

"Heavens above!" exclaimed Ned Land.

"But remember that all of us, including passengers, sailors, and officers, probably do not form a tenth of that number."

"Even a fifteenth of 625 men would prove a fairly stiff job for three men to tackle," murmured Conseil.

The Canadian shook his head despairingly, passed his hand once or twice across his forehead, and left the room without further parley.

"May I make one observation, sir?" queried Conseil. "Poor Ned is longing for everything he cannot have. His past life is always present before him. Every single thing that is denied him he regrets. His head is full of memories."

"I must say," I remarked tartly, "that I do not entirely sympathize with his condition."

"That's just it, sir," Conseil persisted, "you must understand him! Pardon me if I continue. What has this harpooner to do on board here? Nothing. For he is not learned like you sir, and he has not that taste for the beauties of the sea which we share in common. He would risk his very life to be able once more to go to a tavern in his own native country."

I felt all at once that Conseil was right. I was glad that he had given me a new angle from which to approach the Canadian's case. Certainly the monotony of our existence must be intolerable to him, accustomed as he was to a life of action and not one of thought. There had been but few events which could rouse him to any show of spirit, I must acknowledge.

And yet that selfsame day an event did occur which recalled his happy days as a harpooner. About eleven o'clock in the morning, while floating on the surface of the ocean, our ship fell in with a troop of whales. This encounter, while rare, did not surprise me much, for I knew that these creatures were being so persistently hunted down by whalers that they now sought asylum in high latitudes.

We were seated on the platform with a quiet sea about us. The October of these latitudes gave us some splendid autumnal weather. It was the Canadian, whose clear sight could always be trusted, who first sighted a cetacean on the eastern horizon. Five miles away the animal was, and yet, with close attention, one could see its black back rise and fall with the swaying waves.

"There she blows!" cried Ned Land. "Ah, if I were

aboard a little old whale ship now, I'd like to have a talk with that fellow! It's a monster. See the stream of air and steam its blowholes are throwing up! Hang it, why am I tied to these confounded iron plates!"

"So you haven't lost your old rage for fishing, Ned?"

"Can a whale fisher ever forget his trade, sir? That's where you get excitement! Something doing every minute. I never could get tired of it, Lord love you!"

"Have you ever fished so far south, my boy?"

"Never, sir. I was always up in the northern waters. But I know Behring and Davis Straits like my own front yard, that I do."

"Then the southern whale is still unknown to you. It's the Greenland animal you've been hunting up to this time. And that fellow would never risk passing through the warm seas of the equator. Whales are localized according to their kinds, and stick to certain waters that they never leave. If one of these creatures should go from Behring to Davis Straits, that would surely mean there was a passage from one ocean to the other, on either the American or the Asiatic side."

"Then, as I've never fished down here, I don't know what kind of whales these fellows are."

"Just as I said, my boy."

"All the more reason for making their acquaintance," Conseil suggested.

"Oh, golly, look at 'em!" exclaimed the Canadian angrily. "Here they come! They're laughing at me. They know darn well I can't get at them. They're driving me crazy."

Ned stamped his feet. His hand trembled as he reached out to grasp an imaginary harpoon.

"Are these beasts as big as the ones up north?" he asked.

"Just about."

"Because, sir, believe it or not, I've seen whales that measured over a hundred feet. I've been told, though it's a lie like enough, that there are creatures in Kulammak and Umgallich, of the Aleutian Islands, that are sometimes a hundred and fifty feet long."

"That sounds a little stiff to me, Ned. These creatures are only balaenopterons provided with dorsal fins. Like the cachalots, they are generally much smaller than the Greenland whale."

"Hello!" exclaimed the Canadian, whose eyes had not left the ocean for a moment. "They're coming nearer. They're poaching on our waters right now!"

A moment later he returned to the conversation and said, "You spoke of the cachalot as a small creature, sir. I have heard tell of gigantic ones. They are intelligent fellows. They say some of them cover themselves with seaweed and fucus so as to be mistaken for islands. People camp out on them and settle there—light a fire—"

"And build houses?" inquired Conseil.

"Don't try to be funny, you little frog-eater!" growled Ned Land. "But that's just what people do. And then, one fine day, the whale plunges and carries all the inhabitants on its back down to the bottom of the sea."

"Sounds to me like the travels of Sindbad the Sailor," I could not refrain from saying, with a laugh.

"Gosh all fishhooks!" suddenly squealed the harpooner. "It's not one whale, it's a school of them—ten—twenty—a regular battalion! And here I sit like a bump on a log, not able to do a thing, hands and feet tied."

"But, you old goober," said Conseil, "why don't you ask Captain Nemo's permission to chase them?"

My servant had not finished his question before Ned Land had lowered himself through the panel to seek the commander. A few minutes afterward the two appeared together on the bridge. Our host watched the troop of cetaceans playing on the waters about a mile from the "Nautilus."

"Southern whales," he said. "There goes a fortune for a whole fleet of whalers."

"Well, sir," asked the Canadian impatiently, "what's your decision? May I chase them, please, sir, if only to remind me of my old trade of harpooner?"

"What purpose would it serve?" said Captain Nemo. "It would be killing for the sheer joy of destruction. We have no need of whale oil on board here."

"But you let us hunt down the dugong in the Red Sea."

"That was to procure fresh meat for my crew, Mr. Land. The case here is very different. I know that man jealously reserves his privilege of shooting and hunting just for the sake of excitement, but I do not approve of so murderous a pastime. In destroying the southern whale (like the Greenland cetacean, an inoffensive creature), your colleagues commit a blameworthy deed, Mr. Land. They have already depopulated the whole of Baffin's Bay, and they are annihilating a class of useful animals. Leave these unfortunate fellows alone, that's my advice. They have plenty of natural enemies without your joining in—cachalots, swordfish, and sawfish."

I felt that the captain was right. The barbarous greed of fishermen will one day not far removed cause the disappearance of the last whale from the sea. Ned Land whistled "Yankee Doodle" between his teeth, thrust his hands deep in his pockets, and turned his expressive back upon us. But Captain Nemo continued to watch the troop of cetaceans.

"I was right in saying that whales had natural foes enough without counting man," he said after a moment. "They will have plenty to do before long. Do you see, M. Aronnax, those blackish moving points some eight miles to windward?"

"By Jove, I do!" I replied.

"Those are cachalots—terrible animals which I have sometimes met in troops of two or three hundred. Now, when it comes to cachalots, they are the fellows to exterminate. Cruel, marauding creatures!"

The Canadian whipped around at these words like a flash.

"Well, Captain," he said, "there's still time if we set to work with a will."

"But it is quite needless to expose yourself, my man. The 'Nautilus' will disperse them effectively. It is armed with a steel spur quite as effective as your harpoon would be."

The Canadian did not even bother to shrug his shoulders at this remark. Attack cetaceans with blows of a·spur! Tell that to the marines! Why, who had ever heard of the like?

"Wait a bit, M. Aronnax," continued Captain Nemo. "We'll show you something worth while. I have no pity for these ferocious things. They are nothing but mouth and teeth."

Mouth and teeth! No one could better describe the macrocephalous cachalot, which is sometimes more than seventy-five feet long. Its enormous head occupies a third of its entire body. It is better armed than a whale, whose upper jaw is provided only with whalebone. The cachalot is supplied with twenty-five large tusks about eight inches long, cylindrical and conical at the top, weighing two pounds apiece. It is in the upper part of this huge head, in cavities separated by cartilage, that we find from six to eight hundred pounds of that precious oil known as spermaceti.

The cachalot is a disagreeable creature, more tadpole than fish, to adopt Fredol's description. It is badly formed, the whole of its left side, in a manner of speaking, being a failure. The beast is able to see only with its right eye.

But there was no longer time for general discussion of these matters. The formidable troop was nearing us. They had seen the whales and were preparing to attack them. It was easy to see beforehand that the cachalots would be victorious for several reasons. They were more numerous and better built for attack than their inoffensive adversaries, and they could remain longer under water without coming to the surface. There was only just time to rush to the help of the whales.

The "Nautilus" went under water. Conseil, Ned Land, and I took our places by the window of the saloon. Captain Nemo had joined the pilot in the steering cage, the better to work his apparatus as an engine of destruction. The battle between the cachalots and whales was already in progress when our vessel appeared on the field. At first they did not show any fear at sight of this new monster that joined in the combat. But they soon had to guard against its blows.

What a grewsome, gorgeous fight!

Our submarine turned out to be nothing but a sublimated harpoon brandished in the hand of its skilful captain. It would hurl itself against the fleshy mass chosen as a target, and pass clear through, leaving behind it the two quivering halves of the animal. When one cachalot was thus dispatched, it would run at the next nearest. It tacked from course to course like light itself, so as not to miss its fleeing prey. It darted forward and backward, answering immediately to its helm. It plunged when the cetacean sought the deep waters, it rose when its quarry returned to the surface. It struck front and sidewise, cut and tore in all directions and at any speed, piercing the cachalots with its terrible spur. And itself, it could not feel the hammer blows from their tails upon its sides nor the shock produced when it hit the enemy.

What carnage! What hubbub on the surface of the waves! What sharp hissing and snorting, signs of rage peculiar to these animals. And all this in the midst of a scene generally so peaceful, but now made to rock and sway with the lashing of their tails.

For an hour this wholesale massacre continued. The cachalots were unable to escape us. Several times ten or twelve of them at once would strive to crush the "Nautilus" by their weight. From the safe vantage of the window we could see their immense mouths studded with tusks, and their wicked eyes. Ned Land could not contain himself—he gave way to his proper feelings, threatened, and swore. We could feel how they clung to our vessel, like dogs worrying a wild boar in a copse. But our good ship, working its screw, carried them hither and yon beneath the waves or to the upper levels, caring naught for their ponderous weight nor for the terrific strain upon its sides.

At length the mass of cetaceans broke up, the waves became quiet, and I realized that we were rising to the surface. The panel opened, and we hastened to the platform. The sea was strewn with mutilated bodies. A formidable explosion could not have divided and quartered this hideous mass with greater violence. We were floating in a perfect welter of gigantic corpses, bluish on the back and white underneath and covered with colossal warty protuberances. Some terrified cachalots were speeding toward the horizon. The waves were dyed red for several miles, and the submarine floated on a sea of blood.

Captain Nemo joined us. "Well, Mr. Land," he said, "how now?"

"Sir," replied the Canadian, "it was truly a terrible spectacle. But, now that my blood-lust is somewhat calmed, I am coming to regard it as butchery and not battle. And I, sir, am not a butcher, but a hunter."

"It was a slaughter of mischievous creatures," replied the captain. "And the 'Nautilus' is no butcher's knife."

"I prefer my harpoon," remarked Ned Land curtly.

"Every man to his own tools," the commander answered smoothly enough. But I saw him regard the harpooner fixedly.

I was possessed with a fear the latter would commit some imprudent act of violence. But his anger seemed to be soon turned aside by the sight of a whale which the submersible had just overhauled. The creature had not escaped whole from the cachalot's teeth. I recognized the breed of southern whale by its flat head, which is entirely black. Anatomically it is distinguished from the white whale and its North Cape cousin by the seven cervical vertebrae, and it likewise has two more ribs than its congeners.

This particular unfortunate cetacean was lying on its side, riddled with gaping holes from the bites it had received, and quite dead. From its mutilated fin still hung a young whale which it had been powerless to save from the marauding attack. Its open mouth let the water flow in and out, murmuring like waves breaking on the shore. Captain Nemo steered close to the creature.

Two of his men mounted its side. And I saw, not without surprise, that they were drawing from its breasts all the milk that they contained, that is to say, about two or three tons. The captain offered me a cup of it while it was still warm. I could not help showing my repugnance to the drink. But he assured me that it was excellent, and not to be distinguished in taste from cow's milk. I sipped some of it and was of his opinion. It was a useful reserve for us, since in the form of salt butter and cheese it would furnish an agreeable variety to our ordinary bill of fare.

From that day on I noticed with uneasiness that Ned Land's ill-will toward Captain Nemo increased. And I resolved to keep close tab on the Canadian's actions.

CHAPTER XIII

THE GREAT ICE BARRIER

Our submarine was steadily maintaining its southerly course at considerable speed, following closely the 50th meridian.

The question again became uppermost in my mind: Did our commander wish to reach the pole? I did not think so, if for no other reason, because every attempt hitherto to attain that point had failed miserably. Again, the season was far advanced, for in the antarctic regions the 13th of March corresponds to the northern 13th of September. And they both begin with the equinox.

On the 14th of March I saw floating ice in latitude 55. Mere bits of pale débris, from twenty to twenty-five feet long, had formed into banks over which the sea was curling. The "Nautilus" remained on the surface of the ocean. Ned Land, who had fished the arctic seas, was familiar with icebergs, but Conseil and I were admiring them for the first time in our lives. In the atmosphere toward the southern horizon stretched a dazzling white band to which English seamen give the name of iceblink. However thick the clouds may be, it is always visible, and announces the close proximity of an ice pack or bank.

As was to be expected, then, larger blocks of ice soon appeared, the brilliancy of which changed with the whims of the fog. Some of the masses showed green veins, as if long undulating stripes had been traced on them with sulphate of copper. Others reflected the light of day from a thousand facets of crystals. Still others were shaded with vivid calcareous refractions and resembled a noble city of marble. The more we neared the south, the greater were the number and the importance of these itinerant islands.

At the 60th degree of latitude every passageway and channel through the floating ice had disappeared. After long and careful search, however, Captain Nemo was rewarded by finding a narrow opening through which he boldly slipped, knowing full well, however, that it would close behind him.

In this manner, guided by his clever and practiced hand, the "Nautilus" passed through all the ice with a precision that quite entranced Conseil: icebergs or mountains, ice fields unbroken and limitless, drift ice, floating ice, ice packs, called palchs when they are circular, and streams when they are composed of long strips.

The temperature was very low, the thermometer exposed to the air registering 2 or 3 degrees below zero. But we were warmly clad in furs, at the expense of sea bear and seal. The interior of the ship was warmed regularly by its electric apparatus, and so defied the most intense cold. Besides, it would only have been necessary to submerge some yards to find a more bearable temperature.

Two months earlier in the year we should have had perpetual daylight in these latitudes, but already we were having three or four hours of night, and after a little there would be six months of darkness in these circumpolar districts.

On the 15th of March we were in the latitude of New
Shetland and South Orkney. The captain informed me
that these lands had been inhabited years before by various
tribes of seals. But English and American whalers, in
their rage for destruction, massacred both old and young.
Thus, where there was once upon a time life and animation,
greedy mariners had left behind them silence and death.

About eight o'clock on the morning of March 16 the
"Nautilus," following the 50th meridian still, cut the
antarctic polar circle. Ice surrounded us without a break
on every side and closed the horizon. But Captain Nemo
passed tirelessly onward from one opening to another in
his unceasing southward progress. I simply cannot convey
my amazement at the beauties of these unexplored regions.
The ice assumed the most surprising shapes. Here the
groupings formed an Oriental city, with its innumerable
mosques and minarets. There I saw a fallen city lying,
one that seemed to have been thrown to earth by some
awful convulsion of nature.

The whole aspect of a scene would be constantly
changed by the oblique rays of the sun that struck across
it, or perhaps lost to sight entirely in the grayish mists
amid hurricanes of snow and sleet. Detonations and the
crash of falls were heard everywhere, great overthrows
of icebergs that altered the whole landscape like a diorama.

Often and often I saw no exit and thought that we were
definitely prisoners at last. But, guided by an instinct
that was alive to the least indication of an open path, Captain Nemo would always find it. He was never mistaken
when he saw the thin threads of bluish water trickling

along the ice fields. And I had no doubt that he had before that ventured into the heart of these antarctic seas.

On the 16th of March, however, the ice fields positively blocked our road. It was not the iceberg itself as yet, but vast fields cemented by intense cold that confronted us. Even this obstacle could not cause our commander to falter—he hurled our ship against it with frightful violence. Our ship would enter the brittle mass like a wedge and split it to the accompaniment of the most ear-splitting crackings. It was the battering-ram of the ancients hurled with almost infinite strength. The splintered ice, thrown high into the air, fell like hail around us.

By its own power of impulsion our apparatus made a channel for itself. A few times it carried with such impetus that it lodged on the ice field, crushing the ice with its weight, quite often buried beneath it, dividing it by a simple pitching movement, producing large rents and gaps in it. We did everything possible but one—we never for a second abandoned the fight.

Violent gales assailed us at this time, accompanied by thick fogs through which we could not see from one end of the platform to the other. The wind blew sharply from all points of the compass, and the snow lay in such hard heaps upon our hull that we had to break it with a pickaxe. At a temperature of only 5 degrees below zero, Centigrade, every outward part of our submarine was covered with ice. A rigged vessel never could have worked its way in there, for all the ropes and cables would have stuck in the grooves of the pulleys.

A vessel without sails, with electricity for its motive

power and needing no coal, could alone brave such high latitudes. At length, on the 18th of March, after many fruitless assaults the "Nautilus" for the first time confessed herself defeated. It was no longer a question of streams, packs, or ice fields, but of an interminable and immovable barrier which was formed by mountains soldered fast together and without a crevice.

"The Great Ice Barrier!" said Conseil to me.

I knew that to Ned Land, as well as to other navigators who had preceded us, this was an inevitable obstacle. The sun appeared for an instant at noon, and our commander took an observation with all the accuracy that was possible. This gave our location as 51° 30′ longitude and 67° 39′ south latitude. We had advanced one degree more into this dead antarctic region.

Of the liquid surface of the sea, there was no longer a glimpse. Under the spur of the "Nautilus" lay stretched a vast plain, confusedly strewn with mighty blocks. Here and there from the prairie sharp points and slender needles rose to a height of two hundred feet. Farther on, a succession of cliffs, hewn as if by an axe and clothed in grayish tints, lay half drowned in the fog. Their surfaces, like huge mirrors, reflected dully the few rays of sunshine that caught them.

And over this desolate face of nature a stern silence prevailed, scarcely broken by the flapping wings of petrel and puffin. Everything seemed frozen up—even noise.

The submarine was thus obliged to stop in its adventurous course amid these fields of ice. In spite of our heroic efforts, in spite of the powerful means employed to break up the ice, the ship must remain immovable. Now usually, when we can proceed no farther upon our way, the path of return lies open behind us. But here it was as impossible to go back as to advance, for all channels had closed behind us. And no matter for how short a time our boat remained stationary, it would not fail to be blocked. And now this very thing did happen about two o'clock in the afternoon, the fresh ice forming around our sides with magic swiftness. I was forced to admit that Captain Nemo was more than imprudent. I was on the platform at the moment. Our commander had been observing the situation for some time past when he said to me, "Well, sir, and what do you think of this?"

"I think that we are fairly caught in a vise, Captain."

"So, M. Aronnax, you are perfectly sure that our vessel cannot disengage herself."

"Only with enormous difficulty can she be moved an inch, sir. For the season is already too far advanced for you to reckon on the breaking up of the ice."

"My dear fellow," my host remarked in an ironical tone, "you will never change! You see nothing but difficulties and obstacles. Now, on the contrary, I affirm that the 'Nautilus' can not only free herself at this point, but can go farther south still."

"Farther? Just Heaven!" I exclaimed.

"Yes, M. Aronnax, we are on our way to the pole."

I was unable to repress a gesture of incredulity.

"It is as I say, despite your evident attitude of denial," continued the captain coldly. "We shall find the Antarctic Pole, that untrodden spot from whence springs every meridian of the globe. You should know by this time, Professor, whether I can wreak my will upon this ship or not."

Alas! I knew that fact well enough. I had learned that this eccentric man was bold even to rashness. But to conquer those obstacles which fairly bristle around the South Pole—was it not as mad an enterprise as could have presented itself to the brain of a maniac? The South Pole was much more inaccessible than the North Pole, and this had not been reached by even the boldest navigators. It then flashed into my mind to ask Captain Nemo whether he had perhaps already discovered this pole which had hitherto been unattained by any human creature.

"Not yet, no, sir," he replied. "But we shall discover it together. Where others have lamentably failed, I shall succeed. I have never before driven my ship so far into southern seas, that is true. But I repeat, I shall go on to the end."

"Very well, my dear sir," I said, not entirely innocent of sarcastic intent, "I believe you. Let us go ahead full steam. Obstacles for us simply do not exist—we blow them away with a breath. A wave of the hand, and presto! they are gone. Let us smash this Great Ice Barrier. Let us explode it! And, if it resists our efforts, let us give the 'Nautilus' wings and fly over it."

"Over it, sir?" asked Captain Nemo quietly. "No, not over it, but under it lies my pathway."

"Aha, I see!" I exclaimed, for the first time gaining an idea of what my host's project really was. I understood now to the full how the submarine's wonderful qualities were going to serve us in this superhuman enterprise.

"I am glad," said the commander, smiling, "that you are beginning to recognize the successful issue of this attempt. That which is impossible for any other vessel is easy for mine. Of course, if a continent lies before the pole, then we must stop where land begins. But if, as I suspect, the pole is washed by the open sea, then go to the pole we shall."

"Certainly," I agreed, carried away by the captain's fine assurance, "you will attain it. For, if the surface of the sea is solidified by ice, the lower depths are free from it. This is because of the providential law that has placed the maximum of density of the waters of the ocean one degree higher than the freezing point. And, if I am not mistaken, the portion of this iceberg which is above the water is as one to four to that which is not."

"Very nearly, Professor. For one foot of iceberg above the sea there are three below it. Now, if these ice mountains are not more than three hundred feet above the surface, they are not more than nine hundred beneath. And what are nine hundred feet to the 'Nautilus'?"

"A negligible trifle, sir."

"It could even seek at greater depths that uniform temperature of sea water which would permit it to set at defiance the thirty or forty degrees of surface cold."

"You are absolutely right, sir," I replied with great animation.

"The only difficulty," mused my host, "would be to remain several days without renewing our provision of air."

"Is that all! Why, your ship, Captain, has vast reservoirs. We can fill them, and they will supply us with all the oxygen we want."

"Well thought of, M. Aronnax!" replied the captain, smiling. "I thought I would give you all my objections first, so that you could not justly accuse me of rashness."

"Have you any other obstacles to suggest?"

"Only one, sir. It is possible, if the sea exists at the South Pole, that it may be covered. And, consequently, we should be unable to come to the surface."

"Very good! But do you forget that your vessel is armed with a powerful spur? And could we not send this weapon diagonally against these fields of ice, which would open at the shock?"

"You are full of ideas today, Professor."

"Besides," I added enthusiastically, "why should we not expect to find the sea open at the South Pole as well as at the North? The frozen poles and the poles of the earth do not coincide at either extremity of the globe. And, until the contrary is proved, we may suppose either a continent or an ocean free from ice at these two points of our oblate spheroid."

"I think as you do," replied Captain Nemo. "But do you realize that you are now crushing me with arguments in favor of my project, after having made so many objections?"

Our preparations for this audacious adventure now began.

The powerful pumps of the submarine worked air into the great tanks and stored it there under high pressure. About four o'clock our commander announced the closing of the panels on the platform. I cast one last look at the massive iceberg that we were going to pass.

The weather was clear, the atmosphere pure enough. The cold was very great, being 12 degrees below zero, Centigrade. But as the wind had died down this temperature was not so unbearable as might be imagined. About ten men mounted the sides of the ship, armed with pickaxes to break the icy clutch in which the craft was held. This operation was quickly performed, for the fresh ice was still quite thin, and the "Nautilus" was soon free. We all went below.

The usual reservoirs were filled with the newly liberated water, and the submarine began to sink. I had taken my place beside Conseil in the saloon; through the open window we could see the lower beds of the Southern Ocean. The thermometer rose, the needle of the manometer deviated on the dial. At about nine hundred feet, as Captain Nemo had foreseen, we were floating beneath the undulating surface of the iceberg.

But we went lower still. The ship descended to the depth of four hundred fathoms. The temperature of the water at the surface showed 12 degrees; it was now only 10. We had gained two. I need not say that the warmth of our vessel inside was raised by its heating apparatus to a much higher degree. Every maneuver was accomplished with wonderful precision.

"If you please, sir, we're sure to pass it," said Conseil.

"I believe we shall," I answered in a tone of firm conviction.

In this open corridor of under-the-sea the "Nautilus"

had chosen the course direct for the pole, without once leaving the 52d meridian. From 67° 30′ to 90°, 22½ degrees of latitude remained for her to travel; that is, about five hundred leagues. The ship maintained an average speed of twenty-six miles per hour—the rate of an express train. If that was held, in forty hours or so we should be at our final goal.

For part of the night the novelty of the experience held us to our observation window. The sea was lighted as usual by the rays from the faithful electric lantern But it was as empty as church on a week-day afternoon. Fishes did not care to sojourn in these dead, imprisoned waters. At best, they found in this closed corridor of under-the-sea only a passageway to lead from the Antarctic Ocean to the open polar sea. Our progress was smooth and uneventful—we could not lose the sense of our swift gait because of the rhythmic quivering of the frame of the ship's long steel body. About two o'clock in the morning I snatched a few hours' repose, and so did Conseil. While crossing the waist on my way to bed I did not run across Captain Nemo. I supposed him to be in the pilot's cage and felt the easier in mind because of his direction of our nocturnal dash.

The next morning, March 19, I took up my post once more in the drawing-room. The electric log at once informed me that the speed of our craft had been reduced. It was at that moment on its way toward the surface, but emptying its reservoirs of compressed air slowly and prudently.

My heart beat faster than its wont. Were we on the

point of emerging at the surface and regaining the open atmosphere of the pole? No, apparently not. For a jar told me that the submarine had struck the underbase of the Great Ice Barrier, which was still very thick, to judge by the dead sound of concussion that met my ears.

We had indeed struck (to use a sea expression), but in an inverse sense, and at a depth of three thousand feet. This would give four thousand feet of ice above us, one thousand being above the water line. The Great Ice Barrier, then, was higher here than at the border—not a fact that tended to calm nerves already taut with dread of the unknown.

Several times that day the "Nautilus" tried again to reach a higher level, and each time it struck against the wall that lay like a ceiling above it. Sometimes it met with the ice barrier at a depth of but nine hundred yards, only two hundred of which lay above the surface. The barrier must be twice the height it was when the ship submerged. I carefully noted the different depths, and thereby won a submarine profile chart of the chain of ice mountains as it was developed.

That night no change had taken place in our situation. Still ice between four and five hundred yards in depth. The vertical measurement was evidently diminishing, but yet what a thickness in the cover that separated us from the top level of the sea! It was then eight o'clock. According to the daily custom on board, our supply of air should have been renewed four hours before. But I did not suffer from lack of it, although Captain Nemo had as yet made no demand upon his reserve supply of oxygen.

My sleep was painful that night. One nightmare of oppression followed the other. I scarcely knew whether I was asleep or waking. Hope and fear beset me by turns. I rose and walked about uneasily several times. The deliberate groping of the "Nautilus" for a place of freedom above the water continued.

About three in the morning watch I went back to the saloon for a moment. I noticed that the lower surface of the ice barrier was only about fifty yards deep. One hundred and fifty feet therefore now separated us from the surface of the waters. It would seem that the ice barrier by degrees was becoming an ice field, the mountain a plain. My eyes at this time did not leave the manometer. We were still rising diagonally to the surface, which sparkled under the electric rays. Both above and beneath, the ice barrier was stretching out more horizontally into lengthening slopes. Mile after mile it was growing thinner.

At length, at six o'clock in the morning of that memorable day, the 19th of March, the door of the saloon was torn open, and Captain Nemo appeared.

"The sea is open!" was all he said.

CHAPTER XIV

THE SOUTH POLE

I rushed up to the platform.

Yes, as I lived and breathed! The open sea, with but a few scattered pieces of ice and moving icebergs, a long stretch of ocean water. A world of birds was in the air above me. Myriads of fishes swam beneath the surface. The waters varied in color from an intense blue to an olive green, according to the bottom. The thermometer stood at 3 degrees above zero, Centigrade. It was comparatively spring weather, shut in as we were behind this barrier of ice, whose lengthened mass was dimly seen on the northern horizon.

"Are we at the pole?" I called to the captain, with a beating heart. It was a foolish, if an excusable question.

"I don't know," my companion replied. "At noon, when I get the bearing, we'll be sure."

"But will the sun show itself through this fog?" I asked, looking anxiously at the leaden sky that was our canopy.

"However little of himself Sol shows, it will be enough, sir."

About ten miles to the southward a solitary island rose to a height that I estimated to be over a hundred yards. We made for it, but cautiously, for the sea might be strewn with reefs. An hour later we had reached its shore, another hour after that we had circumnavigated it. It measured four or five miles around. A narrow channel separated it from a considerable stretch of land, perhaps a continent, for we could not see any indication of its limits even with the aid of a high-powered lens.

The existence of this land seemed to lend color to the hypothesis of Maury. This ingenious American has remarked that between the South Pole and the 60th parallel the sea is covered with floating ice of enormous size, which is never met with in the North Atlantic. From this fact he has deduced that the antarctic circle incloses considerable continents, as icebergs cannot form in the open waters of the sea, but only on coasts.

According to these computations, the mass of ice surrounding the South Pole forms a vast cap, the circumference of which must be at least twenty-five hundred miles.

Now the "Nautilus," for fear of running aground, had halted some three cable lengths from a strand above which a superb cliff of rocks reared its proud head. The pinnace was launched. The captain, two of his men with instruments, Conseil, and I were in it. It was ten o'clock in the morning. I had not seen hide or hair of Ned Land. Doubtless the Canadian refused to admit the existence of the South Pole, at any rate at this particular place. A few strokes of the oars brought us to the sandy beach, where we ran ashore. Conseil was preparing to jump from the gunwale of the pinnace to the land when I restrained him.

"Sir," I said to the captain, "to you belongs the honor of first setting foot on this strip of soil."

"Thank you for your courtesy, Professor," the commander replied. "And if I do not hesitate to step on dry land here, it is because up to this moment no human being has left any trace of his presence."

With these rather vindictive words, the strange man jumped lightly upon the sand. His heart must have beat with strong emotion, no matter how successfully his outward mien might disguise the fact. He scaled a rock that sloped up toward a small promontory. And there, with his arms crossed on his breast, mute and motionless, he stood.

With the eager look of an eagle from its eerie he seemed to take possession of these southern regions. After five minutes or more of such rapt contemplation he turned to us.

"When you like, sir," he said to me.

I landed, followed by Conseil. We left the two men in the boat. For a long way, as we strolled together, the soil was composed of a reddish sandy stone, something like crushed brick. Scoriae, streams of lava, pumice stones were strewn about everywhere. It was of unmistakably volcanic origin. In fact, in certain parts, slight curls of smoke emitted a sulphurous smell. This proved to me that the internal fires beneath us had lost nothing of their expansive powers. And yet, when I had ascended a steep escarpment, I could see no sign of a volcano within a radius of several miles.

We know that in these antarctic countries James Ross found two craters in full activity, the Erebus and the Terror, on the 167th meridian, latitude 77° 32′.

The vegetation of this desolate continent seemed to me to be curiously restricted. A few lichens of the species

Usnea melanoxantha lay upon the black rocks. Some microscopic plants, rudimentary diatomas (a kind of cell), I discovered struggling out from between two quartz shells. Long purple and scarlet fuci were supported on little swimming bladders which the breakers brought to shore. These constituted, so far as I could see, the meager flora of this region.

The beach was strewn with mollusks, tiny mussels, limpets, smooth heart-shaped bucards, and particularly some curious clios. These had membranous bodies, the head of which was composed of two rounded lobes. I likewise noted myriads of northern clios, one and a quarter inches long, of which a whale would swallow a whole world at a single mouthful. And, lastly, several charming pteropods, perfect sea butterflies, animated the waters on the skirts of the shore.

Among other zoöphytes there appeared on the high bottoms certain coral shrubs of the sort that, according to James Ross, lives in the antarctic seas to a depth of more than a thousand yards. Then there were little halcyons, belonging to the species *Procellaria pelagica,* as well as a large number of asteriads peculiar to these climates. Star-fish everywhere studded the soil.

But where life was most abounding and intense was in the air. There thousands of birds fluttered and flew. They were of all kinds and fairly deafened us with their shrill cries. Other feathered folk crowded the rocks and looked down at us without fear as we passed. They even pressed familiarly close to our feet, and one had to exercise unusual caution not to harm them in an unwary moment.

There were penguins, of course. Heavy as these odd customers are when on the land, in the water they are so agile that they have frequently been mistaken for bonitos. They constituted a large congregation and were most sober in gesture and attitude, but they kept uttering the harshest sort of cry and were most extravagant in their clamor.

Among the birds I noticed the chionis, of the long-legged family. These are as large as pigeons, white and with a conical beak, the eyes framed in a red circle. Conseil eagerly laid in a stock of them, for these winged creatures, when properly prepared, make a most agreeable meat.

Albatrosses passed us, birds that are with great justice called the vultures of the ocean. Their expanse of wing is at least four and one-half yards. Gigantic petrels swooped lazily to land. Damiers, a kind of small duck, were represented by hundreds. The under part of their body is black and white, checkered. Then there was a whole series of ordinary petrels, some whitish with brown-bordered wings, others blue all over. This fowl is peculiar to antarctic seas and, as I told Conseil, so oily that the inhabitants of the Ferroe Islands have nothing further to do, when they use them as lamps, but stick a wick in them.

"When this species evolves a bit more," Conseil said, with mock gravity, "perhaps Mother Nature will have provided each member with that necessary little wick."

About half a mile farther on, the soil was riddled as if with a storm of cannon shot. Here was the laying ground for ruffs, many of which birds might be seen issuing from their buried nests. Captain Nemo had them hunted and killed by the hundred. They were nearly the size of geese, but they gave vent to an unearthly cry, much like the braying of an ass. Their body was slate-colored, white beneath, and with a yellow stripe around their throats. They allowed themselves to be killed with stones, not even trying to escape.

Now the sun did not lift the fog and had not shown itself by a single glimmer as late as eleven o'clock. Its absence somehow made me quite uneasy, for without its aid observations were impossible. How could we then decide whether we had reached the pole or not?

When I rejoined Captain Nemo, I found him leaning on a piece of rock, silently watching the sky. He seemed impatient and vexed, but what was there to do to mend the situation? This rash and powerful man could not command the sky as he could the sea. Thus noon arrived and passed without the sun's showing itself for an instant. We could not even guess its approximate position behind the curtain of impenetrable fog. And soon the fog turned to snow!

"Till tomorrow, my friends," said the captain quietly.

And we returned heavy-hearted to the "Nautilus," whipped by a gathering wind of great force and a very tempest of stinging snow.

These atmospheric disturbances continued until the next day. It was impossible to stay on the platform. From the drawing-room, where I was writing my notes of the incidents during our excursion to the polar continent, I could catch the cries of petrels and albatrosses sporting on the wings of the hurricane.

The submarine did not lie idle. It worked its way carefully along the coast, advancing ten miles more to the south. This was done in the half-light left by the sun as it skirted the edge of the horizon.

Next day, the 20th of March, the snow had ceased. The cold was slightly greater, the thermometer registering 2 degrees below zero, Centigrade. The fog seemed to be definitely rising, and I had hopes that on this day our observations might be taken. As Captain Nemo had not yet put in an appearance, the pinnace landed Conseil and myself.

The soil in this new spot was still of a volcanic nature. Everywhere were the traces of lava, scoriae, and basalt. But, as on yesterday, I could find no trace of the volcano which had spewed them forth. The land again was fairly alive with birds, but they now shared their dominion with large troops of sea mammals which regarded us from soft eyes. There were present several varieties of seal. Some were stretched on the earth, some reposed on cakes of ice, but many were going in and out of the sea for bath and breakfast. As they had never had any experience with man and his ways, they did not flee on our approach, a fact that made me feel as if I were walking in a dream. And I calculated that here alone there was provision for hundreds of vessels.

"Sir," said Conseil, "will you tell me the names of these creatures which resemble the seals and yet are not of them?"

"Walruses, my lad. Let us go where we can observe their actions to greater advantage."

It was now eight o'clock in the morning. Four hours, at least, remained to us before exact observations could be gained from the sun. I therefore directed our steps toward a vast bay that cut into the steep granite shore. There (I swear it) earth and ice were literally lost to sight because of the numbers of sea mammals that covered them. Involuntarily I looked about me in search of old Proteus, the mythological shepherd that tended the immense flocks of Neptune.

Here were more seals than anything else, divided into distinct groups, male and female—the father watching over his family, the mother suckling her young, some of the little ones already strong enough to waddle a few steps. When they wished to change their location, the seals took short jumps, made by the contraction of their bodies and aided, rather awkwardly, by their imperfect fin. This member, in the case of the seal's congener, the lamantin, constitutes a perfect forearm. I must add that, because of their flexible spine, their smooth close skin, and their webbed feet, these creatures swim most admirably. Water is their native element.

When resting on the earth the seals assume the graceful attitudes of a beautiful woman. The ancients observed their soft and wistful glances, which cannot be outdone by the most expressive look a woman gives, their clear velvety eyes, their charming poses, and the poetry of their muscular ripplings. And rightly the old poets metamorphosed them, the male into a triton, the female into a mermaid.

I called Conseil's attention to the considerable development of the lobes of the brain in these very interesting cetaceans. Except for man, no mammal has such a quantity of cerebral matter. They are thus capable of receiving a certain amount of education, are easily domesticated, and, naturalists believe, seals, if properly taught, would be of great service as fishing dogs, both trackers and retrievers. The greater part of those in our purview slept on the sand or the rocks.

Among the seals, properly so called, which have no external ears (herein they differ from the otter, whose ears are prominent), I noticed several varieties of stenorhynchi. These latter are some three yards in length, with a white coat and bulldog heads. They are armed with ten teeth in each jaw, four incisors above and below and two large canines cut in the form of a fleur-de-lis. Among these stenorhynchi glided sea elephants, a sort of seal that has a short flexible trunk. The full-grown of this species measured twenty feet around and ten and one-half yards in length. But they did not move an inch as we approached.

"These fellows are not as dangerous as they look?" asked Conseil.

"They are placid enough unless you attack them. But when they are called upon to defend their young, their rage is terrible. And it is not uncommon for them to break fishing boats in pieces."

"You can't blame them for that, sir."

"Nor do I wish to, Conseil."

Two miles farther on we were halted by the promontory that shelters the bay from southerly winds. Beyond this point we heard loud bellowings such as a troop of ruminants might utter.

"Good heavens!" said Conseil, somewhat disconcerted. "Are we listening to a concert of bulls?"

"Let us say rather to a concert of walruses."

"They must be having a Homeric battle!"

"Or an unusual amount of fun. I have a fancy they are playing."

We now began to scale the blackish rocks to the accompaniment of many an unforeseen stumble and over stones made slippery by ice. More than once I practiced a neat half-somersault, but at the expense of my lumbar muscles. Conseil, more prudent or more sure-footed, kept his equilibrium. And he offered me good advice in this matter:

"If you'll be kind enough to spread your feet more widely, sir, you'll preserve a better balance."

On our arrival at the upper ridge of the promontory I saw a vast white plain covered with walruses. My conjecture had been right—they were playing games together, and the bellowings we had heard had been cries of joy and not of anger.

We passed as close to these curious animals as we cared to, for they did not budge from their locations. I examined them leisurely. Their skins were thick and wrinkled, of a yellowish tint akin to red, and their hair was short and scant. Some of them were four and a quarter yards long. They seemed at once more placable and less timid than their congeners of the north, and therefore did not place sentinels around the outskirts of their encampment.

After a protracted study of this city of walruses I

began to consider our return. It was eleven o'clock, and if Captain Nemo should find conditions favorable for his observations, I wished to be present when they were made. We followed a narrow trail which ran along the summit of the steep shore. By fast walking, at half-past eleven we reached the spot where we landed hours before. The boat had run aground, bringing the captain with it. I saw him standing on a rock of basalt, his instruments beside him, his eyes fixed on the northern horizon, near which the sun was then describing a lengthened curve. Without speaking, I took up a position beside him and waited.

Noon arrived. As on the day before, the sun did not appear. It was nothing less than a fatality. Observations must await the pleasure of the sun, but they could not tarry more than one day longer. For, if they were not successfully accomplished on the morrow, we should be compelled to give up all idea of getting any.

It was the 20th day of March. Tomorrow was the equinox. The sun would then disappear below the horizon for six months, and coincident with its vanishing the long polar night would begin. Since the September equinox, it had emerged from the northern horizon, rising by lengthened spirals until the 21st of December. At this period, when the summer solstice of the northern regions occurs, it had begun to descend, and on the morrow was to shed its last rays upon us. I communicated my fears and my observations to Captain Nemo.

"You are right, M. Aronnax," he said. "If I cannot take the altitude of the sun tomorrow, I shall be unable to measure it for six months. On the other hand, precisely because fate has led me to these seas on the 21st of March, my bearings will be easy to secure if at twelve o'clock we can see the sun."

"But why, sir? I should imagine the direct opposite to be the case. For then the sun will describe such lengthened curves that it should be difficult and not easy to measure exactly its height above the horizon. In fact, at such a time the gravest errors are made in reading the instruments, and excusably so."

"Granted, Professor. But I shall not bother to measure the altitude of the sun in the way you imagine."

"Not measure it!" I cried.

"I shall use only my chronometer," replied the commander. "If tomorrow, March 21, the disk of the sun, allowing for refraction, is exactly cut by the northern horizon, this will show conclusively that I am at the pole."

"Just so," I agreed. "But this statement is not mathematically correct, because the equinox does not necessarily begin at noon."

"Very likely, sir, it does not. But the error possibly will not exceed one hundred yards, and that is near enough for me. Till tomorrow, then!"

The commander returned on board. Conseil and I remained behind to survey the shore. And we studied and examined our materials both animate and inanimate until five o'clock. I went to bed very early that evening, but not before invoking the favor of the sun as a North American Indian would have done.

Next day, March 21, at five o'clock in the morning I mounted to the platform. I found Captain Nemo there.

"The weather is lightening a bit," he said at once. "My hopes are in the ascendant. We might go ashore right after breakfast and choose a good post for observation."

This important matter settled to mutual satisfaction, I went off in search of Ned Land. I wanted to take him with us. But the obstinate Canadian refused, and I noticed that his taciturnity and his evil humors were becoming more pronounced with each new day. In a way I was not sorry to have him refuse to go with us. For there were, indeed, too many seals on shore for so unregenerate a harpooner. And we ought not to lay such temptation to murder in this unreflecting mariner's path.

Breakfast was eaten with dispatch, and we went on shore. I found that during the night the "Nautilus" had gone some miles farther up the coast. It was now stationed a whole league from the shore, above which a sharp peak loomed some five hundred yards in height. Besides my unworthy self, the boat carried Captain Nemo, two members of the crew, and the instruments, consisting of chronometer, telescope, and barometer.

While crossing to the mainland I saw numerous whales of the three kinds that are peculiar to the southern seas. The English right whale which has no dorsal fin; the finback, of a yellowish brown, the liveliest of all cetaceans; and the humpback (or balaenopteron), with reeved chest and large whitish fins which, in spite of its name, do not form wings—these three species were before me. The finback is an especially powerful creature, and it can be heard a long distance off when it is throwing to a great height columns of air and vapor which look like whirlwinds of smoke.

These various mammals were disporting themselves in troops in the quiet, friendly waters. And I could realize that this basin of the Antarctic Pole served as a place of refuge to the cetaceans which were too closely pursued and tracked down by whalers. I also noticed the presence of long whitish lines of salpae, a sort of gregarious mollusk, and also large medusae floating between the eddies of the waves.

At nine o'clock we landed. The sky was brightening, the clouds were scudding southward, and the fog seemed to be taking a tearful but definite farewell of the cold surface of the waters. Captain Nemo stalked off toward the peak, which he doubtless meant to use as his observatory.

It was a painful ascent over sharp lava and pumice stones. And we were in an atmosphere impregnated with a sulphurous odor which rose from smoking crevices underfoot. For a man accustomed to walk on firm ground, the commander scaled the steep slopes with an agility that I never saw equaled elsewhere, and one which a practiced hunter would have envied. We were full two hours reaching the summit of this peak, which was made half of porphyry, half of basalt.

From this bastion we looked out upon a vast sea which distinctly traced its northern boundary upon the sky. At our feet lay ice fields of dazzling whiteness. Over our heads the canopy swam in pale azure, free from taint of mist or fog. To the north the disk of the sun appeared like a ball of fire already horned by the cutting of the horizon. From the bosom of the waters rose liquid jets in sheaves of hundreds. In the distance lay the graceful "Nautilus" like a good-humored cetacean asleep on the waves. And behind us, to the south and east, an immense country ran to the horizon and beyond it, for its limits were not visible even through the glass; a chaotic heap of rocks and ice—nothing further.

The moment we arrived at the summit Captain Nemo carefully took the mean height of the barometer, for this would have to be considered in establishing his observations. At a quarter of twelve the sun, then seen only by refraction, looked like a golden disk that was shedding its last rays upon this deserted continent and upon seas which the prows of man have never yet plowed.

Captain Nemo, furnished with a lenticular glass which, by means of a mirror, corrected the refraction, watched the sun sinking slowly on its lengthened diagonal below the horizon. My heart beat as if it would burst. If the disappearance of the half-disk of the sun coincided with noon as marked by the chronometer, we were standing at the pole itself.

"Twelve o'clock!" I called in a choking voice.

"The South Pole!" replied Captain Nemo in grave tones.

He handed me the glass, which showed the sun's disk cut into two exactly equal parts by the horizon.

I looked at the last rays of light crowning the peak and at the shadows that were silently stealing up its slopes. And then it was that the commander, resting his hand on my shoulder, spoke as follows: "I, Captain Nemo, on this

21st day of March, 1868, have reached the South Pole on the 90th degree. And I hereby take possession of this portion of the globe, equal in extent to one-sixth of the continents now known to man."

"In whose name, sir?" I asked.

"In my own, M. Aronnax."

Having said which, Captain Nemo unfurled a black banner which bore an *N* in gold quartered on its bunting. Then he turned toward the orb of day, whose last rays were lapping the horizon of the sea.

"Adieu, sun!" he exclaimed. "Disappear, thou radiant shield! Rest beneath this open ocean, and let a night of six months spread its protecting wings over my new domains!"

CHAPTER XV

AN OVERTURNED MOUNTAIN

Next day, March 22, at six o'clock in the morning preparations for departure from Nemo Land began.

The last gleams of twilight were melting into night. The cold was great; the constellations were shining with an undreamed-of intensity. At the zenith glittered the wondrous Southern Cross, the North Star of the antarctic regions. The thermometer showed 12 degrees below zero, Centigrade. And, when the wind freshened, the weather was most biting. Pieces of ice appeared in the open water.

The open sea began to congeal everywhere. Numerous blackish patches spread their tentacles out on the surface, showing the formation of fresh ice. Evidently the southern basin, frozen during the six winter months of impenetrable night, became absolutely inaccessible.

But what fate met the whales during that season? Doubtless they escaped under the icebergs and sought more practicable seas. The seals and walruses, accustomed to life in the harshest climate, remained on these ice-bound shores. These creatures by instinct know how to break holes in the ice fields and keep them open. To these holes they come for breath. And when the birds, driven away by the cold, have migrated to the north, these sea mammals remain sole masters of the polar continent, monarchs, like Alexander Selkirk, of all they survey.

Our reservoirs were filling with water, and the "Nautilus" was slowly descending. At one thousand feet it stopped. Its screw then beat the waters and it advanced straight northward at a speed of fifteen miles an hour. Toward night it was already floating under the immense mass of the Great Ice Barrier.

At three o'clock in the morning I was awakened by a violent shock. I sat up in bed and listened in the darkness for sounds of some sort which would give me a clue to what had happened. Just then I was hurled from my bed to the floor. The submarine, after having struck, rebounded violently.

I groped blindly along the partition of my cabin and found my way stumblingly to the saloon, which was lighted by its luminous ceiling. The furniture was topsy-turvy. Fortunately the windows were most firmly imbedded and had held fast. The pictures on the starboard side, instead of being vertical, were clinging to the tapestry which backed them, while those of the port wall were hanging out at least a foot from the partition. The submarine was not only badly listing, it was actually lying on its starboard side! And perfectly motionless, you may be sure. I heard confusion of voices and running footsteps. But Captain Nemo did not appear. As I was crawling out of the saloon Ned Land and Conseil entered it.

"What the deuce has happened?" I called to them.

"That's what we want to know," said Conseil.

"Dash my scuppers!" exclaimed the Canadian. "I don't need to ask anybody what's up. I know well enough. The 'Nautilus' has struck, and, judging by the way she lies, she won't right herself again as she did that time in Torres Straits."

"But tell me, my lads, has she at least come to the surface of the ocean?"

"Ask us something easy, sir," said the harpooner.

"Well, we can find that out without much trouble," I answered. I consulted the manometer. To my great surprise, it registered a depth of over a hundred and eighty fathoms.

"That gets me!" I said.

"Let's ask Captain Nemo what it means," advised Conseil.

"Where'll we find him?" inquired the Canadian.

"Follow me," I remarked. "We'll run across him somewhere."

We left the saloon. There was no one in the library. By the berthrooms of the crew, near the center staircase, there was not a living soul. I thought that Captain Nemo must be in the pilot's cage, and counseled waiting for him. So we all returned to the saloon.

For twenty minutes or upward we remained thus, straining our ears to hear the slightest sound that might be made on board. And then, just as our taut nerves were ready to snap, Captain Nemo entered. He seemed not to see us. His face, generally so impassive, showed signs of uneasiness. He studied the compass silently, then the manometer. He went to the planisphere, placed his finger on a spot that represented our part of the southern seas, and ruminated. I refused to interrupt his musing. But some minutes later, when he turned to me, I said (making use of one of his own expressions when we were caught in the Torres Straits), "An incident, Captain?"

"No, sir. This time it is an accident that has befallen us."

"A very serious one?"

"To the best of knowledge, yes."

"Is there any immediate danger?"

"No. But perhaps we may later come to wish there had been."

I puzzled to find the meaning of this cryptic remark. But I understood it all too clearly in the long time that followed. Finally, when I saw that no explanation of his sentence might be expected of our commander, I returned to my questioning.

"The submarine has definitely stranded?"

"Yes, M. Aronnax."

"And this happened—how?"

"From a caprice of nature, Professor, and not through the ignorance or carelessness of man. No mistake has been made in the navigation of our vessel. But we cannot prevent equilibrium from producing its effects. We may brave or outwit human laws, but we have no power to resist natural ones."

The commander had chosen a strange moment for uttering this philosophical reflection. Who else would have preached a homily at such a moment of disaster? Again, his answer had helped me little to understand our precarious situation.

"May I inquire, sir, what is the cause of the accident?"

"An enormous block of ice, a whole mountain in fact,

has turned over," he replied calmly. "When icebergs are undermined at their base by warmer water or by reiterated shocks, their center of gravity rises, and the whole thing topples over. This is what has happened. And one of these mountains of ice, as it fell, struck the 'Nautilus.' Thereafter the berg, gliding under the ship's hull, raised it with irresistible force, throwing it into an ice bed which is not so dense. And here it is lying on its side."

"But, don't you think we might get the vessel off by emptying its reservoir tanks so it can regain its equilibrium?"

"That's the very thing we are this moment at work on. If you listen well, you can hear the pumps going full-tilt. Look at the needle of the manometer. It shows that our ship is rising, but the block of ice is likewise rising with it. Our position cannot be altered."

Surely enough, the submersible still held the same position to starboard. Perhaps it would right itself when the block ceased to exert untoward pressure. Aha! But who knows whether at just that moment of release the ship will not strike against the upper part of the Great Ice Barrier and then get frightfully crushed and mangled between the two glassy surfaces? I reflected gloomily on all the possible chances of our situation. Meanwhile the commander never removed his gaze from the dial of the manometer. Since the fall of the iceberg and our collision with it, the "Nautilus" had risen about one hundred and fifty feet, but it still listed at the same angle from the perpendicular.

Suddenly a slight movement was felt in the hold beneath us. Evidently we were righting ourselves somewhat. The things that hung along the walls of the saloon were sensibly returning to their normal position. The partitions were nearing their proper upright line. No one spoke a word. With beating hearts we watched the progress of events and felt the straightening. The boards beneath our feet became again horizontal. Ten more minutes slowly passed.

"At last we have righted," I said with a deep sigh. "But shall we float?"

Captain Nemo paused on his way to the door of the saloon.

"Certainly," he replied. "As soon as our reservoirs are emptied, then the submarine must rise to the surface of the ocean."

We were in the open sea. But at a distance of about ten yards on either side of us there rose a dazzling wall of ice. Above and beneath our ship there was the same wall—above, because the lower surface of the Great Ice Barrier stretched over us like an immense ceiling; beneath, because the overturned block, having slipped down gradually, had found a final resting place on the lateral walls of ice, which held it firmly in that position.

Thus the vessel was imprisoned in a perfect tunnel of ice more than twenty yards in width and filled with quiet water. It seemed easy for us to escape from the tunnel by going either forward or backward, and later take an open passage beneath the ice barrier, some hundreds of yards lower down.

The luminous ceiling of the saloon had been extinguished, but the room was still resplendent with intense light. This was due to the fact that the glittering walls of ice reflected back to us ever more powerfully the rays of the ship's lantern. I cannot hope to describe the effect of the voltaic rays upon the great blocks, cut into such capricious and unearthly shapes, of which every angle, ridge, and facet cast a different light, depending on the way the ice was veined. We were fairly blinded by a gleaming mine of gems, particularly sapphires, their blue rays crossing with the green of the emerald. Here and there were opal shades of wonderful softness mingling with gleaming points, which were like diamonds of fire, so brilliant that the undimmed eye could not bear them. The power of the lantern seemed to be increased a hundred fold, like a lamp shining through the lenticular plates of a great modern lighthouse.

"How beautiful!" cried Conseil.

"A sight such as it has been given to but few men to see since the creation of the world."

"Blast it!" exclaimed Ned Land. "It is superb. I am mad at being obliged to admit it. No one ever saw the like before. But I have a feeling that the sight may cost me dear. For, if I'm going to say just what I think about it, I'm afraid we're among things here that God never intended man to catch a glimpse of."

The harpooner was right. It was too beautiful. Suddenly a cry of pain from Conseil made me wheel around.

"Are you hurt—injured? What's the matter, my boy?"

"Shut your eyes, sir, please! Oh, don't look, sir!"

Saying which, Conseil promptly clapped both hands tight down over his eyes and held them there.

"Are you in terrible pain?" I asked him fearfully.

"Oh, I am blind, sir, stone-blind!"

Involuntarily my eyes turned again to the panel, but I found that I too could not endure the fire that seemed to devour them. In a flash I realized what had occurred. The "Nautilus" had put on full speed. All the quiet luster of the ice walls was in a second changed into blasts of lightning. The fire from these myriads of diamonds was too dazzling to be borne. It required several minutes before we could once more open our smarting eyes without pain. At last our hands were lowered, however, and our sight restored.

"My faith!" ejaculated Conseil. "I should never have believed it."

It was then five o'clock in the morning. And just as the clock was announcing the hour a shock was felt at the bows of the submarine. It must have been the result of some false maneuver, for this undersea tunnel obstructed by blocks could not be easy of navigation. I judged that Captain Nemo, by changing his course somewhat, would either turn these obstacles or else follow the windings of the tunnel. In any case, I thought, the road before us could not be entirely blocked.

But, contrary to my expectations, our vessel now took a decided retrograde motion.

"Aren't we going backward?" asked Conseil.

"Yes, my boy. It looks as if this end of the tunnel can have no proper egress."

"What's the next move, then, sir?"

"An elemental one. We'll just go right back to where we came from and keep going farther in the same direction. We'll get out by the southern opening."

In speaking as I did, I took pains to appear more confident than I really felt. But the retrograde motion of the submarine was increasing. With reversed screw, we were being transported with great speed.

"It will be a hindrance to our plans to go out the back door," complained Ned Land.

"What do a few hours matter, one way or the other, provided we get out at last, you old croaker?"

"Just so, sir," retorted the Canadian, "if we get out at last and alive."

I got up from my chair in the saloon and, to rest my tired bones a little, went into the library. My companions were silent after I left them, so I threw myself on an ottoman and took up a book, which my eyes began to read quite mechanically. A quarter of an hour later Conseil appeared by my side and asked, "Is what you are reading interesting, sir?"

"Very interesting, indeed," I answered.

"I should imagine it might be, sir. It's your own book, you know."

And indeed, on examination, I saw that I was holding in my hands the work I had written on submarine depths. Besides, I was holding it upside down! Thereafter my friends and I determined to remain together until we had successfully passed out of the block.

Some hours passed. I often consulted the instruments.

The manometer showed that the "Nautilus" kept at a constant depth of more than three hundred yards. The compass still pointed to the south. The log indicated a speed of twenty miles an hour, which, in so cramped a space, was exceedingly high. But Captain Nemo understood that he could hardly hasten too fast, and that minutes might be worth ages to us.

At twenty-five minutes past eight a second shock took place, this time from behind. I turned pale. My companions were close by my side. I seized Conseil's hand. Our looks expressed our feeling better than words could have done. At this moment the commander entered the saloon. I went up to him.

"Our course is barred on the south?" I asked.

"Yes, M. Aronnax. The iceberg in turning over has closed every outlet."

"We are walled in on every side, then?"

"I regret to report that we are, sir."

CHAPTER XVI

A LIVING TOMB

Around the "Nautilus," above and below it, was an impenetrable wall of ice. We were prisoners to the Great Ice Barrier.

I watched the captain narrowly. His face was as calm as ever.

"Gentlemen," he said imperturbably, "there are two ways of dying in the circumstances in which we find ourselves placed. The first is to be crushed; the second is to die of suffocation."

(Really, it was too absurd! This strange person had the air of a professor of mathematics lecturing to his students.)

"I do not speak of a third possibility, dying of hunger. For the supply of provisions in our larder is certain to last longer than we shall. Let us calculate our chances, if you please."

"As to suffocation, sir," I suggested, "that is hardly to be feared. Because our reservoirs are full."

"Exactly. But they will yield only a two days' supply of air. Now, for thirty-six hours we have already been hidden beneath the water, and the heavy atmosphere of our ship requires renewal at this very instant. In forty-eight hours our reserve will be exhausted."

"But may we not hope for deliverance before that time?"

"We shall try, at least, to escape our trap. We shall pierce the wall that surrounds us."

"On which side, Captain?"

"Sound will tell us that, Professor. I am going to run the ship aground on the lower bank, and my men will attack the iceberg on the wall that is least thick."

Captain Nemo left the room. Soon afterward I discovered by a hissing noise that the water was entering our tanks. The submarine sank slowly, and finally came to rest on the ice at a depth of three hundred and fifty yards, the level at which the lower base of the berg was immersed.

"My dear friends," I said to my two companions, "this is a very serious business, but I can rely upon your energy and courage."

"Oh, Professor," replied the harpooner, "I'm ready to do my bit for the general safety, as you know I am."

"I do, indeed, Ned," I asserted vigorously, and I held my hand out for him to grasp.

"And there's another thing," he continued. "I'm just as handy with the pick as with the harpoon. And if the captain finds any use for my services, he has only to shout for me."

"Come on, my lad. He will not refuse your offer."

I conducted him to the room where at that moment the crew of the "Nautilus" were getting into their cork jackets. I told the commander of Ned's proposal, which he delightedly accepted. The Canadian put on his sea costume and was ready as soon as any of his companions.

When Ned was dressed, I went back to the drawing-room, where the panels were open. Posted near Conseil,

I examined through the panes of glass the encompassing beds that supported our submarine. Some instants later we saw a dozen of the crew set foot on the bank of ice, and in their midst walked our friend, noticeable because of his great stature. Captain Nemo was with them.

Before anyone proceeded to dig at the walls the commander took his soundings, to make sure that they would work in the right direction. Long sounding lines were sunk in the side walls, but after fifteen yards they were again brought to a stop by the thick mass of ice. It was evidently useless to attack the ice on the ceiling-like surface, since the Great Barrier itself measured more than four hundred yards in height.

The commander then sounded the lower surface. There he discovered that ten yards of ice separated him from the water, so great was the thickness of the ice field. It was therefore necessary to cut from this substance a piece equal in extent to the water line of the submarine. That meant that there would be about six thousand cubic yards to detach so as to dig a hole by which we could descend.

The work was commenced at once and carried on with tireless energy. Instead of having his men dig around the frame of the submarine itself, Captain Nemo bade them make an immense trench at eight yards from the port quarter. First, the men set to work simultaneously with their great screws and wedges at several points of the indicated circumference of the trench to be excavated. Presently the pickaxe attacked this compact matter vigorously, and large blocks were thus laboriously separated from the mass.

By a curious result of specific gravity, these blocks, which were lighter than water, flew to the vault of the tunnel, the moment they were released from their restraining bed. The vault therefore grew in thickness at the top in proportion as it diminished at the base. But that fact was of trivial importance just so long as the lower part grew thinner. After two hours of exhausting, heart-straining labor, Ned Land returned, thoroughly done in. He and his fellows were replaced by new workers, whom Conseil and I joined.

The second officer of the "Nautilus" superintended our efforts. The water seemed singularly cold in the beginning, but I soon warmed through by handling a pickaxe. My movements were free enough, although they were being made under a pressure of thirty atmospheres. When I reëntered the ship, after two hours of the hardest work I had ever thought to do, I found a perceptible difference between the pure fluid air supplied me by the Rouquayrol apparatus and the atmosphere of the "Nautilus," which was already somewhat charged with carbonic acid. The air had not been renewed for forty-eight hours, and its vivifying qualities were consequently so enfeebled that I scarcely found enjoyment either in my food or in my rest from strenuous labor.

After a lapse of twelve hours, however, it was discovered that we had succeeded in raising only one block one yard thick on the marked surface, which was about six hundred cubic yards. Reckoning that it had consumed twelve hours to accomplish this much, it would require five nights and four days to bring our undertaking to a satisfactory conclusion.

"Jerusalem crickets!" said Ned when informed of this fact. "Five nights and four days! With only enough air in reserve for two days? And without taking into account that, even if we do get out of this infernal tunnel, we shall still be imprisoned beneath the iceberg, and so shut off from all possible communication with the air."

True enough! And who could prophesy the minimum of time necessary for our entire deliverance? We might be suffocated after our escape from the tunnel, but before the submarine could reach the surface of the waves! Was this unique ship destined to perish in this tomb of ice, together with all its precious contents? The situation was desperate. But by now each one of us had looked the danger squarely in the face, and each was resolved to do his duty to the bitter end.

As I expected, during the night another block a yard square was carried away. The immense hollow sank thereby still farther. But in the morning when, dressed in my cork jacket, I traversed the slushy mass in a temperature of 6 or 7 degrees below zero, I noticed that the side walls were gradually closing in. The beds of water farthest from the trench, that had not been warmed by the men's working, likewise showed a tendency to solidification. In the presence of this new and imminent danger, what would become of our chances for safety? And by what means could we prevent the solidification of this liquid medium, an event that would burst the partitions of the submarine like glass?

I said nothing of this fearful discovery to my comrades. What possible use could it serve to dampen the energy they were displaying in the painful work of liberation? But when I went on board again, I informed Captain Nemo of the grave complication.

"I already knew it," he said in that calm tone which could counteract the most hysterical apprehensions. "It is one danger added. But I see no way of avoiding it. Our only chance of safety is to work faster than solidification does. We must beat it at the barrier; that is all we can do."

On this day I handled the pickaxe vigorously for several hours. The work kept my spirit from fainting. Besides, hard as the outside labor was, it gave me a chance to quit the submarine and to breathe directly the pure air drawn from the reservoirs and supplied by our apparatus instead of the impoverished and vitiated atmosphere of the ship. Toward evening the trench was dug one yard deeper. When I returned on board, I was nearly choked by the carbon dioxide with which the air was filled.

Ah, if we only had the chemical means to drive away this deleterious gas!

We had plenty of oxygen. All this water contained a considerable quantity of it, and by dissolving it with our powerful piles the vivifying fluid would be restored. I had pondered the matter well. But of what good was that, since the carbon dioxide produced by our breathing had already invaded every part of the vessel? To absorb it, it would be necessary to fill some jars with caustic potash, and to shake them incessantly. Now, as I happened to know, this substance was wanting on board, and nothing else could replace it.

On that evening Captain Nemo ought to open the taps of his reservoirs and let some pure air into the interior of the "Nautilus." Except for this precaution, we could not get rid of the terrible, ever-present sense of suffocation.

The next day, March 26, I resumed my miner's work in the beginning of the fifth yard of our excavation. The side walls and the lower surface of the ice barrier had thickened visibly. It was now evident that they would meet before the submarine could disengage itself. Despair so seized hold on me for a moment that I nearly let the pickaxe fall from my hands. What was the good of this eternal, back-breaking, heart-bursting digging if we must be suffocated in the end just the same? Crushed by the water that was inevitably turning to stone! A punishment that the ferocity of savages itself would not have invented!

Just then Captain Nemo passed near me. I touched his hand and pointed out to him the walls of our prison. The side to port had advanced to at least four yards from the hull of our ship. The commander understood my silent gesture and signaled me to follow him. We went on board. I took off my cork jacket and accompanied him into the drawing-room.

"M. Aronnax," he said, "we must attempt some desperate means or we shall be sealed up in this solid water as in cement."

"Dear God, yes!" I cried. "But what is there to do?"

"Ah, if my ship were only stout enough to withstand this pressure without being crushed!"

"A foolish wish!" I said, not catching the captain's idea.

"You do not understand," he replied. "Why, man, this congelation of water might help us. Can't you see that, by its very solidification, it would burst through this field of ice that imprisons us? Just as, when it freezes, ice bursts the hardest stones? Do you not perceive that it would be an agent of deliverance and not of destruction?"

"Yes, Captain, perhaps. But, whatever resistance your vessel possesses, it could not support this terrible pressure, and it would be flattened thinner than a pancake."

"I know it, sir. Therefore, we must not trust to the aid of nature, but rather rely upon our own exertions. We must stop this solidification. Our danger at present is not only from the side walls pressing together. There is now not ten feet of water before or behind the submarine. The congelation is gaining on us from every side."

"How much longer will the air in the reservoirs last for us to breathe on board?"

The captain looked me in the face. "After tomorrow they will be empty," he said.

A cold sweat broke out on me. And yet, after all, ought I to have been astonished at the answer? On March 22 the submarine was in the open polar seas. It was now the 26th. For five days we had lived on the reserve on board. And what was left of the respirable air must now be kept for the workers. The thought seemed to deflate my lungs utterly of air. Meanwhile Captain Nemo was reflecting silently. It was evident that a new idea had come to him, but he seemed ready to reject it. At last these words escaped his lips, "Boiling water might do it."

"Boiling water?" I asked.

"Certainly, sir. We are inclosed in a space that is relatively confined. Would not jets of boiling water, constantly injected by the pumps, raise the temperature in this part and stay the congelation?"

"Let us try it, anyway," I said, excitedly.

"That's just what we will do, M. Aronnax."

The thermometer then stood at 7 degrees outside. Captain Nemo took me with him to the galleys, where stood the vast distillatory machines which made sea water drinkable by evaporation. Men filled these machines with water, and all the electric heat from the piles was thrown through the coils in the midst of the liquid. In a few minutes this water reached 100 degrees Centigrade.

It was then directed toward the pumps, while fresh water replaced it in proportion. The heat developed by the piles was soon such that cold water, drawn from the sea, after having but gone through the machines, came boiling into the body of the pump. The injection was then begun, and three hours afterward the thermometer marked 6 degrees below zero, outside. One degree had thus been gained. Two hours later the thermometer marked only 4 degrees.

"We shall succeed," I said to the captain, after I had anxiously watched the result of the operation for some time.

"I think," he said, "that we shall not be crushed, at least. We have only suffocation to fear now."

During the night the temperature of the water rose to one degree below zero. The injections from the pumps

could not bring it to a higher point. But for them to hold
it there was sufficient to guard against congelation of sea
water. And I was finally sure that danger from solidification was past.

The next day, March 27, six yards' depth of ice had
been disposed of, and only four more remained to be cleared
away. This meant that there was yet full two days' work
to do. The air could no longer be renewed on the "Nautilus," and from now on things must therefore get steadily
worse. An intolerable weight oppressed me. Toward
three o'clock in the afternoon this burdensome feeling increased to a violent degree. Yawns fairly dislocated my
jaws. My lungs panted as they inhaled the burning fluid
of air, which was becoming more and more rarified.

And now a torpor of my brain and moral sense took
hold of me. I grew powerless to exercise my will and was
almost unconscious. My brave servant (may heaven
reward him for his kindness!), though exhibiting the same
symptoms and suffering in like manner, never left my side.
He took my hand and encouraged me to persevere. As
if through a veil of sleep I heard him murmur, "Oh, if I
could but stop breathing, so as to leave more air for my
good master!"

Tears of weakness and emotion came into my eyes as
I heard this loyal speech.

The situation in the interior of the vessel was as
unbearable to others as to ourselves. With what joy and
haste, therefore, did we put on our cork jackets when our
turn to work came! Pickaxes rang unintermittently on
the frozen ice beds. Our joints ached, the skin was torn

from our hands. But what did such things matter—
fatigues, wounds, death itself—compared to the fact that
vital air was entering our lungs, and that we breathed!
breathed!

And yet, through all this time no one cheated to prolong his task outside beyond the time prescribed. The
moment his task was accomplished, each one would hand
over to his panting companion the apparatus that was sup-
plying him with life. Captain Nemo, in this as in all
else, set the shining example. And he submitted strictly
to the iron discipline which he had himself inaugurated.
When the time came for him to yield up his apparatus, he
did so and went back on board, calm and unflinching.

On that day the usual labor was accomplished with
extraordinary vigor. At the end of it but two yards
remained to do. Six feet only separated us from the open
sea and salvation. But the reservoirs were practically
empty. The little air that remained ought to be kept for
the workers. Not a particle could be used for the "Nautilus." When I returned on board I was half suffocated.
I do not know how to describe the night that followed. The
next day my breathing was oppressed and stertorous. To
the pain in my head was added nausea and vertigo—I
staggered and reeled about like a drunken man. My companions exhibited similar symptoms. Some of the crew
acquired permanent phlegm in their throats, which rattled
as they breathed.

On that day, the sixth of our confinement in an underworld inferno, Captain Nemo suddenly decided that the
axes were working too slowly. He resolved to crush the

final bed of ice that still held us from the liquid sheet beneath our feet. This strange man's coolness and energy did not forsake him for an instant. He subdued his physical pains by moral force.

By his command the vessel was lightened, that is to say, raised from the ice bed by a change of specific gravity. When it finally floated, the crew towed it with ropes and cables, so as to bring it above the immense trench made on a level with the water line. Then, after the ship's reservoirs were filled with water, she descended and slipped into the groove.

Everyone else hastened on board, and the double door of communication was shut. The "Nautilus" was then resting on a bed of ice which was not one yard thick and which the sounding leads had already penetrated in a dozen different places. The taps of the tanks were then opened, and a hundred cubic yards of water were admitted, increasing the submarine's weight to eighteen hundred tons.

We waited. We listened. We forgot our sufferings in this last mad moment of hope. Our safety depended on this one chance. And, notwithstanding the horrible humming in my head, I heard a rending sound under the ship's hull. The ice was cracking with a singular noise, like paper being torn. And the boat sank!

"We are off!" whispered Conseil, as if speaking from some vast distance.

I could not answer. I could but seize his hand and press it convulsively. All at once, carried down by its frightful overcharge of ballast, the ship descended like a bullet beneath the waters. It fell like a meteorite in a vacuum.

Every bit of electric force was switched to the pumps, which soon began to drain the water from the reservoirs. After some breathless instants our fall was stopped. Not long thereafter the manometer indicated an ascending movement. The screw, now revolving at top speed, made the iron hull tremble to its very bolts. We were drawn lightning-like northward.

But should this navigation under the iceberg last another day before we reached the open sea I should be dead.

Half stretched upon a divan in the library, I choked and sobbed in the early stages of actual suffocation. My face was purple, my lips blue, my faculties almost suspended. I neither saw nor heard. All notion of time had gone from my mind. My muscles could no longer contract. I shall, of course, never know how many hours passed thus, but I was conscious of the awful agony that was finally coming to me. I felt that I was dying.

Of a sudden I revived somewhat. Some breaths of air were entering my lungs. Had we risen to the surface of the waves? Were we free from the shackles of the Great Ice Barrier?

No. Conseil and Ned, my two brave friends, were sacrificing their own chances to save me. Some particles of air had been discovered to remain at the bottom of one apparatus. Instead of using it themselves, they had treasured it for me. While they were being suffocated, they were giving me life drop by drop.

I tried to push the thing away from my lips, but they held my hands and prevented me. For some blessed moments I breathed freely. I glanced at the clock—it was eleven o'clock in the morning. It should, by rights, be the 28th of March.

The "Nautilus" was tearing along at a frightful pace— forty miles an hour. It literally ripped the waters apart.

Where was Captain Nemo? Had he succumbed? Were his companions dead with him? At the moment the manometer was registering our depth as twenty feet. A mere plate of ice separated us from the atmosphere. Could we break through it? Perhaps. In any case, the submarine was going to make the attempt. I felt that it was in an oblique position, lowering the stern, raising its bows. The introduction of water was the means by which its equilibrium had been disturbed until it could assume the inclination desired.

Then, impelled by its powerful screw, the ship attacked the ice field from below like a formidable battering-ram. It broke the mass by backing off and then rushing forward against it. The field gave way. The ship shot through and forward out on the icy pack, crushing it beneath its weight.

The panels were torn open, one might almost say torn off.

And pure air—oceans of it—flooded every part of the interior of the "Nautilus."

CHAPTER XVII

FROM CAPE HORN TO THE AMAZON

How I reached the platform I neither know nor care. It is likely I was carried there by the stalwart Canadian. (Boyish, hulking Ned, who never failed to complain of a scratch on his hide or his soul, but who had made no moan when clutched by the agony of impending death!) But there I was, breathing, inhaling the quickening sea air. My two friends were getting drunk with their great draughts of the fresh particles. Unhappy men who have been long without food cannot at first indulge in even the simplest nourishment that can be given them. But we, on the contrary, had no need to restrain ourselves. We could draw this air freely down into our lungs. And it was the breeze, and that alone, that served to afford us the keenest enjoyment of our lives.

"Aha! Such nice oxygen!" babbled Conseil. "You need now no longer fear to breathe it in, sir. For there's enough for everybody, and quite a little left over to be sent back to the kitchen."

Ned Land wasted no energy in words, but he opened his jaws widely enough to frighten a shark. Our strength soon came back, and when I looked around me I saw that we were alone on the platform. Apparently the foreign seamen in the submarine had been content to breathe the air that now circulated throughout the interior. At least, no one of them had come up to drink in the open air.

As might be expected, the first words I spoke expressed my gratitude to my two companions. They had prolonged my life during the final hours of my great agony. All my gratitude could never repay such heroic devotion.

"My friends," I said, much moved by my thoughts, "we are bound to one another forever. I am under infinite obligations to both of you, nor would I have it otherwise."

"I shall take advantage of your feelings," the Canadian said.

"Just what do you mean, old fellow?" asked Conseil.

"Why, that, because of the close bond that unites us, I shall take you people along with me whenever I leave this dodgasted 'Nautilus.' "

"Well, anyhow," remarked my servant, "now that we've decided to go on living, and now that Ned here has had his say regarding our escape, may I ask a question? Are we headed in the right direction?"

"Yes," I replied. "For we are going the way of the sun, and at this point the sun is in the north."

"No doubt of that, sir," interpolated the harpooner. "But it remains to be seen whether Captain Nemo will bring his ship into the Pacific or the Atlantic Ocean—into frequented or deserted seas."

That question I was unable to answer. But in my heart I feared our commander would prefer to lead us to that vast ocean which washes the coasts of Asia and America at the same time. He would thus complete our tour around the submarine waters of the globe and get back to that sea in which the "Nautilus" could sail freely.

This point ought to be cleared up before long, for our

ship was traveling at a rapid pace. The polar circle was soon passed, and our course shaped for Cape Horn. We were off the American point March 31 at seven o'clock in the evening. Then were all our past sufferings forgotten. The remembrance of our terrible imprisonment in the ice grew pale and was well-nigh effaced from our minds. We thought only of the future.

Captain Nemo did not show his face again, either in the drawing-room or on the bridge. Each day without fail the second in command marked our location on the planisphere, and the exact direction of the ship was therefore clear to me. Now on that last evening in March it became evident, to my great satisfaction, that we were going back north by the Atlantic route.

The next day, April 1, when the submersible rose to the surface a few minutes before noon, we sighted land to the westward. It was Tierra del Fuego, to which the first navigators assigned this queer name when they saw great quantities of smoke issuing from the native huts. The shore seemed low to me, but in the distance high mountains towered aloft. I even fancied I caught a glimpse of Mount Sarmiento, which rises two thousand and seventy yards above the level of the sea. It has an extremely pointed summit that indicates what the weather is going to be, according as it is misty or clear. At this moment of my observation the peak was clearly defined against the sky.

Our ship dove again beneath the waves and approached the coast, which was but a few miles off. From the glass windows in the saloon I saw long seaweeds, gigantic fuci, and varech. The open polar sea contains very many varieties of this last weed, all of them with sharp polished filaments. They measure about three hundred yards in length, and are real cables thicker than one's thumb. Because of their great tenacity they are frequently used as ropes by vessels.

Another weed, known as velp, with leaves four feet long buried in the coral concretions, carpeted the floor of the ocean. It served both as a nesting place and as food for myriads of crustaceans and mollusks, crabs and cuttle-fish. Otters and seals had splendid repasts of it, too— eating their fish flesh with sea vegetables according to the fashion of English dinner tables. Over this fertile and luxuriant ground the submarine passed with great rapidity.

Toward evening it approached the Falkland group, the rugged summits of which I recognized the following day. The depth of the sea was moderate. Off the shores of these islands our nets brought in some beautiful specimens of seaweed, and particularly a certain fucus the roots of which are laden with the best mussels in all the world, bar none. Geese and ducks fell by dozens on our platform and soon took their places in the pantry on board.

With regard to fish, I specially observed a few speci-mens of the goby species, nearly two feet long and plastered all over with white and yellow spots. I admired also numerous medusae; in fact I found the finest sort of them in the crysaora, which is peculiar to the Falkland Isles. I should have liked to preserve some specimens of the deli-cate zoöphytes, but they are without life, like clouds, shadows and apparitions that evaporate and fade away when they are removed from their native element.

When the last headlands of the Falkland Isles had disappeared below the horizon, the "Nautilus" sank to a depth of twenty yards or more and followed the American coast. Our commander disappeared utterly from our ken. We did not quit the shores of Patagonia until April 3, when we passed beyond the large estuary formed by the mouth of the Plata. On the 4th of April we were fifty-six miles off Uruguay. The direction of our ship was northward, and it followed the excessively long windings of the broken coast line of South America. We had by this time made sixteen thousand leagues since our embarkation in the seas of Japan.

About eleven o'clock in the morning the tropic of Capricorn was crossed on the 37th meridian, and we sighted Cape Frio standing out to sea. To Ned Land's great displeasure, Captain Nemo did not seem to care for the neighborhood of the inhabited coasts of Brazil, for we shot ahead at a giddy speed. Not a bird, not a fish of the swiftest habit of flight could keep pace with us, and so it came about that the natural curiosities of these waters quite escaped our observation. I was somewhat disappointed at all this, but, being a fatalist in my attitude toward life, I shrugged my shoulders and thought of other things.

This burst of speed was maintained for several days without let-up, and in the evening of the 9th of April we sighted that most easterly point of all South America which forms Cape San Roque. At this spot the "Nautilus" swerved again and sought the lowest depth of a submarine valley which lies between this cape and Sierra

Leone on the far-off African coast. This valley bifurcates in the latitude of the Antilles and terminates at the north by the enormous depression of nine thousand yards. In this place the geological basin of the ocean forms, as far as the Lesser Antilles, a cliff of three and one-half miles of perpendicular height. And in the latitude of the Cape Verde Islands the basin forms another wall no less considerable. These thus inclose all the sunken continent of Atlantis.

The floor of this unthinkably immense valley is dotted with several mountains that lend to these undersea regions a picturesque aspect. In my description I am speaking, of course, from what I saw at this time through the window panels of the saloon. But beyond this I had for consultation the manuscript charts from the library of the "Nautilus"—evidently the work of Captain Nemo's hand and made from his personal observations. For two whole days the deep deserted waters were visited by means of the inclined planes. Besides these, the submarine was furnished with long diagonal broadsides, which carried it to any desired elevation. But on the 11th of April the ship rose suddenly, and land appeared at the mouth of the Amazon River, a vast estuary the embouchure of which is so great that it freshens the water of the sea for the distance of several leagues.

The equator was passed. Twenty miles to the west were the Guianas, a French territory on which we might easily have found asylum. But a stiff breeze was blowing, and the furious waves would not have permitted a small boat to live a minute in them. Ned Land undoubtedly realized this fact, no doubt, for he made no mention of an attempt to escape. For my part, I was glad enough to speak no word regarding flight, since I was not minded to urge him to engage in an undertaking that I felt was foredoomed to failure.

I managed to pass my time pleasantly in interesting studies. During the days of April 11 and 12 the ship did not leave the surface of the ocean, and the nets brought in a most marvelous haul of zoöphytes, fish, and reptiles. Some zoöphytes had been caught by the chain of the nets. They were for the most part beautiful phyctallines belonging to the actinidian family, and among other species the *Phyctalis protexta,* peculiar to that part of the ocean. This has a small cylindrical trunk ornamented with vertical lines and is speckled with red dots and crowned by a wonderful blossoming of tentacles.

As to mollusks in this district, they consisted largely of those I had already observed: turritellas, olive porphyras, odd peteroceras, translucent hyaleas, argonauts, cuttlefish (excellent eating!), and certain species of calmars that naturalists of antiquity classified with the flying fish, and that nowadays serve principally as bait in the glorious sport of cod fishing. The peteroceras resemble petrified scorpions. The porphyras have regular lines intercrossed, with red spots that contrast plainly with their gray flesh.

Several species of fish that inhabit these coasts I had heretofore had no adequate opportunity to study. But how well I knew them at second hand! Among the cartilaginous ones was petromyzons-pricka, a sort of eel fifteen ınches long. It has a greenish head, violet fins, gray-blue back, and brown belly silvered and sown with bright spots. The pupil of its eye is encircled with gold—a gaudy, curious animal that the current of the Amazon had drawn into the sea, for it prefers to dwell in fresh water. Then, to go on with my list, there were tuberculated streaks, with their pointed snouts and a long loose tail armed with a long jagged sting; and little sharks a yard long, with gray and whitish skin and several rows of teeth bent backward— these are generally known by the familiar name of pan-touffles; and vespertilios, a kind of red isosceles triangle half a yard in length, to which pectorals are attached by fleshy prolongations that make them resemble bats. Their horny appendage, situated near the nostrils, has given them the name of sea unicorns. And lastly, there were several species of balistae, the curassavian, whose spots are of a brilliant gold color, and the capriscus, of clear violet and with varying shades like a pigeon's throat.

And here I end this catalog, which is somewhat dry, I fear, and yet quite exact, with a series of bony fish that I observed: passans which belong to the apteronotes, and their snout is as white as snow. Their body is a beautiful black, marked by a prolonged loose and fleshy strip. There were odontognathes, armed with spikes; sardines nine inches long, glittering with a bright silver light; a species of mackerel provided with two anal fins; centronotes of a blackish tint that are fished for with torches; long fish, two yards in length, with fat flesh, but white and firm (when fresh, they taste like eels; when dried, like smoked sal-mon); labres, half red, covered with scales only at the end of the dorsal and anal fins; chrysoptera, on whose bodies gold and silver blend their brightness with that of the ruby and the topaz; golden-tailed spares, whose flesh is extremely delicate and whose phosphorescent properties betray them in the midst of the waters; orange-colored spares with a long tongue; maigres with golden caudal-fins; dark thorn tails; and anableps of Surinam. And so forth!

Notwithstanding this "and so forth," I must not omit to mention fish that Conseil will long remember, and for the best of reasons. Now, one of our nets had caught a kind of very flat rayfish which, when the tail was cut off, formed a perfect disk and weighed twenty ounces. It was white on the underside and red above, with large round spots of dark blue encircled with black. Its skin was very glossy, terminating in a bilobed fin. When laid out on the platform, it struggled, tried to turn over with convulsive movements, and finally made so many efforts that one last turn was going to send it back into the sea, when Conseil, who attached great importance to this fish, rushed over and, before I could prevent it, had seized the small animal with both hands. In a second he was overthrown, his legs were in the air, and half his body paralyzed. He shrieked, "Oh, master, master, help me!"

It was the first time the poor boy had ever made so personal and pitiful an appeal. The Canadian and I picked him up and rubbed his contracted limbs vigorously, until he became sensible of things. The poor chap had grasped a crampfish of the most dangerous kind, the cumana. This exotic animal, in a conductive medium like water, strikes fish at several yards' distance, so great is the power of its electric organ, the two principal surfaces of which do not measure less than twenty-seven square feet.

The next day, April 12, the "Nautilus" approached the Dutch coast near the mouth of the Maroni River. There several groups of sea cows herded together. They were manatees which, like the dugong and the stellera, belong to the order of sirenians. These beautiful animals, peaceable and inoffensive, from eighteen to twenty-one feet in length, weigh at least sixteen hundredweight. I informed Ned Land and Conseil that provident nature had assigned an important rôle to these mammalia. For they, like the seals, are designed to graze on the submarine prairies and thus destroy the accumulation of weed that obstructs tropical rivers and impedes navigation.

"And, do you know," I added, "what has been the result since man has almost annihilated this useful race? Putrified weeds have poisoned the air, and this causes yellow fever, that dread desolator of these beautiful countries."

"I did not know the cause was discovered," interrupted Conseil.

"It is a recent thing," I acknowledged. "Venomous vegetation has increased under these torrid seas, and thus the evil is irresistibly developed from the mouth of the Rio de la Plata to Florida. But, if we are to believe Toussenel, this plague is as nothing to what it will become when the oceans are cleared of whales and seals. For in that case, infested with poulps, medusae, and cuttlefish, the seas would become immense centers of infection;

because then the waves would not possess 'these vast stomachs that God has charged to scour the surface of the waters.' "

While we were discussing the scientific angle of these matters, the crew of the "Nautilus," without disputing our theories, took possession of half a dozen manatees. They provided the larders with excellent flesh, superior to beef and veal. The sport of killing was not a whit interesting. The manatees permitted themselves to be hit without defending themselves. Several thousand pounds of meat were stored up on board to be dried.

On this day, also, a successful haul of fish increased the stores of the submarine, so full of game were these seas.

In their number were echeneids, belonging to the third family of the malacopterygians. Their flattened disks were composed of movable transverse cartilaginous plates by which the animal was able to create a vacuum and could thus adhere to any object like a cupping-glass. The remora that I noted in the Mediterranean is a member of this species, but the one of which we are speaking now was the echeneis osteochera, peculiar to this part of the ocean.

The hunting and fishing accomplished, the ship neared the coast. Hereabouts a number of sea turtles were asleep on the surface of the sea. It would have been next to impossible to capture these precious reptiles by any ordinary means. For they are awakened by the slightest sound, and their solid shell is proof against the heaviest harpoon.

But the echeneis effects their capture with extraordinary precision and certainty. In fact, this creature is a living fishhook which should make the fortune of an inexperienced fisherman.

The crew of the submarine tied to the tail of these fish a ring not too large to encumber their movements. And to this ring they knotted a long cord, the other end of which was lashed to the ship's side. The echeneids, thrown into the sea, began the game without delay by affixing themselves to the breastplate of the turtles. Their tenacity was such, after they had secured their hold, that they were torn to pieces rather than relinquish their grip. The men of the crew calmly hauled them back up to the ship, and with them the great turtles to which they adhered.

We also bagged several cacouannes a yard long, weighing four hundred pounds apiece. Their carapace is covered with large horny plates, thin, transparent, brown, with white and yellow spots, and for this reason they bring a good price in the market. Besides, they were excellent in an edible way, having quite as good a flavor as the turtles.

This day's fishing brought to an end our stay on the shores of the Amazon. And by nightfall the submarine had regained the high seas.

CHAPTER XVIII

THE POULPS

And now for several days the "Nautilus" kept away from the American coast. I suspected it did not care to risk the tides of the Gulf of Mexico, or perhaps of the sea of the Antilles.

On April 16 we spoke Martinique and Guadaloupe from a distance of about thirty miles. I saw their tall peaks and was quite content to view them thus, shrouded in the mystery of their distant veils. But the Canadian, who undoubtedly had been counting upon attaining his cherished chance to escape while in the Gulf, was disconsolate. He had dreamed of carrying out his project either by landing or by hailing one of the swarm of boats that coast from one island to another.

Now flight would have been simple enough if Ned Land had only been able to get possession of the pinnace without the captain's knowledge. But while we were out in the open sea such a thing could not be seriously thought of.

The Canadian, Conseil, and I had a long and serious talk regarding our plan of running away. What follows is the gist of it:

For six months we had been prisoners hand and foot. We had traveled seventeen thousand French leagues, and there was no reason to believe our trip would ever come to an end. We could hope for no aid from the captain of our prison ship, but must look only to ourselves. Besides, for some time past the commander had become graver, more retiring, less sociable. He seemed to shun us. We met him rarely. Formerly he had been disposed to explain submarine marvels to us; now he left us to our own devices and came no more to the saloon.

What did this change in his demeanor signify? At any rate, it was disconcerting to us who must look forward to an indefinite term of submission to his caprices. So far as I personally was concerned, I did not wish to bury with me at sea the results of my novel and curious studies. I had now the power to write the naturalist's true book of the sea. And I very much wanted this work of mine to see the light of day, whether sooner or later.

But still! Right there through the open window of the drawing-room, ten yards below the surface of the waters of the Antilles, were the intensely interesting products of the ocean that I still had to enter among my daily notes. And when would the day definitely come on which I should willingly leave them all for the poor sake of my physical liberty of movement?

For outside the panels I could see, among other zoöphytes, those called physalis pelagica, a sort of large oblong bladder, with mother-of-pearl rays. They held out their membranes to the wind (and also to me!) and allowed their blue tentacles to float like threads of silk. To the eye they were charming medusae, to the touch they were actual nettles that distil a corrosive fluid. And how could I abandon, perhaps forever, those annelids that were just floating by the panel? Curious fellows, a yard and a half long, furnished with a pink horn and seventeen hundred locomotive organs! They wind sinuously through the waters and throw lazily forth in passing all the colorful light of the solar spectrum.

In the fish category there were some Malabar rays, enormous and gristly things ten feet long, weighing six hundred pounds. Their pectoral fin triangular in the center of a slightly humped back! The eyes fixed in the extremities of their face! The face itself seemed beyond the head proper, which floated like weft and often looked like an opaque shutter against our glass window.

There were American balistae, to whom nature has given only the workday dress of plain black and white; gobies with yellow fins and prominent jaw; mackerel sixteen feet long, with short-pointed stubs of teeth, covered with small scales and belonging to the albicore species. And then in swarms appeared the gray mullet, covered with stripes of gold from head to tail, beating their resplendent fins which seemed to be masterpieces of the jeweler's art. They were formerly consecrated to the goddess Diana, and were particularly sought after for the dinner tables of rich Romans. And yet the Latin proverb says of them: "Whoever takes them on a hook does not take them down his throat."

Lastly, I cast covetous looks at the pomacanthe dorés, ornamented with emerald bands, dressed (as it were) in velvets and silks, that sailed proudly by us like Veronese lords; and at the spurred spari with their pectoral fins; and at the clupanodons, fifteen inches long, enveloped in their mist of phosphorescent lights. Mullet beat the sea with their large jagged tails. Red vendaces seemed to mow the waves with their showy fins. And silvery selenes, worthy of their name, rose on the horizon of the waters like so many moons with whitish rays.

On April 20 the land nearest us was the archipelago of the Bahamas. There rose high submarine cliffs covered with large weeds, giant laminariae, and fuci—a perfect trellis of hydrophytes worthy of a Titan world. It was about eleven o'clock when Ned Land called my notice to a formidable movement among the large seaweeds.

"Well," I said, "these are just the sort of caverns for poulps. And I shouldn't be the least surprised to see some of these monsters turn up most any minute now."

"Honest true?" demanded Conseil. "Real cuttlefish of the cephalopod class?"

"No, my boy. But poulps of huge dimensions."

"You can't get me to believe such things exist," said Ned.

"Oh, can't I?" retorted Conseil, with the most serious face in the world. "Let me just tell you that I have a perfect recollection of seeing a great vessel dragged down beneath the waves by the arm of Mr. Cephalopod."

"You saw what?" asked the Canadian, his eyes wide with amazement.

"I surely did, Ned."

"And you were right there when it was happening?"

"Not ten yards from the fearful scene."

"Criminy! And what place was that, little cabbage?"

"At St. Malo," answered my servant, grave as a judge.

"In the open harbor, I suppose?" inquired the harpooner ironically, for he was beginning to smell a rat.

"Oh, no.   It was in a church."

"Oho, in a church!   Somebody must have been drinking wine that day, and got a wee bit befuddled."

"Nary a drink, Ned.   It was all there in the picture over the altar.   A fine large poulp and a great big boat."

"Good!" said the Canadian, bursting out laughing and slapping his leg with a hairy hand.

"Conseil is telling the truth," I asserted.   "I have heard of this picture.   But the scene of it is taken from a legend, and you know what is left of natural history after a legend gets through with it!   Besides, there's no limit to people's imaginations when they're on the subject of monsters.   Why, these poulps are not only able to draw down ships, according to Olaus Magnus.   He tells us of a cephalopod a mile long, and more like an island than an animal."

"Haha!" exclaimed Conseil.   "That makes me think of the gigantic cachalot Ned told us about that day the 'Nautilus' attacked several hundreds of them."

"And one legend tells a bigger whopper still," I continued.   "It says that the bishop of Nidros built an altar on an immense rock.   When mass had been celebrated, the rock began to stroll and walked into the sea.   The rock was a poulp.   Another bishop, the devout Pontoppidan, speaks of a poulp on which a regiment of cavalry could maneuver.   And ancient historians of nature speak calmly of monsters whose mouths were gulfs, and who were too large to pass through the Straits of Gibraltar."

"How much of such yarns is true?" asked Ned Land.

"Not a stitch of any of them, at least of all fables and

legends. Nevertheless, there must be some ground of truth for the exaggerations of the more honest kind of story. Where there is smoke, there is fire. And one can't deny that there do exist poulps and cuttlefish of a large species—although inferior in size to the cetaceans. Aristotle has given the dimensions of a cuttlefish as five cubits, or nine feet two inches."

"But I thought, sir, the largest ones our fishermen find today are hardly more than four feet," objected Conseil.

"True, my boy. Still some skeletons of poulps in the museums of Trieste and Montpelier measure two yards in length. Besides, if we believe the statements of some naturalists, one of these animals only six feet long would have tentacles that stretch twenty-seven feet. That would suffice to make a formidable monster."

"But they don't really fish for them, do they, sir?" asked Ned.

"Not often, I admit. But sailors see them, at least. One of my friends, Captain Paul Bos of Havre, has often sworn he met one of these monsters, of colossal dimensions, in the Indian seas. But the most astonishing fact of all, well established, too, happened some years ago, in 1861."

"Tell us about it," the Canadian urged.

"Why, in 1861, to the northeast of Teneriffe, much the same latitude as our present one, the crew of the dispatch boat 'Alecton' sighted an enormous cuttlefish. Captain Bouguer went near the animal and attacked it with both harpoons and guns, but with no particular success, for both bullets and harpoons glided over the soft flesh, which was like jelly without any consistency."

"I wish I'd been there!" cried Ned Land. "My blows don't glide over soft flesh, they stay where they hit."

"Well, Ned, in your absence, and after several fruitless attempts, the crew tried to pass a slip knot around the body of the mollusk. The noose slipped on as far as the caudal fins, and there it stopped. They tried to haul the horror on board. But its weight was so great that the rope tore the tail from the body. And, deprived of this ornament, Mr. Cuttlefish disappeared under the water."

"And that's a true story, sir?"

"An indisputable fact, my brave Ned. And naturalists have named the poulp Bouguer's cuttlefish."

"How long was his nibs?"

"It measured about six yards, did it not, sir?" inquired Conseil. He was seated by the window and seemed to be examining the irregular windings of the cliff.

"Precisely that," I replied.

"And was its head not crowned with eight tentacles that beat the water like a nest of serpents?" continued my servant.

"Your description fits to a hair."

"And weren't its eyes very highly developed and placed at the back of its head, sir?"

"Exactly as you say."

"And its mouth was like a parrot's beak?"

"To the very life, Conseil."

"Very well! I hope you will pardon my intrusion, sir," my servant said quietly. "But if this fellow here is not Bouguer's cuttlefish, why then it must be at least his twin brother."

I looked in some amazement at Conseil. But Ned Land, who never wasted any time in meditation, rushed to the window.

"What an impossibly awful beast!" he cried aloud.

I looked in my turn, and could not repress a gesture of disgust. Before our eyes was a horrible monster worthy of figuring in any tale of monstrosities.

It was an immense cuttlefish, at least eight yards long. It swam backward toward the "Nautilus" and at great speed, watching us the while with its huge staring green eyes. Its eight arms (or rather, feet) were twice as long as its body and twisted like the snakes in the Furies' hair. They were fixed to its head and thus justified its name of cephalopod.

We could clearly see the two hundred and fifty little vacuum cups on the inner side of the tentacles, like so many semi-spherical capsules. Every once in a while these little cups stuck to the glass of the window through which we were looking, there making a vacuum. The monster's mouth, a horned beak like a parrot's, opened and shut vertically. Its tongue was of horn substance and furnished with several rows of pointed teeth. It came forth quivering from this veritable pair of shears. What a freak of nature it seemed, a bird's beak on a mollusk! Its spindle-shaped body constituted a fleshy mass that might weigh four to five thousand pounds. Its color changed rapidly from livid gray to reddish brown, a sure sign that the beast was deeply enraged.

What on earth had got on the nerves of this mollusk? The presence of the submarine, no doubt, which was more formidable than itself and upon which its suckers and its jaws had no hold.

Strange with what vitality the Creator has endowed these monster poulps! What vigor in their movements, fed by the three hearts which they possess! Fate herself had brought us into the presence of this cephalopod, and I was not minded to lose the opportunity I had of studying thoroughly this magnificent specimen. So I mastered the disgust with which I was almost overcome and, taking up a pencil, began to draw it.

"This may be the very one the 'Alecton' saw," Conseil remarked.

"No, it can't," replied the Canadian dogmatically. "For this one is whole, and the other fellow sloughed off his tail."

"Which, as a matter of fact, is no reason at all," I said. "The arms and tails of these animals grow on again. And in the seven years since Bouguer's cuttlefish had its little accident, he doubtless has had ample time to acquire a new one."

While we talked thus, other poulps appeared at the port light. I counted seven of them. They formed a sort of procession in the wake of the "Nautilus." Frequently I heard their beaks gnashing against its iron hull. I continued with my work. The monsters maintained their position with regard to us with such precision that it seemed as if they were motionless. Suddenly the submarine stopped. A shock made it tremble in every plate.

"Do you suppose we've struck something or run aground?" I asked.

"At any rate," answered the Canadian, "we must be already free, for we are floating."

Well, our ship might be afloat, all right, but we certainly were not moving. A minute passed, and Captain Nemo, followed by his lieutenant, entered the saloon. I had not seen him for some time, and he appeared duller and more worn than I had remembered him. Without speaking or noticing us in any way, he walked to the panel and looked out at the poulps. Then he spoke a few words to the second officer, and the man departed. Soon the panels were closed. The ceiling was lighted. I approached the commander.

"An interesting collection of poulps," I ventured.

"Very," he replied, more courteously than perhaps I had expected. "And we intend to fight them, Sir Naturalist, man to beast."

I glanced at him in some alarm. I thought I might have misunderstood his meaning.

"Did you say man to beast, sir?"

"Yes, M. Aronnax. The screw is stopped as you doubtless noticed. I think the horny jaw of one of the cuttlefish has got entangled in the blades. That's what keeps us from moving."

"What are you planning to do in the matter, Captain?"

"Rise to the surface and slaughter the vermin."

"That will prove a difficult thing to do, will it not, sir?"

"Quite hard indeed, I fancy. You see, the electric bullets are pretty likely to be powerless against them, because they do not find resistance sufficient to detonate them. But we shall assail them with the hatchet."

"And the harpoon, unless you forbid it a second time, sir," declared the Canadian.

"I shall accept your proffer of assistance most thankfully, I assure you, Mr. Land."

"And we will follow," I said.

So we all left the saloon together and went toward the central staircase.

There we found gathered about ten men with boarding axes, ready for the battle. Conseil and I were given one of the hatchets, Ned seized a harpoon. By this time the "Nautilus" had risen to the surface. One of the sailors, posted on the top step of the iron ladder, unscrewed the bolts of the panels.

But hardly had the screws been loosened, when the panel flew up with great violence, evidently drawn irresistibly by the suckers of a poulp's arm. Immediately one of these arms slid like a snake down the opening, and twenty other such were waiting above. With one blow of the hand axe, Captain Nemo severed this formidable tentacle, and it slid wriggling down the steps. But, just as we were all crowded in a mass, swarming up to reach the platform, two other arms came down, lashing furiously about in the air. They seized hold of a seaman who was placed in front of our commander, and they lifted him up with unbelievable power. Captain Nemo uttered a sharp cry and rushed out through the hatchway. We followed.

What a scene presented itself to our awestruck gaze!

The unhappy sailor, fast clutched by the tentacle and fixed to the suckers, as if for all eternity, was brandished in the air at the caprice of this huge trunk. His throat rattled, he was choking, he could but cry out the one word, "Help!" This word startled me, for it was spoken in French. And so I had a fellow countryman on board and, for aught I knew, several of them.

That cry I shall hear throughout my life—that heart-rending shriek! For the unfortunate man was lost before we could reach him. And what human force could rescue him from that awful pressure?

None the less, Captain Nemo plunged toward the poulp and with a single blow of the axe had cut clear through one arm. His lieutenant was struggling furiously against the other monsters that crept along the flanks of the submarine. The crew fought savagely with their axes, as if they were painted Indians using the war tomahawk. The Canadian, Conseil, and I kept burying our weapons in the fleshy masses. A stifling scent of musk permeated the atmosphere. It was horrible. For one instant I thought the poor fellow who was entangled with the poulp might be wrenched loose from its mighty suction. Seven of the eight arms of the monster had already been hacked clean away. Only one still wriggled in the air, swinging its victim about like a feather. But just as Captain Nemo and his second officer threw themselves upon this last tentacle, the beast ejected a black stream of foul liquid. We were blinded with it.

When the cloud had disappeared, the cuttlefish had vanished from sight, and with it my wretched countryman. Ten or twelve poulps now invaded the platform and sides of our vessel. We rolled pell-mell into the midst of this nest of snakes that was wallowing in waves of blood and ink on the bridge. It almost seemed as if these slimy tentacles grew forth again like hydras' heads. At each recurrent stroke Ned Land's harpoon was driven into the staring eyes of the cuttlefish. But my comrade, bold as a lion though he was, fell into the tentacles of a monster he hadn't been able either to escape or to kill.

How my pulses now hammered with pity and horror. The truly terrible beak of the cuttlefish was open above Ned Land. The poor chap would be cut in two—unless—

I rushed to his succor with all my might and main, but our commander was there before me. His axe disappeared between the two enormous jaws. Miraculously saved, the Canadian jumped unharmed to his feet and jammed his harpoon to its heft into the triple heart of the nauseating poulp.

"I owed myself this revenge!" the captain said to Ned.

The harpooner bowed without replying. He was beyond speech. The grewsome combat had lasted a quarter of an hour. The monsters, vanquished and mutilated, left us at last and fled beneath the waves. Captain Nemo, covered with blood and almost overcome with exhaustion, gazed out upon the sea that had swallowed up one of his cherished companions. And great tears gathered in his eyes.

CHAPTER XIX

THE GULF STREAM

The terrible battle of April 20 none of us can ever forget. I wrote down my first description of it while still under the influence of the violent emotions it stirred in me. But since that time I have revised it and submitted it to both Ned Land and Conseil for perusal and correction. They found it exact as to its facts, but insufficient in its effects. To paint such pictures, I now see, the author must have the magic pen of that most illustrious of our poets, the author of *The Toilers of the Sea.*

I have said that our commander wept at the conclusion of our conflict with the poulps. As he stood and looked out across the waves his grief was evident. This was the second comrade that he had lost since our arrival on board. And what a death this recent one had been! This friend, crushed and stifled by the dreadful arms of a gigantic mollusk, and ground by its iron jaws, would not be laid to rest with his companions in the peaceful coral cemetery.

It was the man's despairing outcry that had wrung my heart. The poor Frenchman, in the moment of his direst need, had forgotten the artificial language in which he had been schooled. And he had turned to his mother tongue to utter one final appeal. Among the crew of the "Nautilus," leagued hand and foot to the captain, renouncing the brotherhood of man, I had a fellow countryman. In this mysterious association of men who recoiled from contact with their mates did he alone represent France?

It was one of the many insoluble problems that rose unceasingly before my mind.

Captain Nemo disappeared behind the closed door of his cabin, and I saw him no more for some time. That he was gloomy and of changeful mood, I could guess from the conduct of the vessel, of which he was the very soul. The "Nautilus" seemed to receive and record his every impression.

The ship kept to no settled course. It floated about like the dead body of a man, a prey to the will of the waves. It went here and there quite at random. It was as if the ship and its commander could not bear to tear themselves finally away from the scene of the last struggle, from this sea that had devoured one of their men.

Ten days passed thus. And it was not until the first day of May that the submarine resumed its northerly course, after having sighted the Bahamas at the mouth of the Bahama Channel. We were then following the current of the largest river in the ocean, one that has its banks, its fish, and its own temperatures. I mean the Gulf Stream. For this is really a river which flows freely in the middle of the Atlantic, one whose waters do not mingle with the waves of the adjacent seas. It is a salt river, more saline than the surrounding liquid element. Its depth on the average is fifteen hundred fathoms, its mean breadth sixty miles. In certain places the current flows at the rate of two and one-half miles an hour. The body of its water is more considerable than that of all the rivers on the globe. It was on this ocean-river that our ship was sailing.

This stream carried with it all sorts of living creatures. Argonauts, so common to the Mediterranean, swarmed in the current. Of the gristly sort, the most remarkable were the rays, whose slender tails form almost a third of their bodies. They looked something like an elongated lozenge twenty-five feet long. Small sharks we saw in great numbers. These were perhaps a yard in length, with large heads, short rounded muzzles, pointed teeth in rows, and bodies covered with what looked like scales.

Among the bony fish I recognized some gray gobies, peculiar to these waters, also black giltheads, whose iris shines like fire. Then there were sirenes three feet long, which uttered little cries like those of ailing human babies. Their large snouts were thickly sown with tiny teeth. Side by side with these swam and sported blue coryphaenes, clad in gold and silver; likewise parrot fish that could outrival in colors the most beautiful tropical birds—they made rainbows wherever they darted through the lucid water.

There were bluish rhombs destitute of scales, and blennies with triangular heads; batrachoides covered with transverse yellow bands shaped in a design that resembled the Greek *t;* heaps of little gobies spotted with yellow; dipterodons with silvery heads and yellow tails; several specimens of salmon; mugilomores, slender in shape, shining with a soft light; and lastly, the American knight, a beautiful fish which, decorated with all kinds of orders and ribbons, frequents the shores of that great nation that esteems orders and ribbons so little.

During the night, especially in the stormy weather that

threatened us so frequently at this season, the phosphorescent waters of the Gulf Stream rivaled the electric power
of our searchlight.

On May 8 we were athwart Cape Hatteras, in the
latitude of North Carolina. At this point the width of
the Gulf Stream is seventy-five miles and its depth two
hundred and ten yards. The "Nautilus," so far as I could
discover, still wandered on more or less at random. All
supervision seemed to be abandoned. It began to occur to
me that, under these circumstances, escape would be possible. Hereabouts the inhabited shores offered an easy
refuge. The sea itself was incessantly ploughed by the
steamers that ply between New York or Boston and the
Gulf of Mexico. It was overrun day and night by small
coastwise schooners that tramped the shore lines of these
parts.

We could therefore reasonably count upon being picked
up after but a short interval of drifting. It was not only
a favorable, but an exceptional opportunity, notwithstanding the all but thirty miles that we were distant from the
edge of the Union.

And yet at this point, as at previous ones in his experience, an ironical circumstance thwarted the Canadian's
plans: the weather was most unpropitious. We were
nearing the spots where tempests are so frequent and so
terrible, that country of waterspouts and cyclones that
are actually engendered by the current of the Gulf Stream.
To tempt the fates in a frail boat now spelled almost certain destruction. Ned Land himself was reluctantly
forced to confess this fact. But he fretted like a spoiled

child, and was possessed with an acute homesickness that escape from the "Nautilus" alone could cure.

"Professor," he said one day to me, "this life I am leading must come to an end. I'm going to make a clean breast of my feeling to the commander. This fool Nemo is leaving land behind once more and heading for the north. But I swear I've had all I want at the South Pole, and I'll be dashed if I follow him to the other one."

"But what else can you do, Ned, since you can't get away now?"

"You said nothing, sir, when we were in your native seas. But by criminy, now that we are in mine, I'll do a little talking! When I think that before long the ship will be off Nova Scotia, I'm simply furious. There's a big bay there by Newfoundland, and the St. Lawrence empties into it, and Quebec, my native town, is on that river. I'll tear my hair out by the roots if we pass that bay without at least a try for freedom. I'll throw myself into the sea. I won't stick it here any longer. I'm choking to death."

The Canadian was evidently losing all patience. His vigorous nature sickened under our prolonged captivity. His face grew daily thinner and more wan. His temper, at best uncertain, now developed a morose and surly streak. And I knew from personal experience well enough what the poor fellow must be suffering, for I was by no means free from violent spells of homesickness myself.

Nearly seven months had passed without our having any news from land. And the altered spirits of our captain, his isolation since the day of our battle with the cuttlefish, his taciturnity—all these things were bringing me to view our situation in a new light.

"Well, sir, have you nothing to say?" asked Ned.

"Out with it, my lad! Do you want me to ask Captain Nemo what his intentions regarding us are?"

"That's the very idea, sir."

"Even if he has already indicated what they are?"

"Yes, sir, even so. I want the thing black on white. Speak to him in my name only, if you think best."

"But, confound it, I almost never see him! He avoids me."

"That's all the more reason for hunting him up."

I went to my room. From there I heard the sound of walking in the commander's cabin. It would not do to let this opportunity slip. Ned was right.

I knocked at the door of Captain Nemo's room. There was no response. I knocked again, and then gently turned the handle. The panel opened and I entered. The captain was there, bending over his work table. It was evident that he had not heard me. Firmly resolved not to go away before our talk was had, I approached him. He raised his head quickly, frowned, and said in a rough tone that I had never heard him use before, "You here, sir? What do you want?"

"I want a few words with you, Captain."

"But I am busy, M. Aronnax, as you see. I leave you liberty to shut yourself away. Can you not grant me the same privilege?"

This reception was anything but encouraging. However, I was determined not to be frightened away. And I demanded an answer.

"Sir," I said coolly, "I have to speak to you of a matter that brooks no delay."

"Oho! What is this that I hear?" he asked ironically. "Have you discovered something that has escaped my notice? Or has the sea yielded any new secrets?"

We were at cross-purposes. I felt that further talk at present would only lead to unhappy misunderstandings. But, luckily, before I could frame a new sentence in reply to his query, the captain showed me an open manuscript that lay before him on the table. And he said in a more serious tone, "Here, Professor, is a manuscript written in several languages. It contains the sum of my knowledge of the sea. If it please God, it shall not perish with me. This book, signed with my name, ended with the story of my life, will be found locked in an insubmersible case. The last survivor of all of us now on board the 'Nautilus' will throw this case into the sea, and it will go whithersoever it is borne by the waves."

This man's real name! A history written by himself! His mystery was, then, fated to be revealed some day.

"Captain Nemo," I said, "of course I approve of your idea regarding the manuscript. It must be published abroad among men, for the result of your studies must not be lost. But don't you think the means you employ to deliver the book are a trifle—er—primitive? For who knows where the four winds of heaven may carry this insubmersible case? Into whose hands will it fall—savage or cultured, silly or wise? Could you not make use of far better ways to achieve your object? You, yourself, or one of your men might leave this—"

"Never, sir! Under no conceivable circumstances!" the commander hurriedly interrupted me.

"But just consider! My companions and I are willing and ready to devote ourselves to the preservation of your work. If you will set us at liberty—"

"What's that you say?" the captain asked, rising.

"Why, simply this. It's the very subject about which I wanted to question you. For seven months now we have been on board here. And our continued imprisonment, and the uncertainty of our future, are fair killing us, sir. What do you mean to do with us? Keep us here always, buried alive?"

"M. Aronnax, my answer today is the same that it was seven months ago. Whoever enters the 'Nautilus' does not leave it until he is carried out feet foremost in a coffin."

"You impose slavery upon us then?"

"Call it anything you like."

"But by heaven! Even the cringing slave has the divinely appointed right to secure his freedom."

"Who denies you this right? I do not. Have I ever tried to chain you by means either physical or spiritual? Did I ask you to take an oath or give a bond?"

He stood before me with his arms crossed and fixed me with a concentrated gaze not easy to endure.

"My dear sir," I observed, "there is no point in our ever mentioning this subject again. It is distasteful to us both. But, as we have hit upon it this once, let us go through to the end. Remember I am not pleading for myself alone. Study is to me a relief, a sport, a passion even, that can make me forget everything else. Like you, my captain, I am willing to lead an obscure life of selfless effort, because I have the frail hope of some day bequeathing the result of my studies to the future. But it is far different with Ned Land. And he, like any other man who is worth a penny, is entitled to some consideration."

"He gets it," the commander said sharply.

"No, not to his own way of thinking, at least. And have you thought that hatred of enslavement, love of liberty, may in a nature like this Canadian's give birth to wild schemes of revenge? Don't you see that he might think—might attempt—or try—"

I could not continue, in the face of the cold contempt written in the manner of my companion. I fell silent. Captain Nemo said, "It is no concern of mine what Ned Land thinks or tries. I did not seek his company. Nor do I hold him here for any pleasure or profit to myself. As for you, M. Aronnax, you are one of those who can understand anything, including silence. I have nothing more to say. Let this be the only time you raise this subject. A second time I should refuse to listen to you."

I retired from the fray defeated, but I had entertained no other hope from the start. Our situation was critical. I related my conversation to my two comrades.

"Well, we know now, anyway," said Ned. "That may not be much, but it's something. There's nothing to hope for except escape, whatever the weather may be. The 'Nautilus' is nearing Long Island."

The sky was becoming more and more threatening.

Symptoms of a hurricane were growing manifest. The atmosphere was clouded with a white mist. On the far horizon fine streaks of cirrose clouds were being swiftly succeeded by cumuli. Other clouds, lower down, swept by in flight. The sea, already swollen, was rising into huger billows.

Except for the stormy petrels, friends of the tempest, birds had disappeared from our view. The barometer fell even while one glanced at it. The mixture in the storm-glass was decomposing under the influence of the electricity with which the air was charged. The war of the elements burst, May 18, just as the submarine was floating off the shore of Long Island, some miles from the port of New York City.

I can describe the terrible scene of strife and tumult, for, by some unaccountable caprice, Captain Nemo decided to brave it out upon the surface of the waves. At first the wind blew from the southwest. During the preliminary squalls our commander had taken up his post on the platform. He had lashed himself fast, to keep from being washed overboard by the monstrous mountain of water. I had likewise crept outside and made myself tight with ropes. I was divided in my mind between admiration of the storm itself and of the extraordinary man who was here to cope with it.

The raging sea was swept by vast cloud drifts that were actually saturated with the water of heaven-aspiring waves. Our ship rolled and pitched unbelievably, now on its side, now erect as a mast. About five o'clock a torrent of rain fell, but it lulled neither the sea nor the wind. The hurricane blast blew forty leagues an hour. At such times trees are felled, houses overturned, twenty-four-pounders lifted like straws from their carriage. And in the midst of this inferno the submarine justified the words of a great engineer—"There is no rightly built hull but can defy the sea."

Our boat was not a resisting rock, else had it broken. It was a steel spindle, obedient and movable without rigging or spars. And so it was the plaything of the fury which it could not conquer.

Still, you may imagine that I watched these raging waves with a polite attention. They measured fifteen feet in height and one hundred and fifty to one hundred and seventy-five yards long. Their speed of propagation was thirty feet per second. Their bulk and power of course increased with the depth of the water. At the Hebrides such waves as these have displaced a mass weighing well over four tons. In the tempest of December 23, 1864, after destroying the Japanese town of Yeddo, such waves broke the same day on the shores of western America.

The intensity of the tempest increased with the night. During a cyclone at Réunion in 1860 the barometer fell to 710 millimeters at the close of day. The like case was now our evil lot.

I saw a large vessel pass across the horizon laboring most painfully. She was endeavoring to lie to, under half-steam, in order to keep her nose above the waves. This was probably a steamer of the line from New York to Havre or Liverpool. It soon disappeared in the all-enveloping gloom.

At ten o'clock in the evening the sky was on fire. The atmosphere was streaked with lightning so vivid that I could not bear the brightness of it. But the captain, gazing upon it, seemed to envy and to emulate the spirit of the tempest. A terrible noise filled the air. It was a complex roaring, made up of the howls of the crushed waves, the growling of the wind, and the claps of thunder. The wind would veer suddenly to any point of the horizon. And the cyclone, rising in the east, actually returned after passing by the north, west, and south, in the inverse course to that pursued by the circular storms of the southern hemisphere.

Gulf Stream! Thou deservest the title of King of Tempests.

It is this current which causes these formidable cyclones, because of the difference in temperature between the air above it and its own currents. A shower of fire had succeeded the downpour of rain. Drops of water were in a twinkling changed to luminous aigrettes. One would have thought that Captain Nemo, desiring a death worthy of him, was courting annihilation by lightning. For as the "Nautilus," pitching dreadfully, would raise its steel spur high in air, this would act as a conductor, and I saw long sparks burst from it.

Crushed and without further strength of either body or spirit, I crept to the panel, opened it, and descended to the saloon. The storm was then at its height. It was impossible to stand upright in the interior of the ship.

Captain Nemo came down about twelve. I heard the reservoirs filling by degrees, and we sank slowly beneath the waves. Through the opened casements in the saloon

I saw large fish terrified, passing like phantoms in the water. Some of them were struck and blasted before my wondering eyes. The submarine was still descending.

I thought that at about eight fathoms deep we should find a calm. But no. The upper levels were too violently stirred for that to be the case. We did not find repose until we were more than twenty-five fathoms submerged in the bowels of the deep. But, once there, what silence! And what peace! None could have told that hell had loosed its fury on the face of that ocean.

CHAPTER XX

WE VISIT A TOMB

As a consequence of the storm we had been thrown eastward once more. All hope of escape on the shores of New York or the St. Lawrence had faded away to nothingness. Poor Ned, in his grim despair, had isolated himself like Captain Nemo.

Conseil and I, however, never left each other's side. I have said the "Nautilus" had veered to the east. But it would have been more exact to say northeast. For some days then we wandered first on the surface and then beneath it, amid the fogs so dreaded by mariners.

What accidents are due to these white fogs! What shocks of collision between vessels, in spite of warning lights, whistles, and alarm bells! What wrecks upon reefs hidden in the thick wool-wrapping of mist, when the wind drowns the breaking of the waves! And the bottoms of these seas look like a field of battle, where still lie the conquered of the ocean—some ships old and already incrusted, others fresh and reflecting from their iron bands and copper plates the brilliance of our watch lantern.

On May 15 we were at the extreme south of the Banks of Newfoundland. These banks consist of alluvia, or large heaps of organic matter. This has been brought either from the equator by the Gulf Stream, or from the North Pole by that counter-current of cold water which skirts the American coast. There also are piled those erratic blocks which are carried along by broken ice. And close by there is the charnel house of mollusks and zoöphytes which perish here by the million. The depth of the sea is not great at Newfoundland, not more than some hundreds of fathoms, but toward the south the ocean floor falls away in a depression of fifteen hundred fathoms. Here the Gulf Stream widens. It loses some of its speed and some of its warmth. For it has become itself a sea.

It was on the 17th of May, about five hundred miles from Heart's Content, at a depth of more than fourteen hundred fathoms, that I saw the electric cable lying on the ground. I had not mentioned the fact to Conseil, and he thought at first that it was a gigantic sea serpent. But I quickly undeceived the worthy fellow and, to console him for his very natural blunder, related several particulars concerning the laying of the cable. The first one was laid in the years 1857, 1858. But after it had transmitted about four hundred telegrams, it refused to work any longer. In 1863 the engineers constructed another one, measuring two thousand miles in length and weighing forty-five hundred tons, which they embarked on the "Great Eastern." This attempt also failed.

On May 25 the "Nautilus," at a depth of more than 1918 fathoms, came to the precise spot where the rupture occurred which ruined the enterprise. It was within 638 miles of the Irish coast. At two o'clock one afternoon it was noticed that communication with Europe had just ceased. The electrical experts on board the cable ship resolved to sever the strands before fishing them up. By eleven that night they had recovered the damaged part.

They made another contact point and spliced it. Again the cable was submerged. But some days later it broke once more, and in the depths of the ocean it could not be recovered. Were the Americans discouraged by these frequent failures? By no manner of means. Cyrus Field, the bold promoter of the undertaking, had lost every penny of his own great fortune. But he set a new subscription on foot, which met with a surprising popular response. Another cable was constructed along better principles.

The bundles of conducting wires were each enveloped in gutta-percha and protected by a wadding of hemp contained in a metallic sheath. The "Great Eastern" sailed July 13, 1866. But one incident occurred this time to mar the operation. Several times, in unrolling the cable, it was noticed that nails had recently been forced into it. This was probably with the design of destroying its usefulness. Captain Anderson consulted with the officers and engineers. Thereafter a notice was posted that the offender, if caught, would be thrown without trial into the sea. From that time forward the criminal attempts were never repeated.

On July 23 the "Great Eastern" was not more than five hundred miles from Newfoundland when from Ireland was telegraphed the news of an armistice concluded between Austria and Prussia, after the battle of Sadowa. On the 27th, in the midst of heavy fogs, the cable ship reached the port of Heart's Content. The great adventure was thus successfully terminated. And for its first dispatch young America addressed to old Europe those wise words so often misinterpreted: "Glory to God in the highest, and on earth peace, good-will toward men."

Naturally, we did not expect to find the electric cable in its primitive state of splendor, such as it was on leaving the factory. So, in a sense, we discovered only what we anticipated seeing. The long serpent was covered with the remains of shells and bristled with foraminiferae. It was incrusted with a stout coating which served as an effective protection against all boring mollusks. It lay quietly sheltered from the motions of the sea. And the pressure it endured was favorable to the transmission of the electric spark which passes from Europe to America in a third of a second.

Doubtless this cable will last for a great length of time, for it has been found that the gutta-percha envelope is improved by the action of sea water. Besides, on this level, so well chosen, the cable is never so deeply submerged as to cause it to break.

The "Nautilus" followed it to the lowest depth, which was more than 2212 fathoms. And there the serpent lay without anchorage of any sort. Finally we reached the spot where the accident of the year 1863 had taken place. The bottom of the ocean there formed a valley about one hundred miles broad, in which Mont Blanc might have been stood upright without having its summit appear above the waves. This valley is closed at the east by a perpendicular wall over two thousand yards high. We arrived there May 28, and the submarine was then not more than one hundred and twenty miles from Ireland.

It looked a bit as though Captain Nemo intended to

land on the British Isles. But no. To my great surprise, he made for the south, once more returning toward European seas. In rounding the Emerald Isle for one short instant I caught sight of Cape Clear and the light that guides the thousands of vessels annually from Glasgow or Liverpool. An important question then arose in my mind: Did our ship dare entangle itself in the English Channel? Ned Land, who had reappeared since we were nearing land, did not cease to interrogate me. But how could I answer him? Captain Nemo remained invisible. Was he going to show me the coast of France after having given the Canadian a glimpse of the American shores?

The submarine was still forging southward. On May 30 it passed in sight of Land's End, between the extreme point of England and the Scilly Isles, which were left to starboard. If he wished to enter the English Channel, he must steer straight to the east. He did not do so.

During the whole of the 31st of May the "Nautilus" described a series of circles on the water in a way that interested me greatly. It seemed to be seeking a spot which it had particular trouble in locating. At noon Captain Nemo himself came to work the ship's log. He exchanged no word with me, and he seemed more gloomy and distracted than ever. What could thus sadden him? Was it his proximity to European shores? Had he haunting or remorseful recollections of the country he had abandoned? For a long while these thoughts occupied my mind, and I had a sort of presentiment that before long chance might lead me to stumble upon the commander's secrets.

Next day, June 1, the submarine repeated the process of searching. It was evidently hunting for a particular nook of the sea. The captain took the sun's altitude as he had done the previous day. The sea was beautiful, the sky was guiltless of cloud. About eight miles to the east a large steamer could be discerned on the horizon. No flag fluttered from its mast, and I could therefore gain no hint of its nationality. Some minutes before the sun passed the meridian our commander took his sextant and watched with great attention. The absolute calm of the water greatly helped this operation. The submarine was motionless; it neither rolled nor pitched.

I was on the platform when the altitude was taken. And thus I heard the captain pronounce the words, "It is here."

He turned away and went below. What had he seen? Was it the vessel which was now changing its direction and seeming to draw nearer to us? I could not tell. But hardly had I gone down to the saloon when the panels closed and I heard the hissing of the water in the reservoirs. Our ship began to sink, following an almost vertical line, for its screw communicated no motion to it. Some minutes later we had stopped at a depth of more than four hundred and twenty fathoms and were resting on the ground. The luminous ceiling was then darkened, the casements of the drawing-room opened, and through the glass I saw the sea brilliantly illuminated by the rays of our lantern for at least half a mile around us.

I looked to the port side and saw nothing but an immensity of waters. But to starboard, on the floor of the sea, appeared a large protuberance that at once drew my attentive gaze. One might almost have thought it a ruin buried beneath a coating of white shells that much resembled a covering of snow. But, upon studying the mass more minutely, I could recognize the ever-thickening form of a vessel bare of its masts. It must have sunk head foremost. This disaster certainly dated from a time long dead. The wreck, to be so incrusted with the lime of the water, undoubtedly could count weary seasons spent on the bottom of the ocean.

What was this ship? Why did our submarine visit its tomb? Could it have been anything but accident that had sent it below the waters? I was debating what to think when near me in a slow voice I heard Captain Nemo speaking.

"At one time this ship was called the 'Marsellais.' It carried seventy-four guns and was launched in 1762. In 1778, commanded by Lapoype-Vertrieux, it fought boldly against the 'Preston.' In 1779 it was at the taking of Granada with the squadron of Admiral Estaing. In 1781 it took part in the battle of Comte de Grasse in Chesapeake Bay. In 1794 the French Republic changed its name, M. Aronnax."

"To what other, Captain Nemo?"

"Have patience, sir. On the 16th of April, in the same year, it joined the squadron of Villaret-Joyeuse at Brest, being intrusted with a cargo of wheat coming from America under the command of Admiral Van Stabel. On the 11th and 12th Prairal of the second year of the Republic this squadron fell in with an English vessel. Sir, today is the 13th Prairal, or the 1st of June, 1868. It is thus now seventy-four years ago, day for day on this very spot, in latitude 47° 24′, longitude 17° 28′, that this vessel, after fighting heroically, losing its three masts, with water in its hold, and one-third of its crew disabled, preferred sinking with its 356 sailors to surrendering. It nailed its colors to the poop and disappeared beneath the waves, to the triumphant cry of 'Long live the Republic!' "

"Ah, now I know!" I exclaimed. "They had changed the name of that heroic ship from the 'Marseillais' to the 'Avenger.' "

"Yes, sir. The 'Avenger'! And it is the best name in all the world," muttered Captain Nemo as he crossed his arms upon his chest.

CHAPTER XXI

HUMAN SACRIFICE

The captain's way of describing the scene impressed itself deeply upon my mind. He had begun to tell the history of the patriot ship so coldly, and yet he had pronounced his concluding words—the name of the "Avenger" —with an emotion so significant that it could not escape the notice of his listener.

My eyes still clung to the commander. With hand stretched out to sea, he was watching the poor wreck with a glowing eye. Perhaps I was never to learn who my companion was, whence he came, whither he was going. But more and more I was able to see the man in him, and not the scientist. It was no common hatred of his kind which had shut Captain Nemo and his comrades within the submarine. It was a wrath, either monstrous or sublime, which age could not stale nor custom wither.

Did this bitterness of his still seek for vengeance? The future would soon teach me that. The "Nautilus" was slowly rising to the surface of the sea, and the outlines of the "Avenger" were gradually fading from my view. Soon a slight rolling informed me that we were in the open air. At that moment a dull boom was heard. I looked at the captain. He did not move.

"May I ask you a question, Captain?" I said.

He did not answer. I left him and mounted to the platform. Ned Land and Conseil were already there.

"Where did that reverberating sound come from?" I demanded.

"It was a gunshot," replied the Canadian.

I looked in the direction of the vessel I had already seen. It was fast nearing the submarine. We could see that its stokers were crowding on steam. It was now within six miles of us.

"What ship is that, Ned?"

"By its rigging and the height of its lower masts," said the harpooner, "I'll bet my bottom dollar she's a ship of war. Let her overhaul us! I say, and sink this prison boat we're on."

"But, my dear friend," replied Conseil, "what earthly harm can it do us? It can't attack beneath the waves. It can't cannonade us while we're resting at the bottom of the sea."

My servant's logic seemed to stump the harpooner, for he had no retort ready.

"Tell me, Ned," I asked after a moment's silence, "can you make out what country she hails from?"

The Canadian knitted his eyebrows, half closed his eyes, and fixed a piercing look upon the vessel.

"Blow me if I can, sir!" he said. "For she doesn't show a stitch of colors anywhere. But man-of-war she is, for there's a long pennant floating from her masthead."

During the following quarter of an hour we watched with some anxiety the ship that was running full-tilt toward us. I could hardly convince myself that she could pick out the "Nautilus" from that distance, and still less believe that she could know what this submarine machine was. Soon the Canadian informed me that she was a large armored two-decked ram.

A thick black smoke issued from her funnels. Her close-furled sails were strapped to her yards. She hoisted no flag at her mizzenpeak. The distance still prevented our distinguishing the colors of her pennant, which floated out like a thin ribbon. She advanced rapidly. If Captain Nemo allowed her to approach to close quarters before he submerged, there was still a chance of salvation for us.

"Lookee here," said Ned Land. "If that cruiser passes anywhere within a mile of us, I'm going into the sea. And I advise you lads to follow suit."

I did not reply to the Canadian's suggestion, but continued to watch the oncoming ship. Whether English, French, American, or Russian, she would be sure to take us castaways in if we could only make her sides. Presently a white smoke burst from the fore part of the vessel. Some seconds afterward the water near us was agitated by the fall of a heavy body and splashed the stern of the submarine. An instant later a loud explosion almost shattered my ear drums.

"Merciful heavens!" I exclaimed. "They are firing at us."

"Sure thing," said Ned, almost amiably now that there was a good chance for a ruction. "They've recognized the unicorn and are letting fly at us proper."

"But good Lord! Can't they see that there are innocent men in the case?"

"That's why they're wasting good powder and shot," replied Ned Land, with a curious glance in my direction.

A whole blinding flood of light penetrated my brain. Doubtless the world knew by this time how much and how little credence to give the stories of the pretended monster. Doubtless when he ran afoul of the "Nautilus," on board the "Abraham Lincoln," and Ned struck it with his harpoon, Commander Farragut must have recognized in the fictitious narwhal a submarine boat, more dangerous to society at large than any supernatural cetacean. And now on every sea of Christendom they were on the sharp lookout for this engine of destruction.

And our situation was terrible indeed if Captain Nemo employed the "Nautilus" to carry out his works of vengeance. On the night when we were imprisoned in that cell had he not attacked some vessel in the midst of the Indian Ocean? And the man buried in the coral cemetery —had he not been a victim of the shock caused by the submarine when she rammed her antagonist below the water line? Yes, that is the way it must have happened. One part of the mysterious existence had been unveiled.

All the ghastly past rose before my mind. If the identity of our commander had not been learned as yet, the nations which were banded together for his destruction knew, at least, that they were not hunting a fabulous creature, but a man who had vowed a deadly hatred against them. So, instead of meeting friends on board the fast approaching ship, we could expect to find only pitiless enemies.

The shot now rattled about us. Some of them struck the sea and ricochetted, losing themselves in the distance, but none touched the submarine. Our adversary was not more than three miles away now. In spite of this rather serious cannonade, Captain Nemo did not appear out on the platform. And yet, if one of the conical projectiles raining down so near at hand had struck the shell of the "Nautilus," it would have been all day with us.

"Sir," said the harpooner eagerly, "we must do all we can to get out of this pickle. Let's flag them. Perhaps they'll understand then that we are honest folks."

Ned Land took his sizable bandana handkerchief to wave in the air. But he had scarcely displayed it, when he was struck down by an iron hand. Despite his great strength, he was felled like an ox to the platform.

"Idiot!" cried the captain, who had come upon us unawares. "Do you long to be pierced by the spur of this boat before it is hurled against the ribs of our enemy?"

Captain Nemo was terrible to hear. He was, if possible, more dreadful to see. His face was deathly pale, apparently from a spasm of his heart. For an instant it must have ceased to beat. His pupils were curiously contracted. And he did not speak as, with body thrown forward, he wrung the Canadian's shoulders—he *roared*.

Then he turned his heel contemptuously upon the fallen harpooner and stared at the ship of war that was loosing a perfect hailstorm of shot at him.

"Ship of an accursed nation!" he cried with a powerful voice. "You know me at last, do you? I know who you are, without colors to tell you by. Look! and I will show you mine."

On the fore part of the bridge our commander unfurled a black flag similar to the one he had placed at the

South Pole. At this moment a shot struck the shell of the "Nautilus" obliquely without piercing it, rebounded near the commander, and was lost in the sea. He shrugged his shoulders mockingly. Then he said to me, "Down below, you and your companions! Go down, sir!"

"Are you going to attack this ship?" I asked.

"Certainly. And sink it."

"You must not do that, sir."

"And who are you to give commands, pray? And I advise you to withhold your judgment, M. Aronnax. Fate has shown you what you should not have seen. The attack has begun. Down with you!"

"What is this vessel?" I asked firmly.

"Aha! So you do not know? So much the better, sir. Its nationality to you, at least, will remain a secret. For the last time, below with you!"

What could we do but obey?

About fifteen sailors surrounded the captain, looking with implacable hatred at the vessel bearing down upon them. One could feel that the same desire for vengeance animated every soul of them. As I passed through the panel to the iron staircase another projectile struck the "Nautilus," and I heard the captain call, "Strike, mad vessel! Shower your useless shot! And then let us see if you can escape our wrath. But it is not here that you shall perish by the spur. I will not have your ruins mingle with those of the 'Avenger'!"

I reached my cabin in a daze. The captain and his second officer had remained up on the platform. The screw was set in motion, and the submarine, moving with high speed, was soon out of range of the ship's guns. But the pursuit continued, and Captain Nemo contented himself with keeping his distance.

Toward four o'clock in the afternoon I could no longer master my impatience. I slipped quietly and unobserved to the central staircase. The panel was open, and I ventured out on the platform. The captain was pacing the narrow deck with restless tread. He did not remove his gaze from the enemy, who was by now five or six miles to leeward.

He was describing great circles about the hostile vessel, always out of gunshot range and yet always drawing the foe eastward in determined if futile pursuit. But he did not attack. Perhaps he still hesitated before the grewsome deed? I wished to interfere once for all. But I had scarcely addressed Captain Nemo when he imposed silence with an imperious gesture of his hand, and said, "I am the law and the judge of law. I am the oppressed and there is my oppressor, flaunting his idle power. Through him I have lost all that I venerated and held most dear: country, wife and children, father and mother. I saw them perish miserably. All that I hate is there before me. Hold your peace!"

I cast a last look at the man-of-war that was crowding on every ounce of steam. I rejoined Ned and Conseil.

"We will fly!" I called to them.

"That's the talk!" said Ned. "What vessel is she?"

"I've not the ghost of an idea. But whoever and whatever she is, she'll be sunk before night is past. In any case, it is better for us to perish with her than be made accomplices in a retaliation the justice of which it is beyond our power to understand."

"You've taken the words from my lips, sir," remarked Ned coolly. "Let us only wait for night."

Night came. Deep silence reigned on board. The compass showed that the "Nautilus" had not altered its course. It was on the surface, rolling slightly. My companions and I resolved to fly when the vessel should be near enough either to hear or see us. For the moon, which would be full in two or three days, was shining with unwonted brightness. Once on board the other ship, if we could not prevent the blow that threatened it, we would at least do anything that circumstances permitted.

Several times I thought the submarine was preparing for the attack. But Captain Nemo merely allowed his adversary to approach and then once more fled before it.

The first part of the night passed without any incident. We watched the opportunity for action. We spoke but little to one another, since we were too much moved for easy utterance. Ned Land would have thrown himself into the sea and risked all if I had not forced him to wait. My idea now was that the "Nautilus" would attack the ship at her water line, and then it would not only be possible but easy to fly.

At three o'clock in the morning, nervous beyond power of expression, I again mounted to the platform. Captain Nemo had not left it. He was planted at the fore part of the bridge near his flag, which a slight breeze unfurled above his head. He kept his gaze riveted on the foe. It seemed as if the ship were drawn onward toward him by the attraction of that intense look as definitely as if he had it in tow. The moon at that moment was passing the meridian. Jupiter was rising in the eastern sky. Amid this peaceful scene of nature water and firmament rivaled each other in tranquillity. The sea was offering to the stars the finest mirror they could ever have in which to reflect their image. I compared the deep abiding calm of the elements with the passions brooding inside the submarine. And I shuddered.

The vessel was within two miles of us. It was drawing nearer and nearer to that phosphorescent light which betrayed the presence of the "Nautilus." I could see its green and red light and the white lantern suspended from its large mizzenmast. An indistinct vibration quivered through its rigging, showing that the boilers were heated to the utmost. Sheaves of sparks and red ashes flew from the two funnels, shining through the clear night like passionate stars.

I remained thus until six in the morning. And I firmly believe that our commander never once noticed me. The hostile ship stood about a mile and a half from us, and with the first break of dawn the firing started afresh. The moment could not be now far delayed when the submarine would be attacking its foe, and then my comrades and I should leave this man. I was on the point of going down below to remind them, when the second officer mounted the platform, accompanied by several sailors. Their commander either did not see them or did not wish to recognize their presence.

Some very simple steps were taken which might be

called clearing the ship for action. The iron balustrade around the platform was lowered. The lantern and the pilot cages were pushed within the shell of the submarine until they were flush with the deck. The long surface of the steel cigar had no longer a single obstacle to check its maneuvers. I returned to the saloon. The "Nautilus" was still floating on the face of the waters. Some streaks of light were still filtering through the liquid beds. The windows were brightened by the red beams of the rising sun. The dreadful day of June 2 had arrived.

At five o'clock the log indicated that the speed of the submarine was slackening. I knew this was for the purpose of allowing the enemy to get into closer quarters. Besides, the detonations of the guns were heard more clearly. And the projectiles, as they plunged through the environing waves, were extinguished with a louder hissing noise.

"My friends," I said, "the moment has arrived. A shake of the hand! And may God protect us!"

Ned Land (of course) was resolute, and Conseil (naturally) was calm about it all. But, I confess, I was so shaky that I could scarcely hold myself together. We all passed into the library. But the moment I pushed open the door that led to the central staircase I heard the upper panel close sharply.

The Canadian rushed onto the stairs, but I stopped him. A hissing noise that I recognized perfectly well informed me that the water was running into the reservoirs. And in a few moments the ship was several yards beneath the surface. I understood the proceeding. It was too late

482 TWENTY THOUSAND LEAGUES

for us to act. The "Nautilus" did not wish to strike at the impenetrable cuirass of the enemy's vessel, but below the water line in a place where no metallic covering protected it.

We were again imprisoned, unwilling witnesses of the dire tragedy that was in process of enactment. We had scarcely any time to reflect upon our disappointing situation. We took refuge in my cabin, where we huddled together and looked at one another without saying a word. A deep stupor had taken hold of my mind. I was in that painful state of expectancy which precedes an awaited explosion. I listened, with my every sense merged in that of hearing.

The speed of our ship was suddenly accelerated. It was beginning its fatal charge. The whole frame trembled—

All at once I screamed.

I had felt the shock, although it was a comparatively light one. I felt the penetrating power of the steel spur. I heard the sound of scraping and rending. But the submarine, carried along by its seemingly inexhaustible propelling force, passed through the mass of the vessel as a needle goes through sail cloth.

I could endure the suspense no longer. Out of my proper mind—quite mad, in fact—I rushed from my confined cabin into the spacious saloon. Captain Nemo was there. Mute, gloomy, implacable, he was gazing through the port panel. A vast mass cast a shadow on the water. And that its men might lose no whit of the foe's agony, the submarine was accompanying the scuttled vessel down into the abyss. Ten yards from me I saw the open shell of the ship, through which the water was rushing with a sound like thunder. Then I glimpsed the double line of guns, and after that the netting. The bridge swarmed with black agitated shadows.

The water was rising for its prey. Poor creatures were crowding the ratlines, clinging to the masts, struggling beneath the waves. It was a human ant heap overtaken by the sea.

Rigid with anguish, paralyzed by my emotions, I stood by and looked on. With eyes wide open, my hair standing on end, gasping for breath, and mute, I was watching. An irresistible attraction seemed to glue me to the glass.

Suddenly an explosion occurred.

The compressed air blew up the decks of the lost ship as if her magazines had caught fire. Then indeed she began to sink rapidly. Her topmast, laden with victims, now hove into view; then her spars, which were literally bent beneath their human weight; last of all, the top of her mainmast. Then the dark mass disappeared with a rush, and with it the dead and dying crew, drawn down by the strong eddy.

I turned to Captain Nemo. That terrible avenger, a perfect archangel of hatred, was still studying the details of the catastrophe. When all was over, but not till then, he returned to his room, opened the door, and entered it.

I followed him with my eyes. On the end wall, beneath the portraits of his heroes, I saw the picture of a woman, still young, and her two little children. Captain Nemo stared at this group for some moments and stretched his arms out toward them as if they were alive. Then he knelt down and burst into uncontrollable sobbing.

CHAPTER XXII

CAPTAIN NEMO'S LAST WORDS

The panels had closed on this dreadful vision, but the luminous ceiling of the saloon was still unlighted. All was silence and darkness within the "Nautilus." A hundred feet beneath the waves, at wonderful speed, the ship was fleeing from this desolate spot.

Where were we going—north or south? Toward what was this most strange mortal rushing after such cruel retaliation?

I felt an insurmountable horror of Captain Nemo. Whatever he may have suffered at the hands of these men, or of others like them, he had no right to punish thus. He had made me, if not exactly an accomplice, at least a witness of the vengeance he had wreaked.

At eleven o'clock the electric light flashed on. I had gone to my cabin to sit with Ned Land and Conseil, but they had been under the spell of a brooding silence, and so I passed back again to the drawing-room. It was deserted. I consulted the different instruments. The submarine was flying northward at the rate of twenty-five miles an hour, now on the surface, now thirty feet below it. On taking the bearings by the chart I noted that we were passing the mouth of the English Channel and that our course was hurrying us toward the northern seas at frightful speed.

That night we had cleared two hundred leagues of the

Atlantic. The shadows fell, and the sea was covered with darkness until the moon should rise. I went to my room, but not to sleep—the sinking of the man-of-war had murdered sleep. I was troubled with waking nightmare. The horrible scene of destruction was continually before my mind's eye.

From that day forward who could tell into what part of the North Atlantic basin the "Nautilus" would take us, still at unaccountable speed, still in the midst of icy fogs? Would it touch at Spitsbergen, or at the shores of Novaya Zemlya? Should we explore those unknown briny wastes the White Sea, the Sea of Kara, the Gulf of Ob, the archipelago of Liakov? I could not say.

I could also not judge of the passage of time. The clocks on board had been stopped. It seemed, however, as in polar regions, that night and day no longer followed their appointed course. I felt myself being lured into that strange no-man's land wherein the foundered imagination of Edgar Poe roamed at will.

Like the fabulous Gordon Pym, at any moment I expected to see "that veiled human figure, of larger proportions than those of any inhabitant of the earth, thrown across the cataract which defends the approach to the pole."

I may be mistaken, but I estimated this adventurous wandering of the submarine to have lasted fifteen or twenty days. And I do not know how much longer it might have lasted but for the catastrophe which ended this voyage.

Of Captain Nemo and his second officer I saw nothing. Not a man of the crew was visible for an instant.

The ship was almost incessantly submerged. If we came to the surface, the panels were opened and shut by a mechanical device. There were no new marks on the planisphere. I knew not where we were.

The Canadian's strength and patience were at an end. He, too, appeared no more. Conseil could not extract a word from him. Fearing that he might kill himself in some dreadful access of madness, my servant watched his friend with constant devotion.

One morning (I cannot say the date), I had fallen into a fitful slumber toward the early hours when I was suddenly awakened. Ned Land was leaning over me, saying in a low voice, "We're going to fly. The decision is made."

"When shall we start?" I asked.

"Tonight, irrevocably. All inspection on this boat has ceased. Everybody seems to be stupefied as if by drugs. You will be sure to be ready, sir?"

"Count upon me. Whereabouts are we?"

"In sight of land. I took the reckoning this morning in the fog. There are hills twenty miles to the east of us."

What country is it?"

None that I know about, sir. But, whatever it may prove to be, there's refuge of some sort there."

"I'm with you, Ned, heart and soul. We go tonight, even if the sea swallows us up."

"The waves are bad, sir, and the wind is blowing a gale. But a matter of twenty miles in the pinnace of the 'Nautilus' does not frighten me. Without anyone's knowledge I have been able to stow away some food and several bottles of water."

"I'll follow where you lead, my lad."

"It may be to your death, M. Aronnax. For, if I am surprised, I shall defend myself. They will be forced to kill me."

"In that case we shall die together, my friend."

I had made up my mind to endure the worst with equanimity. The Canadian left me. I reached the platform, to which I could cling only with great difficulty because of the thudding shock of the waves. The sky was lowering, but if land lay far across those threatening billows, we must seek it. I returned to the saloon, fearing and yet hoping to see Captain Nemo. Why did I wish to meet him there? What could I possibly have said to him? Could I have hidden the involuntary horror with which he inspired me? Alas, no. It was better that I should not again confront him, it was wisest to forget him quite. And yet—and yet—

How endless was that day! The last that I should spend in the submarine! I remained alone with my thoughts. Tomorrow I should be a corpse tossing on this wild waste of waters or a man among my fellows, erect and free.

Ned Land and Conseil avoided speech, fearing lest they betray themselves. At some hour (six, perhaps) I dined, although I was not hungry. In spite of my distaste for food, I forced myself to eat that I might conserve my full strength.

In half an hour or so Ned Land came to my cabin and said, "We shall not see each other again before our departure. At ten the moon will not yet be risen. We shall profit by the darkness. Come to the boat, simply. Conseil and I will await you there."

The Canadian went away without giving me an opportunity to answer. Wishing to verify the course of the "Nautilus," I went to the saloon. We were running N.N.E. at frightful speed and more than fifty yards beneath the surface.

I cast a last look on the wonders of nature about me. I gazed long at the riches of art heaped up in this museum. It seemed strange to think this unrivaled collection was destined to perish at the bottom of the sea, together with him who had gathered it. I wished to fix in my mind an indelible impression of it. And so I remained an hour thus, bathed in the light of the luminous ceiling and passing in review those treasures shining under the glass cases. Then I returned to my room.

I dressed myself in my stoutest sea garments. I collected my notes and placed them carefully about me. My heart was beating loudly; I was unable to check its pulsations. Certainly my troubled appearance and my agitation would betray me to Captain Nemo.

What was he doing this very moment? I listened stealthily at the door of his room. I heard steps inside it. Captain Nemo was there and had not gone to rest. At every moment I expected him to appear and ask me why I wished to flee. I was constantly on the alert for this. My imagination magnified everything. My nervous fears at last became so poignant that I almost persuaded myself it would be better to go to the commander's room, confront him with my plan, face him down with look and gesture.

It was the inspiration of a madman. Fortunately I resisted the desire and stretched myself upon the bed to quiet my bodily ills.

My nerves grew somewhat calmer, but still in my excited brain I saw reviewed my whole existence on board the "Nautilus." Every incident, happy or sad, that had happened since my disappearance from the "Abraham Lincoln" recurred to me: the submarine hunt; Torres Straits; the savages at Papua; the coral cemetery; the passage of Suez; the island of Santorin; the Cretan diver; Vigo Bay; Atlantis; the iceberg; the South Pole; imprisonment in the ice; fight with the poulps; storm in the Gulf Stream; the "Avenger"; horrible scene of the vessel sunk with all her crew.

All these events passed before my eyes like scenes in a drama. Then Captain Nemo seemed to become immeasurably larger, his features assumed superhuman proportions. He was no longer my equal, but a creature of the waters, the genie of the sea.

Suddenly I awoke to a realization of the fact that it was half-past nine. I held my head between my hands to keep it from bursting. I closed my eyes tight and decided that I would do no more thinking. There was another half-hour to wait, a session of further nightmare that might drive me mad.

At that moment I heard the distant strains of the organ. They were the mournful harmony of an indefinable chant, and to my aroused mood they seemed the wail of a tormented soul longing to break its earthly bonds. I listened with every sense, scarcely breathing. Like

Captain Nemo, I was plunged in that musical ecstasy which was drawing him in spirit to the very edge of life.

Then a sudden thought terrified me. The commander had left his room. He was in the saloon, which I must cross to get to the central staircase. There I should meet him for the last time. He would see me, would speak to me perhaps. A gesture of his would have power to destroy me; a single word from him, and I might be chained on board forever.

Ten was about to strike.

The moment had come for me to leave my room and seek for my companions.

I must not hesitate now, even if Captain Nemo himself should place himself before me and bar the way. I opened my door with extreme caution, but as it turned upon its hinges it seemed to make a most unusual amount of noise. I had come to such a state that I could not tell whether the creaking sound was real or existed only in my imagination.

I crept forward through the dark waist of the "Nautilus," stopping at every step to check the insane pounding of my heart. I reached the door of the saloon and pushed it gently open. The apartment was plunged into profound darkness! The strains of the organ sounded faintly. Captain Nemo was there almost within my reach. But apparently he did not know of my presence. If the room had been in full light, I do not think he would have noticed me, so entirely was he absorbed in his ecstasy.

I stole along the carpet, avoiding the least sound that would indicate where I was. It took me at least five minutes to reach the door at the opposite end which opened into the library.

I was about to open that, when a deep sigh from Captain Nemo rooted me to the spot. I knew that he was rising. I could even see him, though very dimly, for the light from the library filtered through to the saloon. He came toward me silently, with his arms crossed, gliding like a specter rather than walking. His breast was swelling with sobs. And I heard him murmur these words, the last of his that ever struck my ear, "Almighty God! Enough! Enough!"

Was it a confession of remorse which thus escaped a tortured conscience?

In desperation I rushed through the library, flew up the central staircase, and, following the upper passageway reached the boat. I crept through its opening, which had already admitted my two companions.

"Let us go! Oh, let us go!" I begged.

"Directly!" replied the Canadian.

The orifice in the plates of the "Nautilus" was now closed and locked by means of the false key with which Ned Land had provided himself. The opening in the boat was also shut. The harpooner began to loosen the bolts which still fastened us to the submarine.

Suddenly a shout was heard from the interior below us. Voices clamored and called loudly to others. What had happened? Had the crew discovered our flight? I felt Ned Land slip a dagger into my hand.

"Yes," I muttered, "we know how to die."

My comrade had stopped in his work of releasing the

pinnace. A single word many times repeated, a dreadful word, revealed the cause of the agitation which was spreading on board the "Nautilus." It was not we whom the crew were seeking.

"The maelstrom!" I exclaimed.

The maelstrom! In a dreadful situation such as ours, could a word of more dire significance have sounded in our ears? We were, it seems, off the dangerous coast of Norway. Was our vessel being drawn into this gulf at the moment the pinnace was about to leave its sides? We knew that at the turn of the tide the pent-up waters between the islands of Ferroe and Lofoden rush forward with irresistible force. And they form a whirlpool from which no ship ever escapes.

From the four corners of the horizon enormous waves come plunging and form a vast eddy which sailors justly call the Navel of the Ocean. Its power of attraction is fatal to a distance of twelve miles, so inconceivably strong is the lure of this engulfing maw. Whatever nears it is sacrificed unalterably. Not vessels alone, but whales, white bears from the northern regions—

And it was to that point that the "Nautilus," whether wittingly or no, had been directed by the captain.

The ship was describing a spiral the circumference of which was narrowing perceptibly. Our pinnace, still fastened to the ship, was spun along at giddy speed. I felt that nauseating vertigo that arises from long-continued whirling. My head whirled like a top.

We were in the grip of dread. Our horror had reached its possible limit. All nervous influence had been annihilated, and we were bathed in cold sweat, like a sweat of agony.

The noise about our frail bark was terrific. Roarings were repeated in echoes from miles away. And we began to hear the uproar of the waters which dashed on the sharp rocks of the gulf's bottom where the hardest substances are ground to powder and great trees worn away. "It rubs off all the fur" is the Norwegian phrase for the maelstrom's activity.

What a situation to encounter!

We rocked frightfully. The "Nautilus" seemed to defend herself like a human being driven into the last trench. Her steel muscles cracked. At times she seemed to rear herself upright.

"We must hold on," Ned managed to gasp, "and screw down the bolts again. If we stick to the ship, we may still be saved, and—"

He had not finished his words when we heard a crashing noise. The bolts gave way as if they were made of tissue paper, and the pinnace, torn from its groove, was hurled like a stone from a sling into the midst of the whirlpool.

My head struck against a piece of iron. And with a violent concussion I lost all consciousness.

CHAPTER XXIII

CONCLUSION

Thus ends the voyage under the seas. What passed during that night no one of us can tell. For we do not know how the pinnace escaped from the eddies of the maelstrom, how we ever came out of the gulf.

When I returned to the world of reality, I was lying in a fisherman's hut on the Lofoden Isles. My two comrades, safe and sound, were at the bedside holding my hands. We embraced one another heartily.

There was no possible way for us to return to France for a long time to come. The means of communication between the north and the south of Norway are scant and rare. And therefore we are compelled to await the monthly steamer from North Cape.

Thus, among the kindly people who have welcomed us back to earth, I sit and revise my record of these adventures one last time. Not a salient fact has been omitted, not a detail exaggerated. It is the faithful narrative of this incredible expedition in an element inaccessible to man. But in the near future Progress will one day open a road in it, for exploration and discovery, at least, if not for life.

Shall I be believed? I do not know. And, after all, what matters it if my book be distrusted? All that I affirm is, that I have authority to speak of those seas, under which in ten months I crossed twenty thousand leagues in that submarine tour of the world which revealed so many wonders.

What became of the "Nautilus"?

Did it resist the pressure of the maelstrom? Does Captain Nemo still live? And beneath the surface of the sea does he still pursue his course of frightful retaliation? Or after that hecatomb near the ruins of the "Avenger" has the grim commander withheld his hand?

Will the waves some day carry to him this manuscript containing the history of his life? Shall I ever know the name of this eccentric soul? Will the missing vessel tell us Captain Nemo's nationality by revealing its own?

I hope so.

And I also hope that his powerful submarine conquered the ocean at its most terrible gulf, that it survived where other hundreds have found their grave. If this be so, if our commander still inhabits the ocean as his adopted country, then let us pray that the hatred in his savage heart may be appeased. May the contemplation of so many undersea wonders dim forever the spirit of his vengeance!

May the judge of human wrongs disappear in him, and the philosopher that he really is continue the peaceful exploration of the sea!

If his destiny be strange, it is also sublime. Have I myself not come to understand it? Did I not share ten months of his unnatural life? And to the question asked by Ecclesiastes six thousand years ago, "That which is far off and exceeding deep, who can find it out?" two men alone of all now living have the right to give an answer—

CAPTAIN NEMO AND MYSELF.

Printed in U.S.A.